La ratonera

Austral Educación

LA RATONERA
Agatha Christie

....

Traducción de
Miguel Temprano

**Estudio preliminar
y propuestas de trabajo
a cargo de**
Rosa Solé

Ilustraciones de
Guillermo Berdugo

AUSTRAL
EDUCACIÓN

🌐 Planeta

Obra editada en colaboración con Editorial Planeta – España

Título original: *The Mousetrap*

© 1952, Agatha Christie

© 2022, Traducción: Miguel Temprano García

© Ilustraciones del interior y de la portada: Guillermo Berdugo

© Imágenes del Estudio preliminar: Alamy / ACI

© 2022, Editorial Planeta, S. A. – Barcelona, España

Derechos reservados

© 2023, Editorial Planeta Mexicana, S.A. de C.V.
Bajo el sello editorial AUSTRAL M.R.
Avenida Presidente Masarik núm. 111,
Piso 2, Polanco V Sección, Miguel Hidalgo
C.P. 11560, Ciudad de México
www.planetadelibros.com.mx

Diseño de portada: Austral / Área Editorial Grupo Planeta

Primera edición impresa en España en Austral: marzo de 2022
ISBN: 978-84-670-6524-4

Primera edición impresa en México en Austral: enero de 2023
ISBN: 978-607-07-9509-1

Impreso en los talleres de Impresora Tauro, S.A. de C.V.
Av. Año de Juárez 343, Colonia Granjas San Antonio, Iztapalapa
C.P. 09070, Ciudad de México.
Impreso en México - *Printed in Mexico*

Biografía

Agatha Christie es conocida en todo el mundo como la Dama del Crimen. Es la autora más publicada de todos los tiempos, tan solo superada por la Biblia y Shakespeare. Sus libros han vendido más de cuatro mil millones de ejemplares en todo el mundo. Escribió un total de ochenta novelas de misterio y colecciones de relatos breves, diecinueve obras de teatro y seis novelas escritas con el pseudónimo de Mary Westmacott. Probó suerte con la pluma mientras trabajaba en un hospital durante la Primera Guerra Mundial, y debutó con *El misterioso caso de Styles* en 1920, cuyo protagonista es el legendario detective Hércules Poirot, que luego aparecería en treinta y tres libros más. Alcanzó la fama con *El asesinato de Roger Ackroyd* en 1926, y creó a la ingeniosa Miss Marple en *Muerte en la vicaría*, publicado por primera vez en 1930. Se casó dos veces, una con Archibald Christie, de quien adoptó el apellido con el que es conocida mundialmente como la genial escritora de novelas y cuentos policiales y detectivescos, y luego con el arqueólogo Max Mallowan, al que acompañó en varias expediciones a lugares exóticos del mundo que luego usó como escenarios en sus novelas. En 1961 fue nombrada miembro de la Real Sociedad de Literatura y en 1971 recibió el título de Dama de la Orden del Imperio Británico, un título nobiliario que en aquellos días se concedía con poca frecuencia. Murió en 1976 a la edad de ochenta y cinco años. Sus misterios encantan a lectores de todas las edades, pues son lo suficientemente simples como para que los más jóvenes los entiendan y disfruten, pero a la vez muestran una complejidad que las mentes adultas no consiguen descifrar hasta el final.

www.agathachristie.com

ÍNDICE

ESTUDIO PRELIMINAR

1. INTRODUCCIÓN

La ratonera es casi la única obra que Agatha Christie escribió para el teatro exprofeso y, sin embargo, ostenta un récord envidiable: es el título que más tiempo se ha mantenido en escena de forma ininterrumpida. Se estrenó en 1952 y, durante casi siete décadas, más de once millones de espectadores han podido disfrutarla en unas treinta mil funciones. También cuenta con una larga trayectoria más allá de las fronteras británicas, con funciones prácticamente en todos los países del mundo, desde Turquía hasta Sudáfrica, pasando por Escandinavia o Venezuela. En España se estrenó en octubre de 1954 con un reparto de lujo: María Luisa Ponte, Irene y Julia Gutiérrez Caba, Mariano Azaña, Antonio Casas... Permaneció dos años en cartel con más de setecientas representaciones y siguió así hasta hace bien poco: en 2014 fue la obra más vista en la ciudad de Barcelona. ¿A qué se debe semejante éxito? La crítica parece unánime: es uno de los mejores ejemplos de lo que llamamos «suspense», un género que ha ocupado miles de páginas de libros, escenas de teatro y pantallas de cine o televisión. Son relatos con una incógnita, una verdad oculta, que mantiene en vilo a lectores y espectadores porque estos quieren conocer su desenlace, lo que ha ocurrido realmente. La «intriga» (según nuestro diccionario, una «acción que se ejecuta con astucia y ocultamente para conseguir un fin») mueve, así, los hilos de la trama, mientras quienes escuchamos, vemos o leemos disfrutamos con lo que va ocurriendo, a la vez que intentamos destapar esa verdad oculta. Esa atracción seguramente no es más que algo derivado de nuestra propia curiosidad, la que nos ha llevado a investigar y nos ha hecho avanzar en todos los campos de la ciencia, pero también la misma que nos ha deleitado, desde tiempos inmemoriales, con enigmas por descubrir o acertijos por resolver. A este respecto, nuestra autora, Agatha Christie, es una maestra, la «gran dama del misterio», según se la conoce. En todo su universo narrativo el argumento ofrece unos hechos con una explicación oculta que al principio de la obra no entendemos y que poco a poco se va desvelando de una manera muy particular, a través de ciertas claves o «pistas». Con estas, nosotros, los lectores o espectadores de *La ratonera* en este caso, intentamos desentrañar la verdad casi a la vez que los personajes y nos identificamos con ellos de forma cada vez más intensa conforme avanza la acción. A esto hay que añadir un entorno sencillo (con pocos personajes y apenas referencias al exterior, un escenario simple y único) que focaliza la atención en la acción y, sobre todo, un desenlace sorprendente y magistral. Este, de hecho, es tan importante que,

12

cuando acaba una representación, los actores piden al público asistente que mantenga en secreto el nombre del asesino para permitir que futuros espectadores puedan disfrutar plenamente del misterio y el suspense de la obra.

Agatha Christie fotografiada en 1957.

Agatha Mary Clarissa Miller nació el 15 de septiembre de 1890 en el pueblo de Torquay, en la idílica campiña de Devon, condado situado en el suroeste de Inglaterra. Fruto del feliz matrimonio entre el corredor de bolsa estadounidense Fred Miller y la británica Clarissa Boehmer, fue la menor de tres hermanos. La acomodada familia residía en la bella mansión de Ashfield y allí la niña viviría una alegre infancia que le dejó una profunda huella. La escritora recibió su educación en casa, tutelada por su madre, que le dio una visión intelectual abierta aunque en consonancia con los hábitos y las costumbres de la clase alta inglesa. Su progenitora pensaba que la mejor manera de educar a una niña era dejarla libre y no forzarla con ninguna disciplina, así que la pequeña creció conociendo el amor por los libros a través de su madre y el gusto por las matemáticas y los acertijos gracias a las aficiones de su padre. Varias profesoras particulares le enseñaron distintas materias y a tocar el piano, pero hasta su adolescencia no recibió una educación reglada. Ávida lectora desde muy pequeña, devoraba las aventuras de Sherlock Holmes y disfrutaba con las novelas góticas y de detectives.

Aquel ambiente se vio truncado en 1901 con la muerte del progenitor. La triste viuda descubrió entonces que su situación económica no era tan desahogada como todos creían, de modo que Margaret (Madge), la hija mayor, se casó y se trasladó a Cheadle Hall, mientras que Monty, el menor, se unió al ejército. Así, Agatha y su madre se quedaron solas en Ashfield, una mansión que resultaría, en tales circunstancias, difícil de mantener. Dado que toda la familia se sentía muy ligada a ella y no quería venderla, procuraron alquilarla y recibir rentas mientras viajaban y residían en el extranjero —por aquel entonces, algo más económico— o pasaban largas temporadas en casa de familiares. Vivieron mucho tiempo, por ejemplo, en Abney Hall, propiedad del marido de la hermana, o en el londinense hogar de la acaudalada tía abuela Margaret. Este entorno familiar, extenso y abierto, con una madre luchadora que siempre animó a sus hijos a que persiguieran sus ideales, fue muy importante para la escritora.

Agatha de pequeña junto a su padre, Fred Miller.

Todos formaban parte de un mundo particular y maravilloso en el que Agatha se sentía muy cómoda y que acabaría reflejándose en sus futuras creaciones.

En Torquay, por su parte, Agatha gozaba de un buen círculo de conocidos y amigos con quienes se divertía y junto a quienes se fue convirtiendo en una adolescente atractiva que disfrutaba asistiendo a bailes y a fiestas o yendo a patinar por el muelle. Sin embargo, a los dieciséis años, Clarissa decidió que su hija menor debía completar su formación en el extranjero. Así que la llevó a París, donde la chica pasó una larga temporada estudiando sobre todo música, aunque pronto se dio cuenta de que no poseía el don necesario para hacer carrera. Acabados los estudios, volvió en seguida a Inglaterra, donde encontró a su madre con la salud muy delicada, y ambas decidieron pasar el invierno en Egipto. La jovencita tenía edad de ser presentada en sociedad, pero como no podían permitirse organizar semejante evento en la capital británica, el traslado también servía para esquivar aquel compromiso. Ese viaje de 1910 fascinó a Agatha. El Cairo fue el lugar donde alternó con la colonia británica, ya como miembro de pleno derecho, y donde venció su timidez. Por aquel entonces los monumentos y su historia no la impresionaron tanto como las relaciones que fue contemplando: los tenues hilos que tejían unas y enredaban otras, las sutilezas del lenguaje gestual, la comunicación sin palabras desplegada en los salones... Estos serían materiales de los que más adelante haría buen uso para urdir sus tramas.

En esa época la joven escribía ya de forma regular: aquel era su pasatiempo favorito y al que dedicaba todo su tiempo libre. Envió varios relatos, cuentos y poemas a diferentes revistas. También su primer relato extenso, aunque solo recibió amables cartas de rechazo.

3. EL NACIMIENTO DE UNA AUTORA DE SUSPENSE

De vuelta en Torquay, Agatha conoció a Archibald Christie, oficial del Ejército del aire británico. Ambos se enamoraron y tras un largo compromiso, contrajeron matrimonio en 1914. El inmediato estallido de la Gran Guerra, sin embargo, separó a los recién casados: él se fue a Europa con la aviación británica y ella comenzó a trabajar como voluntaria en el primer hospital público de Torquay. Ejerció de enfermera y descubrió una vocación: le gustaba cuidar de los heridos y no le importaba llevar a cabo las tareas menos agradecidas. Más adelante se ocupó del dispensario médico, convertido en una gran farmacia. Con su curiosidad habitual, quiso formarse en este campo para hacer bien su trabajo y configurar adecuadamente las preparaciones que se le pedían. Entre preparación y preparación, rodeada de productos químicos y con cierto saber farmacológico, Agatha dio a luz la que sería su primera novela publicada, *El misterioso caso de Styles*.

La novela se sitúa en la mansión Styles, cuya rica propietaria aparece muerta en la cama. Todo parece indicar que se ha tratado de un ataque cardíaco, pero, ante el asombro de todos los invitados allí reu-

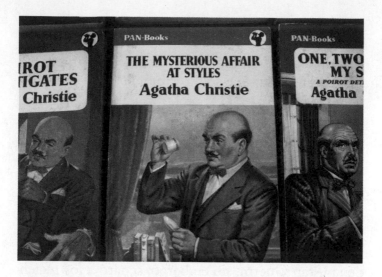

nidos, el médico dice sospechar que se trata de un asesinato por envenenamiento. En *El misterioso caso de Styles* encontramos ya el esquema que acabará siendo característico de la autora: un inicio en el que aparece un grupo variopinto de personajes, que incluye a la víctima y el verdugo, al que sigue después un recorrido de pistas y enigmas que retarán al lector a descubrir quién ha cometido el crimen. Para ello se siguen las hipótesis de un detective particular, aunque siempre será la narradora quien cierre su obra con una sorpresa para resolver el crimen. Y todo ello con el telón de fondo de una confortable residencia en la apacible campiña inglesa. El carismático investigador que se estrena aquí para resolver el caso es ya el personaje que hará a Christie famosa: Hércules Poirot. Para su creación la autora se inspiró sin duda en un hecho real, y es que, con la invasión de Bélgica por parte de Alemania en 1914, más de un millón de ciudadanos de aquel país se vieron obligados a huir y muchos buscaron refugio en las islas británicas. Seguía, también, la línea que habían abierto los primeros creadores de la llamada novela de misterio, focalizada en un caso criminal enigmático que debe resolver su protagonista. La obra *Mademoiselle de Scuderi*, publicada por E. T. A. Hoffmann en 1819, parece la primera inspiración del gran precursor de esta tradición: Edgar Allan Poe y su libro *Los crímenes de la calle Morgue*. El detective aficionado de Poe, Auguste Dupin, será el modelo en que se base más adelante (en 1887) sir Arthur Conan Doyle para crear al celebérrimo investigador Sherlock Holmes, cuyas aventuras alcanzaron en seguida una enorme popularidad y afianzaron la forma clásica de esta narrativa, que, además, solía publicarse por entregas en los periódicos, lo que contribuía a aumentar la tensión ficcional. En esta misma línea, ya a comienzos del siglo xx (en 1910), G. K. Chesterton dio forma a su carismático padre Brown, un humilde sacerdote de la vieja guardia capaz de desentrañar crímenes que parecían escapar a la razón. Así, y siguiendo el camino trazado por Dupin o Sherlock Holmes, Agatha nos presenta a un policía belga retirado que, trasladado a Inglaterra, ayuda en algunos casos a Scotland Yard. Para resolverlos, el flemático detective, de bigote peculiar, utiliza unos métodos muy diferentes a los desplegados por el cuerpo policial, basándose en la psicología e interesándose por detalles que parecen insignificantes pero que acaban revelándose decisivos para la resolución del enigma. Su forma de proceder y su desprecio por las pistas más evidentes

19

le valdrán las burlas de los agentes uniformados, quienes, sin embargo, al final, tendrán que rendirse ante la maestría del arrogante Poirot.

Agatha acabó de escribir la novela hacia 1916, aunque se publicaría años más tarde. Paralelamente, al terminar el conflicto bélico, Archibald volvió a casa y el matrimonio se mudó a Londres. La adaptación fue difícil, pues la posguerra exigía una enorme

David Suchet encarnó al famoso detective Hércules Poirot con enorme éxito para la serie de televisión británica *Agatha Christie's Poirot* (1989-2013), basada en las novelas y relatos cortos de la autora.

austeridad y al excombatiente le costó encontrar trabajo. En 1919 nació Rosalind, la que sería la única hija de nuestra autora. Poco después, en los primeros años veinte, por fin la editorial de John Lane, The Bodley Head, accedió a dar a luz *El misterioso caso de Styles*. El libro no tuvo una mala acogida, pero la novelista no había firmado un contrato demasiado ventajoso y recibió muy poco dinero por las ventas. En cualquier caso, la escritura comenzó a perfilarse como posible fuente de ingresos para la familia, que seguía con una situación económica apurada y con la necesidad de mantener Ashfield. Así, animada también por su esposo, la joven se decidió por fin a escribir su segunda novela, *El misterioso señor Brown*, que también fue publicada por Lane, pero esta vez por entregas, que aportaron más beneficios a su creadora. Muy pronto le siguió otro título, *Asesinato en el campo de golf*, un segundo caso para Hércules Poirot. La prensa ya había tomado buena nota de que la nueva pluma ofrecía al lector un misterio apasionante e inusual, que además jugaba limpio con el lector al facilitarle toda la información necesaria para resolver el enigma. El éxito empezaba a asomarse, y la popularidad que estaba adquiriendo Poirot hizo surgir por fin un suculento encargo: una serie de doce relatos interpretados por el detective y su ayudante, el capitán Hastings —su particular Watson—, que daría a luz una prestigiosa revista semanal. Agatha no solo estaba cada vez más vinculada a las novelas de misterio, sino que también había creado un personaje que hacía las delicias de los lectores. Junto con la posterior Miss Marple, Poirot granjeó a la autora la complicidad y estima del gran público, que los seguirá con atención en las treinta y tres novelas y cincuenta relatos cortos que acabaron protagonizando.

Poco después de la publicación de su tercera novela, su marido recibió una propuesta de trabajo que cambió sus vidas. La propuesta estaba relacionada con la organización de la Exposición del Imperio Británico que iba a celebrarse en 1924. Para este tipo de eventos, centrados fundamentalmente en el comercio y la presentación de avances tecnológicos, las autoridades necesitaban contratar a ciudadanos competentes que lograran la colaboración de todo tipo de representantes en sus dominios. Para Archibald y Agatha era una oportunidad única de ganar dinero y viajar por todo el mundo. Decidieron arriesgarse y la familia emprendió el viaje como parte de la misión británica. Canarias, Sudáfrica, Australia, las islas Fiyi o Hawái formaron parte de su itinerario. De todos estos lugares la escritora recogerá ingredientes pintorescos, motivos y escenarios para sus futuras narraciones. En su última etapa, en Honolulu, el matrimonio pudo permitirse dos semanas de vacaciones, y la intrépida señora aprendió a surfear antes de emprender la difícil vuelta a casa.

4. LA ECLOSIÓN DEL ÉXITO

Ya en Inglaterra, y a pesar del viaje enriquecedor, los Christie volvieron a sufrir apuros económicos en un país todavía sumido en la posguerra. Agatha volvió a tomar la pluma y en 1924 publicó por entregas en el periódico *The Evening News* —y con un generoso anticipo— *El hombre del traje marrón*. En esta ocasión, la hija de un antropólogo es testigo de la muerte de un hombre en el metro de Londres y de una serie de extraños sucesos posteriores que la llevarán a querer descubrir qué se esconde detrás de todo el asunto sin importarle correr riesgos. El género policíaco se mezclaba aquí con la novela de aventuras y el público siguió la obra con expectación. Archie, por su parte, consiguió por fin un buen trabajo en el sector financiero, de modo que la situación de la familia se fue estabilizando. Se trasladaron a una bonita casa en el campo, y Agatha pudo cumplir uno de sus sueños: comprarse un coche que le permitiera libertad e independencia. Y así, por fin, en 1926 llegó el gran éxito, la primera edición de *El asesinato de Roger Ackroyd*, que vendió rápidamente más de cincuenta mil ejemplares. La novela recibió numerosos elogios y generó gran revuelo por la forma en que la escritora cambiaba las reglas tradicionales del género policíaco. Su protagonista es un médico rural que se convierte en hábil ayudante de Hércules Poirot, y su final está considerado uno de los más sorprendentes e inesperados de la obra de Christie.

Dos infortunios, sin embargo, golpearon a la escritora para hacerla descender varios peldaños en aquella escalera de la fama. Por un lado, la muerte de su querida madre y, por el otro, la infidelidad confesa de su esposo la sumieron en una tristeza rayana en la depresión que la llevó a desaparecer. Durante trece días nadie supo dónde estaba. Solo un músico que tocaba en un hotel de Yorkshire la reconoció y puso fin a uno de los capítulos más misteriosos y extraños

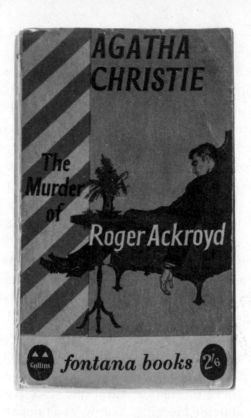

en la vida de la autora. Aquello llamó la atención de la prensa porque se parecía demasiado a sus propias novelas, así que durante casi dos semanas la señora Christie ocupó páginas de periódicos repletas de especulaciones. Ella, no obstante, se limitó a alegar una pérdida de memoria debido a los nervios y jamás volvió a hablar del suceso. Poco después, en 1928, el matrimonio se divorció y Agatha publicó *El misterio del tren azul,* novela que nunca acabó de convencer a su autora pero que supuso su profesionalización. A partir de ese momento, su situación económica y el bienestar de su hija dependerían totalmente de sus ingresos como escritora.

La prensa hizo muchas especulaciones sobre la desaparición de Agatha Christie. *The Daily News* incluso llegó a publicar cómo habría podido disfrazarse la escritora para pasar desapercibida.

5. EL VIAJE DECISIVO

Ya divorciada y con su niña en un internado, la autora decidió trasladarse a Siria en el mítico Orient Express, el tren de larga distancia más lujoso de su época. Viajar sola en aquel momento y hacerlo a semejante destino resultaba del todo inusual para una mujer, pero Agatha no dudó en embarcarse en aquella aventura con determinación. Visitó Estambul, Damasco e Irak, y quedó absolutamente prendada del encanto de Oriente y sus tesoros. Gracias a las amistades que entabló durante tan largo viaje, tuvo la oportunidad de visitar el yacimiento arqueológico de Ur acompañada por el matrimonio Woolley. Leonard era el arqueólogo responsable de la excavación y su esposa, Katherine, una gran admiradora de las novelas de Christie, por lo que la invitaron a pasar una temporada con ellos. Más allá de los monumentos, aquella estancia le permitió enamorarse del lugar y sus gentes, de la belleza de los atardeceres, de los infinitos paisajes de arena o de las huellas del pasado que se revelaban excavación tras excavación.

De otra parte, sus obras se vendían a buen ritmo y la escritora disfrutaba del éxito. En 1930 publicó *Muerte en la vicaría*, una novela en la que presentó a otro de sus inolvidables personajes, Miss Marple. Lejos del estereotipo del detective, en este caso quien resuelve los enigmáticos crímenes es una anciana solterona y algo inocente que posee una enorme curiosidad y una gran capacidad analítica. Interesada por las vidas ajenas y gran observadora, a menudo alardea del conocimiento del comportamiento humano que ofrece la vejez y que muchas veces permite traspasar los límites de las sesudas investigaciones policiales.

Ese mismo año volvió a visitar al matrimonio Woolley en Ur y allí conoció a Max Mallowan, un distinguido arqueólogo mucho más joven que ella, que acabó convirtiéndose, poco después, en su segundo marido. Con él alcanzaría la felicidad en esta nueva etapa de su vida. Apoyó la carrera de su marido y lo acompañó en todos los proyectos, lo que supuso pasar largas temporadas en Oriente. En ninguna de estas ocasiones Christie ejerció de mera consorte, sino que se implicó de forma activa tanto en las excavaciones e investigaciones como en asuntos relacionados con la restauración y la clasificación de los hallazgos. Su interés por la fotografía la convirtió en pieza clave

Agatha Christie y su segundo esposo, Max Mallowan, en una excavación arqueológica en Nimrud.

para la documentación de los yacimientos y su pasión por conocer a las personas e integrarse en las comunidades locales resultó decisiva para el buen funcionamiento de los proyectos. En el ámbito literario, los años treinta fueron muy prolíficos para la autora, que empezó a plasmar de forma clara sus experiencias viajeras en obras como *Asesinato en el Orient Express* (1934), donde la muerte de una pasajera convertirá en sospechosos a todos los ocupantes de un vagón del famoso convoy; *Asesinato en Mesopotamia* (1936), cuyo crimen ocurre en el seno de una excavación arqueológica; o *Muerte en el Nilo* (1937), en la que la víctima es una joven recién casada que viaja en un crucero. A estos títulos hay que sumar otros igualmente populares, como *Peligro inminente* (1932), una curiosa novela en la que Poirot deberá resolver un crimen aún no cometido, *El misterio de la guía de ferrocarriles* (1936), donde el famoso detective se enfrenta a su primer asesino en serie, y *Diez negritos* (1939), una de las más sorprendentes en cuanto a su trama y su siniestro final.

6. AÑOS DE MADUREZ

Con el estallido de la Segunda Guerra Mundial, Oriente Medio dejó de ser un lugar tranquilo para el matrimonio, que decidió entonces volver a Inglaterra. Se instalaron en el número 48 de Sheffield Terrace en Londres y compraron también una casa de campo en Winterbrook, cerca de Wallingford. Estas dos residencias constituyeron un verdadero hogar en el que pudieron dedicarse a sus respectivas y apasionantes profesiones. Con el tiempo, a las anteriores vino a sumarse Greenway House, una mansión cercana a Torquay que a la autora le recordaba a Ashfield.

En 1943, Rosalind dio a luz a Mathew, pero un año después moría su padre, víctima de la batalla de Normandía, y Agatha se volcó en el cuidado de su hija y de su nieto. Durante este nuevo conflicto bélico, la escritora también prestó sus servicios en el hospital y trabajó activamente para paliar las terri-

Agatha Christie y Max Mallowan en su casa de campo Greenway House, en Devon.

bles consecuencias que volvían a sufrir su entorno y su país. La guerra, sin embargo, no le impidió seguir escribiendo: entre otras novelas, publicó *Un triste ciprés* (1940), protagonizada por una rica heredera sospechosa de haber asesinado a su tía; *Maldad bajo el sol* (1941), en la que el asesinato ocurre en un balneario durante las vacaciones de Poirot; *Un cadáver en la biblioteca* (1942), protagonizada por Miss Marple; o *El caso de los anónimos* (1943), donde la astucia de la anciana investigadora deberá resolver un misterio que parece involucrar a todos los habitantes de un pequeño pueblo. En sus últimos años de vida, la escritora y su marido recibieron honores por su labor en pro de su país: ella fue nombrada Dama del Imperio Británico y él, Caballero del Reino. Agatha Christie murió por causas naturales el 12 de enero de 1976, a los ochenta y cinco años, en su casa de campo. Había vivido sin más preocupaciones económicas gracias a los ingresos que fue generando su extensa obra.

El éxito de las novelas de Christie atrajo la atención de los productores de cine y de teatro. Las primeras que contaron con adaptación teatral fueron *Café solo* (1930) y *Diez negritos* (1943). Ambas triunfaron desde las primeras representaciones, de modo que les siguieron muchas más: *Asesinato en el Nilo* (1944), *Cita con la muerte* (1945), *Sangre en la piscina* (1951), etc. En la gran pantalla, la película más conocida y que ha pasado a formar parte del canon clásico es *Testigo de cargo* (1957), basada en un libro de relatos de la autora, dirigida con maestría por Billy Wilder e interpretada por Charles Laughton, Tyrone

Power y Marlene Dietrich. Otros largometrajes basados en sus obras y que han gozado de gran reconocimiento son *El tren de las 4:50* (George Pollock, 1961), *Asesinato en el Orient Express* (Sidney Lumet, 1974; Kenneth Branagh, 2017) y *Muerte en el Nilo* (John Guillermin, 1978). En total se han realizado veintisiete películas basadas en su trabajo, así como varias series de televisión e incluso varios videojue-

Cartel de la película *Testigo de cargo*.

gos, como *The ABC Murders* (2016) y *Hercule Poirot: The First Cases* (2021).

Agatha Christie ostenta varios récords que la convierten en una figura legendaria. Según el *Libro Guinness de los récords*, es la novelista con más libros vendidos de todos los tiempos, precedida únicamente por William Shakespeare y la Biblia. También es la más traducida de la historia, a más de cien idiomas, y es la única autora que ha llegado a tener tres obras en cartel en el famoso West End de Londres.

7. *LA RATONERA*
7.1. *Génesis y contexto*

Por expreso deseo de la reina consorte María, gran admiradora de la autora, en 1947 la BBC telefoneó a Agatha Christie con una propuesta. Querían que escribiera una obra corta para el programa radiofónico que conmemoraría el octogésimo cumpleaños de la soberana. La sugerencia atrajo a la escritora y en poco tiempo redactó *Tres ratones ciegos*, inspirada en el caso real del asesinato de un niño adoptado por unos granjeros. Poco tiempo después, la novelista volvió a recibir el encargo de alargar su creación y convertirla en una pieza teatral de suspense. Christie añadió personajes e hizo más compleja la trama para retrasar el momento del clímax. Al advertir que ya existía una obra titulada *Tres ratones ciegos*, tuvo que pensar en un nuevo título y acabó optando por *La ratonera (The Mousetrap)*, quizá inspirada por Shakespeare. Concretamente, por el tercer acto de *Hamlet*, cuando tiene lugar una representación teatral con la intención de desenmascarar al culpable del asesinato del rey y a la que Hamlet llama «la ratonera», porque será la trampa en la que caerá el homicida.

No era la primera vez que Christie se enfrentaba a las tablas. En 1943 ella misma había adaptado al teatro *Diez negritos*, para lo que había tenido que cambiar el final. Aunque la obra gozó de cierto éxito, la escritura dramática nunca motivó demasiado a nuestra autora. La consideraba un mero divertimento frente a la labor creativa profunda, disciplinada y atenta al detalle que requería la novela. Con todo, como era de esperar, no solo supo crear un ambiente y una acción impagables, sino que, además, según parece, asistió con frecuencia a las representaciones y se acercó a los directores teatrales para dar algunas indicaciones sobre cómo mejorar sus puestas en escena. *La ratonera* subió a escena por primera vez el 6 de octubre de 1952 en el Royal Theatre de la ciudad de Nottingham y estuvo de gira durante siete semanas hasta que se estrenó oficialmente el 25 de noviembre del mismo año en el Ambassadors Theatre de Londres. En marzo de 1974, la pieza se trasladó al St. Martin's Theatre, donde todavía hoy continúa representándose y donde ha acabado por erigirse en el gran reclamo turístico.

La obra se estrenó, pues, en plena posguerra. El país trataba de reinventarse y la población hacía todo lo posible por recuperarse de las terribles heridas sufridas tras más de cinco años de conflicto. El racionamiento de alimentos se había superado hacía muy poco (1950), las ciudades se reconstruían después de

Representación de *La ratonera* en el Ambassadors Theatre de Londres.

los terribles bombardeos, la industria y el comercio seguían en crisis y encontrar empleo, especialmente para los jóvenes, no era una tarea fácil. Con la independencia de la India en 1947 y la retirada de las colonias africanas, el antaño orgulloso y potente Imperio Británico se desintegraba. Y, ante la patente decadencia británica, Estados Unidos y la Unión Soviética tomaban el relevo en la geopolítica mundial.

En contraste con toda esa realidad, el escenario de *La ratonera* se sitúa en la acogedora casa de huéspedes Monkswell Manor, un entorno que permite al espectador evadirse de sus penurias para concentrarse en la poderosa trama, si bien a lo largo de la obra aparecen algunas referencias a la realidad del momento. Por ejemplo, cuando algún personaje teme que haya escasez de alimentos o cuando se queja del elevado precio del carbón. En todo caso, al subir el telón, la escena nos ofrece el típico entorno de las obras de Christie que tan bien retratan la vida de la alta sociedad británica y sus mansiones aisladas en la campiña inglesa. Allí, entre personajes decadentes que intentan con todas sus fuerzas resistirse al cambio que exigen los nuevos tiempos, pueden suceder los crímenes más inesperados. La señora Boyle es en *La ratonera* la viva encarnación de ese antiguo orden en el que resulta imposible concebir una casa sin servicio o un matrimonio no acordado y bendecido por los progenitores. Es la representante de una adusta moral, herencia de la época victoriana, a la que la Segunda Guerra Mundial vino a dar su estocada de muerte. La jerarquía de amos y criados ya no tiene cabida en ese mundo que necesita renacer de sus cenizas con mayor justicia social. La nostalgia por lo antiguo está así tan presente en la obra como la lucha de la nueva pequeña burguesía personificada en el joven matrimonio Ralston.

7.2. *Estructura*

La ratonera es una obra de misterio en dos actos. El primero se abre con una escena expositiva, en la que poco a poco van entrando y se nos van presentando todos los personajes a excepción de uno, que aparecerá solo en la segunda. En el segundo acto, de una sola escena, la acción se ralentiza hasta el conflicto final, el giro donde se revela la intriga y su resolución. Todo ocurre en el salón de una antigua mansión convertida en casa de huéspedes y situada a unos cuarenta kilómetros de Londres. La trama se sitúa en un tiempo prácticamente contemporáneo al del espectador, una tarde de invierno en que una intensa nevada ha dejado incomunicada la residencia, y acabará por resolverse al ocaso del día siguiente. Agatha Christie se mantiene fiel, así, a las tres unidades aristotélicas: una sola acción, un solo lugar y también un solo día, pues todo transcurre en un lapso inferior a las veinticuatro horas.

7.3. *Personajes y temas*

La ratonera arranca efectivamente en el confortable salón de Monkswell Manor, donde la radio está emitiendo noticias poco tranquilizadoras. Se ha cometido un terrible crimen, y la información nos inquieta tanto como resulta acogedora la escenografía, que ofrece el ambiente característico de muchas obras de Christie: una casa de campo confortable cuya decoración da sensación de seguridad, transmitiendo la idea de que entre sus paredes estaremos a salvo de todo lo malo que pueda ocurrir en el exterior. Este entorno sin estridencias ayuda a focalizar la atención del espectador en la trama sin despistarlo con elucubraciones sobre dónde ocurren los acontecimientos. Y, sin embargo, esta capa de protección se resquebraja pronto cuando a través de la radio se cuelan desde el exterior los detalles de un asesinato cometido en Londres, a la vez que se detalla la descripción del asesino dado a la fuga y se anuncia una fuerte nevada. La oposición entre el mundo exterior y el interior de la casa es también recurrente en el universo de la autora, que juega sutilmente con los elementos para hacer sentir un peligro difícil de concebir siquiera dentro de nuestra zona de confort. Una vez creado el ambiente, hacen su entrada los personajes. Los primeros en aparecer son el matrimonio Ralston. Mollie es una mujer joven y guapa, algo ingenua, que ha heredado una vieja mansión y ha decidido montar una pequeña casa de huéspedes en lugar de venderla. Ya desde aquí podemos suponer que, a pesar de su inocencia, la chica es una persona capaz de tomar decisiones arriesgadas. Giles, su marido, aparece como un joven apuesto, algo arrogante, que se esfuerza por llevar a buen fin la empresa que acaba de emprender el matrimonio. El diálogo que mantienen desprende auténtica ternura, pero sus movimientos en torno a los objetos de la casa también inducen a pensar que no son del todo sinceros. Tras ellos aparece el primer huésped: Christopher Wren, un joven atolondrado, neurótico y estrafalario que establece casi de inmediato una relación de confianza con Mollie. La siguiente en entrar en escena es la señora Boyle, encarnación de la Inglaterra anterior a la guerra, severa y cargada de convenciones morales y sociales que chocan con el entorno, que critica sin ningún tipo de comedimiento. El comandante Metcalf, por su parte, es un hombre maduro, de porte militar, pero en su primera aparición ya se muestra servicial y con un talante cordial y conciliador. La siguiente visitante en llegar es la señorita Casewell, una joven de aspecto varonil, que parece acostumbrada a valerse por sí misma y cuyas réplicas ponen en evidencia tanto su inteligencia como sus ganas de no desvelar ningún detalle sobre sí misma. Cuando ya no se espera a ningún huésped más, llega la figura más curiosa del reparto: el señor Paravicini, un hombre con un sentido del humor muy negro cuyas constantes bromas y comparaciones con asesinatos harán muy poca gracia a los demás. La primera escena acaba con Mollie y Giles observándolo con inquietud.

En la segunda escena, la primera impresión que nos hemos hecho de los personajes se ve reforzada por diálogos en los que se descubren, y también se encubren, muchas cosas. A través de estas conversaciones, el espectador comienza a notar que todos tienen algo que esconder. La casa ha quedado incomunicada y nos encontramos ante un universo en el que ha coincidido un grupo variopinto, con cuya observación sin duda disfrutamos. A continuación, una llamada de teléfono avisando de la inminente llegada de un policía parece incomodarlos a todos, a pesar de que no tenemos ningún dato por el que podamos justificar esa reacción, lo que contribuye a aumentar el suspense. El recién llegado es el oficial Trotter. Su aparición genera la sensación de peligro inminente, pues tiene relación directa con la noticia que habíamos oído en la radio: hay motivos suficientes para pensar que las personas que se encuentran en Monkswell Manor pueden ser los siguientes objetivos del asesino. La sospecha de que todos allí ocultaban algo se hace evidente cuando el oficial, muy metódico en su trabajo, empieza a hacer preguntas. El espectador o el lector advierte de inmediato los nervios y la incomodidad de los huéspedes y de los propietarios. La escena y este primer acto acaban con el clímax de la obra: alguien muere asesinado en la casa.

El acto segundo tensa la acción ante la certeza de que el asesino se encuentra entre los presentes y ante la posibilidad de que se cometa un nuevo crimen. Suena repetidamente en la obra una canción que parece avisar de las acciones del criminal y que habla de tres ratoncitos, de manera que quizá haya, pues, tres víctimas. Por otra parte, el hecho de que todo el mundo guarde un secreto deja la puerta abierta a la duda y todos se convierten en sospechosos. Asimismo, al no revelar nada más sobre los personajes, la autora integra al espectador en su universo dramático. Cada pista, cada información valiosa, se muestra a la vez a los huéspedes de la mansión y a quienes están viendo la escena, y así hasta la resolución final del enigma,

Aún hoy se sigue representando la obra en el St. Martin's Theatre de Londres.

que sorprende por igual a unos y a otros. Este final, tan revelador y verosímil como inesperado y asombroso, se ha considerado el mejor elemento de la trama, su punto más fuerte y destacado.

Esta conclusión es, a la vez, la que acaba abriendo el argumento de la obra a otras cuestiones como el poder de la venganza, el peso de la justicia, los límites de la locura o la criminalización de algunas víctimas. Y es que, a pesar de ser una obra con trama y personajes muy determinados, *La ratonera* acaba planteando temas universales.

LA RATONERA

PERSONAJES

Mollie Ralston
Giles Ralston
Christopher Wren
Sra. Boyle
Comandante Metcalf
Srta. Casewell
Paravicini
Oficial de policía Trotter

PRIMER ACTO

Lugar: El gran salón de Monkswell Manor. Última hora de la tarde.

La casa no parece tanto un edificio de época como una casa en la que han vivido varias generaciones de una misma familia con recursos cada vez más escasos. Hay unos ventanales altos en el centro; un gran arco a la derecha lleva al vestíbulo, la puerta principal y la cocina; y otro arco a la izquierda lleva arriba, a las habitaciones. A la izquierda, en el primer rellano, está la puerta de la biblioteca; abajo a la izquierda está la puerta de la salita, y abajo a la derecha, la puerta (que da al escenario) del comedor; a la derecha hay una chimenea y debajo de la ventana en el centro un asiento y un radiador.

El salón está amueblado como un cuarto de estar. Hay bastantes muebles de roble antiguo, entre ellos una gran mesa de comedor al lado de la ventana en el centro y un baúl de roble a la derecha del vestíbulo. Las cortinas y los muebles tapizados (un sofá en el centro a la izquierda, un sillón en el centro, un sillón

43

grande de cuero a la derecha y una butaca victoriana a la derecha), están raídos y anticuados. Hay un escritorio y una estantería a juego a la izquierda con una radio y un teléfono encima y una silla al lado. Hay otra silla en el centro al lado de la ventana, un atril con periódicos y revistas sobre la repisa de la chimenea y una mesita para jugar a los naipes semicircular detrás del sofá. Hay dos lámparas en la pared, encima de la repisa de la chimenea, que se encienden juntas; y otra en la pared de la izquierda, una a la izquierda de la puerta de la biblioteca y otra en el vestíbulo, que también se encienden juntas. Hay interruptores dobles a la izquierda del arco de la derecha y la puerta de la parte izquierda del escenario, y un interruptor sencillo en la parte derecha al lado de la puerta. Sobre la mesita del sofá hay una lámpara.

Antes de que se levante el telón las luces de la casa se apagan y se oye la música de *Tres ratones ciegos*.[1]

Cuando se alza el telón el escenario está totalmente a oscuras. La música se apaga y deja paso a un silbido agudo de la misma canción, *Tres ratones ciegos*. Se oye el grito desgarrador de una mujer y luego varias voces masculinas y femeninas que dicen: «Dios mío, ¿qué ha sido eso?», «¡Se ha ido por ahí!», «¡Ay, Dios mío!». Luego suena un silbato de la policía, seguido de varios más, hasta que todo va quedándose en silencio.

1. Canción infantil inglesa muy popular.

Voz en la radio.—…y según Scotland Yard, el crimen ocurrió en el veinticuatro de Culver Street, en Paddington. (*Las luces se encienden y muestran el salón de Monkswell Manor. Es la última hora de la tarde y casi ha oscurecido. Se ve caer la nieve copiosamente por las ventanas del centro. El fuego está encendido. Hay un cartel recién pintado apoyado de lado en las escaleras contra el arco de la izquierda; en grandes letras dice: «Casa de huéspedes Monkwell Manor».*) La mujer asesinada era una tal señora Maureen Lyon. En relación con el asesinato, la policía está interesada en interrogar a un hombre al que se vio en las proximidades con un abrigo oscuro, una bufanda clara y un sombrero blando de fieltro. (*Mollie Ralston entra por el arco de la derecha. Es una joven alta y guapa de aire ingenuo, de unos veintitantos años. Deja el bolso y los guantes en el sillón del centro, después cruza hasta la radio y la apaga. Deja un paquetito en la estantería de encima del escritorio.*) Se advierte a los conductores de la presencia de hielo en las carreteras. Se espera que continúen las nevadas, y habrá heladas en todo el país, en particular en puntos de la costa norte y noreste de Escocia.

Mollie.—(*Llama.*) ¡Señora Barlow! ¡Señora Barlow! (*Como nadie contesta, cruza hasta el sillón del centro del escenario, recoge el bolso y un guante y sale por el arco de la derecha. Se quita el abrigo y vuelve.*) ¡Brr! Hace frío. (*Va hasta el interruptor que hay en la pared y enciende las lámparas de encima de la chimenea. Va a la ventana, toca el radiador y echa las cortinas. Luego va hasta la mesita del sofá y enciende la lámpara de mesa. Se vuelve y repara en el cartel que*

hay de lado en las escaleras. Lo recoge y lo coloca contra la pared a la izquierda del hueco de la ventana. Retrocede y asiente con la cabeza.) La verdad es que queda muy bien..., ¡oh! *(Se da cuenta de que falta la ese en el cartel.)* Qué tonto ha sido Giles. *(Mira su reloj de pulsera y luego el reloj de pared.)* ¡Cielos!

(MOLLIE sube a toda prisa las escaleras de la izquierda. GILES entra por la puerta principal a la derecha. Es un joven arrogante, pero atractivo, de unos veintitantos años. Da unas patadas en el suelo para sacudirse la nieve, abre el baúl de roble y mete dentro una enorme bolsa de papel. Se quita el abrigo, el sombrero y la bufanda y los deja en el sillón del centro. Después va al lado del fuego y se calienta las manos.)

GILES.—*(Llama.)* ¿Mollie? ¿Mollie? ¿Mollie? ¿Dónde estás?

(MOLLIE entra por el arco de la izquierda.)

MOLLIE.—*(Contenta.)* Haciendo todo el trabajo, caradura. *(Cruza hacia GILES.)*

GILES.—¡Ah, estás ahí...! Déjame el trabajo a mí. ¿Quieres que eche carbón a la calefacción?

MOLLIE.—Ya lo he hecho yo.

GILES.—*(La besa.)* Caramba, cariño. Tienes la nariz fría.

MOLLIE.—Acabo de llegar. *(Cruza el escenario hacia la chimenea.)*

GILES.—¿Por qué? ¿Dónde has estado? ¿No habrás salido con este frío?

MOLLIE.—He tenido que bajar al pueblo a por unas cosas que había olvidado. ¿Has traído la cerca de los pollos?

GILES.—No tenían la que yo quería. *(Se sienta en el reposabrazos izquierdo del sillón que hay en el centro del escenario.)* Luego fui a otro sitio, pero tampoco me gustó. He perdido todo el día. Dios mío, estoy medio congelado. No imaginas cómo patinaba el coche. Está nevando mucho. ¿Qué te apuestas a que mañana estamos bloqueados por la nieve?

MOLLIE.—Dios mío, espero que no. *(Va hasta el radiador y lo toca.)* Ojalá que no se congelen las tuberías.

GILES.—*(Se levanta y va hacia* MOLLIE.*)* Tendremos que tener la calefacción central siempre encendida. *(Toca el radiador.)* No es que caliente demasiado... Ojalá envíen pronto el carbón. Ya no queda mucho.

MOLLIE.—*(Va hacia el sofá y se sienta.)* ¡Oh! Espero que todo vaya bien desde el principio. Las primeras impresiones son muy importantes.

GILES.—*(Va a la derecha del sofá.)* ¿Está todo listo? Supongo que aún no habrá llegado nadie.

MOLLIE.—No, gracias a Dios. Creo que todo está preparado. La señora Barlow se ha ido pronto. Supongo que tenía miedo del tiempo.

GILES.—Qué fastidio son estas asistentas. Eso deja toda la carga en tus hombros.

MOLLIE.—¡Y en los tuyos! Somos socios.

GILES.—*(Cruza el escenario hacia la chimenea.)* Con tal de que no me pidas que cocine.

MOLLIE.—(*Se levanta.*) No, no, ese es mi departamento. En cualquier caso, tenemos latas de sobra por si nos quedamos bloqueados por la nieve. (*Va hacia* GILES.) ¡Ay, Giles!, ¿crees que todo irá bien?

GILES.—Tienes miedo, ¿eh? ¿Te arrepientes de que no vendiéramos la casa cuando tu tía te la dejó, en vez de tener la absurda idea de convertirla en una casa de huéspedes?

MOLLIE.—No, qué va. Me encanta. Y hablando de la casa de huéspedes. ¡Mira eso! (*Señala hacia el cartel con gesto acusador.*)

GILES.—(*Complacido.*) Ha quedado bien, ¿eh? (*Va hacia la izquierda del cartel.*)

MOLLIE.—¡Es un desastre! ¿No lo ves? Te has olvidado la ese. Has escrito «Monkwell» en vez de «Monkswell».

GILES.—Dios mío, es verdad. ¿Cómo he podido? Pero no tiene tanta importancia, ¿no? Monkwell es un nombre igual de bueno.

MOLLIE.—Te mereces un castigo. (*Va hacia el escritorio.*) Ve a echar carbón en la calefacción.

GILES.—¡Al otro lado de ese patio helado! ¡Uf! ¿Le echo para toda la noche?

MOLLIE.—No, espera hasta las diez o las once.

GILES.—¡Qué horror!

MOLLIE.—Date prisa. En cualquier momento puede llegar alguien.

GILES.—¿Están listas todas las habitaciones?

MOLLIE.—Sí. (*Se sienta al escritorio y coge una hoja de papel.*) La señora Boyle en la habitación que tiene la cama con dosel. El comandante Metcalf en la habitación azul. La señorita Casewell, en la habitación este. El señor Wren, en la habitación con los paneles de roble.

GILES.—*(Va a la derecha de la mesita del sofá.)* Vete a saber cómo será esa gente. ¿No deberíamos haberles cobrado por adelantado?

MOLLIE.—Oh, no, no lo creo.

GILES.—Somos novatos en este negocio.

MOLLIE.—Traen equipaje. Si no pagan, nos quedamos con sus maletas. Es muy sencillo.

GILES.—No dejo de pensar que deberíamos haber hecho un curso por correspondencia para regentar un hotel. Seguro que nos timan. Las maletas podrían estar llenas de ladrillos envueltos en papeles de periódico. ¿Y qué haríamos entonces?

MOLLIE.—Todos tienen señas muy respetables.

GILES.—Igual que los criados con referencias falsas. Algunas de esas personas podrían ser criminales que huyen de la policía. *(Va hacia el cartel y lo recoge.)*

MOLLIE.—Me da igual lo que sean, con tal de que nos paguen siete guineas a la semana.

GILES.—Eres una mujer de negocios maravillosa, Mollie.

(GILES sale con el cartel por el arco de la derecha. MOLLIE enciende la radio.)

VOZ EN LA RADIO.—Y según Scotland Yard, el crimen ocurrió en el veinticuatro de Culver Street, en Paddington. La mujer asesinada era una tal señora Maureen Lyon. En relación con el asesinato, la policía... *(MOLLIE se levanta y va hasta el sillón del cen-*

tro.)... está interesada en interrogar a un hombre al que se vio en las proximidades con un abrigo oscuro... (MOLLIE *recoge el abrigo de* GILES.)..., una bufanda clara... (MOLLIE *recoge su bufanda.)*... y un sombrero blando de fieltro. (MOLLIE *recoge el sombrero y sale por el arco de la derecha.)* Se advierte a los conductores de la presencia de hielo en las carreteras. *(Suena el timbre de la puerta.)* Se espera que continúen las nevadas, y habrá heladas en todo el... (MOLLIE *entra, va hasta el escritorio, apaga la radio y sale a toda prisa por el arco de la derecha.)*

MOLLIE.—*(Fuera de escena.)* ¿Cómo está usted?

CHRISTOPHER.—*(Fuera de escena.)* Muchas gracias. (CHRISTOPHER WREN *entra por el arco de la derecha con una maleta que deja a la derecha de la mesa de comedor. Es un joven de aspecto neurótico y desquiciado. Lleva el pelo largo y despeinado y una bufanda de punto de fantasía. Sus modales son casi infantiles.* MOLLIE *entra y va hacia el centro del escenario.)* Hace un tiempo sencillamente espantoso. Mi taxi se rindió al llegar a la verja. *(Cruza el escenario y deja el sombrero encima de la mesita del sofá.)* No se atrevió con el camino de entrada. No tenía espíritu deportivo. *(Va hacia* MOLLIE.*)* ¿Es usted la señora Ralston? ¡Qué encantadora! Soy Christopher Wren.

MOLLIE.—¿Cómo está usted, señor Wren?

CHRISTOPHER.—¿Sabe? No se parece en nada a como la había imaginado. Pensé que sería la viuda de un general retirado del Ejército del Raj Británico. Pensaba que sería lúgubre y muy Memsahib, y que la casa estaría abarrotada de objetos de latón de Benarés.[2] Y en vez de eso, este sitio es celestial... *(Cruza por delante del sofá y se queda la izquierda de la mesita del sofá.)*, celestial. Las proporciones son preciosas. *(Señala hacia el escritorio.)* ¡Ese es falso! *(Señala a la mesita del sofá.)* ¡Ah!, pero esta mesa es auténtica. Me va a encantar este sitio. *(Va hacia el sillón del centro.)* ¿Tiene flores de cera o aves del paraíso?

MOLLIE.—Me temo que no.

CHRISTOPHER.—¡Qué lástima! Bueno, ¿y qué me dice de un aparador? Un aparador de caoba de color ciruela con grandes frutas talladas en él.

MOLLIE.—Sí, tenemos uno... en el comedor. *(Mira hacia la puerta que hay a la derecha.)*

CHRISTOPHER.—*(Sigue su mirada.)* ¿Aquí? *(Va hacia la derecha y abre la puerta.)* Tengo que verlo.

> (CHRISTOPHER *sale por la puerta del comedor y* MOLLIE *lo sigue.* GILES *entra por el arco de la derecha. Mira a su alrededor y ve la maleta. Al oír voces en el comedor, sale por la derecha.)*

MOLLIE.—*(Fuera de escena.)* Venga a calentarse.

> (MOLLIE *entra desde el comedor, seguida de* CHRISTOPHER. MOLLIE *va hacia el centro del escenario.)*

---

2. Con la palabra *Memsahib* se aludía a las mujeres blancas de clase alta que vivían en la India. Benarés es una ciudad india situada en la riba del Ganges.

CHRISTOPHER.—*(Al entrar.)* Es perfecto. De una respetabilidad sólida como una roca. Pero ¿por qué no han puesto una mesa de centro de caoba? *(Mira a la derecha.)* Las mesitas estropean el efecto.

(GILES *entra por la derecha y se queda a la derecha del sillón del centro del escenario.)*

MOLLIE.—Pensamos que los huéspedes las preferirían... Le presento a mi marido.

CHRISTOPHER.—*(Va hacia* GILES *y le estrecha la mano.)* Encantado. Qué tiempo tan espantoso, ¿eh? Me recuerda a Dickens y a Scrooge y al cargante del pequeño Tim.[3] Qué impostado. *(Se vuelve hacia el fuego.)* Por supuesto, señora Ralston, tiene usted toda la razón en lo de las mesitas. Me estaba dejando llevar por mi afición a los muebles antiguos. Si tuviese una mesa de comedor de caoba, necesitaría sentar alrededor la familia indicada. *(Se vuelve hacia* GILES.) Un padre serio y apuesto con barba, una madre prolífica y cansada, once niños de edades diversas, una lúgubre gobernanta, y alguien llamado «la pobre Harriet», ¡la pariente pobre siempre a disposición de todos que se siente muy *muy* agradecida de que le hayan dado un buen hogar!

GILES.—*(Con desagrado.)* Le subiré la maleta. *(Coge la maleta. A* MOLLIE.) Has dicho a la habitación con paneles de roble, ¿no?

MOLLIE.—Sí.

3. Ambos, Scrooge y Tim, son personajes dickensianos y aparecen en la obra *Canción de Navidad* (1843).

CHRISTOPHER.—Espero que tenga una cama con dosel y pequeñas rosas de cretona.

GILES.—Pues no.

(GILES *sale y sube por las escaleras de la izquierda con la maleta.*)

CHRISTOPHER.—Creo que a su marido no le caigo bien. *(Da unos pasos hacia* MOLLIE.*)* ¿Cuánto tiempo llevan casados? ¿Está usted muy enamorada?

MOLLIE.—*(Con frialdad.)* Llevamos casados justo un año. *(Va hacia las escaleras de la izquierda.)* ¿No quiere subir a ver su habitación?

CHRISTOPHER.—¡Me merezco la regañina! *(Va hacia la mesita del sofá.)* Pero me encanta saberlo todo de la gente. Quiero decir que la gente es muy interesante. ¿No le parece?

MOLLIE.—Bueno, supongo que hay quien lo es y *(Se vuelve hacia* CHRISTOPHER.*)* quien no lo es.

CHRISTOPHER.—No, no estoy de acuerdo. Todo el mundo es interesante, porque nunca se sabe cómo es nadie en realidad... ni en qué está pensando. Por ejemplo, usted no sabe en qué pienso ahora, ¿a que no? *(Sonríe como si pensara en una broma privada.)*

MOLLIE.—No tengo ni la menor idea. *(Va hacia la mesita del sofá y coge un cigarrillo de la caja.)* ¿Un cigarrillo?

CHRISTOPHER.—No, gracias. *(Va a la derecha de* MOLLIE.*)* ¿Lo ve? Las únicas personas que saben cómo son los demás son los artistas... ¡y no saben por qué lo saben! Pero si son retratistas *(Va hacia el cen-*

tro del escenario.) sale a relucir... *(Se sienta en el reposabrazos derecho del sofá.)* en el lienzo.

MOLLIE.—¿Es usted pintor? *(Enciende el cigarrillo.)*

CHRISTOPHER.—No, soy arquitecto. Mis padres
me bautizaron Christopher con la esperanza de que
me hiciese arquitecto. ¡Christopher Wren! *(Se ríe.)*
Ya tenía la mitad del camino hecho. En realidad, claro, todo el mundo se burla y hace bromas sobre la
catedral de San Pablo.[4] Aunque, ¿quién sabe? Todavía puedo ser el que ría el último. (GILES *entra por el
arco de la izquierda y cruza hasta el de la derecha.)*
¡Las casas prefabricadas de hormigón Chris Wren
aún pueden pasar a la historia! *(A* GILES.*)* Voy a estar
a gusto aquí. Su mujer me parece *muy* simpática.

GILES.—*(Con frialdad.)* No me diga.

CHRISTOPHER.—*(Volviéndose para mirar a* MOL-
LIE.*)* Y muy guapa, la verdad.

MOLLIE.—¡Oh! No sea absurdo.

(GILES *se apoya en el respaldo del sillón.)*

CHRISTOPHER.—Bueno, ¿no le parece típico de una
auténtica inglesa? Los cumplidos siempre las aver-
güenzan. Las mujeres europeas dan los cumplidos
por descontados, pero a las inglesas sus maridos les
aplastan todo espíritu femenino. *(Se vuelve y mira a*
GILES.*)* Los maridos ingleses tienen un no sé qué muy
grosero. ¿No le parece?

4. Uno de los monumentos arquitectónicos más célebres de
Londres, de cuyo diseño se encargó el famoso arquitecto inglés
Christopher Wren (1632-1723).

Mollie.—*(Atropellada.)* Suba a ver su habitación. *(Va hacia el arco de la izquierda.)*

Christopher.—¿Puedo?

Mollie.—*(A* Giles.*)* ¿Podrías echar carbón en la caldera del agua caliente?

> (Mollie *y* Christopher *salen y suben las escaleras de la izquierda.* Giles *frunce el ceño y va hacia el centro del escenario. Suena el timbre de la puerta. Se produce una pausa y el timbre vuelve a sonar varias veces con impaciencia.* Giles *sale apresuradamente por la derecha hacia la puerta principal. Por un instante se oyen el viento y la nieve.)*

La Sra. Boyle.—*(Fuera de escena.)* Esto debe de ser Monkswell Manor, ¿no?

Giles.—*(Fuera de escena.)* Sí...

> (La Sra. Boyle *entra por el arco de la derecha, cargada con una maleta, unas revistas y sus guantes. Es una mujer imponente y corpulenta y está de muy mal humor.)*

La Sra. Boyle.—Soy la señora Boyle. *(Deja la maleta en el suelo.)*

Giles.—Yo soy Giles Ralston. Por favor, caliéntese un poco junto al fuego, señora Boyle. (La Sra. Boyle *se acerca al fuego.)* Qué tiempo tan espantoso, ¿verdad? ¿Es este todo su equipaje?

La Sra. Boyle.—Un tal comandante... ¿Metcalf, puede ser?... se está encargando de él.

Giles.—Dejaré abierta la puerta para que pueda entrar.

(Giles *va a la puerta principal.*)

La Sra. Boyle.—El taxi no se ha atrevido a subir por el camino de entrada. (Giles *vuelve y se queda a la izquierda de* La Sra. Boyle.) Se ha parado en la verja. Hemos tenido que compartir un taxi desde la estación... y hasta *eso* ha sido difícil. *(En tono acusador.)* Por lo visto nadie había avisado de que fuesen a recogernos.

Giles.—Lo lamento mucho. No sabíamos en qué tren vendrían; de lo contrario, por supuesto, habríamos, ¡ejem!, enviado a alguien.

La Sra. Boyle.—Deberían haber enviado a alguien a la llegada de todos los trenes.

Giles.—Deje que le coja el abrigo. (La Sra. Boyle *le da a* Giles *los guantes y las revistas y se queda junto al fuego calentándose las manos.*) Mi mujer vendrá en seguida. Iré un momento a ayudar a Metcalf con las bolsas.

(Giles *sale por la derecha hacia la puerta principal.*)

La Sra. Boyle.—*(Va hacia el arco al ver marcharse a* Giles.) Deberían haber despejado al menos la nieve del camino de entrada. *(Después de que salga.)* Tengo que decir que todo me parece muy improvisado. *(Va hacia el fuego y mira a su alrededor con un gesto de desaprobación.)*

(Mollie *llega corriendo desde las escale-*
ras de la izquierda, le falta un poco el
aliento.)

Mollie.—Lo siento mucho, yo...
La Sra. Boyle.—¿Es usted la señora Ralston?
Mollie.—Sí... *(Va hacia* La Sra. Boyle, *le tiende*
la mano con indecisión, luego la aparta, sin saber qué
suelen hacer los dueños de las casas de huéspedes.)

(La Sra. Boyle *observa a* Mollie *con de-*
sagrado.)

La Sra. Boyle.—Es usted muy joven.
Mollie.—¿Joven?
La Sra. Boyle.—Para regentar un establecimien-
to como este. No puede tener mucha experiencia.
Mollie.—*(Retrocediendo.)* Todo el mundo tiene
que empezar en algún momento, ¿no cree?
La Sra. Boyle.—Entiendo. Sin experiencia. *(Mira*
a su alrededor.) Es una casa vieja. Espero que no haya
carcoma. *(Olisquea con suspicacia.)*
Mollie.—*(Con indignación.)* ¡Por supuesto que
no!
La Sra. Boyle.—Mucha gente no se da cuenta de
que tiene carcoma hasta que es demasiado tarde.
Mollie.—La casa está en perfectas condiciones.
La Sra. Boyle.—¡Hum!..., no le vendría mal una
mano de pintura. Esa mesa de roble tiene carcoma.
Giles.—*(Fuera de escena.)* Por aquí, comandante.
(Giles *y* El comandante Metcalf *entran por la dere-*
cha. El comandante Metcalf *es un hombre de me-*

diana edad, ancho de hombros, de porte y modales castrenses. GILES *se dirige al centro del escenario.* EL COMANDANTE METCALF *deja la maleta que lleva en el suelo y va hacia el sillón del centro del escenario;* MOLLIE *acude a su encuentro.)* Le presento a mi mujer.

METCALF.—*(Estrechándole la mano a* MOLLIE.*)* ¿Cómo está usted? Ahí fuera sopla una auténtica ventisca. Ha habido un momento en que he pensado que no llegábamos. *(Ve a* LA SRA. BOYLE.*)* ¡Oh!, le ruego que me disculpe. *(Se quita el sombrero.* LA SRA. BOYLE *sale por la derecha.)* Si continúa así, yo diría que tendremos entre metro y medio y dos metros de nieve por la mañana. *(Cruza hacia el fuego.)* No había visto nada igual desde que estuve de permiso en 1940...

GILES.—Yo le subiré las maletas. *(Coge las maletas. Se dirige a* MOLLIE.*)* ¿Qué habitaciones dijiste? ¿La habitación azul y la rosa?

MOLLIE.—No... He instalado a Wren en la habitación rosa. Le encantó la cama con dosel. Así que la señora Boyle irá a la habitación con paneles de roble y el comandante Metcalf, a la habitación azul.

GILES.—*(En tono autoritario.)* ¡Comandante! *(Va a la izquierda hacia las escaleras.)*

METCALF.—*(Responde instintivamente como un soldado.)* ¡Señor!

> (EL COMANDANTE METCALF *sigue a* GILES *y salen ambos por las escaleras de la izquierda.* LA SRA. BOYLE *entra por la derecha y va hacia la chimenea.)*

LA SRA. BOYLE.—¿Tienen muchos problemas con los criados?

MOLLIE.—Tenemos una señora muy servicial que viene del pueblo.

LA SRA. BOYLE.—¿Y el personal de la casa?

MOLLIE.—No hay más personal. Solo nosotros. *(Va por delante del escenario hasta la izquierda del sillón.)*

LA SRA. BOYLE.—Ya. Tenía entendido que esta era una casa de huéspedes en pleno funcionamiento.

MOLLIE.—Acabamos de empezar.

LA SRA. BOYLE.—Yo habría dicho que los criados eran esenciales para este tipo de establecimiento. Su anuncio me parece muy engañoso. ¿Puedo preguntar si soy la única huésped... además del comandante Metcalf, quiero decir?

MOLLIE.—¡Oh, no!, hay varios más.

LA SRA. BOYLE.—Y encima con este tiempo. Una ventisca... *(Se vuelve hacia el fuego.)* Nada menos... Todo muy desafortunado.

MOLLIE.—Pero ¡no podíamos prever que haría este tiempo!

(CHRISTOPHER WREN *entra sin hacer ruido desde las escaleras de la izquierda y se acerca* MOLLIE *por detrás.)*

CHRISTOPHER.—*(Canta.)*

*Sopla el viento del norte
y traerá la nieve
¿y qué será del pobre petirrojo?*

Me encantan las cancioncillas infantiles, ¿a usted no? Siempre tan trágicas y *macabras*. Por eso les gustan a los niños.

MOLLIE.—¿Me permite presentarles? El señor Wren..., la señora Boyle.

CHRISTOPHER.—¿Cómo está usted, señora?

(CHRISTOPHER *inclina la cabeza.*)

LA SRA. BOYLE.—(*Con frialdad.*) Encantada.

CHRISTOPHER.—Es una casa preciosa. ¿No le parece?

LA SRA. BOYLE.—He llegado a ese momento de la vida en el que las comodidades de un establecimiento son más importantes que su apariencia. (CHRISTOPHER *retrocede hacia la derecha.* GILES *entra desde las escaleras de la izquierda y se queda debajo del arco.*) Si no hubiese creído que esta era una casa seria, jamás habría venido. Entendí que estaba totalmente equipada y con todas las comodidades domésticas.

GILES.—No tiene por qué quedarse si no está a gusto, señora Boyle.

LA SRA. BOYLE.—(*Cruza el escenario hacia la derecha del sofá.*) No, desde luego. Ni se me pasaría por la cabeza.

GILES.—Si ha habido algún malentendido, tal vez sería mejor que se fuese usted a alguna otra parte. Puedo telefonear al taxi para que vuelva. Las carreteras aún no están bloqueadas. (CHRISTOPHER *se adelanta y se sienta en el sillón del centro del escenario.*) Hemos tenido tantas solicitudes de habitaciones que podremos ocuparla fácilmente. En cualquier caso, el mes que viene vamos a subir los precios.

LA SRA. BOYLE.—Por supuesto que no voy a marcharme antes de haber probado cómo es este sitio. No crea que va a poder echarme ahora. (GILES *va hacia la izquierda del escenario.*) ¿Podría llevarme a mi dormitorio, señora Ralston? (*Se dirige majestuosa hacia la escalera de la izquierda.*)

MOLLIE.—Por supuesto, señora Boyle. (*Sigue a* LA SRA. BOYLE. *A* GILES, *en voz baja, al pasar a su lado.*) Cariño, has estado maravilloso...

(LA SRA. BOYLE *y* MOLLIE *salen por las escaleras de la izquierda.*)

CHRISTOPHER.—(*Se levanta, con un gesto infantil.*) Qué mujer tan espantosa. No me gusta nada. Debería haberla echado usted y haberla dejado bajo la nieve. Se lo habría merecido.

GILES.—Es un placer al que me temo que tendré que renunciar. (*Suena el timbre de la puerta.*) Dios, ahí llega otro. (GILES *sale hacia la puerta principal. Fuera de escena.*) Adelante..., adelante.

(LA SRTA. CASEWELL *entra por la derecha. Es una joven de aspecto masculino y va cargada con una maleta. Lleva un abrigo largo y oscuro, una bufanda de color claro y no lleva sombrero.* GILES *entra.*)

CASEWELL.—(*Con voz profunda y masculina.*) Me temo que mi coche está atascado a casi un kilómetro por la carretera... He chocado con un montón de nieve.

GILES.—Deje que le lleve esto. (*Coge la maleta y la pone a la derecha de la mesa de comedor.*) ¿Ha dejado algo más en el coche?

CASEWELL.—(*Se acerca al fuego.*) No, viajo ligera de equipaje. (GILES *se pone detrás del sillón del centro.*) Uf, me alegro de que tengan un buen fuego. (*Se pone delante de la chimenea con gesto masculino.*)

GILES.—Ejem... Señor Wren... ¿La señorita...?

CASEWELL.—Casewell. (*Saluda a* CHRISTOPHER *con un movimiento de cabeza.*)

GILES.—Mi mujer bajará en un minuto.

CASEWELL.—No hay prisa. (*Se quita el abrigo.*) Tengo que descongelarme. Me parece que se van a quedar ustedes aislados. (*Saca un periódico vespertino del bolsillo.*) El pronóstico del tiempo dice que se esperan fuertes nevadas. Avisan a los conductores y demás. Espero que tengan suficientes provisiones.

GILES.—Oh, sí. Mi mujer es una administradora excelente. Además, siempre podríamos comernos las gallinas.

CASEWELL.—Antes de empezar a comernos unos a otros, ¿eh?

(*Se ríe con estridencia y lanza el abrigo a* GILES, *que lo coge al vuelo. Se sienta en el sillón del centro del escenario.*)

CHRISTOPHER.—(*Se levanta y va hacia el fuego.*) ¿Alguna noticia interesante en el periódico... aparte del tiempo?

CASEWELL.—Los líos políticos de costumbre. ¡Ah, sí, y un asesinato de lo más jugoso!

CHRISTOPHER.—¿Un asesinato? *(Se vuelve hacia* LA SRTA. CASEWELL.) ¡Oh, me encantan los asesinatos!

CASEWELL.—*(Le da el periódico.)* Por lo visto, creen que ha sido un maníaco homicida. Estranguló a una mujer cerca de la estación de Paddington. Un maníaco sexual, supongo. *(Mira a* GILES.)

> (GILES *cruza a la izquierda de la mesita del sofá.)*

CHRISTOPHER.—No dice gran cosa, ¿no? *(Se sienta en la butaca de la derecha y lee.)* «La policía está interesada en interrogar a un hombre al que se vio en las proximidades de Culver Street en el momento de producirse los hechos. De estatura mediana, con un abrigo oscuro, una bufanda clara y un sombrero blando de fieltro. Se han emitido mensajes por la radio al respecto todo el día.»

CASEWELL.—Una descripción muy útil. Encajaría con cualquiera, ¿no creen?

CHRISTOPHER.—Cuando dicen que la policía está interesada en interrogar a alguien, ¿es una manera educada de insinuar que es el asesino?

CASEWELL.—Es posible.

GILES.—¿Quién es la mujer asesinada?

CHRISTOPHER.—La señora Lyon. La señora Maureen Lyon.

GILES.—¿Joven o vieja?

CHRISTOPHER.—No lo dice. No parece que haya sido un robo...

CASEWELL.—(*A* GILES.) Se lo dije: un maníaco sexual.

(MOLLIE *baja las escaleras y va al lado de* LA SRTA. CASEWELL.)

GILES.—Esta es la señorita Casewell. Mollie, mi mujer.

CASEWELL.—(*Poniéndose en pie.*) Encantada. (*Le estrecha la mano a* MOLLIE. GILES *coge su maleta.*)

MOLLIE.—Hace una noche espantosa. ¿Quiere subir a su habitación? Hay agua caliente, si quiere darse un baño.

CASEWELL.—Tiene usted razón, debería.

(MOLLIE *y* LA SRTA. CASEWELL *salen por las escaleras de la izquierda.* GILES *va detrás de ellas cargando con la maleta. Cuando lo dejan a solas,* CHRISTOPHER *se levanta y empieza a explorar la habitación. Abre la puerta de la izquierda, se asoma y luego sale. Un momento después reaparece en las escaleras de la izquierda. Cruza hasta el arco de la derecha y se asoma. Canturrea* Little Jack Horner, *se ríe para sus adentros y da la impresión de estar un poco desequilibrado. Pasa detrás de la mesa de comedor.* GILES *y* MOLLIE *entran desde las escaleras de la izquierda charlando.* CHRISTOPHER *se esconde detrás de la cortina.* MOLLIE *pasa por detrás del sillón del centro y* GILES *va al extremo derecho de la mesa de comedor.*)

MOLLIE.—Tengo que ir a la cocina. El comandante Metcalf es muy amable. No nos dará problemas. La que me asusta es la señora Boyle. La cena *tiene* que salir bien. Estaba pensando en abrir un par de latas de carne en conserva, cereales, una lata de guisantes y preparar un puré. También tenemos higos confitados y natillas. ¿Crees que está bien?

GILES.—¡Oh!, yo creo que sí. No..., tal vez no sea muy original.

CHRISTOPHER.—(*Sale de detrás de la cortina y se coloca entre* GILES *y* MOLLIE.) Deje que la ayude. Me encanta cocinar. ¿Por qué no hacemos una tortilla? Tienen huevos, ¿no?

MOLLIE.—Sí, hay huevos de sobra. Tenemos muchas gallinas. No ponen tanto como deberían, pero hemos acumulado un montón de huevos.

(GILES *se aparta a la izquierda.*)

CHRISTOPHER.—Y si tienen una botella de vino barato, de cualquier clase, podrían echárselo a la... ¿ha dicho carne en conserva? Le dará un toque más europeo. Dígame dónde está la cocina y qué es lo que tiene y creo que algo se me ocurrirá.

MOLLIE.—Venga por aquí. (MOLLIE *y* CHRISTOPHER *salen por el arco de la derecha en dirección a la cocina.* GILES *frunce el ceño, murmura para sus adentros y va hacia la butaca de la derecha. Coge el periódico y lo lee con mucha atención. Da un respingo cuando* MOLLIE *vuelve a la sala y le habla.*) ¿No te parece que es un encanto? (*Va detrás de la mesita del sofá.*) Se ha puesto un delantal y lo está preparando todo. Me ha dicho que lo deje todo en sus manos y que no vuelva hasta dentro de media hora. Si nuestros clientes quieren preparar su propia comida, nos ahorrarán mucho trabajo.

GILES.—¿Por qué le has dado la mejor habitación?

MOLLIE.—Ya te lo dije, le gustó la cama con dosel.

GILES.—Le gustó la bonita cama con dosel. ¡Idiota!

MOLLIE.—¡Giles!

GILES.—No me gustan los tipos así. *(En tono elocuente.)* Tú no has cargado con su maleta, yo sí.

MOLLIE.—¿Tenía ladrillos dentro? *(Va hacia el sillón del centro y se sienta en él.)*

GILES.—No pesaba nada. Mi opinión es que dentro no había *nada*. Quizá sea uno de esos jóvenes que van por ahí estafando a los dueños de los hoteles.

MOLLIE.—No lo creo. Me gusta. La señorita Casewell me parece muy peculiar, ¿a ti no?

GILES.—Es una mujer horrible..., suponiendo que sea una mujer.

MOLLIE.—También es mala pata que todos nuestros huéspedes sean raros o antipáticos. En fin, el comandante Metcalf no está mal, ¿verdad?

GILES.—¡Probablemente beba!

MOLLIE.—¡Oh! ¿Tú crees?

GILES.—La verdad es que no. Solo estoy un poco desanimado. En fin, en cualquier caso, ahora ya sabemos a qué atenernos. Han llegado todos.

(Suena el timbre de la puerta.)

MOLLIE.—¿Quién puede ser?

GILES.—Casi seguro el asesino de Culver Street.

MOLLIE.—*(Se levanta.)* ¡No digas eso!

(GILES *sale por la derecha hacia la puerta principal.* MOLLIE *va en dirección a la chimenea.)*

GILES.—*(Fuera de escena.)* ¡Oh!

(EL SR. PARAVICINI *entra tambaleándose por la derecha cargado con una maleta pequeña. Es extranjero, moreno y anciano, con un bigote muy llamativo. Es una versión un poco más alta de Hércules Poirot, lo cual puede dar una impresión equivocada al público. Lleva un abrigo grueso de piel. Se apoya en el lado izquierdo del arco y deja la maleta en el suelo.* GILES *entra.)*

PARAVICINI.—Mil perdones. Estoy en... ¿dónde estoy?

GILES.—Esta es la casa de huéspedes Monkswell Manor.

PARAVICINI.—¡Pero qué buena suerte la mía! ¡Señora! *(Va hacia* MOLLIE, *le toma la mano y la besa.* GILES *pasa por detrás del sillón del centro del escenario.)* Es una respuesta a mis plegarias. Una casa de huéspedes... y una anfitriona encantadora. Mi Rolls Royce, ¡ay!, ha chocado con un montón de nieve. La nieve apenas deja ver nada. No sé dónde estoy. Tal vez, me digo a mí mismo, muera congelado. Y luego cojo un bolso de mano. Voy dando tumbos por la nieve, veo ante mí una enorme verja de hierro. ¡Una casa! Estoy salvado. Dos veces me caigo en la nieve al subir por el camino de entrada, pero por fin llego y en el acto... *(Mira a su alrededor.)* la desesperación se convierte en alegría. *(Cambia de actitud.)* Me alquilarán una habitación, ¿verdad?

GILES.—Oh, sí...

MOLLIE.—Me temo que es muy pequeña.

PARAVICINI.—Claro..., claro..., tienen otros huéspedes.

MOLLIE.—Acabamos de abrir la casa de huéspedes hoy mismo, y somos... muy nuevos en esto.

PARAVICINI.—*(Mira lascivamente a* MOLLIE.*)* Encantadora..., encantadora...

GILES.—¿Y su equipaje?

PARAVICINI.—No tiene importancia. He cerrado el coche con llave.

GILES.—Pero ¿no sería mejor ir a buscarlo?

PARAVICINI.—No, no. *(Va a la derecha de* GILES.*)* Puedo asegurarle que en una noche como esta no habrá ladrones por ahí. En cuanto a mí, mis necesidades son muy sencillas. Tengo todo lo que necesito... aquí..., en este bolso. Sí, todo lo que necesito.

MOLLIE.—Vale más que se caliente un poco. *(EL SR. PARAVICINI cruza el salón para ir a la chimenea.)* Iré a prepararle la habitación. *(Va hacia el sillón del centro del escenario.)* Me temo que es un poco fría, porque da al norte, pero todas las demás están ocupadas.

PARAVICINI.—Entonces, ¿tiene usted muchos huéspedes?

MOLLIE.—Están la señora Boyle, el comandante

Metcalf, la señorita Casewell, un joven llamado Christopher Wren... y ahora... usted.

PARAVICINI.—Sí... el huésped inesperado. El huésped al que no han invitado. El huésped recién llegado de ninguna parte..., salido de la tormenta. Suena muy teatral, ¿no cree? ¿Quién soy? No lo sabe. ¿De dónde vengo? No lo sabe. Soy un hombre misterioso. *(Se ríe.* MOLLIE *se ríe y mira a* GILES, *que esboza una vaga sonrisa.* PARAVICINI *asiente con la cabeza y mira a* MOLLIE *de muy buen humor.)* Pero deje que le diga una cosa. Conmigo se completa el cuadro. A partir de ahora no vendrá nadie más. Ni tampoco se irá. A partir de mañana..., tal vez incluso ahora..., estaremos apartados de la civilización. Ni carnicero, ni panadero, ni lechero, ni cartero, ni periódicos diarios, ni nadie ni nada, solo nosotros. Es admirable... admirable. No podía convenirme más. Por cierto, me llamo Paravicini. *(Va hacia la butaca de la derecha.)*

MOLLIE.—¡Ah, sí! Nosotros somos los Ralston.

*(*GILES *va a la izquierda de* MOLLIE.)*

PARAVICINI.—¿El señor y la señora Ralston? *(Asiente con la cabeza cuando ellos se lo confirman. Mira a su alrededor y va hacia la derecha de* MOLLIE.)* ¿Y esta... es la casa de huéspedes Monkswell Manor, dice usted? Bien. La casa de huéspedes Monkswell Manor. *(Se ríe.)* Perfecto *(Se ríe.)* Perfecto. *(Se ríe y va hacia la chimenea.)*

*(*MOLLIE *mira a* GILES *y los dos miran in-*

cómodos a PARAVICINI *mientras... cae el telón.)*

ESCENA II

Mismo lugar. La tarde siguiente.

Cuando se levanta el telón no está nevando, pero se ve la nieve amontonada contra la ventana. EL COMANDANTE METCALF está sentado en el sofá leyendo un libro, y LA SRA. BOYLE está sentada en el sillón grande justo delante del fuego, escribiendo en un cuaderno que tiene sobre la rodilla.

LA SRA. BOYLE.—Me parece muy poco honrado por su parte no habernos avisado de que acababan de abrir este sitio.

METCALF.—Bueno, todo tiene que empezar alguna vez, ya me entiende. El desayuno esta mañana ha sido excelente. Buen café. Huevos revueltos, mermelada casera de naranja. Y todo muy bien presentado. Esa jovencita lo hace todo ella sola.

LA SRA. BOYLE.—Son unos aficionados: deberían tener personal como es debido.

METCALF.—La comida también ha sido excelente.

LA SRA. BOYLE.—Carne en conserva.

METCALF.—Pero muy bien aderezada. Con vino tinto. La señora Ralston ha prometido hacernos una empanada de carne para cenar.

LA SRA. BOYLE.—*(Se levanta y va hacia el radiador.)* Estos radiadores no calientan nada. Me quejaré.

METCALF.—Las camas son comodísimas. Al menos la mía. Espero que la suya también.

LA SRA. BOYLE.—No estaba mal. *(Vuelve al sillón grande y se sienta.)* No acabo de entender por qué han tenido que darle la mejor habitación a ese joven *tan* raro.

METCALF.—Él llegó antes. Los primeros en llegar se llevan lo mejor.

LA SRA. BOYLE.—El anuncio me dio una idea *muy* diferente de cómo sería este sitio. Un salón cómodo, un sitio mucho más grande... con mesas de bridge y otras distracciones.

METCALF.—Un auténtico paraíso de las solteronas.

LA SRA. BOYLE.—¿Cómo ha dicho?

METCALF.—Ejem..., que sí, que puede que tenga razón.

(CHRISTOPHER entra desde las escaleras de la izquierda sin que lo vean.)

LA SRA. BOYLE.—No, desde luego, no me quedaré mucho aquí.

CHRISTOPHER.—*(Se ríe.)* No. No creo.

(CHRISTOPHER sale hacia la biblioteca de arriba a la izquierda.)

LA SRA. BOYLE.—La verdad es que es un joven muy peculiar. No me extrañaría que fuese un desequilibrado.

METCALF.—Parece que se haya escapado de un manicomio.

La Sra. Boyle.—No me sorprendería.

(Mollie *entra por el arco de la derecha.*)

Mollie.—*(Grita hacia las escaleras.)* ¿Giles?
Giles.—*(Fuera de escena.)* ¿Sí?
Mollie.—¿Puedes volver a quitar la nieve de la puerta de atrás?
Giles.—*(Fuera de escena.)* ¡Ya voy!

(Mollie *desaparece por el arco.*)

Metcalf.—Le echaré una mano, ¿quiere? *(Se levanta y va hacia la derecha en dirección al arco.)* Es un ejercicio muy saludable. Hay que hacer ejercicio.

(El comandante Metcalf *sale.* Giles *entra desde las escaleras, cruza el escenario y sale por la derecha.* Mollie *vuelve con un plumero y una aspiradora, cruza el vestíbulo y sube por las escaleras. Choca con* La Srta. Casewell, *que estaba bajando.)*

Mollie.—¡Lo siento!
Casewell.—No pasa nada.

(Mollie *sale.* La Srta. Casewell *va despacio hacia el centro del escenario.)*

La Sra. Boyle.—¡Vaya! Qué joven tan increíble.

¿Es que no sabe cómo llevar una casa? Cargar con la aspiradora por el vestíbulo. ¿Es que no hay escaleras de servicio?

CASEWELL.—*(Saca un cigarrillo de una cajetilla que lleva en el bolso.)* ¡Oh, sí! Unas escaleras de servicio estupendas. *(Va hacia la chimenea.)* Muy prácticas en caso de incendio. *(Enciende el cigarrillo.)*

LA SRA. BOYLE.—¿Y por qué no las usa? Además, debería hacer la limpieza por la mañana antes de comer.

CASEWELL.—Supongo que tiene que preparar la comida.

LA SRA. BOYLE.—Todo muy improvisado y poco profesional. Debería haber personal cualificado.

CASEWELL.—No es fácil de encontrar en estos tiempos, ¿no cree?

LA SRA. BOYLE.—No, desde luego, las clases inferiores parecen ignorar cuáles son sus responsabilidades.

CASEWELL.—Pobres clases inferiores. No tienen mucha elección, ¿verdad?

LA SRA. BOYLE.—*(Con gelidez.)* Supongo que es usted socialista.

CASEWELL.—Oh, yo no diría eso. No soy roja..., solo rosa pálido. *(Va hacia el sofá y se sienta en el reposabrazos derecho.)* Pero no estoy muy interesada en la política..., vivo en el extranjero.

LA SRA. BOYLE.—Supongo que en el extranjero las condiciones son mucho más fáciles.

CASEWELL.—No tengo que limpiar y cocinar... como tengo entendido que hace la mayoría de la gente en este país.

LA SRA. BOYLE.—Por desgracia este país está en

decadencia. No es lo que era. El año pasado vendí mi casa. Todo era demasiado difícil.

CASEWELL.—Los hoteles y las casas de huéspedes son más fáciles.

LA SRA. BOYLE.—Desde luego solucionan muchos problemas. ¿Va a pasar mucho tiempo en Inglaterra?

CASEWELL.—Depende. Tengo que ocuparme de unos asuntos. Cuando los resuelva... volveré.

LA SRA. BOYLE.—¿A Francia?

CASEWELL.—No.

LA SRA. BOYLE.—¿A Italia?

CASEWELL.—No. *(Sonríe.)*

> (LA SRA. BOYLE *la mira intrigada, pero* LA SRTA. CASEWELL *no le responde.* LA SRA. BOYLE *empieza a escribir.* LA SRTA. CASEWELL *sonríe, va hasta la radio, la enciende, al principio no muy alta, luego sube el volumen.)*

LA SRA. BOYLE.—*(Irritada mientras escribe.)* ¡Le importaría no poner eso tan alto! La radio siempre me despista cuando estoy intentando escribir una carta.

CASEWELL.—¿Ah, sí?

LA SRA. BOYLE.—Si no tiene especial interés en escucharla ahora...

CASEWELL.—Es mi programa favorito. Tiene una mesa allí. *(Hace un gesto en dirección a la puerta de la biblioteca a la derecha.)*

LA SRA. BOYLE.—Lo sé. Pero aquí se está mucho más caliente.

Casewell.—Sí, mucho más. (*Baila al son de la música.* La Sra. Boyle, *después de echarle una mirada furiosa, se levanta y va a la biblioteca de arriba a la izquierda.* La Srta. Casewell *sonríe, va a la mesita del sofá y apaga el cigarrillo. Va a la parte de atrás del escenario y coge una revista de la mesa de comedor.*) Puñetera vieja bruja. (*Va hacia el sillón grande y se sienta.*)

(Christopher *entra desde la biblioteca y va a la izquierda del escenario.*)

Christopher.—¡Oh!
Casewell.—Hola.
Christopher.—(*Hace un gesto en dirección a la biblioteca.*) Vaya donde vaya, esa mujer parece perseguirme..., y luego me mira furiosa..., furiosa de verdad.
Casewell.—(*Señala a la radio.*) Bájela un poco.

(Christopher *baja la radio hasta que casi no se oye.*)

Christopher.—¿Así mejor?
Casewell.—¡Oh, sí, ya ha cumplido su propósito!
Christopher.—¿Qué propósito?
Casewell.—Tácticas, muchacho.

(Christopher *parece confundido.* La Srta. Casewell *señala hacia la biblioteca.*)

81

CHRISTOPHER.—¡Ah!, lo dice por *ella*.

CASEWELL.—Estaba sentada en el mejor sillón. Ahora lo tengo yo.

CHRISTOPHER.—La ha echado usted. Me alegro. Me alegro mucho. No me gusta nada. *(Va deprisa hacia* LA SRTA. CASEWELL.) Pensemos qué podemos hacer para molestarla, ¿le parece? Ojalá se fuese.

CASEWELL.—¿Con este tiempo? Abandone toda esperanza.

CHRISTOPHER.—Pues cuando se derrita la nieve.

CASEWELL.—¡Oh! Cuando se derrita la nieve pueden haber pasado muchas cosas.

CHRISTOPHER.—Sí..., sí..., eso es cierto. *(Va a la ventana.)* La nieve es preciosa, ¿no cree? Tan pacífica... y pura... Hace que uno se olvide de las cosas.

CASEWELL.—A mí no me hace olvidar.

CHRISTOPHER.—¡Qué feroz parece usted!

CASEWELL.—Estaba pensando.

CHRISTOPHER.—¿En qué? *(Se sienta en el asiento de la ventana.)*

CASEWELL.—Hielo en la jarra de una habitación, sabañones sangrantes, una manta fina deshilachada..., un niño que tiembla de miedo y frío.

CHRISTOPHER.—Dios mío, suena demasiado..., demasiado lúgubre, ¿qué es? ¿Una novela?

CASEWELL.—No sabía que era escritora, ¿a que no?

CHRISTOPHER.—¿Lo es? *(Se levanta y va a su lado.)*

CASEWELL.—Siento decepcionarle. La verdad es que no. *(Se pone la revista delante de la cara.)*

(CHRISTOPHER *la mira dubitativo, luego*

va a la izquierda, enciende la radio, la pone muy alta y se dirige hacia la salita. Suena el teléfono. MOLLIE *baja corriendo las escaleras, plumero en mano, y va hacia el teléfono.)*

MOLLIE.—*(Descuelga el auricular.)* ¿Sí, dígame? *(Apaga la radio.)* Sí... aquí la casa de huéspedes Monkswell Manor. ¿Qué...? No, me temo que el señor Ralston no puede ponerse al teléfono ahora mismo. Soy la señora Ralston. ¿Quién...? ¿La policía de Berkshire? *(LA SRTA. CASEWELL baja la revista.)* Oh, sí, sí, subcomisario Hogben, me temo que es imposible. No podría llegar. Estamos bloqueados por la nieve. Totalmente. Las carreteras están cerradas... *(LA SRTA. CASEWELL se levanta y va hacia el arco de la izquierda.)* No puede pasar nadie... Sí... Muy bien... Pero ¿qué...? Oiga..., oiga... *(Cuelga el auricular.)*

*(*GILES *entra por la derecha con un abrigo. Se lo quita y lo cuelga en el vestíbulo.)*

GILES.—Mollie, ¿sabes dónde hay otra pala?
MOLLIE.—*(Va hacia el centro del escenario.)* Giles, acaba de llamar la policía.
CASEWELL.—Problemas con la policía, ¿eh? ¿Es que venden alcohol sin licencia?

*(*LA SRTA. CASEWELL *sale por las escaleras de la izquierda.)*

MOLLIE.—Van a enviar a un inspector, un oficial o algo por el estilo.

GILES.—*(Va a la derecha de* MOLLIE.) Pero no podrá llegar.

MOLLIE.—Ya se lo he dicho. Pero parecían convencidos de que sí podría.

GILES.—Tonterías. Ni siquiera un *jeep* podría pasar hoy. Pero ¿qué ocurre?

MOLLIE.—Es lo que le he preguntado. Pero no me lo ha dicho. Solo que le dijese a mi marido que escuchara con mucha atención al oficial Trotter, creo que ha dicho, y que siguiese sus instrucciones implícitamente. ¿No te parece rarísimo?

GILES.—*(Va hacia el fuego.)* ¿Qué demonios crees que hemos hecho?

MOLLIE.—*(Va a la izquierda de* GILES.) ¿Crees que será por aquellas medias de contrabando?

GILES.—Me acordé de pagar la licencia de radio, ¿verdad?

MOLLIE.—Sí, está en el armario de la cocina.

GILES.—El otro día estuve a punto de chocarme con el coche, pero fue culpa del otro tipo.

MOLLIE.—Debemos de haber hecho alguna cosa...

GILES.—*(Se arrodilla y echa un tronco al fuego.)* Es probable que sea algo que tenga que ver con regentar este lugar. Imagino que habremos hecho caso omiso de alguna norma absurda de algún ministerio. Hoy en día es casi imposible no hacerlo. *(Se levanta y se sitúa delante de* MOLLIE.)

MOLLIE.—¡Ay, cariño! Ojalá no hubiésemos abierto este sitio. Nos vamos a pasar días bloqueados y todo el mundo está enfadado y se nos acabarán las reservas de latas.

GILES.—Anímate, cariño. *(Coge a* MOLLIE *entre sus brazos.)* Por ahora todo va bien. He llenado todos los cubos de carbón y metido la leña, he avivado la calefacción y guardado las gallinas. Ahora iré a echar carbón en la caldera y cortaré un poco de leña... *(Se interrumpe.)* ¿Sabes, Mollie? *(Va despacio a la derecha de la mesa de comedor.)* Ahora que lo pienso, tiene que ser algo muy grave para que envíen a un oficial andando hasta aquí. Debe de ser algo muy urgente...

> (GILES y MOLLIE *se miran incómodos.* LA SRA. BOYLE *llega desde la biblioteca a la izquierda.)*

LA SRA. BOYLE.—*(Va a la izquierda de la mesa de comedor.)* ¡Ah!, está usted aquí, señor Ralston. ¿Sabe que la calefacción en la biblioteca está casi fría?

GILES.—Lo siento, señora Boyle, estamos un poco cortos de carbón y...

LA SRA. BOYLE.—Pago siete guineas a la semana..., siete guineas, y no quiero congelarme.

GILES.—Iré a echar más carbón. (GILES *sale por la derecha.* MOLLIE *le sigue hasta el arco.)*

LA SRA. BOYLE.—Señora Ralston, si no le importa que se lo diga, ese joven que se aloja aquí es muy peculiar. Sus modales... y sus corbatas... ¿Es que no se peina nunca?

MOLLIE.—Es un joven arquitecto muy brillante.

LA SRA. BOYLE.—¿Cómo dice?

MOLLIE.—Christopher Wren es arquitecto...

LA SRA. BOYLE.—Mi querida señora. Naturalmente que he oído hablar de sir Christopher Wren. (*Cruza hasta el fuego.*) Y ya sé que era arquitecto. Construyó la catedral de San Pablo. Ustedes los jóvenes piensan que los demás no hemos tenido una educación.

MOLLIE.—Digo *este* Wren. Se llama Christopher. Sus padres lo llamaron así con la esperanza de que se hiciese arquitecto. (*Cruza hasta la mesita del sofá y saca un cigarrillo de la caja.*) Y lo es, o casi, así que les salió bien.

LA SRA. BOYLE.—¡Hum! No sé si creerme esa historia. (*Se sienta en el sillón grande.*) En su lugar haría algunas averiguaciones. ¿Qué sabe usted de él?

MOLLIE.—Más o menos lo mismo que sé de usted, señora Boyle: que ambos nos pagan siete guineas por semana por alojarse aquí. (*Enciende el cigarrillo.*) En realidad, es lo único que necesito saber, ¿no cree? Y es lo único que me interesa. Da igual si me gustan mis huéspedes o (*En tono elocuente.*) no.

LA SRA. BOYLE.—Es usted joven e inexperta y debería dar gracias cuando le aconseja alguien que sabe más que usted. ¿Y qué me dice de ese extranjero?

MOLLIE.—¿Qué le pasa?

LA SRA. BOYLE.—No lo esperaban, ¿no?

MOLLIE.—Echar a un viajero *bona fide* va contra la ley, señora Boyle. Precisamente usted debería saberlo.

LA SRA. BOYLE.—¿Por qué dice eso?

MOLLIE.—(*Va hacia el centro.*) ¿No era usted magistrada, señora Boyle?

LA SRA. BOYLE.—Solo digo que el tal Paravicini, o como quiera que se llame, me parece...

(PARAVICINI *entra sin hacer ruido.*)

PARAVICINI.—Vaya con cuidado señora. Habla usted del rey de Roma y por la puerta asoma. Ja, ja.

(LA SRA. BOYLE *da un respingo.*)

LA SRA. BOYLE.—No le he oído entrar.

(MOLLIE *se pone detrás de la mesita del sofá.*)

PARAVICINI.—He entrado de puntillas..., así. *(Hace una demostración y va al centro del escenario.)* Nadie me oye si yo no quiero. Me parece muy divertido.

LA SRA. BOYLE.—¿De verdad?

PARAVICINI.—*(Se sienta en el sillón del centro del escenario.)* Había una joven que...

LA SRA. BOYLE.—*(Poniéndose en pie.)* En fin, tengo que seguir con mis cartas. Veré si hace más calor en la salita. (LA SRA. BOYLE *sale hacia la salita por la izquierda.* MOLLIE *la sigue hasta la puerta.*)

PARAVICINI.—Mi encantadora anfitriona parece disgustada. ¿Qué le ocurre, querida señora? *(La mira lascivamente.)*

MOLLIE.—Esta mañana todo es más complicado por culpa de la nieve.

PARAVICINI.—Sí, la nieve lo dificulta todo, ¿verdad? *(Se pone en pie.)* O lo facilita. *(Va hacia la mesa de comedor.)* Sí, lo facilita mucho.

MOLLIE.—No sé por qué lo dice.

PARAVICINI.—No, hay muchas cosas que no sabe. Por ejemplo, creo que no sabe muy bien cómo llevar una casa de huéspedes.

MOLLIE.—*(Va hacia la izquierda de la mesita del sofá y apaga el cigarrillo.)* Me temo que no. Pero nuestra intención es llegar a tener éxito.

PARAVICINI.—¡Bravo..., bravo! *(Aplaude y se pone en pie.)*

MOLLIE.—No soy tan mala cocinera.

PARAVICINI.—*(Con lascivia.)* Sin duda es usted una cocinera encantadora. *(Va detrás de la mesita del sofá y le coge la mano a MOLLIE. Ella la aparta y pasa por delante del sofá mientras se dirige al centro del escenario.)* ¿Me permite que le haga una pequeña advertencia, señora Ralston? *(Va delante del sofá.)* No conviene que usted y su marido sean demasiado confiados. ¿Tiene usted referencias de todos sus huéspedes?

MOLLIE.—¿Es lo habitual? *(Se vuelve hacia PARAVICINI.)* Siempre pensé que la gente... venía sin más.

PARAVICINI.—Es recomendable saber un poco más de la gente que duerme bajo su techo. Piense en mí, por ejemplo. Llego aquí diciendo que mi coche ha chocado con un montón de nieve. ¿Qué sabe de mí? ¡Nada! Podría ser un ladrón, un atracador *(Se acerca despacio a MOLLIE.)*, un fugitivo de la justicia, un loco, incluso un asesino.

MOLLIE.—*(Retrocede.)* ¡Ay!

PARAVICINI.—¡Ya lo ve! Y probablemente tampoco sepa nada de los otros huéspedes.

MOLLIE.—Bueno, en el caso de la señora Boyle...

(LA SRA. BOYLE *entra desde la salita.* MOL-
LIE *va hacia el centro de la mesa de comedor.*)

LA SRA. BOYLE.—En la salita hace demasiado frío.
Escribiré mis cartas aquí. *(Cruza en dirección al sillón
grande.)*
PARAVICINI.—Permita que le avive el fuego. *(Va a
la derecha y lo aviva.)*

(EL COMANDANTE METCALF *entra por el
arco de la derecha.*)

METCALF.—*(Se dirige a* MOLLIE *con anticuada mo-
destia.)* Señora Ralston, ¿está su marido? Me temo
que las tuberías del, ejem, guardarropa de abajo se
han congelado.
MOLLIE.—Dios mío, qué día tan espantoso. Primero las tuberías y luego la policía. *(Va hacia el arco
de la derecha.)*

(PARAVICINI *suelta el atizador con estrépi-
to.* EL COMANDANTE METCALF *se queda
paralizado.*)

LA SRA. BOYLE.—*(Sobresaltada.)* ¿La policía?
METCALF.—*(En voz alta, como con incredulidad.)*
¿Ha dicho usted la policía? *(Va hacia el extremo izquierdo de la mesa de comedor.)*
MOLLIE.—Acaban de telefonear. Dicen que van a
enviar a un oficial. *(Mira hacia la nieve.)* Aunque no
creo que pueda llegar.

(GILES *entra por el arco de la derecha con una cesta de leña.*)

GILES.—El puñetero carbón no se enciende. Y eso que lo pago a... Caramba, ¿pasa algo?

METCALF.—He oído que la policía viene para aquí. ¿Por qué?

GILES.—¡Ah, no se preocupe por eso! Nadie puede pasar con esta nevada. Los montones de nieve deben de tener más de metro y medio de altura. Las carreteras están todas bloqueadas. Hoy no vendrá nadie. (*Lleva los troncos a la chimenea.*) Disculpe, señor Paravicini. ¿Me permite que deje esto en el suelo?

(PARAVICINI *va hacia la chimenea. Se oyen tres golpes secos en la ventana y* EL OFICIAL DE POLICÍA TROTTER *aprieta la cara contra el cristal y se asoma al interior.* MOLLIE *da un grito y señala hacia él.* GILES *va hacia allí y abre la ventana.* EL OFICIAL DE POLICÍA TROTTER *lleva esquís y es un joven alegre y normal con un ligero acento cockney.*[5])

TROTTER.—¿Es usted el señor Ralston?

GILES.—Sí.

TROTTER.—Gracias, señor. Soy el oficial Trotter, de la policía de Berkshire. ¿Puedo quitarme estos esquís y dejarlos en algún sitio?

5. Acento de una zona determinada del este de Londres.

GILES.—(*Señala hacia la derecha.*) Dé la vuelta por ese lado hasta la puerta principal. Iré a abrirle.

TROTTER.—Gracias, señor.

(GILES *deja la ventana abierta y sale por la derecha hacia la puerta principal.*)

LA SRA. BOYLE.—Supongo que para eso pagamos hoy en día a la policía, para que vayan por ahí disfrutando de los deportes de invierno.

(MOLLIE *pasa por delante de la mesa de comedor mientras se dirige a la ventana.*)

PARAVICINI.—(*Va hacia la mesa de comedor y le susurra con enfado a* MOLLIE.) ¿Por qué ha llamado a la policía, señora Ralston?

MOLLIE.—Pero si no les he llamado. (*Cierra la ventana.*)

(CHRISTOPHER *entra desde la salita de la izquierda y va a la izquierda del sofá.* PARAVICINI *va al extremo derecho de la mesa de comedor.*)

CHRISTOPHER.—¿Quién es ese? ¿De dónde ha salido? Ha pasado con unos esquís por delante de la ventana de la salita. Por encima de la nieve y con un aspecto de lo más jovial.

LA SRA. BOYLE.—Lo creerá o no, pero ese hombre es policía. ¡Un policía esquiando!

(Giles y Trotter llegan de la puerta principal. Trotter se ha quitado los esquís y los lleva a cuestas.)

Giles.—*(Va a la derecha del arco de la derecha.)* Ejem... Les presento al oficial de policía Trotter.

Trotter.—*(Va a la izquierda del sillón.)* Buenas tardes.

La Sra. Boyle.—No puede ser usted oficial. Es demasiado joven.

Trotter.—No soy tan joven como aparento, señora.

Christopher.—Pero sí muy jovial.

Giles.—Dejaremos sus esquís debajo de las escaleras, oficial.

(Giles y Trotter salen por el arco de la derecha.)

Metcalf.—Disculpe, señora Ralston, pero ¿podría utilizar su teléfono?

Mollie.—Por supuesto, comandante Metcalf.

(El comandante Metcalf va al teléfono y marca un número.)

Christopher.—*(Se sienta en el extremo más alejado del sofá.)* Es muy atractivo, ¿no les parece? Los policías siempre me han parecido muy atractivos.

La Sra. Boyle.—No es muy listo. Se nota nada más verle.

METCALF.—*(Por teléfono.)* ¡Oiga! ¡Oiga...! *(A* MOLLIE.*)* Señora Ralston, el teléfono no funciona... Está estropeado.

MOLLIE.—Hace un rato funcionaba.

METCALF.—Supongo que la línea debe de haberse cortado por el peso de la nieve.

CHRISTOPHER.—*(Riéndose con histerismo.)* Ahora sí que estamos aislados. Aislados del todo. Es gracioso, ¿no les parece?

METCALF.—*(Va a la izquierda del sofá.)* No le veo la gracia.

LA SRA. BOYLE.—Desde luego que no.

CHRISTOPHER.—¡Ay!, son cosas mías. ¡Chis! Aquí vuelve el sabueso.

(TROTTER *entra desde el arco de la derecha, seguido de* GILES. TROTTER *va al centro mientras* GILES *cruza a la izquierda de la mesita del sofá.)*

TROTTER.—*(Saca su cuaderno de notas.)* Bueno, ¿podemos ir al grano, señor y señora Ralston?

(MOLLIE *va hacia el centro del escenario.)*

GILES.—¿Quiere que hablemos a solas? Si es así, podemos ir a la biblioteca.

TROTTER.—*(De espaldas al público.)* No es necesario, señor. Ahorraremos tiempo si todos están presentes. ¿Puedo sentarme a esta mesa? *(Va hacia el centro de la mesa de comedor.)*

94

Paravicini.—Disculpe. *(Va por detrás de la mesa hasta el otro extremo de la sala.)*

Trotter.—Gracias. *(Se instala con aire oficial en el centro detrás de la mesa.)*

Mollie.—¡Ay!, dese prisa y díganos. *(Va hacia el extremo de la derecha de la mesa de comedor.)* ¿Qué hemos hecho?

Trotter.—*(Sorprendido.)* ¿Qué han hecho? ¡Oh!, no es nada de *eso*, señora Ralston. No tiene nada que ver. Es más bien una cuestión de protección policial, ya me entiende.

Mollie.—¿Protección policial?

Trotter.—Tiene que ver con la muerte de la señora Lyon..., la señora Lyon del veinticuatro de Culver Street, en Londres, a quien asesinaron ayer, el día quince del presente mes. ¿Tal vez haya oído o leído algo sobre el caso?

Mollie.—Sí. Lo he oído en la radio. ¿Es la mujer a la que estrangularon?

Trotter.—Exacto, señora. *(A Giles.)* Lo primero que quiero saber es si conocían a la tal señora Lyon.

Giles.—No había oído hablar de ella en mi vida.

(Mollie niega con la cabeza.)

Trotter.—Es posible que no la conocieran por el nombre de Lyon. Lyon no era su verdadero nombre. Tenía antecedentes policiales y sus huellas dactilares estaban en los archivos, así que pudimos identificarla sin dificultad. Su verdadero nombre era Maureen Stanning. Su marido era John Stanning, un granjero que residía en la granja Longridge, no muy lejos de aquí.

GILES.—¡La granja Longridge! ¿No fue allí donde esos niños...?

TROTTER.—Sí, el caso de la granja Longridge.

(LA SRTA. CASEWELL *entra desde las escaleras de la izquierda.*)

CASEWELL.—Tres niños... (*Cruza hasta el sillón de la derecha y se sienta. Todos la miran.*)

TROTTER.—Eso es, señorita. Los Corrigan. Dos niños y una niña. El tribunal dictaminó que necesitaban cuidados y protección. Les buscaron una casa con el señor y la señora Stanning en la granja Longridge. Uno de los niños murió después por malos tratos y abandono. El caso dio bastante que hablar en su época.

MOLLIE.—(*Muy conmovida.*) Fue horrible.

TROTTER.—A los Stanning los condenaron a varios años de prisión. Él murió en la cárcel. La señora Stanning cumplió su sentencia y la pusieron en libertad. Ayer, como he dicho, la encontraron estrangulada en el veinticuatro de Culver Street.

MOLLIE.—¿Quién lo hizo?

TROTTER.—Ahora iremos a eso, señora. Cerca de la escena del crimen recogieron un cuaderno de notas. En él había escritas dos direcciones. Una era el veinticuatro de Culver Street. La otra (*Hace una pausa.*) era Monkswell Manor.

GILES.—¿Qué?

TROTTER.—Sí, señor. (*Mientras dura el siguiente parlamento,* PARAVICINI *va despacio hacia las escaleras de la izquierda y se apoya en la parte más alejada del arco.)* Por eso el subcomisario Hogben, al recibir esta información de Scotland Yard, ha creído imprescindible que viniese y averiguara si saben de alguna relación entre esta casa, o alguien de la casa, y el caso de la Granja Longridge.

GILES.—*(Va al extremo izquierdo de la mesa de comedor.)* No hay ninguna... absolutamente ninguna. Tiene que ser una coincidencia.

TROTTER.—El subcomisario Hogben no cree que sea una coincidencia, señor. (EL COMANDANTE METCALF *se vuelve y mira a* TROTTER. *Mientras duran los siguientes parlamentos saca la pipa y la rellena.)* Habría venido él mismo si hubiese podido. En vista del tiempo que hace, y como yo sé esquiar, me ha enviado para recopilar los datos personales de todos los presentes en la casa, informarle por teléfono y tomar las medidas que considere necesarias para garantizar la seguridad de la casa.

GILES.—¿La seguridad? ¿Cree que corremos algún peligro? Dios mío, no querrá decir que van a asesinar a nadie aquí.

TROTTER.—No quiero asustar a las señoras... pero, con franqueza, sí, esa es la idea.

GILES.—Pero... ¿por qué?

TROTTER.—Eso es lo que he venido a averiguar.

GILES.—Pero ¡todo esto es una locura!

TROTTER.—Sí, señor. Y por eso mismo es peligroso.

LA SRA. BOYLE.—¡Tonterías!

CASEWELL.—Debo decir que parece un poco traído por los pelos.

CHRISTOPHER.—A mí me parece maravilloso. *(Se vuelve y mira al* COMANDANTE METCALF.)

(EL COMANDANTE METCALF *enciende la pipa.)*

MOLLIE.—¿Hay algo que no nos haya dicho, oficial?

TROTTER.—Sí, señora Ralston. Al pie de las dos direcciones habían escrito «Tres ratones ciegos». Y sobre el cadáver de la mujer había un papel que decía: «Esta es la primera», y debajo había un dibujo de tres ratoncitos y una partitura musical. La música era la melodía de la cancioncilla infantil *Tres ratones ciegos.* Ya saben cómo suena. *(Canta.)*

Tres ratones ciegos...

MOLLIE.—*(Canta.)*

Mira cómo corren.
Todos corrieron detrás de la mujer del granjero,
que les cortó...

¡Ay, es horrible!

GILES.—¿Había tres niños y uno murió?

TROTTER.—Sí, el pequeño, un niño de once años.

GILES.—¿Qué fue de los otros dos?

TROTTER.—A la niña la adoptaron. No hemos podido dar con su paradero actual. El mayor debe de tener ahora unos veintidós años. Desertó del ejército y no se ha vuelto a saber de él. Según el psicólogo del ejército, era un auténtico esquizofrénico. *(Sigue explicándoles.)* Es decir, que estaba un poco mal de la cabeza.

MOLLIE.—¿Creen que es él quien mató a la señora Lyon..., a la señora Stanning? *(Va hacia el sillón del centro del escenario.)*

TROTTER.—Sí.

MOLLIE.—Y que es un maníaco homicida *(Se sienta.)* y que piensa presentarse aquí para intentar asesinar a alguien..., pero ¿por qué?

TROTTER.—Eso es lo que tengo que averiguar de ustedes. El subcomisario opina que tiene que haber alguna relación. *(A GILES.)* ¿Entonces dice usted, señor, que nunca ha tenido la menor relación con el caso de la granja Longridge?

GILES.—No.

TROTTER.—¿Y lo mismo usted, señora?

MOLLIE.—*(Incómoda.)* Yo... no..., quiero decir..., ninguna relación.

TROTTER.—¿Y qué hay de los criados?

(LA SRA. BOYLE *hace constar su desaprobación.)*

MOLLIE.—No tenemos criados. *(Se levanta y va hacia la derecha del arco.)* Eso me recuerda que... ¿Le importa, oficial TROTTER, si voy a la cocina? Estaré allí, si me necesita.

TROTTER.—Está bien, señora Ralston. (MOLLIE *sale por el arco de la derecha.* GILES *cruza a la derecha del arco, pero se detiene al oír a* TROTTER.) En fin, ¿pueden darme sus nombres, por favor?

La Sra. Boyle.—Esto es ridículo. Solo nos alojamos en una especie de hotel. Llegamos ayer mismo. No tenemos nada que ver con este sitio.

Trotter.—Sin embargo, todos planearon venir aquí de antemano. Hicieron las reservas con antelación.

La Sra. Boyle.—Pues, sí. Todos menos el señor... *(Mira a* Paravicini.*)*

Paravicini.—Paravicini. *(Va hacia el extremo izquierdo de la mesa de comedor.)* Mi coche chocó con un montón de nieve.

Trotter.—Entiendo. Lo que quiero decir es que cualquiera que les haya seguido podría saber que iban a venir aquí. Necesito saber una cosa cuanto antes. ¿Quién de ustedes es el que tiene algo que ver con lo que pasó en la granja Longridge? *(Se produce un silencio sepulcral.)* No están siendo muy sensatos. Uno de ustedes corre peligro..., un peligro mortal. Tengo que saber quién es. *(Se produce otro silencio.)* Muy bien, tendré que preguntarles uno por uno. *(A* Paravicini.*)* Usted primero, puesto que parece haber llegado aquí más o menos por accidente, señor Pari...

Paravicini.—Para... Paravicini. Pero, mi querido inspector, yo no sé nada, nada de lo que ha estado contando. Soy extranjero. No sé nada de los asuntos locales del pasado.

Trotter.—*(Se levanta y va a la izquierda de* La Sra. Boyle.*)* ¿Señora...?

La Sra. Boyle.—Boyle. No veo..., en realidad me parece una impertinencia... ¿Por qué iba a tener nada que ver con... este desdichado incidente?

(EL COMANDANTE METCALF *la mira fija-mente.*)

TROTTER.—(*Mira a* LA SRTA. CASEWELL.) ¿Señorita...?

CASEWELL.—(*Despacio.*) Casewell. Leslie Casewell. Nunca había oído hablar de la granja Longridge
y no sé nada del asunto.

TROTTER.—(*Va a la derecha del sofá y se dirige al*
COMANDANTE METCALF.) ¿Y usted, señor?

METCALF.—Metcalf..., comandante Metcalf. Leí
acerca del caso en los periódicos en su momento. En
aquella época estaba en Edimburgo. No tengo ningún vínculo personal con él.

TROTTER.—(*A* CHRISTOPHER.) ¿Y usted?

CHRISTOPHER.—Christopher Wren. Era solo un
niño en esa época. No recuerdo haber oído hablar
siquiera de ello.

TROTTER.—(*Va detrás de la mesita del sofá.*) ¿Y
eso es todo lo que tienen que decir... todos ustedes?
(*Se produce un silencio. Va hacia el centro.*) Bueno,
si asesinan a uno de ustedes, la culpa será suya. En
fin, señor Ralston, ¿puedo echar un vistazo a la
casa?

(TROTTER *sale por la derecha con* GILES.
PARAVICINI *se sienta en el asiento de la
ventana.*)

CHRISTOPHER.—(*Se pone en pie.*) Amigos míos,
qué melodramático. Es muy atractivo, ¿verdad? (*Va
hasta la mesa de comedor.*) La verdad es que admiro a

101

la policía. Tan duros y serios. Todo este asunto es muy emocionante. *Tres ratones ciegos*. ¿Cómo es la canción? *(La silba.)*

La Sra. Boyle.—¡La verdad, señor Wren!

Christopher.—¿No le gusta? *(Va a la izquierda de La Sra. Boyle.)* Pero es una melodía de apertura..., la firma del asesino. Imagínese lo que debe de gustarle.

La Sra. Boyle.—Tonterías melodramáticas. No me creo ni una palabra.

Christopher.—*(Se le acerca con disimulo por detrás.)* Pero espere, señora Boyle. Hasta que me acerque a su espalda con disimulo y note mis manos en el cuello.

La Sra. Boyle.—Pare... *(Poniéndose en pie.)*

Metcalf.—Ya es suficiente, Christopher. Una broma sin ninguna gracia. De hecho, ni siquiera es una broma.

Christopher.—¡Oh, claro que sí! *(Va por detrás del sillón del centro.)* ¡Es justo eso! La broma de un loco. Eso es lo que la hace tan deliciosamente *macabra. (Va hasta el arco, mira a su alrededor y se ríe.)* ¡Si pudieran verse la cara!

(Christopher *sale por el arco.)*

La Sra. Boyle.—*(Va hacia el arco por la derecha.)* Un joven particularmente maleducado y neurótico.

(Mollie *entra desde el comedor a la derecha y se queda al lado de la puerta.)*

MOLLIE.—¿Dónde está Giles?

CASEWELL.—Ha llevado al policía a hacer una visita guiada de la casa.

LA SRA. BOYLE.—*(Va hasta el sillón grande.)* Su amigo, el arquitecto, se ha portado de un modo de lo más extraño.

METCALF.—Hoy en día los jóvenes son muy nerviosos. Seguro que se le pasará.

LA SRA. BOYLE.—*(Sentándose.)* ¿Nervios? No tengo paciencia con la gente que dice ser nerviosa. Yo no soy nerviosa.

(LA SRTA. CASEWELL *se levanta y va hacia las escaleras de la derecha.)*

METCALF.—¿No? Tal vez sea una ventaja para usted, señora Boyle.

LA SRA. BOYLE.—¿Qué quiere decir?

METCALF.—*(Va hacia la derecha del sillón del centro.)* Creo que en la época era usted magistrada. De hecho, fue usted responsable de enviar a esos tres niños a la granja Longridge.

LA SRA. BOYLE.—La verdad, comandante Metcalf. No se puede decir que fuese responsable. Recibimos informes de los asistentes sociales. Los granjeros parecían personas muy agradables y estaban deseosos de recibir a los niños. Nos pareció de lo más conveniente. Huevos, leche fresca y una vida saludable al aire libre.

METCALF.—Patadas, golpes, hambre y una pareja de lo más cruel.

MOLLIE.—Sí, yo tenía razón. *(Va al centro del es-*

cenario y mira fijamente a LA SRA. BOYLE.) Fue usted...

(EL COMANDANTE METCALF *mira muy serio a* MOLLIE.)

LA SRA. BOYLE.—Te esfuerzas en cumplir con un deber público y lo único que consigues es que te insulten.

(PARAVICINI *se ríe jovial.*)

PARAVICINI.—Deben perdonarme ustedes, pero la verdad es que esto me parece de lo más divertido. Me estoy divirtiendo mucho.

(*Sin dejar de reír,* PARAVICINI *sale por la izquierda del salón.* MOLLIE *va a la derecha del sofá.*)

LA SRA. BOYLE.—¡Ese hombre no me gusta un pelo!

CASEWELL.—(*Va hacia la izquierda de la mesita del sofá.*) ¿De dónde salió anoche? (*Saca un cigarrillo de la caja.*)

MOLLIE.—No lo sé.

CASEWELL.—Me parece un poco falso. Y lleva maquillaje. Polvos cosméticos y colorete. Es repugnante. Y debe de ser bastante viejo. (*Enciende el cigarrillo.*)

MOLLIE.—Pues se mueve como si fuese joven.

METCALF.—Va a hacer falta más leña. Iré a por ella.

(EL COMANDANTE METCALF *sale por la derecha.*)

MOLLIE.—Ya casi ha oscurecido y son solo las cuatro de la tarde. Encenderé las luces. *(Va a la derecha y enciende las lámparas de encima de la chimenea.)* Así está mejor.

> *(Se hace una pausa.* LA SRA. BOYLE *mira incómoda primero a* MOLLIE *y luego a* LA SRTA. CASEWELL, *que la están mirando.)*

LA SRA. BOYLE.—*(Recoge sus artículos de escritorio.)* Vaya, ¿dónde he dejado la pluma? *(Se levanta y va hacia la izquierda.)*

> *(*LA SRA. BOYLE *sale por la izquierda en dirección a la biblioteca. Se oye un piano donde alguien toca la melodía de* Tres ratones ciegos *con un dedo.)*

MOLLIE.—*(Va hasta la ventana para echar las cortinas.)* Qué cancioncilla tan horrible.

CASEWELL.—¿No le gusta? ¿Le recuerda a su infancia tal vez...? ¿Fue una infancia infeliz?

MOLLIE.—De niña fui muy feliz. *(Da la vuelta hasta el centro de la mesa de comedor.)*

CASEWELL.—Fue usted afortunada.

MOLLIE.—¿Usted no?

CASEWELL.—*(Cruza hacia el fuego.)* No.

MOLLIE.—Lo siento.

CASEWELL.—Pero de eso hace mucho tiempo. Una va superando las cosas.

MOLLIE.—Supongo que sí.

CASEWELL.—¿O tal vez no? Es muy difícil decirlo.

MOLLIE.—Dicen que lo que ocurre en la niñez es lo más importante.

CASEWELL.—Dicen..., dicen... ¿Quién lo dice?

MOLLIE.—Los psicólogos.

CASEWELL.—Menudo hatajo de farsantes. Un puñetero montón de tonterías. No quiero saber nada de psicólogos ni psiquiatras.

MOLLIE.—*(Pasa por delante del sofá.)* La verdad es que nunca he tenido mucho que ver con ellos.

CASEWELL.—Esa suerte que tiene. Pura palabrería. La vida es lo que tú hagas con ella. Hay que seguir y no mirar atrás.

MOLLIE.—No siempre se puede evitar volver la vista atrás.

CASEWELL.—Tonterías. Es cuestión de fuerza de voluntad.

MOLLIE.—Tal vez.

CASEWELL.—*(En tono enérgico.)* Lo sé. *(Va hacia el centro del escenario.)*

MOLLIE.—Supongo que tiene usted razón... *(Suspira.)* Pero a veces ocurren cosas... que te hacen recordar...

CASEWELL.—No se rinda. Deles la espalda.

MOLLIE.—¿Es esa la manera? A veces me gustaría saberlo. Tal vez se equivoque. A lo mejor lo que habría que hacer en realidad es... enfrentarse a ellas.

CASEWELL.—Depende de a qué se refiera.

Mollie.—(*Con una leve risita.*) A veces no sé qué cosas digo. (*Se sienta en el sofá.*)

Casewell.—(Va en dirección a Mollie.) No dejo que me afecte nada del pasado..., a no ser que yo quiera.

(Giles y Trotter *entran desde las escaleras de la izquierda.*)

Trotter.—Bueno, arriba todo está en orden. (*Ve la puerta abierta del comedor, cruza el escenario y va al comedor. Reaparece por el arco de la derecha.* La Srta. Casewell *sale hacia el comedor y deja la puerta abierta.* Mollie *se pone en pie y empieza a ordenarlo todo y coloca los cojines, después va hacia las cortinas.* Giles *va a la derecha de* Mollie. Trotter *cruza hacia la izquierda. Mientras, abre la puerta que hay al fondo a la izquierda.*) ¿Qué hay aquí, una salita? (*Con la puerta abierta el piano se oye con mucha más fuerza.* Trotter *va a la salita y cierra la puerta. En seguida reaparece por la puerta de la izquierda.*)

La Sra. Boyle.—(*Fuera de escena.*) ¿Le importaría cerrar esa puerta? Este sitio está lleno de corrientes de aire.

Trotter.—Lo siento, señora, pero tengo que familiarizarme con la casa. (Trotter *cierra la puerta y luego sube por las escaleras.* Mollie *pasa por detrás del sillón del centro del escenario.*)

Giles.—(*Va a la izquierda de* Mollie.) Mollie, ¿qué es todo este...?

(TROTTER *reaparece por las escaleras.*)

TROTTER.—Bueno, esto completa la visita. No he visto nada sospechoso. Creo que informaré al subcomisario Hogben. (*Va hacia el teléfono.*)

MOLLIE.—(*Va a la izquierda de la mesa de comedor.*) Pero no podrá utilizar el teléfono. La línea está cortada...

TROTTER.—(*Se vuelve con brusquedad.*) ¿Qué? (*Descuelga el auricular.*) ¿Desde cuándo?

MOLLIE.—El comandante Metcalf lo intentó justo después de que usted llegara.

TROTTER.—Pero antes funcionaba. El subcomisario Hogben llamó sin problemas.

MOLLIE.—Sí. Supongo que después los cables han debido caerse por culpa de la nieve.

TROTTER.—Vete a saber. Podrían haberlos cortado. (*Cuelga el auricular y se vuelve hacia ellos.*)

GILES.—¿Cortado? Pero ¿quién iba a querer cortarlos?

TROTTER.—Señor Ralston... ¿Qué sabe usted de estas personas que se alojan en su casa?

GILES.—Yo..., nosotros..., en realidad no sabemos nada de ellos.

TROTTER.—¡Ah! (*Va detrás de la mesita del sofá.*)

GILES.—(*Va a la derecha de* TROTTER.) La señora Boyle hizo la reserva desde un hotel en Bournemouth, el comandante Metcalf desde una dirección en..., ¿dónde era?

MOLLIE.—Leamington. (*Va a la izquierda de* TROTTER.)

GILES.—Wren reservó desde Hampstead y la tal

Casewell desde un hotel en Kensington. Paravicini, como le hemos dicho, llegó caído del cielo. Pero supongo que todos podrán identificarse. Todavía tendrán sus cartillas de racionamiento, o algo por el estilo.

TROTTER.—Lo comprobaré, claro. Pero ese tipo de documentación no es muy fiable.

MOLLIE.—Pero incluso si ese..., ese loco quiere venir aquí a matarnos a todos... o a uno de nosotros, estamos a salvo. Gracias a la nieve. Nadie puede llegar hasta que se funda.

TROTTER.—A no ser que ya esté aquí.

GILES.—¿Aquí?

TROTTER.—¿Por qué no, señor Ralston? Toda esta gente llegó aquí ayer por la noche. Unas horas después del asesinato de la señora Stanning. Hay tiempo de sobra de llegar.

GILES.—Pero, excepto Paravicini, todos reservaron con antelación.

TROTTER.—¿Y por qué no? Los crímenes estaban planeados.

GILES.—¿Crímenes? Solo se ha cometido un crimen. En Culver Street. ¿Por qué está tan seguro de que se cometerá otro aquí?

TROTTER.—De que se cometerá, no..., espero impedirlo. Pero de que se intentará, sí.

GILES.—(*Va hacia la chimenea.*) No puedo creerlo. Es tan inverosímil.

TROTTER.—No tiene nada de inverosímil. Son solo hechos.

MOLLIE.—¿Tiene una descripción del aspecto de ese hombre de Londres?

TROTTER.—Altura media, complexión indeterminada, abrigo oscuro, sombrero blando de fieltro, el rostro oculto por una bufanda. Hablaba con susurros. *(Cruza a la izquierda del sillón del centro del escenario. Hace una pausa.)* Hay tres abrigos oscuros colgados en el vestíbulo ahora mismo. Uno de ellos es suyo, señor Ralston... Hay tres sombreros blandos de fieltro...

(GILES *se dirige hacia el arco de la derecha, pero se detiene cuando oye hablar a* MOLLIE.)

MOLLIE.—Sigo sin poder creerlo.

TROTTER.—¿Ve lo que quiero decir? Lo que me preocupa es el corte de la línea telefónica. Si la han cortado... *(Va hasta el teléfono, se inclina y observa el cable.)*

MOLLIE.—Tengo que ir a terminar de preparar las verduras.

(MOLLIE *sale por el arco de la derecha.* GILES *recoge el guante de* MOLLIE *que hay en el sillón y lo sostiene con aire ausente, alisándolo. Saca un billete de autobús londinense, lo observa con sorpresa, a continuación mira el arco por donde ha salido* MOLLIE *y luego nuevamente el billete.)*

TROTTER.—¿Hay algún supletorio?

(G<small>ILES</small> *mira el billete de autobús con el ceño fruncido y no responde.*)

G<small>ILES</small>.—Perdone. ¿Ha dicho usted algo?

T<small>ROTTER</small>.—Sí, señor Ralston, le he preguntado si hay algún supletorio. (*Cruza hacia el centro del escenario.*)

G<small>ILES</small>.—Sí, en el dormitorio.

T<small>ROTTER</small>.—Suba a ver si funciona, ¿quiere?

> (G<small>ILES</small> *sale por las escaleras con aire confundido y con el guante y el billete de autobús en la mano.* T<small>ROTTER</small> *sigue comprobando el cable hasta la ventana. Aparta la cortina y abre la ventana intentando seguir el cable. Va hasta el arco de la derecha, sale y vuelve con una linterna. Va hacia la ventana, sale por ella de un salto, se inclina mirando a su alrededor y después desaparece de la vista. Casi ha oscurecido.* L<small>A</small> S<small>RA</small>. B<small>OYLE</small> *entra por la izquierda desde la biblioteca, se estremece de frío y mira la ventana abierta.*)

L<small>A</small> S<small>RA</small>. B<small>OYLE</small>.—(*Va hacia la ventana.*) ¿Quién ha vuelto a dejarse esa ventana abierta? (*Cierra la ventana y echa la cortina, después va hacia el fuego y echa otro tronco en la chimenea. Va hasta la radio y la enciende. Va a la mesa de comedor, coge una revista y la hojea. Hay un programa musical en la radio.* L<small>A</small> S<small>RA</small>. B<small>OYLE</small> *frunce el ceño, vuelve a la radio y sintoniza otro programa.*)

Voz en la radio.—... para entender lo que podemos llamar la mecánica del temor, es necesario estudiar los efectos que produce en la imaginación humana. Imaginen, por ejemplo, que están solos en una habitación. Es la última hora de la tarde. Una puerta se abre despacio a su espalda.

> (*La puerta de la derecha se abre. Se oye silbar la melodía de* Tres ratones ciegos. La Sra. Boyle *se vuelve con un sobresalto.*)

La Sra. Boyle.—(*Con alivio.*) ¡Ah!, es usted. No consigo encontrar un programa que valga la pena. (*Va hacia la radio y vuelve a sintonizar el programa de música. Se ve una mano que asoma por la puerta abierta y pulsa el interruptor. Las luces se apagan de pronto.*) ¡Eh...! ¿Qué hace? ¿Por qué ha apagado la luz?

> (*La radio está sonando a pleno volumen, y mezclado con ella se oyen ruidos ahogados y una pelea. El cadáver de* La Sra. Boyle *cae al suelo.* Mollie *entra por el arco de la derecha y se queda de pie confundida.*)

Mollie.—¿Por qué está tan oscuro? ¡Cuánto ruido!

> (*Enciende las luces desde el interruptor de la derecha y va hacia la radio para apagar-*

la. Entonces ve a La Sra. Boyle *que yace estrangulada delante del sofá y grita mientras cae el telón a toda prisa.)*

FIN DEL PRIMER ACTO

SEGUNDO ACTO

Mismo lugar. Diez minutos después.

Cuando se levanta el telón han retirado el cadáver de La Sra. Boyle y todos están en el salón. Trotter está al mando al otro lado de la mesa de comedor. Mollie está de pie a la derecha de la mesa de comedor. Los demás están todos sentados; El comandante Metcalf está en el sillón situado a la derecha, Christopher en la silla del escritorio, Giles en la silla de la izquierda, La Srta. Casewell a la derecha del sofá, y Paravicini a la izquierda.

Trotter.—Vamos, señora Ralston, intente recordar...

Mollie.—(*Al borde del ataque de nervios.*) No puedo pensar. Estoy aturdida.

Trotter.—Cuando usted entró, acababan de matar a la señora Boyle. Usted entró desde la cocina. ¿Está segura de que no vio ni oyó a nadie al llegar por el pasillo?

Mollie.—No, no creo. Solo la radio a todo volumen. No entendí quién podía haberla puesto tan alta. Así no se podía oír nada, ¿no cree?

TROTTER.—Eso fue lo que pensó el asesino... o *(En tono elocuente.)* la asesina.

MOLLIE.—¿Cómo quiere usted que yo oyese nada así?

TROTTER.—Pudo oír algo. Si el asesino salió del salón por ahí *(Señala hacia la izquierda.)* pudo oírla llegar desde la cocina. Tal vez subiera por las escaleras de servicio... o se escabullera al comedor.

MOLLIE.—Creo, no estoy segura, que oí rechinar una puerta y luego cerrarse, justo al salir de la cocina.

TROTTER.—¿Qué puerta?

MOLLIE.—No lo sé.

TROTTER.—Piense, señora Ralston, intente *recordar*. ¿Arriba? ¿Abajo? ¿Cerca? ¿A la derecha? ¿A la izquierda?

MOLLIE.—*(Llorosa.)* Le digo que no lo sé. Ni siquiera estoy segura de haber oído algo. *(Va hacia el sillón en el centro del escenario y se sienta.)*

GILES.—*(Se levanta y va a la izquierda de la mesa de comedor; con enfado.)* ¿No puede dejar de acosarla? ¿No ve que está muy nerviosa?

TROTTER.—*(En tono cortante.)* Estamos investigando un asesinato, señor Ralston. Hasta el momento nadie se ha tomado esto en serio. Es lo que hizo la señora Boyle. Me ocultó información. Todos me han ocultado información. Pues bien, la señora Boyle está muerta. A no ser que lleguemos al fondo de esto, y cuanto antes, podría haber otra muerte.

GILES.—¿Otra? ¿Tonterías? ¿Por qué?

TROTTER.—*(Con seriedad.)* Porque los ratones ciegos eran *tres*.

GILES.—¿Una muerte por cada uno de ellos? Pero tendría que haber alguna relación..., quiero decir, otra relación... con el asunto de la granja Longridge.

TROTTER.—Sí, tendría que haberla.

GILES.—Pero ¿por qué otra muerte *aquí*?

TROTTER.—Porque en el cuaderno de notas que encontramos solo había dos direcciones. En el veinticuatro de Culver Street solo había una víctima posible. Está muerta. En cambio, aquí, en Monkswell Manor hay más posibilidades. *(Mira a su alrededor con elocuencia.)*

CASEWELL.—Tonterías. Sería una coincidencia rarísima que *dos* personas relacionadas con el caso de la granja Longridge acabaran aquí por casualidad.

TROTTER.—Dadas ciertas circunstancias, no sería tanta coincidencia. Piénselo, señorita Casewell. *(Se pone en pie.)* Quiero saber con total claridad dónde estaban todos cuando mataron a la señora Boyle. Ya tengo la declaración de la señora Ralston. Estaba usted en la cocina preparando las verduras. Salió de la cocina, por el pasillo, a través de la puerta basculante y vino aquí. *(Señala al arco de la derecha.)* La radio estaba a todo volumen, pero la luz estaba apagada y el salón estaba a oscuras. Encendió usted la luz, vio a la señora Boyle y gritó.

MOLLIE.—Sí. Grité y grité. Hasta que por fin llegó gente.

TROTTER.—*(Va a la izquierda de* MOLLIE.*)* Sí. Como usted dice, llegó gente, mucha gente de todas partes, y todos llegaron más o menos al mismo tiempo. *(Hace una pausa, va hacia el centro del escenario y*

CHRISTOPHER.—Y quería peinarme y, ejem, adecentarme un poco.

TROTTER.—(*Mira muy serio el pelo despeinado de* CHRISTOPHER.) ¿Quería peinarse?

CHRISTOPHER.—¡El caso es que estaba allí! (GILES *va a la izquierda de la puerta.*)

TROTTER.—¿Y oyó gritar a la señora Ralston?

CHRISTOPHER.—Sí.

TROTTER.—¿Y bajó usted?

CHRISTOPHER.—Sí.

TROTTER.—Es raro que el señor Ralston y usted no coincidieran en las escaleras.

> (CHRISTOPHER *y* GILES *se miran el uno al otro.*)

CHRISTOPHER.—Bajé por las escaleras de servicio. Están más cerca de mi habitación.

TROTTER.—¿Subió usted a su habitación por las escaleras de servicio o pasó por aquí?

CHRISTOPHER.—Subí también por las escaleras de servicio. (*Va hasta la silla del escritorio y se sienta.*)

TROTTER.—Entiendo. (*Va a la derecha de la mesita del sofá.*) ¿Señor Paravicini?

PARAVICINI.—Ya se lo he dicho. (*Se levanta y va a la izquierda del sofá.*) Estaba tocando el piano en el salón..., por aquí, inspector. (*Hace un gesto hacia la izquierda.*)

TROTTER.—No soy inspector..., solo oficial, señor Paravicini. ¿Le oyó alguien tocar el piano?

PARAVICINI.—(*Sonriendo.*) No lo creo. Toqué muy muy bajito... con un solo dedo..., así.

le da la espalda al público.) Veamos, cuando salí por esa ventana de ahí (*Señala a la ventana.*) para comprobar el cable del teléfono, usted, señor Ralston, fue al piso de arriba, a la habitación que ocupan usted y la señora Ralston, a ver si funcionaba el supletorio del teléfono. (*Va hacia el fondo del escenario.*) ¿Dónde estaba usted cuando gritó la señora Ralston?

GILES.—Estaba aún en el dormitorio. El supletorio tampoco funcionaba. Me asomé a la ventana por si veía algún indicio de que hubiesen cortado la línea, pero no vi nada. Justo después de cerrar la ventana, oí gritar a Mollie y bajé a toda prisa.

TROTTER.—(*Apoyándose en la mesa de comedor.*) Tardó usted bastante en hacer esas cosas tan sencillas, ¿no, señor Ralston?

GILES.—No lo creo. (*Retrocede hacia las escaleras.*)

TROTTER.—Yo diría que, sin lugar a duda, se tomó usted su tiempo.

GILES.—Estaba pensando en algo.

TROTTER.—Muy bien. Veamos, señor Wren, dígame dónde estaba.

CHRISTOPHER.—(*Levantándose y poniéndose a la izquierda de* TROTTER.) Había ido a la cocina a ver si podía ayudar en algo a la señora Ralston. Me encant[a] cocinar. Luego subí a mi cuarto.

TROTTER.—¿Por qué?

CHRISTOPHER.—Es algo de lo más natural subi[r a] tu cuarto, ¿no cree? Quiero decir que *a veces* [se] quiere estar a solas.

TROTTER.—¿Fue usted a su cuarto porque q[uería] estar a solas?

MOLLIE.—Tocó usted *Tres ratones ciegos*.

TROTTER.—*(En tono cortante.)* ¿Ah, sí?

PARAVICINI.—Sí. Es una cancioncilla muy pegadiza. Es..., ¿cómo decirlo?, una cancioncilla muy ¿evocadora? ¿No están de acuerdo?

MOLLIE.—A mí me parece horrible.

PARAVICINI.—Tal vez. Y sin embargo... se te mete en la cabeza. También había alguien silbándola.

TROTTER.—¿Silbándola? ¿Dónde?

PARAVICINI.—No estoy seguro. Tal vez en el vestíbulo, tal vez en las escaleras, tal vez incluso arriba en un dormitorio.

TROTTER.—¿Quién estaba silbando *Tres ratones ciegos*? *(No hay respuesta.)* ¿Se lo ha inventado usted, señor Paravicini?

PARAVICINI.—No, no, inspector, disculpe, oficial. Nunca se me ocurriría hacer tal cosa.

TROTTER.—Continúe, estaba usted tocando el piano.

PARAVICINI.—*(Extiende un dedo.)* Con un dedo..., así... Y luego oí la radio muy alta... Alguien gritaba en ella. Me hizo daño en los oídos. Y luego... de pronto... oí gritar a la señora Ralston. *(Se sienta en el extremo izquierdo del sofá.)*

TROTTER.—*(Va hacia el centro de la mesa de comedor mientras hace gestos con los dedos.)* El señor Ralston estaba arriba. El señor Wren también arriba. El señor Paravicini en la salita. ¿Señorita Casewell?

CASEWELL.—Estaba escribiendo cartas en la biblioteca.

TROTTER.—¿Oyó lo que pasaba aquí?

CASEWELL.—No, no oí nada hasta que gritó la señora Ralston.

TROTTER.—¿Y qué hizo usted?

CASEWELL.—Vine aquí.

TROTTER.—En el acto.

CASEWELL.—Eso creo.

TROTTER.—¿Dice que estaba usted escribiendo unas cartas cuando oyó gritar a la señora Ralston?

CASEWELL.—Sí.

TROTTER.—¿Y que se levantó del escritorio y vino aquí corriendo?

CASEWELL.—Sí.

TROTTER.—Sin embargo, no parece haber ninguna carta sin terminar en el escritorio de la biblioteca.

CASEWELL.—(*Levantándose.*) La traje conmigo. (*Abre el bolso, saca una carta, va a la izquierda de* TROTTER *y se la da.*)

TROTTER.—(*La mira y se la devuelve.*) «Queridísima Jess...», ejem, ¿es una amiga o alguien de la familia?

CASEWELL.—Eso no es asunto suyo. (*Se da la vuelta.*)

TROTTER.—Es posible. (*Rodea la mesa de comedor por la derecha y se queda detrás de ella en el centro.*) ¿Sabe? Si yo oyese a alguien gritar que se había cometido un asesinato mientras estaba escribiendo una carta, no creo que me tomase el tiempo de coger la carta inacabada, doblarla y meterla en el bolso antes de correr a ver qué pasaba.

CASEWELL.—¿Ah, no? Qué interesante. (*Va hacia las escaleras y se sienta en el taburete.*)

TROTTER.—(*Va hacia la izquierda del* COMANDAN-

TE METCALF.) Bueno, comandante Metcalf. ¿Y usted? Dice que estaba en la bodega. ¿Por qué?

METCALF.—(*Con amabilidad.*) Estaba echando un vistazo. Solo echando un vistazo. Miré en el armario que hay debajo de las escaleras cerca de la cocina. Muchos trastos y equipo deportivo. Y reparé en que había otra puerta dentro, la abrí y encontré unas escaleras. Me entró curiosidad y bajé. Tienen unas bodegas muy interesantes.

MOLLIE.—Me alegro de que le gusten.

METCALF.—No me gustan ni un pelo. Yo diría que es la cripta de un antiguo monasterio. Probablemente sea la razón por la que este sitio se llama «Monkswell».[1]

TROTTER.—No estamos haciendo una investigación arqueológica, comandante Metcalf. Estamos investigando un asesinato. La señora Ralston nos ha dicho que oyó cerrarse una puerta que rechinaba. (*Va a la derecha del sofá.*) Esa puerta rechina al cerrarse. Es posible que, después de matar a la señora Boyle, el asesino oyese llegar desde la cocina a la señora Ralston (*Va hacia la izquierda del sillón del centro.*) y se escabullera por la puerta del armario y la cerrase tras él.

METCALF.—Muchas cosas son posibles.

(**MOLLIE** *se levanta, va hasta la butaca y se sienta. Se hace una pausa.*)

1. *Monkswell*, en inglés, significa «el pozo del monje». (*N. del T.*)

CHRISTOPHER.—(*Poniéndose en pie.*) Tendría que haber huellas dactilares en la parte interior del armario.

METCALF.—Las mías sin duda estarán ahí. Pero casi todos los criminales usan guantes, ¿no?

TROTTER.—Es lo más frecuente. Pero antes o después todos los criminales acaban cometiendo un error.

PARAVICINI.—Me pregunto, oficial, si eso es cierto.

GILES.—(*Yendo hacia la izquierda de* TROTTER.) Oiga, ¿no estamos perdiendo el tiempo? Hay una persona que...

TROTTER.—Por favor, señor Ralston, yo estoy a cargo de esta investigación.

GILES.—Muy bien, pero... (GILES *sale por la puerta de la izquierda.*)

TROTTER.—(*En tono autoritario.*) ¡Señor Ralston! (GILES *vuelve a regañadientes y se queda al lado de la puerta.*) Gracias. (*Pasa detrás de la mesa de comedor.*) Tenemos que establecer quién tuvo la oportunidad de cometer el crimen y no solo el motivo. Y dejen que les diga una cosa: todos la tuvieron. (*Se oyen varios murmullos de protesta. Levanta la mano.*) Hay dos escaleras: cualquiera pudo subir por una y bajar por la otra. Cualquiera pudo bajar al sótano por la puerta que hay cerca de la cocina y subir por un tramo de escaleras que sube por una trampilla hasta el pie de esas escaleras traseras de ahí. (*Señala a la derecha.*) La clave es que todos ustedes estaban *solos* en el momento en que se cometió el asesinato.

GILES.—Pero, oficial, habla usted como si todos estuviésemos bajo sospecha. ¡Es absurdo!

TROTTER.—En un caso de asesinato, todo el mundo está bajo sospecha.

GILES.—Pero usted sabe muy bien quién mató a esa mujer en Culver Street. Cree que es el mayor de los tres niños de la granja. Un joven mentalmente perturbado. El caso, maldita sea, es que aquí solo hay una persona que encaje con esa descripción. *(Señala a* CHRISTOPHER *y va despacio hacia él.)*

CHRISTOPHER.—¡No es cierto..., no es cierto! Están todos contra mí. Todos han estado siempre contra mí. Y ahora me quieren hacer cargar con un asesinato. Eso se llama acoso *(Pasa a la izquierda del* COMANDANTE METCALF*.)*, sí, señor: acoso.

*(*GILES *lo sigue, pero se detiene al llegar al extremo izquierdo de la mesa de comedor.)*

METCALF.—*(Se levanta, con amabilidad.)* Tranquilo, muchacho, tranquilo. *(Da unas palmaditas a* CHRISTOPHER *en el hombro y luego saca la pipa.)*

MOLLIE.—*(Se levanta y va a la izquierda de* CHRISTOPHER*.)* No pasa nada, Chris. Nadie está contra ti. *(A* TROTTER*.)* Dígale que no pasa nada.

TROTTER.—*(Mirando a* GILES*; con estolidez.)* Nosotros no incriminamos a nadie.

MOLLIE.—*(A* TROTTER*.)* Dígale que no va a detenerlo.

TROTTER.—*(Va hacia la izquierda de* MOLLIE*; con estolidez.)* No voy a detener a nadie. Para eso tengo que tener pruebas. No tengo ninguna... aún.

*(*CHRISTOPHER *va hacia la chimenea.)*

125

GILES.—Creo que te has vuelto loca, Mollie. *(Va hacia el centro del escenario. A* TROTTER.*)* ¡Y usted también! Solo hay una persona que encaje con la descripción y, aunque sea como una medida de seguridad, debería detenerla. Es lo más justo para los demás.

MOLLIE.—Espera, Giles, espera. Sargento Trotter, ¿puedo..., puedo hablar con usted un minuto?

TROTTER.—Por supuesto, señora Ralston. Los demás pasen al comedor, por favor.

> *(Los demás se levantan y van hacia la puerta: primero* LA SRTA. CASEWELL, *luego* EL SR. PARAVICINI, *refunfuñando, seguido de* CHRISTOPHER *y del* COMANDANTE METCALF, *que se detiene un momento para encender la pipa.* EL COMANDANTE METCALF *repara en que le están mirando. Salen todos.)*

GILES.—Yo me quedo.

MOLLIE.—No, Giles, ve tú también por favor.

GILES.—*(Furioso.)* Me quedo. No sé qué mosca te ha picado, Mollie.

MOLLIE.—Por favor.

> *(*GILES *sale detrás de los otros por la derecha y deja la puerta abierta.* MOLLIE *la cierra.* TROTTER *va hacia el arco de la derecha.)*

TROTTER.—Sí, señora Ralston *(Va detrás del sillón del centro del escenario.),* ¿qué quería decirme?

MOLLIE.—(*Va a la izquierda de* TROTTER.) Oficial Trotter, usted piensa que este... (*Pasa delante del sofá.*) asesino perturbado debe ser el... mayor de los dos niños de la granja, pero no lo sabe con certeza, ¿verdad?

TROTTER.—En realidad no sabemos nada con certeza. Lo único que sabemos es que la mujer que, junto con su marido, maltrató e hizo pasar hambre a aquellos niños ha sido asesinada, y que la magistrada que fue la responsable de enviarlos allí ha sido asesinada. (*Va a la derecha del sofá.*) Alguien ha cortado el cable del teléfono que me comunica con el cuartelillo...

MOLLIE.—Ni siquiera sabe usted eso. Podría haber sido la nieve.

TROTTER.—No, señora Ralston, lo han cortado a propósito. Lo han cortado justo al salir por la puerta principal. He visto dónde.

MOLLIE.—(*Impresionada.*) Entiendo.

TROTTER.—Siéntese, señora Ralston.

MOLLIE.—(*Se sienta.*) Pero, aun así, no sabe...

TROTTER.—(*Gira a la izquierda por detrás del sofá y luego a la derecha por delante.*) Me guío por la probabilidad. Todo apunta en la misma dirección; inestabilidad mental, personalidad infantil, deserción del ejército y el informe del psiquiatra.

MOLLIE.—Ya veo, y por tanto todo parece acusar a Christopher. Pero yo no creo que haya sido Christopher. Tiene que haber otras posibilidades.

TROTTER.—(*A la derecha del sofá; se vuelve hacia ella.*) Como por ejemplo...

MOLLIE.—(*Duda.*) Pues... ¿no tenían los niños ningún pariente?

TROTTER.—La madre era una borracha. Murió poco después de que le quitaran a los niños.

MOLLIE.—¿Y el padre?

TROTTER.—Era sargento del ejército, destinado en el extranjero. Si está vivo, probablemente se haya licenciado ya.

MOLLIE.—¿No saben dónde está ahora?

TROTTER.—No tenemos ninguna información. Localizarlo podría llevar un tiempo, pero le aseguro, señora Ralston, que la policía tiene en cuenta todas las posibilidades.

MOLLIE.—Pero no saben dónde podría estar en este momento, y, si el hijo es un desequilibrado, también podría serlo el padre.

TROTTER.—Bueno, es una posibilidad.

MOLLIE.—Si hubiese vuelto, después de ser prisionero de guerra, por ejemplo, y de haber sufrido mucho. Y descubriese que su mujer había muerto y que sus hijos habían sufrido unas vivencias tan terribles y uno de ellos hubiese muerto por ello, podría haber perdido la cabeza y querer... ¡venganza!

TROTTER.—Eso son solo suposiciones.

MOLLIE.—Pero ¿es posible?

TROTTER.—¡Oh!, sí, señora Ralston, es muy posible.

MOLLIE.—De modo que el asesino podría ser un hombre de mediana edad, o incluso viejo. *(Hace una pausa.)* Cuando dije que la policía había telefoneado. El comandante Metcalf se asustó mucho. De verdad. Vi su cara.

TROTTER.—*(Se para a pensar.)* ¿El comandante

Metcalf? (*Va hasta el sillón del centro del escenario y se sienta.*)

MOLLIE.—De mediana edad. Militar. Parece muy amable y de lo más normal..., pero podría ser que no se le notara, ¿no?

TROTTER.—No, no siempre se nota.

MOLLIE.—(*Levantándose y yendo a la derecha de* TROTTER.) Entonces Christopher no es el único sospechoso. También lo es el comandante Metcalf.

TROTTER.—¿Alguna otra sugerencia?

MOLLIE.—Bueno, al señor Paravicini se le cayó al suelo el atizador cuando dije que la policía había telefoneado.

TROTTER.—El señor Paravicini. (*Parece pararse a pensarlo.*)

MOLLIE.—Sé que parece muy viejo... y que es extranjero y demás, pero tal vez no sea tan viejo como aparenta. Se mueve como un hombre más joven y lleva maquillaje en la cara. La señorita Casewell también se dio cuenta. Podría ser, ya sé que suena muy melodramático, pero podría ir *disfrazado*.

TROTTER.—Le preocupa mucho exculpar al joven señor Wren, ¿no?

MOLLIE.—(*Va hacia la chimenea.*) Parece tan... indefenso. (*Se vuelve hacia* TROTTER.) Y tan desdichado.

TROTTER.—Señora Ralston, deje que le diga una cosa. He considerado *todas* las posibilidades desde el principio. El niño Georgie, el padre... y alguien más. Recuerde que había una hermana.

MOLLIE.—¡Ah! ¿La hermana?

TROTTER.—(*Se levanta y va hacia* MOLLIE.) Puede

que una mujer matase a Maureen Stanning. Una mujer. *(Va hacia el centro del escenario.)* Llevaba una bufanda y el sombrero calado, y recuerde que hablaba con susurros. Es la voz lo que delata el sexo. *(Va detrás de la mesita del sofá.)* Sí, podría haber sido una mujer.

MOLLIE.—¿La señorita Casewell?

TROTTER.—*(Va hacia las escaleras.)* Parece un poco mayor para serlo. *(Sube hasta el rellano, abre la puerta de la biblioteca, se asoma y luego cierra la puerta.)* ¡Oh!, sí, señora Ralston, hay muchas posibilidades. Usted misma, por ejemplo.

MOLLIE.—¿Yo?

TROTTER.—Tiene usted la edad indicada. (MOLLIE *hace ademán de quejarse. La contiene.)* No, no. Diga lo que diga, recuerde que ahora no puedo comprobarlo. Y también está su marido.

MOLLIE.—¡Giles! ¡Qué ridiculez!

TROTTER.—*(Cruza despacio a la izquierda de* MOLLIE.*)* Christopher Wren y él son casi de la misma edad. Su marido parece mayor de lo que es, y Christopher Wren parece más joven. La edad es difícil de determinar. ¿Qué sabe usted de su marido, señora Ralston?

MOLLIE.—¿Que qué sé de Giles? ¡Oh, no sea estúpido!

TROTTER.—¿Cuánto llevan casados?

MOLLIE.—Un año.

TROTTER.—¿Y dónde lo conoció?

MOLLIE.—En un baile, en Londres. Fuimos a una fiesta.

TROTTER.—¿Le presentó a sus padres?

MOLLIE.—No tiene parientes. Todos han muerto.

TROTTER.—*(En tono elocuente.)* Todos han muerto.

MOLLIE.—Sí..., pero, ¡ay!, hace que todo suene mal. Su padre era abogado y su madre murió cuando era niño.

TROTTER.—Solo me dice lo que *él* le ha contado.

MOLLIE.—Sí, pero... *(Se vuelve.)*

TROTTER.—No lo sabe por usted misma.

MOLLIE.—*(Se vuelve deprisa.)* Es escandaloso que...

TROTTER.—Se sorprendería usted, señora Ralston, si supiera cuántos casos como el suyo tenemos. Sobre todo, desde la guerra. Hogares rotos y familias desaparecidas. Un tipo dice que estuvo en la Fuerza Aérea, o que acaba de terminar su instrucción militar. Los padres murieron..., no tiene parientes. No hay familia y los jóvenes resuelven sus propios asuntos. Se conocen. Se casan. Antes eran los padres y los parientes quienes hacían averiguaciones antes de dar el visto bueno al matrimonio. A veces ella tarda un año o dos en descubrir que en realidad es un cajero fugado, o un desertor del ejército o algo igual de indeseable. ¿Cuánto tiempo hacía que usted conocía a Giles Ralston cuando se casó con él?

MOLLIE.—Solo tres semanas. Pero...

TROTTER.—¿Y no sabe nada de él?

MOLLIE.—No es verdad. ¡Lo sé todo de él! Sé exactamente qué clase de persona es. Es *Giles. (Se vuelve hacia la chimenea.)* Y es totalmente absurdo insinuar que es un maníaco homicida desquiciado. Caramba, si ni siquiera estaba en Londres ayer cuando se cometió el asesinato.

TROTTER.—¿Dónde estaba? ¿Aquí?

MOLLIE.—Fue al campo a comprar alambre para la cerca de los pollos.

TROTTER.—¿Lo trajo consigo? (*Va hasta el escritorio.*)

MOLLIE.—No, al final no era el que él quería.

TROTTER.—Estamos solo a cuarenta y cinco kilómetros de Londres, ¿no? ¡Ah! ¿Tiene una guía de carreteras? (*Coge la guía de carreteras y la hojea.*) Solo a una hora en tren..., un poco más en coche.

MOLLIE.—(*Da una patada airada en el suelo.*) Le digo que Giles no estuvo en Londres.

TROTTER.—Espere un minuto, señora Ralston. (*Cruza el escenario hacia el vestíbulo y vuelve con un abrigo oscuro. Va hacia la izquierda de* MOLLIE.) ¿Es este el abrigo de su marido?

(MOLLIE *mira el abrigo.*)

MOLLIE.—(*Con suspicacia.*) Sí. ¿Por qué?

(TROTTER *saca un periódico vespertino doblado del bolsillo.*)

TROTTER.—Es el *Evening Standard.* De ayer. Vendido en la calle a eso de las tres y media ayer por la tarde.

MOLLIE.—¡No le creo!

TROTTER.—¿No? (*Va a la derecha del arco con el abrigo.*) ¿Seguro?

(TROTTER *sale por el arco de la derecha con el abrigo.* MOLLIE *se sienta en el sillón*

pequeño de la derecha y mira el periódico
vespertino. La puerta de la derecha se abre
despacio. CHRISTOPHER *se asoma por la*
puerta, ve que MOLLIE *está sola y entra.)*

CHRISTOPHER.—¡Mollie!

(MOLLIE *da un respingo y oculta el perió-*
dico debajo del cojín del sillón del centro
del escenario.)

MOLLIE.—¡Me ha dado un susto! *(Va a la izquier-*
da del sillón del centro del escenario.)
CHRISTOPHER.—¿Dónde está? *(Va a la derecha de*
MOLLIE.) ¿Adónde se ha ido?
MOLLIE.—¿Quién?
CHRISTOPHER.—El oficial.
MOLLIE.—¡Ah!, se ha ido por ahí.
CHRISTOPHER.—Ojalá pudiera marcharme. De
algún modo. ¿Hay algún sitio donde pueda escon-
derme... en la casa?
MOLLIE.—¿Esconderse?
CHRISTOPHER.—Sí..., de *él.*
MOLLIE.—No.
CHRISTOPHER.—Pero, ¡querida!, todos están espan-
tosamente en mi contra. Dirán que yo cometí los asesi-
natos..., sobre todo su marido. *(Va a la derecha del sofá.)*
MOLLIE.—No le haga caso. *(Da un paso a la dere-*
cha de CHRISTOPHER.) Escuche, Christopher, no pue-
de seguir... huyendo de las cosas... toda la vida.
CHRISTOPHER.—¿Por qué dice eso?
MOLLIE.—Bueno, es cierto, ¿no?

CHRISTOPHER.—(*Con impotencia.*) ¡Oh, sí!, muy cierto. (*Se sienta en el extremo izquierdo del sofá.*)

MOLLIE.—(*Sentándose en el otro extremo del sofá; con afecto.*) Alguna vez tendrá que crecer, Chris.

CHRISTOPHER.—Ojalá no tuviese que hacerlo.

MOLLIE.—En realidad no se llama Christopher Wren, ¿verdad?

CHRISTOPHER.—No.

MOLLIE.—Y tampoco está estudiando arquitectura.

CHRISTOPHER.—No.

MOLLIE.—¿Por qué...?

CHRISTOPHER.—¿Que por qué elegí el nombre de Christopher Wren? Me divirtió. En el colegio se burlaban de mí y me llamaban el pequeño Christopher Robin. Robin..., Wren, fue una asociación de ideas.[2] El colegio fue un infierno.

MOLLIE.—¿Y cuál es su verdadero nombre?

CHRISTOPHER.—Qué más da eso. Hui mientras hacía el servicio militar. Era horrible..., lo odiaba. Lo odiaba tanto que me escapé. (MOLLIE *de pronto se siente incómoda y* CHRISTOPHER *se da cuenta. Ella se levanta y se va a la derecha del sofá.* CHRISTOPHER *se levanta y se va hacia la izquierda.*) Sí, igual que el..., el asesino. (MOLLIE *va hacia la izquierda de la mesa de comedor y se aparta de él.*) Ya le he dicho que todo encaja conmigo. Verá, mi madre... mi madre... (*Va a la izquierda de la mesita del sofá.*)

MOLLIE.—¿Sí? ¿Su madre?

CHRISTOPHER.—Todo habría ido bien si no hu-

2. En inglés, *robin* significa «petirrojo», y *wren*, «reyezuelo», dos especies de pájaro.

biese muerto. Se habría preocupado por mí y me habría cuidado...

MOLLIE.—No puede aspirar a que lo cuiden toda la vida. Las cosas pasan. Y hay que soportarlas..., hay que seguir adelante.

CHRISTOPHER.—No puedo.

MOLLIE.—Claro que puede.

CHRISTOPHER.—¿Usted ha podido? *(Va a la izquierda de* MOLLIE.)

MOLLIE.—Sí *(Mirando a* CHRISTOPHER.)

CHRISTOPHER.—¿Cómo fue? ¿Muy difícil?

MOLLIE.—No lo he olvidado nunca.

CHRISTOPHER.—¿Tuvo algo que ver con Giles?

MOLLIE.—No, fue mucho antes de conocer a Giles.

CHRISTOPHER.—Debía de ser usted muy joven. Casi una niña.

MOLLIE.—Tal vez por eso fue tan... espantoso. Fue horrible..., horrible... Intento olvidarlo. Intento no pensar en ello.

CHRISTOPHER.—O sea que usted también huye. ¿También huye de las cosas... en lugar de enfrentarse a ellas?

MOLLIE.—Sí... tal vez en cierto sentido. *(Se hace un silencio.)* Teniendo en cuenta que no nos habíamos visto hasta ayer, parecemos conocernos muy bien.

CHRISTOPHER.—Sí, es raro, ¿verdad?

MOLLIE.—No sé. Supongo que debe de haber una especie de... sintonía entre los dos.

CHRISTOPHER.—De todos modos, cree usted que debo seguir adelante.

MOLLIE.—Con franqueza, ¿qué otra cosa puede hacer?

CHRISTOPHER.—Podría robarle los esquís al oficial. Sé esquiar muy bien.

MOLLIE.—Eso sería una estupidez espantosa. Sería casi como admitir que es usted culpable.

CHRISTOPHER.—El sargento Trotter cree que lo soy.

MOLLIE.—No es cierto. Al menos, que yo sepa. *(Va hacia el sillón del centro del escenario, saca el periódico vespertino de debajo del cojín y se queda mirándolo fijamente. De pronto, con apasionamiento.)* Le odio..., le odio..., le odio...

CHRISTOPHER.—*(Sobresaltado.)* ¿A quién?

MOLLIE.—Al sargento Trotter. Te mete cosas en la cabeza. Cosas que no son ciertas, y que no pueden serlo.

CHRISTOPHER.—¿Por qué lo dice?

MOLLIE.—No le creo..., no le creo...

CHRISTOPHER.—¿Qué es lo que no cree? *(Va despacio hacia* MOLLIE, *le pone las manos en los hombros y le vuelve la cara hacia él.)* Vamos..., ¡dígamelo!

MOLLIE.—*(Le enseña el periódico.)* ¿Ve esto?

CHRISTOPHER.—Sí.

MOLLIE.—¿Qué es? Un periódico vespertino de ayer..., un periódico londinense. Y estaba en el bolsillo de Giles. Pero ayer Giles no fue a Londres.

CHRISTOPHER.—Bueno, si estuvo aquí todo el día...

MOLLIE.—Pero es que no estuvo. Se fue con el coche a comprar una valla para los pollos, pero no encontró.

CHRISTOPHER.—Bueno, no pasa nada. *(Va hacia*

la izquierda en dirección al centro del escenario.) Probablemente sí fuese a Londres.

MOLLIE.—¿Y por qué no me lo dijo? ¿Por qué fingir que se había pasado el día en el campo?

CHRISTOPHER.—Tal vez, cuando se enteró de lo del asesinato...

MOLLIE.—No lo sabía. ¿O sí? ¿Lo sabía? *(Va hacia el fuego.)*

CHRISTOPHER.—Dios mío, Mollie. No pensará que... El oficial no pensará que...

> *(Durante el siguiente parlamento* MOLLIE *cruza despacio el escenario hacia la izquierda del sofá.* CHRISTOPHER *deja el periódico en silencio sobre el sofá.)*

MOLLIE.—No sé qué piensa el oficial. Y sabe cómo hacer que pienses cosas de la gente. Te haces preguntas y empiezas a dudar. Tienes la sensación de que alguien a quien quieres y conoces bien podría ser un... desconocido. *(Susurra.)* Es como en las pesadillas: estás en algún sitio con amigos y de pronto los miras a la cara y ya no son tus amigos..., son otras personas..., están fingiendo. Tal vez no podamos fiarnos de nadie..., a lo mejor todos son desconocidos. *(Se tapa la cara con las manos.)*

> *(*CHRISTOPHER *va al extremo izquierdo del sofá, se arrodilla en él, le coge las manos y las aparta de su cara.* GILES *entra desde el comedor a la derecha, pero se detiene al verlos.* MOLLIE *retrocede y* CHRISTOPHER *se sienta en el sofá.)*

GILES.—(*Desde la puerta.*) Parece que interrumpo algo.

MOLLIE.—No, solo estábamos... hablando. Tengo que ir a la cocina..., tengo que hacer la empanada y las patatas..., y... preparar las espinacas. (*Va a la derecha por detrás del sillón del centro.*)

CHRISTOPHER.—(*Se levanta y va hacia el centro del escenario.*) Iré a echarle una mano.

GILES.—(*Va hacia el fuego.*) No, no va a ir a ninguna parte.

MOLLIE.—Giles.

GILES.—Los *tête-à-têtes* no son muy saludables en este momento. No vaya a la cocina ni se acerque a mi mujer.

CHRISTOPHER.—Pero oiga...

GILES.—(*Furioso.*) Que no se acerque a mi mujer, Wren. No va a ser la próxima víctima.

CHRISTOPHER.—Así que eso es lo que piensa de mí.

GILES.—Ya lo he dicho, ¿no? Hay un asesino en la casa... y a mí me parece que usted encaja con la descripción.

CHRISTOPHER.—No soy el único que encaja.

GILES.—No veo a ningún otro.

CHRISTOPHER.—Qué ciego está usted..., ¿o solo finge estarlo?

GILES.—Ya le he dicho que me preocupa la seguridad de mi mujer.

CHRISTOPHER.—A mí también. Y no pienso dejarle a solas con ella. (*Va hacia la izquierda de* MOLLIE.)

GILES.—(*Va a la derecha de* MOLLIE.) ¿Qué demonios...?

MOLLIE.—Por favor, váyase, Chris.

CHRISTOPHER.—No pienso ir a ninguna parte.

MOLLIE.—Por favor, váyase, Christopher. Por favor, lo digo en serio...

CHRISTOPHER.—*(Va hacia la derecha.)* No estaré muy lejos.

(A regañadientes CHRISTOPHER *sale por el arco de la derecha.* MOLLIE *cruza a la silla del escritorio, y* GILES *la sigue.)*

GILES.—¿A qué viene esto? Mollie, debes de estar loca. Estabas dispuesta a encerrarte en la cocina con un maníaco homicida.

MOLLIE.—No lo es.

GILES.—Solo hace falta mirarlo para darse cuenta de que está chiflado.

MOLLIE.—No lo está. Solo es desdichado. Te digo, Giles, que no es peligroso. Si lo fuese lo sabría. Y, además, sé cuidar de mí misma.

GILES.—¡Eso es lo que decía la señora Boyle!

MOLLIE.—¡Oh! Giles, no... *(Va hacia delante del escenario a la izquierda.)*

GILES.—*(Va hacia la derecha de* MOLLIE.*)* Oye, ¿qué hay entre tú y ese chico desdichado?

MOLLIE.—¿Qué quieres decir con eso? Me da lástima. Nada más.

GILES.—A lo mejor lo conocías de antes. Tal vez le sugeriste venir y que fingiese que no os habíais visto nunca. Lo teníais todo preparado, ¿no?

MOLLIE.—Giles, ¿es que has perdido la cabeza? ¿Cómo te atreves a insinuar algo así?

GILES.—(*Va al centro de la mesa de comedor.*) Es raro que haya venido a alojarse a un sitio tan apartado, ¿no crees?

MOLLIE.—Tanto como que hayan venido la señorita Casewell, el comandante Metcalf y la señora Boyle.

GILES.—Una vez leí en el periódico que esos tipos homicidas atraían a las mujeres. Parece que es cierto. (*Va hacia el centro del escenario.*) ¿Dónde lo conociste? ¿Cuánto tiempo lleváis así?

MOLLIE.—Estás siendo totalmente ridículo. (*Va un poco hacia la derecha.*) No había visto a Christopher Wren hasta que llegó ayer.

GILES.—Eso es lo que tú dices. Tal vez has estado yendo a Londres para verlo a escondidas.

MOLLIE.—Sabes perfectamente que hace semanas que no voy a Londres.

GILES.—(*En un tono peculiar.*) Así que hace semanas que no vas a Londres. ¿Estás segura?

MOLLIE.—¿Qué quieres decir con eso? Es cierto.

GILES.—¿Ah, sí? Entonces, ¿qué es esto? (*Saca del bolsillo el guante de* MOLLIE *y el billete de autobús.* MOLLIE *da un respingo.*) Es uno de los guantes que llevabas ayer. Lo encontré esta tarde mientras hablaba con el oficial Trotter. Mira lo que hay dentro: ¡un billete de un autobús londinense!

MOLLIE.—(*Con aire culpable.*) ¡Ah..., eso!

GILES.—(*Se aparta a la derecha.*) Así que, por lo visto, no solo fuiste al pueblo, sino también a Londres.

MOLLIE.—Está bien, fui a...

GILES.—Mientras yo iba en coche por el campo.

MOLLIE.—(*Subraya las palabras.*) Mientras tú ibas en coche por el campo.

GILES.—Vamos..., reconócelo. Fuiste a Londres.

MOLLIE.—Está bien. Fui a Londres. ¡Y tú también!

GILES.—¿Qué?

MOLLIE.—Que tú también fuiste. Trajiste un periódico vespertino. (*Coge el periódico del sofá.*)

GILES.—¿De dónde has sacado eso?

MOLLIE.—Del bolsillo de tu abrigo.

GILES.—Cualquiera podría haberlo puesto ahí.

MOLLIE.—¿Ah, sí? Estuviste en Londres.

GILES.—De acuerdo. Sí, estuve en Londres. Pero no fui a verme con una mujer.

MOLLIE.—(*Horrorizada; con un susurro.*)... a lo mejor... sí.

GILES.—¿Eh? ¿Qué quieres decir? (*Se acerca a ella.*)

> (MOLLIE *se aparta y retrocede hacia la izquierda.*)

MOLLIE.—Vete. No te me acerques.

GILES.—(*La sigue.*) ¿Qué te pasa?

MOLLIE.—No me toques.

GILES.—¿Fuiste ayer a Londres para verte con Christopher Wren?

MOLLIE.—No seas absurdo. Pues claro que no.

GILES.—Entonces, ¿por qué?

> (MOLLIE *cambia de actitud. Esboza una sonrisa soñolienta.*)

MOLLIE.—No... te lo diré. A lo mejor..., ahora... he olvidado por qué fui... *(Cruza hacia el arco de la derecha.)*

GILES.—*(Va a la izquierda de* MOLLIE.) Mollie, ¿qué te pasa? De pronto estás diferente. Es como si no te conociera.

MOLLIE.—A lo mejor nunca me has conocido. Llevamos casados cuánto tiempo, ¿un año? Pero en realidad no sabes nada de mí. Nada de lo que hice, pensé, sentí o sufrí antes de conocerte.

GILES.—Mollie, estás loca...

MOLLIE.—¡Muy bien, pues estoy loca! ¿Por qué no? ¡A lo mejor estar loca es divertido!

GILES.—*(Enfadado.)* ¿Qué demonios estás...?

(EL SR. PARAVICINI *entra por el arco de la derecha. Se coloca entre ellos.)*

PARAVICINI.—Vamos, vamos. Espero que no se estén diciendo cosas que no quieren decir en realidad. Ocurre a menudo en estas discusiones de enamorados.

GILES.—«¡Discusiones de enamorados!» Esta sí que es buena. *(Va a la izquierda de la mesa de comedor.)*

PARAVICINI.—*(Va a la butaca de la derecha.)* Cierto. Cierto. Sé cómo se siente. Yo también he pasado por eso de joven. *Jeunesse... jeunesse...,* como dice el poeta. No llevan mucho tiempo casados, ¿verdad?

GILES.—*(Cruza hasta el fuego.)* No es asunto suyo, señor Paravicini...

PARAVICINI.—*(Va hasta el centro del escenario.)* No, no lo es. Pero he venido solo a decirles que el oficial no encuentra sus esquís y me temo que está muy enfadado.

MOLLIE.—*(Va a la derecha de la mesita del sofá.)* ¡Christopher!

GILES.—¿Cómo dice?

PARAVICINI.—*(Se vuelve para mirar a* GILES.) Quiere saber si, por casualidad, los ha cambiado de sitio, señor Ralston.

GILES.—No, claro que no.

> (EL OFICIAL DE POLICÍA TROTTER *entra por el arco de la derecha acalorado y disgustado.)*

TROTTER.—Señor Ralston..., señora Ralston, ¿han sacado ustedes mis esquís del armario?

GILES.—Por supuesto que no.

TROTTER.—Alguien se los ha llevado.

PARAVICINI.—*(Va a la derecha de* TROTTER.) ¿Cómo se ha dado cuenta?

TROTTER.—Seguimos rodeados de nieve. Necesito ayuda, refuerzos. Iba a ir a la comisaría de Market Hampton para informar de la situación.

PARAVICINI.—Y ahora no puede..., vaya, vaya. Alguien se ha encargado de que no se vaya. Pero podría haber otra razón, ¿no?

TROTTER.—¿Sí? ¿Cuál?

PARAVICINI.—Alguien podría querer huir.

GILES.—*(Va a la derecha de* MOLLIE; *le habla.)* ¿Por qué has dicho «Christopher» hace un momento?

MOLLIE.—Por nada.

PARAVICINI.—*(Riéndose.)* Así que nuestro joven arquitecto se ha largado, ¿eh? Muy muy interesante.

TROTTER.—¿Es eso cierto, señora Ralston? *(Va hacia el centro de la mesa de comedor.)*

> *(CHRISTOPHER entra por las escaleras de la izquierda y va a la izquierda del sofá.)*

MOLLIE.—*(Va un poco hacia la izquierda.)* ¡Oh, gracias a Dios! Al final no te has ido.

TROTTER.—*(Cruza a la derecha de CHRISTOPHER.)* ¿Se ha llevado usted mis esquís, señor Wren?

CHRISTOPHER.—*(Sorprendido.)* ¿Sus esquís, oficial? No, ¿por qué?

TROTTER.—La señora Ralston parecía pensar que... *(Mira a MOLLIE.)*

MOLLIE.—Al señor Wren le encanta esquiar. Pensé que podría haberlos cogido para hacer... un poco de ejercicio.

GILES.—¿Ejercicio? *(Va hacia el centro de la mesa de comedor.)*

TROTTER.—En fin, escúchenme. Es un asunto muy serio. Alguien se ha llevado mi única posibilidad de comunicarme con el exterior. Quiero que todos vengan aquí ahora mismo.

PARAVICINI.—Creo que la señorita Casewell está arriba.

MOLLIE.—Iré a buscarla.

> *(MOLLIE sube las escaleras. TROTTER va a la izquierda del arco de la izquierda.)*

PARAVICINI.—(*Va hacia la derecha.*) Acabo de ver al comandante Metcalf en el comedor. (*Abre la puerta de la derecha y se asoma.*) ¡Comandante Metcalf! No está.

GILES.—Iré a buscarlo.

> (GILES *sale por la derecha.* MOLLIE *y* LA SRTA. CASEWELL *entran por las escaleras.* MOLLIE *va a la derecha de la mesa de comedor y* LA SRTA. CASEWELL *a la izquierda.* EL COMANDANTE METCALF *llega de la biblioteca por la izquierda.*)

METCALF.—Hola, ¿me buscaban?

TROTTER.—Es por mis esquís.

METCALF.—¿Sus esquís? (*Va a la izquierda del sofá.*)

PARAVICINI.—(*Va al arco de la derecha y llama.*) ¡Señor Ralston!

> (GILES *entra por la derecha y se queda debajo del arco.* EL SR. PARAVICINI *vuelve y se sienta en la butaca de la derecha.*)

TROTTER.—¿Ha sacado alguno de ustedes un par de esquís del armario que hay al lado de la puerta de la cocina?

CASEWELL.—Dios mío, no. ¿Por qué iba a sacarlos?

METCALF.—Y *yo* no los he tocado.

TROTTER.—Pues ya no están. (*A* LA SRTA. CASEWELL.) ¿Por dónde ha ido usted a su habitación?

CASEWELL.—Por las escaleras de servicio.

TROTTER.—Entonces ha tenido que pasar por delante de la puerta del armario.

CASEWELL.—Si usted lo dice..., no tengo ni idea de dónde están sus esquís.

TROTTER.—*(Al* COMANDANTE METCALF.) Usted ha estado dentro de ese armario hoy.

METCALF.—Sí, así es.

TROTTER.—Cuando mataron a la señora Boyle.

METCALF.—Cuando mataron a la señora Boyle yo había bajado al sótano.

TROTTER.—¿Estaban los esquís en el armario cuando pasó por allí?

METCALF.—No tengo ni la menor idea.

TROTTER.—¿No los vio allí?

METCALF.—No lo recuerdo.

TROTTER.—¡Tiene que acordarse de si los esquís estaban ahí!

METCALF.—Oiga, joven, de nada sirve que me levante la voz. No estaba pensando en esos malditos esquís. Solo me interesaba la bodega. *(Va hacia el sofá y se sienta.)* La arquitectura de este lugar es muy peculiar. Abrí la otra puerta y bajé. Así que no puedo decirle si los esquís estaban allí o no.

TROTTER.—*(Va a la izquierda del sofá.)* ¿Se da cuenta de que tuvo una oportunidad excelente de llevárselos?

METCALF.—Sí, sí, lo reconozco. Si hubiese querido, claro.

TROTTER.—La pregunta es: ¿dónde están ahora?

METCALF.—Si los buscamos entre todos deberíamos encontrarlos. No es como buscar una aguja en un pajar. Los esquís son muy voluminosos. ¿Por qué no empezamos cuanto antes? *(Se levanta y cruza a la derecha, en dirección a la puerta.)*

TROTTER.—No tan deprisa, comandante Metcalf. Eso podría ser lo que quiere que hagamos.

METCALF.—¿Cómo? No le entiendo.

TROTTER.—Me veo obligado a ponerme en el lugar de una mente astuta y desquiciada. Tengo que prever qué es lo que quiere que hagamos y qué tiene pensado hacer ella. Tengo que ir un paso por delante. Porque de lo contrario se producirá otra muerte.

CASEWELL.—¿No irá a decirme que se cree eso?

TROTTER.—Sí, señorita Casewell, claro que lo creo. Tres ratones ciegos. Dos ya han sido eliminados... Todavía falta un tercero. *(Va al centro del escenario, de espaldas al público.)* Hay seis personas escuchándome. Uno de ustedes es un asesino. *(Se hace una pausa. Todos se quedan impresionados y se miran incómodos.)* Uno de ustedes es un asesino. *(Va hacia la chimenea.)* Aún no sé quién, pero lo averiguaré. Y otro es la futura víctima del asesino. A ella es a quien me dirijo. *(Cruza el escenario en dirección a* MOLLIE.) La señora Boyle me ocultó cosas... y ahora está muerta. *(Va hacia el centro del escenario.)* Usted, quienquiera que sea, me está ocultando cosas. No lo haga. Está en peligro. Quien ha matado dos veces no dudará en matar una tercera. *(Va hacia la derecha en dirección al* COMAN-DANTE METCALF.) Y ahora mismo no sé quién de ustedes necesita protección. *(Se hace una pausa. Cruza hasta el centro del escenario y da la espalda al público.)* Vamos, cualquiera de los presentes que tenga algo, por nimio que sea, que reprocharse en ese viejo asun-

to, más vale que lo diga. *(Se hace una pausa.)* Está bien..., no quiere. Detendré al asesino, de eso no me cabe duda, pero puede que sea demasiado tarde para alguno de ustedes. *(Va hasta el centro de la mesa de comedor.)* Y les diré una cosa más. El asesino se está divirtiendo. Sí, se lo está pasando en grande. *(Se hace una pausa. Rodea el extremo derecho de la mesa de comedor hasta quedarse detrás. Abre la cortina, se asoma y se sienta en el asiento de la ventana.)* Muy bien..., pueden irse.

MOLLIE.—Tengo que seguir con la comida.

(EL COMANDANTE METCALF *sale al comedor por la derecha del escenario.* CHRISTOPHER *sale por las escaleras de la izquierda.* LA SRTA. CASEWELL *cruza el escenario hasta el fuego y se apoya en la repisa de la chimenea.* GILES *va al centro del escenario y* MOLLIE *lo sigue;* GILES *se detiene y gira a la derecha.* MOLLIE *le da la espalda y va detrás del sillón del centro.* PARAVICINI *se pone de pie y va a la derecha de* MOLLIE.)

PARAVICINI.—Hablando de comida, mi querida señora, ¿ha probado alguna vez los higadillos de pollo servidos en una tostada con una buena capa de *foie gras,* una tira muy fina de beicon y un toque de mostaza francesa? Iré con usted a la cocina y veremos qué podemos preparar juntos. Es una ocupación deliciosa.

(PARAVICINI *coge a* MOLLIE *del brazo derecho y empieza a ir hasta la derecha.)*

GILES.—(*Coge* a MOLLIE *del brazo izquierdo.*) A mi mujer la ayudo yo, Paravicini.

(MOLLIE *se suelta de* GILES.)

PARAVICINI.—Su marido se preocupa por usted. Es muy natural dadas las circunstancias. No quiere que esté a solas conmigo. (MOLLIE *se suelta de* PARAVICINI.) Teme mis tendencias sádicas..., no las deshonestas. (*La mira lascivamente.*) Ay, qué inconvenientes son siempre los maridos. (*Le besa los dedos de la mano.*) A rivederla...

MOLLIE.—Estoy segura de que Giles no cree que...

PARAVICINI.—Es muy inteligente. No corre riesgos. (*Va a la derecha del sillón que hay en el centro del escenario.*) ¿Puedo demostrarle a usted o a él o a nuestro obstinado oficial que no soy un maníaco homicida? Es tan difícil probar una negativa. Y si en vez de eso, resulta que sí lo soy... (*Tararea la melodía de* Tres ratones ciegos.)

MOLLIE.—¡Oh, no haga eso! (*Va detrás del sillón del centro del escenario.*)

PARAVICINI.—Pero si es una cancioncilla preciosa. ¿No les parece? Les cortó la cola con un cuchillo de cocina: zas, zas, zas, deliciosa. Los niños la adoran. Son criaturas crueles, los niños. (*Se inclina hacia delante.*) Algunos no crecen nunca.

(MOLLIE *suelta un grito asustado.*)

GILES.—(*Va a la derecha de la mesa de comedor.*) No vuelva a asustar a mi mujer.

MOLLIE.—Soy una tonta. Pero verá..., la encontré yo. Tenía la cara morada. No puedo olvidarlo...

PARAVICINI.—Lo sé. Es difícil olvidar, ¿verdad? Usted no es de las que olvidan.

MOLLIE.—*(Con incoherencia.)* Tengo que irme..., la comida..., la cena..., preparar las espinacas..., y las patatas se han deshecho..., por favor, Giles.

(GILES *y* MOLLIE *salen por el arco de la derecha.* PARAVICINI *se apoya en el lado izquierdo del arco y los mira sonriente.* LA SRTA. CASEWELL *se queda abstraída al lado de la chimenea.)*

TROTTER.—*(Se pone en pie y va hasta la izquierda de* PARAVICINI.) ¿Por qué ha querido incomodar a la señora?

PARAVICINI.—¿Yo, oficial? ¡Oh, solo quería un poco de diversión inocente! Siempre me han gustado las bromas.

TROTTER.—Hay bromas graciosas... y otras que no lo son tanto.

PARAVICINI.—*(Va hacia el centro del escenario.)* No entiendo qué quiere decir con eso, oficial.

TROTTER.—He estado pensando en usted, señor.

PARAVICINI.—¿Ah, sí?

TROTTER.—He estado pensando en ese coche suyo que chocó con un montón de nieve *(Se detiene y corre la cortina de la derecha.)* de forma tan conveniente.

PARAVICINI.—Querrá decir inconveniente, ¿no, oficial?

TROTTER.—*(Va a la derecha de* PARAVICINI.) Eso

depende de cómo se mire. Y, a propósito, ¿adónde iba cuando tuvo usted el accidente?

Paravicini.—¡Oh, iba a ver a un amigo!

Trotter.—¿En los alrededores?

Paravicini.—No muy lejos de aquí.

Trotter.—¿Y cómo se llama ese amigo y cuáles son sus señas?

Paravicini.—Vamos, oficial Trotter, ¿acaso tiene importancia? Quiero decir que no tiene nada que ver con este embrollo, ¿verdad? *(Se sienta en el extremo izquierdo del sofá.)*

Trotter.—Nos gusta reunir toda la información posible. ¿Cómo ha dicho que se llama su amigo?

Paravicini.—No se lo he dicho. *(Coge un cigarro de una petaca que saca del bolsillo.)*

Trotter.—No, no me lo ha dicho. Y, por lo que veo, no me lo va a decir. *(Se sienta en el reposabrazos derecho del sofá.)* Es muy interesante.

Paravicini.—Pero podría haber... muchos motivos. Un *amour...*, la discreción. Estos maridos celosos. *(Agujerea un extremo del cigarro.)*

Trotter.—Es usted un poco mayor para correr detrás de las faldas a estas alturas de la vida, ¿no cree?

Paravicini.—Mi querido oficial, tal vez no sea tan viejo como aparento.

Trotter.—Eso mismo he pensado yo, señor.

Paravicini.—¿Qué? *(Enciende el cigarro.)*

Trotter.—Que tal vez no sea tan viejo como... intenta aparentar. Mucha gente intenta parecer más joven de lo que es. Cuando alguien intenta parecer más viejo..., en fin, le hace preguntarse a uno por qué.

PARAVICINI.—Después de tanto preguntar a los demás..., ¿también se pregunta cosas a usted mismo? ¿No le parece que es llevar las cosas demasiado lejos?

TROTTER.—A lo mejor así consigo alguna respuesta. Usted no me está dando ninguna.

PARAVICINI.—Bueno, bueno, inténtelo otra vez... si es que tiene algo más que preguntar.

TROTTER.—Una o dos cosas. ¿De dónde venía la otra noche?

PARAVICINI.—Esa es fácil de responder: de Londres.

TROTTER.—¿De qué dirección?

PARAVICINI.—Siempre me alojo en el hotel Ritz.

TROTTER.—Estoy seguro de que debe de ser muy agradable. ¿Cuál es su dirección permanente?

PARAVICINI.—No me gustan las cosas permanentes.

TROTTER.—¿Cuál es su oficio o profesión?

PARAVICINI.—Los mercados.

TROTTER.—¿Agente de bolsa?

PARAVICINI.—No, no me ha entendido usted.

TROTTER.—Le divierte su jueguecito, ¿eh? Y se le ve muy seguro de sí mismo. Pero yo no estaría tan seguro. No olvide que está involucrado en un caso de asesinato. Y los asesinatos no son cosa de risa.

PARAVICINI.—¿Ni siquiera este? (*Suelta una risita y mira de reojo a* TROTTER.) Caramba, es usted muy serio, oficial Trotter. Siempre he pensado que los policías no tienen sentido del humor. (*Se levanta y va a la izquierda del sofá.*) ¿Ha terminado su interrogatorio... de momento?

TROTTER.—Sí..., de momento.

Paravicini.—Muchas gracias. Iré a buscar sus esquís en la salita. No vaya a ser que alguien los haya escondido en el piano de cola.

> (Paravicini *sale por la izquierda.* Trotter *lo mira con el ceño fruncido, va hasta la puerta y la abre.* La Srta. Casewell *cruza en silencio hacia las escaleras de la izquierda.* Trotter *cierra la puerta.)*

Trotter.—*(Sin volver la cabeza.)* Un momento, por favor.

Casewell.—*(Se detiene en las escaleras.)* ¿Me decía usted a mí?

Trotter.—Sí. *(Cruza hasta el sillón del centro del escenario.)* Tal vez quiera usted pasar y sentarse. *(Le prepara el sillón.)*

> (La Srta. Casewell *lo mira con recelo y pasa delante del sofá.)*

Casewell.—Y bien, ¿qué quiere?

Trotter.—Tal vez haya oído lo que le he preguntado al señor Paravicini.

Casewell.—Lo he oído.

Trotter.—*(Va hacia el extremo derecho del sofá.)* Quisiera que me diese cierta información.

Casewell.—*(Va hacia el sillón del centro del escenario y se sienta.)* ¿Qué quiere saber?

Trotter.—Su nombre completo, por favor.

Casewell.—Leslie Margaret *(Hace una pausa.)* Katherine Casewell.

TROTTER.—(*En un tono un poco diferente.*) Katherine...

CASEWELL.—Con K.

TROTTER.—Claro. ¿Dirección?

CASEWELL.—Villa Mariposa. Pine d'Or, Mallorca.

TROTTER.—¿En Italia?

CASEWELL.—Es una isla..., una isla española.

TROTTER.—Entiendo. ¿Y sus señas en Inglaterra?

CASEWELL.—Puede escribir al Banco Morgan, en Leadenhall Street.

TROTTER.—¿No tiene ninguna otra dirección en Inglaterra?

CASEWELL.—No.

TROTTER.—¿Cuánto tiempo lleva en Inglaterra?

CASEWELL.—Una semana.

TROTTER.—¿Y dónde se ha alojado desde su llegada...?

CASEWELL.—En el hotel Ledbury, en Knightsbridge.

TROTTER.—(*Se sienta en el extremo derecho del sofá.*) ¿Qué la ha traído a Monkswell Manor, señorita Casewell?

CASEWELL.—Quería un sitio tranquilo... en el campo.

TROTTER.—¿Cuánto tiempo pensaba, o piensa, quedarse aquí? (*Empieza a retorcerse el pelo con la mano derecha.*)

CASEWELL.—Hasta que termine lo que he venido a hacer. (*Repara en lo del pelo.*)

(TROTTER *alza la vista, sorprendido por el tono de sus palabras. Ella lo mira fijamente.*)

TROTTER.—¿Y qué es? *(Se hace una pausa.)* ¿Y qué es? *(Deja de retorcerse el pelo.)*

CASEWELL.—*(Con el ceño fruncido de perplejidad.)* ¿Qué?

TROTTER.—¿Qué es lo que ha venido a hacer?

CASEWELL.—Disculpe. Estaba pensando en otra cosa.

TROTTER.—*(Levantándose y yendo a la izquierda de* LA SRTA. CASEWELL.) No ha respondido a mi pregunta.

CASEWELL.—La verdad es que no veo por qué, entiéndame, tengo que hacerlo. Es algo que me atañe solo a mí. Un asunto estrictamente personal.

TROTTER.—Aun así, señorita Casewell...

CASEWELL.—*(Se levanta y va hacia el fuego.)* No, no creo que valga la pena hablar de eso.

TROTTER.—*(La sigue.)* ¿Le importaría decirme su edad?

CASEWELL.—Ni lo más mínimo. Está en mi pasaporte. Tengo veinticuatro años.

TROTTER.—Veinticuatro.

CASEWELL.—Había pensado que aparento más. Pues es cierto.

TROTTER.—¿Hay alguien en este país que pueda... responder por usted?

CASEWELL.—Mi banco puede responder de mi situación financiera. También puedo remitirle a un abogado, un hombre muy discreto. No estoy en posición de darle referencias sociales. He vivido casi siempre en el extranjero.

TROTTER.—¿En Mallorca?

CASEWELL.—En Mallorca... y en otros sitios.

TROTTER.—¿Nació usted en el extranjero?

CASEWELL.—No, me fui de Inglaterra a los trece años.

(Se hace una pausa, se nota cierta tensión.)

TROTTER.—¿Sabe, señorita Casewell? No acabo de entenderla. *(Retrocede un poco hacia la izquierda.)*

CASEWELL.—¿Tiene eso alguna importancia?

TROTTER.—No lo sé. *(Se sienta en el sillón del centro del escenario.)* ¿Qué ha venido a hacer aquí?

CASEWELL.—Parece preocuparle mucho.

TROTTER.—Es que me preocupa... *(La mira fijamente.)* ¿Dice que se marchó usted al extranjero a los trece años?

CASEWELL.—Doce..., trece..., por ahí.

TROTTER.—¿Entonces también se llamaba usted Casewell?

CASEWELL.—Me llamo así ahora.

TROTTER.—¿Y cómo se llamaba entonces? Vamos... dígamelo.

CASEWELL.—¿Qué está intentando demostrar? *(Pierde la calma.)*

TROTTER.—Quiero saber cómo se llamaba cuando se marchó de Inglaterra.

CASEWELL.—Ha pasado mucho tiempo. Lo he olvidado.

TROTTER.—Hay cosas que no se olvidan.

CASEWELL.—Es posible.

TROTTER.—La desdicha..., la desesperación...

CASEWELL.—Supongo...

TROTTER.—¿Cuál es su verdadero nombre?

CASEWELL.—Ya se lo he dicho... Leslie Margaret Katherine Casewell. *(Se sienta en la butaca de la derecha.)*

TROTTER.—*(Levantándose.)* ¿Katherine...? *(Se planta delante de ella.)* ¿Qué demonios ha venido a hacer aquí?

CASEWELL.—Yo..., yo... ¡Dios...! *(Se levanta, va al centro del escenario y se desploma en el sofá. Llora mientras se balancea adelante y atrás.)* Ojalá no hubiese venido nunca..., ¿qué voy a hacer? ¿Dios, qué voy a hacer?

> *(TROTTER, sobresaltado, va a la derecha del sofá. CHRISTOPHER entra por la puerta a la izquierda.)*

CHRISTOPHER.—*(Va a la izquierda del sofá.)* Pensaba que la policía no podía aplicar el tercer grado.

TROTTER.—Solo he interrogado a la señorita Casewell.

CHRISTOPHER.—Parece haberla disgustado. *(A LA SRTA. CASEWELL.)* ¿Qué le ha hecho?

CASEWELL.—No, no es nada. Es solo... este... asesinato..., es tan espantoso. *(Se levanta y mira a TROTTER.)* Me ha cogido de sorpresa. Subiré a mi habitación.

> *(LA SRTA. CASEWELL sale por las escaleras de la izquierda.)*

TROTTER.—*(Va a las escaleras y la mira mientras sube.)* Es imposible... No puedo creerlo...

CHRISTOPHER.—*(Se apoya en la silla del escritorio.)* ¿Qué es lo que no puede creer? ¿Seis cosas imposibles antes del desayuno como la Reina Roja?

TROTTER.—¡Oh, sí! Más o menos.

CHRISTOPHER.—Dios mío..., parece que haya visto usted un fantasma.

TROTTER.—*(Vuelve a adoptar la actitud de siempre.)* He visto algo que debería haber visto antes. *(Va hacia el centro del escenario.)* He estado ciego como un topo. Pero ahora creo que llegaremos a alguna parte.

CHRISTOPHER.—*(Con impertinencia.)* Por fin, la policía tiene una pista.

TROTTER.—*(Yendo a la derecha de la mesita del sofá; con un deje amenazador.)* Sí, señor Wren..., por fin la policía *tiene* una pista. Quiero que todos vuelvan aquí. ¿Sabe dónde están?

CHRISTOPHER.—*(Va a la izquierda de* TROTTER.*)* Giles y Mollie están en la cocina. He estado ayudando al comandante Metcalf a buscar sus esquís, hemos mirado en los sitios más divertidos..., pero sin éxito. No sé dónde está Paravicini.

TROTTER.—Iré a buscarle *(Va a la izquierda en dirección a la puerta.)* Usted traiga a los demás. *(*CHRISTOPHER *sale por la derecha. Abre la puerta.)* Señor Paravicini. *(Va hacia el sofá.)* Señor Paravicini. *(Vuelve a la puerta y grita.)* ¡Paravicini! *(Va hasta el centro de la mesa de comedor.* PARAVICINI *entra alegremente por la izquierda.)*

PARAVICINI.—¿Sí, oficial? *(Va hacia la silla de escritorio.)* El pobre policía ha perdido sus esquís y no sabe dónde encontrarlos. Déjelos y ya volverán, arrastrando tras ellos a un asesino. ¿Qué puedo hacer por usted? (*Va al fondo del escenario a la izquierda.*)

> (EL COMANDANTE METCALF *entra por el arco de la derecha.* GILES *y* MOLLIE *entran por la derecha con* CHRISTOPHER.)

METCALF.—¿Qué pasa aquí? (*Va hacia la chimenea.*)

TROTTER.—Siéntense, comandante, señora Ralston...

> (*Nadie se sienta.* MOLLIE *va hacia el sillón del centro del escenario,* GILES *va a la derecha de la mesa de comedor y* CHRISTOPHER *se queda entre ellos.*)

MOLLIE.—¿Tiene que ser *ahora*? Me viene muy mal.

TROTTER.—Hay cosas más importantes que la comida, señora Ralston. La señora Boyle, por ejemplo, ya no necesitará otra comida.

METCALF.—Es una manera de plantearlo con muy poco tacto, oficial.

TROTTER.—Lo siento, pero quiero cooperación y pienso conseguirla. Ralston, ¿le importa ir a pedirle a la señorita Casewell que vuelva a bajar? Ha subido a su habitación. Dígale que serán solo unos minutos.

> (GILES *sale por las escaleras de la izquierda.*)

MOLLIE.—(*Va a la derecha de la mesa de comedor.*) ¿Han encontrado sus esquís, oficial?

TROTTER.—No, señora Ralston, pero puedo decir

161

que tengo una clara sospecha de quién y por qué se los llevó. No diré más de momento.

PARAVICINI.—No, por favor. (*Va hacia la mesa de escritorio.*) Siempre he pensado que es mejor dejar las explicaciones para el final. Ese último capítulo tan emocionante, ya me entiende.

TROTTER.—(*En tono de reproche.*) Esto no es un juego, señor.

CHRISTOPHER.—¿Ah, no? No, en eso creo que se equivoca. Creo que es un juego... para alguien.

PARAVICINI.—Cree que el asesino se está divirtiendo. Es posible..., es posible. (*Se sienta en la mesa de escritorio.*)

(GILES y LA SRTA. CASEWELL, *que ha recobrado la compostura, entran por las escaleras de la izquierda.*)

CASEWELL.—¿Qué pasa?

TROTTER.—Siéntense, señorita Casewell, señora Ralston... (LA SRTA. CASEWELL *se sienta en el reposabrazos derecho del sofá,* MOLLIE *va hacia el frente del escenario y se sienta en el sillón del centro.* GILES *se queda al pie de las escaleras. En tono oficial.*) ¿Quieren prestar atención, por favor? (*Se sienta en el centro de la mesa de comedor.*) Recordarán que, después del asesinato de la señora Boyle, les tomé declaración a todos ustedes. El objeto de dicha declaración era determinar dónde se encontraban en el momento en que se cometió el asesinato. Esto fue lo que declararon (*Consulta su cuaderno de notas.*): la señora Ralston en la cocina, el señor Paravicini tocaba el piano en la salita, el señor Ralston en su cuarto. Lo mismo el señor Wren. La señorita Casewell en la biblioteca. El comandante Metcalf *(Hace una pausa y mira al* COMANDANTE METCALF.) en la bodega.

METCALF.—Así es.

TROTTER.—Eso es lo que declararon. Yo no tenía forma de comprobarlo. Podía ser cierto... o no. Por decirlo con claridad, cinco de esas declaraciones son ciertas, pero una es falsa: ¿cuál? *(Hace una pausa mientras los mira uno por uno.)* Cinco dijeron la verdad, uno mentía. Tengo un plan que puede ayudarme a descubrir al asesino. Y, si descubro que uno de ustedes me mintió, sabré quién es el asesino.

CASEWELL.—No necesariamente. Alguien podría haber mentido... por otros motivos.

TROTTER.—Lo dudo mucho.

GILES.—Pero ¿qué es lo que pretende? Acaba de decir que no tenía forma de comprobar las declaraciones.

TROTTER.—No, pero suponiendo que todos tuviesen que repetir por segunda vez lo que hicieron...

PARAVICINI.—*(Con un suspiro.)* Ah, ese recurso tan manido. La reconstrucción del crimen.

GILES.—Es una idea nueva.

TROTTER.—No una reconstrucción del *crimen*, señor Paravicini. Una reconstrucción de los movimientos de personas aparentemente inocentes.

METCALF.—¿Y qué espera averiguar con eso?

TROTTER.—Me perdonará si no se lo aclaro de momento.

GILES.—¿Quiere... repetir la función?

TROTTER.—Sí, señor Ralston, eso es.

MOLLIE.—Es una trampa.

TROTTER.—¿Qué quiere decir con que es una trampa?

MOLLIE.—Es una trampa. Lo sé.

TROTTER.—Solo quiero que todos hagan exactamente lo que hicieron antes.

CHRISTOPHER.—*(También con suspicacia.)* Pero no acabo de ver, sencillamente no veo qué cree que va a descubrir haciendo que repitamos lo que hicimos antes. Me parece absurdo.

TROTTER.—¿Sí, señor Wren?

MOLLIE.—Bueno, pues conmigo no cuente. Estoy demasiado ocupada en la cocina. *(Se pone en pie y va hacia la derecha.)*

TROTTER.—No puede irse. *(Se pone en pie y mira a su alrededor.)* Viéndolos, casi parece que sean *todos* culpables. ¿Por qué no quieren cooperar?

GILES.—Por supuesto, como usted diga, oficial. Cooperaremos, ¿verdad Mollie?

MOLLIE.—*(A regañadientes.)* Muy bien.

GILES.—¿Wren? (CHRISTOPHER *asiente con la cabeza.)* ¿Señorita Casewell?

CASEWELL.—Sí.

GILES.—¿Paravicini?

PARAVICINI.—*(Levanta las manos.)* Oh, sí, acepto.

GILES.—¿Metcalf?

METCALF.—*(Despacio.)* Sí.

GILES.—¿Tenemos que repetir exactamente lo que hicimos?

TROTTER.—Tienen que repetir exactamente los mismos actos, sí.

PARAVICINI.—*(Se pone en pie.)* Entonces volveré

al piano en la salita y, una vez más, tocaré con un dedo la canción favorita del asesino. *(Canta, haciendo gestos con un dedo.)* Ta, ra, ra..., ra, ra, ra... *(Va hacia la izquierda.)*

TROTTER.—*(Va hacia el centro del escenario.)* No tan deprisa, señor Paravicini. *(A* MOLLIE.*)* ¿Sabe usted tocar el piano, señora Ralston?

MOLLIE.—Sí.

TROTTER.—¿Y se sabe la melodía de *Tres ratones ciegos*?

MOLLIE.—¿No la sabemos todos?

TROTTER.—Entonces podría tocarla al piano con un dedo igual que hizo el señor Paravicini. *(*MOLLIE *asiente con la cabeza.)* Bien. Por favor pase a la salita, siéntese al piano, y prepárese para tocar cuando se lo diga.

> *(*MOLLIE *cruza a la izquierda por delante del sofá.)*

PARAVICINI.—Pero, oficial, había entendido que todos íbamos a repetir nuestros papeles anteriores.

TROTTER.—Repetirán los mismos actos, *pero no necesariamente las mismas personas.* Gracias, señora Ralston.

> *(*PARAVICINI *abre la puerta que hay a la izquierda.* MOLLIE *sale.)*

GILES.—No le veo sentido.

TROTTER.—*(Yendo hacia el centro de la mesa de comedor.)* Lo tiene. Es un modo de comprobar las declaraciones originales, y tal vez una declaración en particular. Bien, escuchen, por favor. Voy a asignarles a cada uno un nuevo papel. Señor Wren, ¿tiene la bondad de ir a la cocina? Ocúpese de la cena de la señora Ralston. Tengo entendido que le gusta mucho la cocina.

(CHRISTOPHER *sale por la izquierda.*)

TROTTER.—Señor Paravicini, ¿quiere usted subir a la habitación del señor Wren? Mejor vaya por las escaleras de servicio. Comandante Metcalf, ¿puede subir a la habitación del señor Ralston y comprobar el teléfono? Señorita Casewell, ¿le importaría bajar a la bodega? El señor Wren le enseñará el camino. Por desgracia, necesito a alguien para reproducir mis propios actos. Siento tener que pedírselo, señor Ralston, pero ¿puede salir por esa ventana y seguir el hilo del teléfono hasta cerca de la puerta principal. Es una misión un poco gélida... pero probablemente sea usted el más fuerte de los presentes.

METCALF.—¿Y usted qué va a hacer?

TROTTER.—*(Cruza hasta la radio y la enciende y la apaga.)* Yo representaré el papel de la señora Boyle.

METCALF.—Un poco arriesgado, ¿no?

TROTTER.—*(Se apoya en el escritorio.)* Quédense donde están y no se muevan de allí hasta que les llame.

(LA SRTA. CASEWELL *se levanta y sale por la derecha.* GILES *va detrás de la mesa de comedor y descorre la cortina de la dere-*

cha. El comandante Metcalf *sale por la derecha.* Trotter *le indica con un gesto de la cabeza a* Paravicini *que se vaya.)*

Paravicini.—*(Se encoge de hombros.)* ¡Juegos de salón! (Paravicini *sale por la derecha.)*

Giles.—¿No le importa que me ponga un abrigo?

Trotter.—Se lo recomiendo, señor. (Giles *coge el abrigo del vestíbulo, se lo pone y vuelve a la ventana.* Trotter *va al centro del escenario por delante de la mesa de comedor y escribe en su cuaderno de notas.)* Llévese mi linterna, señor. Está detrás de la cortina. (Giles *trepa a la ventana y sale.* Trotter *cruza el escenario hasta la puerta de la biblioteca a la izquierda y sale. Al cabo de una breve pausa vuelve a entrar, apaga la luz de la biblioteca, va a la ventana, la cierra y echa la cortina. Cruza hasta la chimenea y se desploma en el sillón. Después de una pausa se pone en pie y va a la puerta de la izquierda. Grita.)* Señora Ralston, cuente hasta veinte y luego empiece a tocar. (Trotter *cierra la puerta de la izquierda, va a las escaleras y se asoma. Se oye tocar* Tres ratones ciegos *al piano. Después de una pausa, apaga las luces de la pared derecha, luego apaga las de la izquierda. Luego enciende la lámpara de la mesa y va hasta la puerta de la izquierda. Grita.)* ¡Señora Ralston, señora Ralston!

(Mollie *entra por la izquierda y pasa delante del sofá.)*

Mollie.—¿Sí? ¿Qué pasa? (Trotter *cierra la puerta de la izquierda y se apoya en la puerta.)* Parece muy pagado de sí mismo. ¿Ya tiene lo que quería?

Trotter.—Tengo exactamente lo que quería.

Mollie.—¿Sabe quién es el asesino?

Trotter.—Sí, lo sé.

Mollie.—¿Quién de ellos es?

Trotter.—*Usted* debería saberlo, señora Ralston.

Mollie.—¿Yo?

Trotter.—Ha sido muy tonta, ¿sabe? Ha corrido el riesgo de que la mataran por no confiar en mí. Y ha estado en grave peligro varias veces.

Mollie.—No sé qué quiere decir.

Trotter.—*(Va despacio por detrás de la mesita del sofá hasta la derecha del sofá; todavía con mucha naturalidad y amabilidad.)* Vamos, señora Ralston. Los policías no somos tan tontos como cree. Desde el primer momento comprendí que conocía de primera mano el asunto de la granja Longridge. Sabía que la señora Boyle fue la magistrada del caso. De hecho, lo sabía todo. ¿Por qué no habló y me lo dijo?

Mollie.—*(Muy afectada.)* No entiendo. Quería..., quería olvidar. *(Se sienta en el extremo izquierdo del sofá.)*

Trotter.—¿De soltera se llamaba usted Waring?

Mollie.—Sí.

Trotter.—La señorita Waring. Era usted la maestra... del colegio al que iban esos niños.

Mollie.—Sí.

Trotter.—¿No es cierto que Jimmy, el niño que murió, consiguió enviarle a usted una carta? *(Se sienta en el extremo derecho del sofá.)* En la carta pedía ayuda..., ayuda a su joven y amable maestra. Usted nunca respondió a la carta.

MOLLIE.—No pude. No la recibí.

TROTTER.—Sencillamente... no hizo caso.

MOLLIE.—Eso no es cierto. Estaba enferma. Contraje neumonía ese mismo día. Dejaron la carta con las demás. No la encontré hasta semanas después. Y para entonces el pobre niño estaba muerto... (*Cierra los ojos.*) Muerto..., muerto... Esperando a que yo hiciese alguna cosa... Esperando... Perdiendo la esperanza poco a poco... ¡Oh!, me ha obsesionado desde entonces... Ojalá no hubiese enfermado... ojalá lo hubiese sabido. ¡Es espantoso que ocurran cosas así!

TROTTER.—(*Su voz se vuelve de pronto más grave.*) Sí, es espantoso. (*Saca un revólver del bolsillo.*)

MOLLIE.—Pensaba que la policía no llevaba armas... (*De pronto ve la cara de* TROTTER *y se queda boquiabierta de espanto.*)

TROTTER.—La policía no..., pero yo no soy policía, señora Ralston. Usted creyó que lo era porque telefoneé desde una cabina y le dije que llamaba desde la comisaría y que el oficial Trotter iba de camino. Corté el cable del teléfono antes de entrar por la puerta principal. ¿Sabe quién soy, señora Ralston? Georgie..., soy el hermano de Jimmy, Georgie.

MOLLIE.—¡Oh! (*Mira desesperada a su alrededor.*)

TROTTER.—(*Se pone en pie.*) Más le vale no gritar, señora Ralston, porque como grite disparará... Me gustaría hablar con usted un momento. (*Se aparta.*) He dicho que me gustaría hablar con usted un momento. Jimmy murió. (*Su actitud se vuelve sencilla e infantil.*) Esa mujer tan cruel lo mató. La metieron en la cárcel. No era lo bastante mala para ella. Dije que un día la mataría... y lo he hecho. En mitad de la niebla. Fue divertido. Espero que Jimmy lo sepa. «Los mataré a todos cuando sea mayor.» Eso me dije. Porque los adultos pueden hacer lo que quieren. (*Alegremente.*) Y voy a matarla a usted dentro de un minuto.

MOLLIE.—Más le vale no intentarlo. (*Se esfuerza todo lo posible en ser persuasiva.*) No podrá escapar.

TROTTER.—(*Malhumorado.*) ¡Alguien ha escondido mis esquís! No los encuentro. Pero da igual. En realidad, me da lo mismo si consigo escapar o no. Estoy cansado. Ha sido muy divertido. Verlos a todos. Y fingir ser un policía.

MOLLIE.—Ese revólver va a hacer mucho ruido.

TROTTER.—Cierto. Es mucho mejor hacerlo de la manera habitual y cogerla del cuello. (*Se acerca despacio a ella, silbando* Tres ratones ciegos.) El último ratoncito en la ratonera. (*Suelta el revólver en el sofá y se inclina hacia ella con la mano izquierda en su boca y la derecha en el cuello.*)

(LA SRTA. CASEWELL y EL COMANDANTE METCALF *aparecen por el arco de la derecha.*)

CASEWELL.—Georgie, Georgie, me conoces, ¿verdad? ¿No recuerdas la granja, Georgie? Los animales, aquel cerdo viejo y gordo y el día que el toro nos persiguió por el campo. Y los perros. (*Cruza a la izquierda de la mesita del sofá.*)

TROTTER.—¿Los perros?

CASEWELL.—Sí, Spot y Plain.

TROTTER.—¿Kathy?

CASEWELL.—Sí, Kathy…, me recuerdas ahora, ¿verdad?

TROTTER.—Kathy, eres tú. ¿Qué haces aquí? *(Se pone en pie y va a la derecha de la mesita del sofá.)*

CASEWELL.—He venido a Inglaterra a buscarte. No te he reconocido hasta que te retorciste el pelo como hacías siempre. *(TROTTER se retuerce el pelo.)* Sí, siempre lo hacías. Georgie, ven conmigo. *(Con firmeza.)* Vas a venir conmigo.

TROTTER.—¿Adónde vamos?

CASEWELL.—*(Con dulzura, como si le hablase a un niño.)* No pasa nada, Georgie. Te voy a llevar a un sitio donde cuidarán de ti, y se asegurarán de que no hagas más daño a nadie…

(LA SRTA. CASEWELL sale por las escaleras, llevándose a TROTTER de la mano. EL COMANDANTE METCALF enciende las luces, va a las escaleras y mira hacia arriba.)

METCALF.—*(Llama.)* ¡Ralston! ¡Ralston!

(EL COMANDANTE METCALF sale por las escaleras. GILES entra por el arco de la derecha. Corre hacia MOLLIE, que está en el sofá, se sienta, la coge entre sus brazos y deja el revólver sobre la mesita del sofá.)

GILES.—Mollie, Mollie, ¿estás bien? Cariño, cariño.

MOLLIE.—¡Ay, Giles!

GILES.—¿Quién iba a imaginar que era Trotter?

MOLLIE.—Está loco, loco...

GILES.—Sí, pero tú...

MOLLIE.—Yo me vi involucrada en todo aquello, daba clases en la escuela. No fue culpa mía..., pero él pensaba que habría podido salvar al niño.

GILES.—Tendrías que habérmelo contado.

MOLLIE.—Quería olvidar.

(EL COMANDANTE METCALF *entra por las escaleras y va al centro del escenario.*)

METCALF.—Todo está controlado. Pronto estará inconsciente con un sedante... Su hermana está cuidando de él. El pobre está como una cabra, claro. Sospeché de él todo el tiempo.

GILES.—¿Ah, sí? ¿No creía que fuese policía?

METCALF.—Sabía que no lo era. Verá, señor Ralston, yo soy policía.

GILES.—¿Usted?

METCALF.—En cuanto encontramos el cuaderno de notas con las palabras «Monkswell Manor», comprendimos que era vital tener a alguien sobre el terreno. Cuando se lo explicamos, el comandante Metcalf aceptó dejarme ocupar su sitio. Me extrañó mucho cuando apareció Trotter. (*Ve el revólver en la mesita del sofá y lo coge.*)

MOLLIE.—¿Y la señorita Casewell es su hermana?

METCALF.—Sí, por lo visto lo reconoció justo antes de que pasara esto. No sabía qué hacer, pero por suerte vino a contármelo, justo a tiempo. En fin, ha empezado a derretirse la nieve, no tardará en llegar ayuda. *(Va hacia el arco de la derecha.)* A propósito, iré a por los esquís. Los escondí encima de la cama con dosel. (EL COMANDANTE METCALF *sale por la derecha.)*

MOLLIE.—Y yo que pensaba que había sido Paravicini.

GILES.—Supongo que registrarán su coche con cuidado. No me sorprendería que hubiese mil relojes suizos en la rueda de recambio. Sí, a eso se dedica, al contrabando. Mollie, creí que pensabas que yo...

MOLLIE.—Giles ¿qué fuiste a hacer ayer a Londres?

GILES.—Cariño, fui a comprarte un regalo de aniversario, hoy hace un año que nos casamos.

MOLLIE.—¡Oh! Para eso fui yo a Londres, por eso no quería que lo supieras.

GILES.—No.

(MOLLIE *se levanta, va al aparador y saca el paquete.* GILES *se levanta y va a la derecha de la mesita del sofá.)*

MOLLIE.—*(Le da el paquete.)* Son cigarros. Espero que te gusten.

GILES.—*(Deshace el paquete.)* Cariño, muchas gracias. Son buenísimos.

MOLLIE.—¿Te los fumarás?

GILES.—*(Heroicamente.)* Me los fumaré.

MOLLIE.—¿Y mi regalo?

GILES.—Ah, sí, casi se me olvida. *(Corre al baúl del vestíbulo, saca la sombrerera y vuelve. Orgulloso.)* Es un sombrero.

MOLLIE.—(*Sorprendida.*) ¿Un sombrero? Pero si casi nunca llevo.

GILES.—Así tienes uno.

MOLLIE.—(*Saca el sombrero de la caja.*) ¡Oh!, es precioso, cariño.

GILES.—Póntelo.

MOLLIE.—Luego, cuando esté bien peinada.

GILES.—Te gusta, ¿verdad? La chica de la tienda dijo que era el último grito en sombreros.

> (MOLLIE *se pone el sombrero.* GILES *pasa delante del escritorio.* EL COMANDANTE METCALF *entra corriendo por la derecha.*)

METCALF.—¡Señora Ralston, señora Ralston! Sale mucho olor a quemado de la cocina.

> (MOLLIE *sale corriendo por la derecha en dirección a la cocina.*)

MOLLIE.—(*Gime.*) ¡Ay, mi empanada!

TELÓN

PROPUESTAS DE TRABAJO

1. ACTIVIDADES PARA TRABAJAR ANTES DE LA LECTURA

1.1. Agatha Christie es una de las escritoras de novela policíaca más conocida de todos los tiempos. Busca información sobre la autora y haz un resumen de su biografía. ¿Piensas que era una mujer avanzada a su tiempo? ¿Crees que algunos rasgos de su vida parecen propios de alguien que escribe sobre crímenes? ¿Te ha sorprendido alguno en concreto?

1.2. *La ratonera* es una obra de teatro que entronca con el género del misterio y el suspense. ¿Has leído algún relato de este tipo? ¿Conoces a algún otro autor de novelas policíacas? Según los especialistas, estas se dividen en dos grandes tradiciones: la escuela inglesa y la americana. En grupos reducidos, buscad información sobre el género y realizad un Power-Point para exponerlo en clase ante vuestros compañeros. No olvidéis especificar a quiénes se considera sus primeros autores.

1.3. Inglaterra participó muy activamente en la Segunda Guerra Mundial. A pesar de estar en el bando de los «vencedores», pagó duramente las consecuencias del conflicto. *La ratonera* se estrenó unos años después de que acabara la guerra. Busca información sobre la situación del país después del armisticio y describe con tus palabras la situación en la que se encontraba la población. Muchos críticos han acusado a Agatha Christie de frivolidad al escribir literatura de evasión en ese contexto. ¿Qué opinas de ello? ¿Crees que es una opción válida en un momento tan difícil para la población? Razona tu respuesta.

1.4. La obra teatral que vas a leer se llama *La ratonera*. Busca en el diccionario qué significa este término. ¿Te parece sugerente para una pieza de misterio? Originalmente se iba a titular *Tres ratones ciegos*, nombre de una canción popular infantil inglesa, pero la autora tuvo que cambiar de idea porque ya existía una obra con ese título. Lee la letra y escucha la canción que aparecerá varias veces durante la trama en este enlace: <http://www.mamalisa.com/?t=ss&p=1553 &c=116#multimediaBoxInternalLink>. ¿Te atreverías a interpretarla? ¿Dirías que esta, como otras canciones infantiles, contienen a veces algo inquietante? Justifica tu respuesta.

1.5. Muchas de las obras de Agatha Christie transcurren en mansiones de la campiña inglesa. Estas casas provienen de la herencia victoriana y con el tiempo se convirtieron en un problema para sus propietarios debido al elevado coste que suponía mantenerlas. Entra en este enlace y observa cómo eran por dentro y por fuera: <https://www.youtube.com/watch?v=XH1Zj2llefU>. ¿Te gustaría vivir en una casa así? ¿Por qué?

2. ACTIVIDADES PARA TRABAJAR DURANTE LA LECTURA

2.1. La obra empieza con una larga acotación. ¿Qué es una acotación? ¿Qué utilidad tiene en el teatro? Léela con atención y haz un dibujo del espacio que se describe.

2.2. En la primera escena se presenta a la mayoría de los personajes. Gracias a las acotaciones, pero también a sus palabras y a cómo se expresan, nos podemos hacer en seguida una idea del tipo de personas que son. Haz una breve descripción física y psicológica de cada uno de ellos.

2.3. El personaje de Paravicini se muestra especialmente inquietante. ¿Por qué? Busca citas que lo evidencien a lo largo de la obra.

2.4. «No, desde luego, las clases inferiores parecen ignorar cuáles son sus responsabilidades» (p. 78). Eso es lo que dice la señora Boyle en una conversación con la señorita Casewell en la que queda patente que los tiempos están cambiando. ¿Por qué asegura ella que es difícil ahora encontrar servicio? ¿De qué acusa a la señorita Casewell? ¿Por qué? Justifica tu respuesta.

2.5. A pesar de la gran nevada y cómo dificulta la movilidad, el oficial Trotter llega a la mansión en la segunda escena. ¿Cómo lo consigue? ¿Por qué se ha desplazado hasta allí de forma tan urgente?

2.6. Antes de finalizar el primer acto descubrimos que la señora Boyle miente. Se ha mostrado implacable con la moralidad y comportamiento de los otros, y sin embargo ha mentido. ¿Qué pretendía esconder?

2.7. En el segundo acto, Mollie dice horrorizada: «No sé qué piensa el oficial. Y sabe cómo hacer que pienses cosas de la gente. Te haces preguntas y empiezas a dudar. Tienes la sensación de que alguien a quien quieres y conoces bien podría ser un... desconocido. (*Susurra.*) Es como en las pesadillas: estás en algún sitio con amigos y de pronto los miras a la cara y ya no son tus amigos..., son otras personas..., están fingiendo. Tal vez no podamos fiarnos de nadie..., a lo mejor todos son desconocidos» (p. 137). ¿Podrías imaginar una pesadilla de este tipo? Escribe un relato breve en el que esta sensación sea el motor de la trama.

2.8. Trotter presiona a Mollie para que le cuente su relación con el caso de la granja Longridge. ¿Qué tiene que ver ella con los niños que vivieron allí?

2.9. La resolución del caso tiene que ver, finalmente, con la identidad de nuestro policía. ¿Quién es en realidad el oficial Trotter?

3. ACTIVIDADES PARA TRABAJAR DESPUÉS DE LA LECTURA

3.1. Una vez leída la obra, volvamos sobre nuestro título: ¿por qué crees que la obra se llama *La ratonera*? ¿Y cómo relacionas ahora la cancioncilla *Tres ratones ciegos* con la trama? Resigue las ocasiones en que aparece en la obra y contextualízalas brevemente. No es la primera vez que Agatha Christie se inspiró en una cancioncilla para crear una trama misteriosa. Algo parecido fue utilizado, por ejemplo, en su novela *Diez negritos*. Busca información sobre esta: ¿de qué trata?

3.2. *La ratonera* ostenta un récord mundial: es el título teatral que más tiempo se ha mantenido en escena, sin interrupción. Mira este vídeo promocional de la obra que hoy en día aún se representa en Londres: <https://www.youtube.com/watch?v=SsexOrG wQqQ>. ¿A qué crees que se debe este éxito?

3.3. Durante toda la representación, la autora juega con el llamado concepto del *whodunnit* (una elisión coloquial del inglés *who has done it?* ['¿Quién lo hizo?']) para despistar al espectador y hacer que vaya sospechando de todos los personajes. ¿Qué pistas argumentales se van dando para que pensemos, erróneamente, que ciertos personajes son el asesino? Escoge alguna característica de cada personaje que lo convierta en el posible criminal.

3.4. Algunos datos biográficos del asesino seguramente harán que sintamos cierta empatía por él. ¿Por qué? Esta es una de las genialidades de la autora: el final de la obra cierra el caso, pero abre otras cuestiones que nos dejan cierto regusto amargo. ¿Georgie es más víctima que verdugo? ¿Hasta qué punto merece castigo quien sufre cierta locura? ¿Cómo se compensa un error de la justicia? Contextualizad estas preguntas y debatidlas en el aula.

3.5. Según algunos críticos, en *La ratonera* podemos encontrar ciertas inverosimilitudes, en concreto algunos hechos poco realistas pero que favorecen la trama y son necesarios para que se mantenga y progrese el suspense. ¿Los has detectado? Comenta al menos dos de ellos.

3.6. Ha llegado el momento de pasar a la acción. En grupos reducidos, escoged un fragmento de la obra y representadlo, ya sea en clase o grabándolo como hicieron estos alumnos de un taller de teatro: <https://www.youtube.com/watch?v=J8yG4MZCtPM>. ¿Seréis capaces de mantener el suspense?

Daniel O'Shaughnessy Dip ION FdSc mBANT CNHC IFMCP is an award-winning nutritionist and certified functional medicine practitioner who has helped over a thousand clients find better health. He discovered his path to nutrition through suffering his own health issues. Through research, Daniel was able to come to understand the factors which helped alleviate his symptoms, giving him more energy, and a full understanding of how his body and mind are meant to function.

NAKED NUTRITION

An LGBTQ+ Guide to Diet and Lifestyle

DANIEL O'SHAUGHNESSY

unbound

First published in 2022

Unbound
Level 1, Devonshire House,
One Mayfair Place, London W1J 8AJ

www.unbound.com

Text design by PDQ Digital Media Solutions Ltd

A CIP record for this book is available from the British Library

ISBN 978-1-80018-093-2 (limited edition)
ISBN 978-1-80018-046-8 (trade pbk)
ISBN 978-1-80018-047-5 (ebook)

Printed and bound in Great Britain by Clays Ltd, Elcograf S.p.A.

To every rejected kid who doesn't quite know their worth yet. It gets better, I promise ♡.

CONTENTS

1. INTRODUCTION

In 2019, I was fortunate enough to be invited onto my first voyage on a gay cruise ship. I was a little hesitant about this but my friends assured me that it would be 'life-changing'. Fast forward to the sail date, I found myself surrounded by 5,000 LGBTQ+ individuals, most of whom identified as gay men.

I think it was at the disco-themed party where it all clicked. I was surrounded by sequins, glitter and metallic jumpsuits on a boat in the middle of the Caribbean Sea, living a week of my life as a majority for once. Some guests had come from parts of the world where it was illegal to be their true self, others from very small towns where they daren't express their sexuality in fear of being disowned by family and others around them. Under the giant disco ball, I found myself thinking about work (hard not to when you're self-employed) and how this community in front of my eyes wasn't catered for. Some people I was introduced to asked my profession. The moment I said that I was a nutritionist, the immediate retort was 'What can I do to recover from this week?' My reply was always the same: 'Pace yourself and get plenty of rest afterwards.' This recurring question set my mind in a frenzy about the many ways in which nutrition and lifestyle interventions could be applied to LGBTQ+ individuals and how important a specific health resource would be for the community. My nutrition work was already largely LGBTQ+ focused but I guess I needed the idea to hit me in the face before I decided to do something about it.

I have been practising as a nutritionist for nearly ten years at the time of writing this book. I qualified as a nutritional therapist in 2012 and furthered my study by becoming a Certified Functional Medicine Practitioner from the Institute for Functional Medicine in 2019. During my time in practice, I have completed over 1,000 hours of one-to-one clinical work and worked with clients – a large percentage of whom identify as LGBTQ+ – for a range of health issues. More and more, I began to see themes emerge which highlighted individual needs among LGBTQ+ individuals. This included specific health issues such as sexual health, supporting a transgender individual while they are transitioning, understanding the needs of someone who is living with human immunodeficiency virus (HIV), fertility nutrition for same-sex couples, mental health considerations for the LGBTQ+ population, addiction, as well as lifestyle behaviours that might be more common in sections of the LGBTQ+ community such as club drug and anabolic steroid use.

When the layperson thinks about nutrition, they think about gym, fitness and eating a balanced healthy diet. The truth is nutrition has developed to encompass so much more than that. Not only can nutrition play a role in maintaining weight but there is also vast research available showing that the food we eat plays a massive role in our everyday health and helps support health conditions we may experience.

Just as with specialisms such as women's health, men's health and children's health, why can't there be a corner for LGBTQ+ health? Our community has specific health requirements that need to be considered. It's important to be able to empathise fully with regard to specific health issues but there are also general issues which need to be tailored to the LGBTQ+ population. An example is digestive health where someone who is having digestion concerns may be seeking advice due to the impact on their sex life. Guidance needs to be tailored to the lifestyle of the person and this is something which is currently not addressed directly to this community.

When thinking about gay health, people may wrongly assume that it's about a man with a ripped six pack and pecs who lives in the gym and gets by on chicken, lettuce and protein shakes. However, this stereotype of a gay man comes from media sources displaying toned male cover models or featuring shirtless fitness routines. Although sex sells, the illustration of a fitness model is not reflective of the gay community, nor does it represent the full LGBTQ+ cohort and their health needs. LGBTQ+ health and well-being, aside from fitness and diet, are rarely considered and ultimately the community is failing itself by either not being aware of how to support specific health issues or being too focused on aesthetics or crisis interventions.

In short, LGBTQ+ health and well-being can span a huge subject area which includes HIV support, transgender nutrition, fertility for those considering having a biological child, substance use and addiction, sexual health, mental health and also weight management and fitness. A lot of these topics have been covered in other books but I wanted to bring these all together, tailored to the LGBTQ+ community. I also believe it is important that our community is inclusive and understands the issues across the spectrum and has the resources in one place, so that anyone can read and really relate to the book.

Naked Nutrition is a comprehensive wellness source for any LGBTQ+ health topic. It is designed to help you, the reader, step up and take responsibility for your health with quick and simple advice to incorporate into your daily life. As I say to most of my clients, I want the recommendations to work for you and your lifestyle. That means if you can only make one or two changes before considering more, that's great. This is a much more effective approach than taking on too much at once and giving up, or just doing nothing. I recommend reading the whole book and then deciding what you can implement into your daily life.

With millions of books, websites and articles on health and well-being out there, it can be hard to know what is the best diet to follow or how you should be eating for your health. Should you be doing a ketogenic diet, or go vegan, or calorie count to lose weight? My aim here is to give you the basics of a healthy diet to provide the foundation on which you can build with targeted support for a particular area. If you do not have the foundations right then the specialised support will just be a drop in the ocean. For example, supplements will do little if your diet is full of junk food and sugar.

Nutrition is quite a complex subject and while the gold standard of proving something works is with a double-blind randomised controlled trial, it's hard to get this with LGBTQ+ interest subjects. For example, there is no concrete evidence available to understand how to avoid a comedown after partying or what you should do for post-cycle therapy after an anabolic steroid course. Additionally, the research around HIV and nutrition can be conflicting and it is hard to fully understand the impact of hormone replacement therapy around transitioning without considering the individual. Nutrition has so many variables to consider, which means it's harder to show something has direct cause and effect. It's challenging to get people to stick to diets in trials long enough to show effect, as nothing really happens in the short term. There are socio-economic factors that may influence research and everyone is unique and responds differently based on genetic and other factors. The point is that you need to apply both the best evidence you can get and also logic to the issue in question for safe, effective, evidence-informed recommendations.

To be an LGBTQ+ individual nowadays is a lot easier than it was twenty years ago. Even though there are countries that still shamefully consider homosexuality a sin and do not recognise that gender is a social construct, we are on the downside of the hill-climb to equality. I hope that this book will add to the equality fight not only to help the community itself but also to give tools to practitioners supporting LGBTQ+ individuals, educate allies, empower someone to come out, make someone get tested for HIV and begin treatment, or ease the mind of a parent wanting to support their child who is transgender.

In this book, you will find an honest picture of the LGBTQ+ community in today's world. I would encourage you to read this with an open mind and without judgement. While some chapters may not be relevant to you, they may be very relevant to someone else and just be the support they need for that particular issue. It's about time we dropped prejudice in all areas. For example, this means not being judgemental or stereotyping if someone takes recreational drugs or uses anabolic steroids. The reason why I cover these aspects is because substance use is a reality in our community. It's a fact that gay men belong to a population that is at higher risk of using steroids, largely due to the macro-stressors of feeling the need to look their best.[1] While I'm not condoning substance use, I want you to be free from shame about it and use the book for harm reduction purposes – the same way a drug treatment centre would not pass judgement but would give you advice on using safely. The difference is that you may think twice and be embarrassed about going to a centre to ask for harm reduction advice but a resource such as this is easy to pick up and read discreetly. That said, if you feel, after reading this book, that you do need to get further support from an addiction or mental health service, do so without delay as this book can only go so far on your wellness journey. I hope by the time you have read *Naked Nutrition* that you feel empowered to be able to ask for help. Remember there is no stigma or shame, and learning to be vulnerable is in itself a wonderful journey.

My story

At school I was severely bullied on a daily basis because I was fat, gay and ginger (what a combo). I think I was living in a stress-induced nightmare for most of my adolescence. I was frozen, as my life was complete hell and abuse was hurled at me every day for just being me. This led to a lot of self-esteem issues and confusion. My mother was a weight loss coach so naturally I tried every single fad diet in order to lose weight, which created an unhealthy relationship with food. I demonised foods, triggering episodes of binge eating, stressing about it and then punishing myself. Add to this the stereotypical gay image that I began learning about; the chiselled muscled look I felt I needed if I were to have any luck with dating or being accepted into the gay world. While I lost weight, I spent my twenties still feeling like I was that fat kid about to get more abuse so I had to make sure I was being perfect with my diet, which obviously led to more binge eating and then restricting. The good thing is that I actually enjoyed going to the gym. I hated team sports at school but as soon as I found the gym, my mind settled and I felt I could accomplish something during each session and not be rejected or be the one picked last for the team.

Looking back, these were toxic thoughts and it was not until my thirties when I actually started to feel comfortable in my own skin. I worked with a psychotherapist to address my past trauma to feel less need to fit into what society wanted me to look like. Don't get me wrong, I still have days where I see myself falling into the trap of comparing myself to others and feel unwanted thoughts arising. Now, though, I act less frequently on them, feel better about myself and give less of a crap what people think of me. I wish I could have had a conversation with my younger self, but then again I had to learn this gradually through life lessons. If you are someone who is fanatically obsessing about your physical side, take a moment to see where that is getting you. Starving yourself so you lose weight, pumping yourself full of steroids, getting a haircut every week, whitening your teeth or getting Botox can make you feel a little better in the short term but you will always be playing catch-up, and will it really make you feel happy in the long term if you don't begin to like the person you are on the inside? You may be afraid to start scratching the surface of the inner child; after all, it is going to be painful. However, like the gym, you don't get a beach-ready mind in just one day of training it. My point is that while the information in this book aims to help with your training and body goals, your health and how you feel about yourself are more important – your mental health is just as important as your physical health. Know your triggers and the first focus should be on your health before training or even nutrition. You can have the 'perfect' body but be very unhealthy on the inside – that includes your mental health.

Functional medicine

'There is no point putting new wood floors down in a burning house'

You may have come across the term 'functional medicine' before or it may be completely new to you. In essence, it's understanding the underlying causes of disease for any particular health issue. It considers the individual as a whole rather than treating symptoms alone. It is different from conventional medicine as it looks at the person holistically rather than at a specific targeted area. Two people may suffer from the same health issue but can be supported differently and there can also be more than one cause for a symptom. With functional medicine, there can be a number of nutrition and lifestyle factors which need to be considered to help someone. For example, someone who is seeking support for depression may find that there are a few factors at play hindering their recovery. This may include lifestyle intervention, genetics, gut health, nutrient deficiencies and more. There is more to it than just needing an antidepressant to treat depression, and applying the functional medicine method can achieve a lot more beyond symptom suppression. That said, I want to stress I am very pro-science and believe there are times when both functional and conventional forms of medicine are needed. Nothing in this book is designed to be a substitute for medical advice or treatment and you should consult your doctor if you have a condition requiring medical support. Together with the correct nutrition and medical care, you can give yourself the best support to live a happy, healthy and long life.

When I see my clients in my clinic, I spend a whole hour with them understanding their health, lifestyle, likes and dislikes, and the timeline of events which brought them to me, which often goes back to their childhood. It's important to spend this time to really understand my patients and get to the root cause of the issue so I can provide personalised diet and lifestyle modifications.

Getting and staying healthy means working on all the systems which are out of balance rather than focusing on one area. I always stress to my clients that there is no point putting new wood floors down in a burning house, so taking a supplement, for example, will do very little if you have an unhealthy diet.

When reading this book, I really want you to take note of what stands out, and perhaps if you are suffering from a health issue then pay attention to the above and plot out your health from childhood on a piece of paper. You may actually be able to find some correlations or triggers.

Naked Nutrition considers each LGBTQ+ health need in the functional way with plain-speaking nutritional advice and lots of great ideas to give you inspiration to fully incorporate this book into your life.

2. THE FOUNDATIONS

The problem with our food

At last, people are waking up and realising that the food we eat has a lot to do with our health and well-being, yet a recent survey shows that more than 50% of total dietary energy comes from ultra-processed foods.[1] Ultra-processed foods have excessive levels of sugar, salt, carbohydrates, fats and additives, which are linked to obesity and thought to be big drivers of disease.[2] The more a food is processed, the more it has been stripped of its nutrition and therefore lacking in essential vitamins and minerals, which are the very things needed by our bodies to drive away disease. What's more, over the years we have been bombarded with mixed messages about what is good for us and then for those messages to be proven wrong and replaced with the completely opposite advice. For example, we were told in the 1980s to stop eating high fat foods as they were high in calories and a driver of cardiovascular disease. This led to a surge in low fat products which, in order to be made to taste OK, had to be loaded with sugar. So these products were lower in fat but of course higher in carbohydrates. We now know that this didn't work to improve the health of the population and in fact led to obesity rates increasing, more people getting sick and needing more medications. Fortunately, we now benefit from more informed research so we know for certain that fats are not the driver of disease. In fact, the message now is that sugar is the new smoking and we should be doing our best to cut down as much as possible.

My concept of 'Naked Nutrition' keeps things as close to nature as possible, using unprocessed food which is rich in nutrients. It's a future-proof fad-free food programme which goes beyond the calorie in, calorie out philosophy of eating.

It's essential to get the basics right to create balance in the body. Eating the right foods, digesting and absorbing well, getting the right amount of sleep and controlling stress are all important factors in supporting your overall health, which then give you the basis to build on with targeted nutrition to address a specific issue. Many LGBTQ+ clients have visited my clinic looking for support for HIV, transitioning or depression, anxiety or other reasons and we have to begin with the basics as the foundations are missing.

I encourage you to check in with yourself when reading the following pages and see if there are any improvements you could make in your daily habits. As I have mentioned, you don't need to radically overhaul your diet if it's too much for you to do. Make a few changes and bit by bit you will be on the road to health and functioning at your best.

Food quality

When looking at what food to buy, the idea is to buy the best quality food you can afford and find. Food that is not organic can be genetically modified, contain pesticides and fungicides. Exposure to pesticides can lead to a number of health issues which can impact fertility, digestion, hormones, skin and breathing, and is also linked to the development of cancer.[3] So if possible, consider investing in a weekly organic fruit and vegetable box which gives you a variety of in-season produce. If you are mindful of your budget then try to buy seasonal fruit and vegetables because they will naturally be lower in pesticides. The Pesticide Action Network UK produces a 'dirty dozen and clean fifteen' food list which shows the percentage of different fruit and vegetables found to have multiple pesticide residues.[4] It's worth checking the updated list each year to know which fruit and vegetables have the most and least pesticides.

When considering meat and fish, it's best to buy organic, wild fish or free-range and grass-fed meats. Not only is it sustainable, free from antibiotics and more ethical, it is richer in vitamins, minerals and fatty acids.[5] Again, if budget is a concern, feel free to use cheaper cuts of meat such as legs or thighs – and remember, you don't need to have meat at every single meal. You can also buy in bulk for better value, batch cook and then freeze to enjoy at a later date.

Essential nutrition

The food we eat is made up of compounds called macronutrients. These are split into three primary categories which provide the body with energy: protein, carbohydrate and fat. Food not only provides us with calories to fuel metabolism but also contains elements that support the body to function and play a role in reversing disease. These are called micronutrients, which are the vitamins and minerals in food, and also phytonutrients, which are the substances in plants that exert a positive effect on your health. The problem we have is that our food chain is peppered with processed foods, hydrogenated oils, sugar, sweeteners and agricultural chemicals which drive disease rather than promote optimal health.

Protein

Protein is essential to life. It is found in all cells and tissues so is essential for good health. Proteins are made up of amino acids which come from food and help make muscles, neurotransmitters (chemical messengers in the brain), hormones, and DNA. It is important to get protein from your diet in order to support growth, repair and help maintain good health.

Good protein sources are meat, poultry, fish, shellfish, eggs, beans and legumes, dairy products, nuts and seeds, and protein powders.

Carbohydrate

Carbohydrates are our main source of energy and the body makes use of them very quickly once we have consumed them. We only need a certain amount of carbohydrate in order to function and the rest is stored to be used later for energy. The source of carbohydrate is important as some are more nutrient dense than others. Good carbohydrate sources include fruit and vegetables, wholegrains and beans and legumes. Carbohydrates are also found in refined grains and sugars such as white breads, pasta, cakes, pastries, cookies, crisps, confectionery and fries. Enjoying these now and then is OK but consuming too much and too often can drive inflammation in the body, a process where the body's immune system activates and results in damage to healthy cells therefore driving chronic disease. It is widely accepted that sugar is not good for you and a key factor in developing cardiovascular disease, type 2 diabetes, dementia, depression and a higher risk of mortality.[6]

Fat

Fat is also a source of fuel for the body and supplies essential fatty acids which help nourish the brain and body, and which the body can't make itself. Fats have been demonised over the years but they are essential to our health and help absorption of vitamins A, D, E and K. Saturated fat, found in meat, poultry, dairy products, coconut oil, palm oil and palm kernel oil, was once thought to be something to be avoided completely because it raises so-called bad cholesterol levels in the body and therefore increases the risk of cardiovascular health issues, but this has now been disproven.

People also worry about eating foods rich in cholesterol such as eggs but the truth is cholesterol is essential to your well-being and makes up all cell membranes and sex hormones. Your body does a good job of regulating the amount of blood cholesterol which is produced by the liver. As there are conflicting views on saturated fats, it's recommended we should consume these moderately and from good quality sources.

Other types of fat
Monounsaturated fat
These are healthy types of fat that support heart health, blood sugar and insulin sensitivity. Insulin sensitivity is how responsive your cells are to the hormone insulin. Improving insulin sensitivity helps balance blood sugar levels and prevent metabolic diseases such as type 2 diabetes. Sources of monounsaturated fats include avocados, olives, olive oil, almonds, cashews, pecans, macadamias and nut butters.

Polyunsaturated fat
These include the omega-3 and omega-6 fats. They are considered essential because the body can't make them and so you need to get them from food. Omega-3 fatty acids help reduce inflammation, and

support heart health, hormone balance, brain health and more. Food sources include oily fish such as herring, mackerel, salmon, sardines, trout, flaxseed, chia seeds and walnuts. You only need a small amount of omega-6 fat in your diet but due to high intake of packaged foods and processed, unhealthy, damaged vegetable oils, we have an abundance of them which can cause inflammation in the body. You should try to keep your intake of sunflower, corn, soybean and cottonseed oils and processed foods low to support your omega-3:omega-6 ratio.

Trans fats
These should be avoided and are known as the 'bad fats', which are made by heating and chemically altering liquid fats to make them more shelf-stable. There are many health risks associated with consuming trans fats as they can interfere with the ways cells communicate. There is even a movement to ban them or remove them from our food supply. Examples of trans fats include margarine and vegetable shortening and the processed foods that are made with them; a good reason to stick to butter in its natural form.

Some fats are better for cooking than others as they have a higher smoke point. This is the point where the oil burns and the fat becomes damaged. Examples of oils with a high smoke point and that are good to cook with include avocado oil, butter, ghee, coconut oil, duck fat, lard and olive oil.

Inversely, use the following cold-pressed and unrefined oils for dressing as they have a low smoke point: macadamia oil, sesame oil and walnut oil.

Micronutrients

Food is also made up of vitamins and minerals which are needed by the body to function properly. In an ideal world, we would get most of what we need from what we eat but there are times when our diet does not provide this, either because of lack of variety in our diet or the food itself does not contain enough nutrients. This is another reason to consider buying organic as the quantity of vitamins and minerals is greater than non-organic.[7] There is also an argument for supplementation. For example, if you needed a therapeutic dose of 500mg of vitamin C, you would need to consume approximately seven oranges. This seems impractical so taking a supplement here would be beneficial. We will look at important considerations when choosing a supplement for LGBTQ+ nutrition on page 55. For reference purposes, Appendix 1 details the food sources of vitamins and minerals.

Phytonutrients

You probably have heard the saying 'eat a rainbow'. This is because there are components in plants called phytonutrients which help support the immune system, cardiovascular health and hormone balance, remove toxins and help prevent illness. Phytonutrients come in a range of colours so it is important you don't just eat the same thing each day or rely only on green vegetables for your daily intake. Try to aim for a variety of colours in your diet. Examples include:

- **Red:** apples, cranberries, plums, pomegranates, radishes, red peppers, strawberries, tomatoes, watermelon
- **Orange:** apricots, carrots, mangoes, oranges, papaya, pumpkin, sweet potato, turmeric
- **Yellow:** bananas, corn, ginger, lemons, pineapple, yellow peppers
- **Green:** apples, avocados, asparagus, beans, broccoli, cabbages, celery, cucumbers, courgettes, edamame, green leaves, green peppers, okra, olives, pears, watercress
- **Purple:** aubergines, berries, cabbages, carrots, figs, grapes, olives, plums, raisins
- **White:** cauliflower, coconut, garlic, legumes, mushrooms, nuts, onions, wholegrains

How to eat for health

It's important to eat in a way that nourishes your body both for general health and to support LGBTQ+ health. Hopefully by now you understand the importance of eating fresh and unprocessed food, making sure you have adequate protein, opting for nutrient-dense carbohydrates, getting enough fibre and healthy fats into your diet, while at the same time avoiding excessive sugar and the fats that aren't so good for us. The next step is to understand how much of this you should have in a balanced diet for everyday health. You can also use this for the basis of weight loss and fitness but this will be covered further in Chapter 3.

At any point you should adapt this to your personal needs and preferences and not become obsessive with it. If you are already feeling slightly overwhelmed by the information, just take one or two changes and implement those before moving forward. You may also wish to reach out to a registered nutrition practitioner to help you with changing your diet on a more personal level. You can find a practitioner in the directory in Appendix 2.

How to balance your plate

Calorie counting can be useful to understand portion sizes but this is the only time I would use it. I would discourage you from feeling you need to count calories each day as this only wears you down emotionally and can lead to an obsessive and unhealthy relationship with food. Additionally, calories, while important, are not always equal. For example, you can have 2,000 calories of diet soda per day and be within a healthy calorie limit, but you will not be getting any nutrients from those calories. By focusing on the quality of the food rather than the quantity, you will soon realise that there is no need to count calories as you will feel better, have a better relationship with food and managing your diet will take a lot less effort.

Blood sugar
'What goes up must come down but what you eat depends on how fast the ride is'

Energy is obtained by the body breaking down the food we eat, namely glucose (sugar). It's important to have the right amount of glucose in our body at any given time. If you have too much or too little, it can prevent your body performing efficiently.

When you eat carbohydrates, they are broken down into glucose in the blood which causes the blood sugar to rise. The body then releases a hormone called insulin from the pancreas which communicates with the body's cells and allows the sugar to enter them and be used as energy. When the blood sugar falls, the hormone glucagon tells the body to release energy stored in the liver and muscles so the blood sugar rises.

How quickly food breaks down into glucose and is released into the blood influences our blood sugar levels throughout the day. If you eat a meal rich in refined sugar, the blood sugar rises rapidly compared to a meal which is low in sugar. A high blood sugar means more insulin is released to compensate and your blood sugar goes on a bit of a rollercoaster ride during the day. This is usually the reason for food cravings, brain fog, tiredness and other mood symptoms. A persistent high blood sugar means the body is going to store the excess in liver and muscles or even fat. In order to maintain a healthy weight and have a good supply of energy through the day you need to keep your blood sugar stable. Over time, an imbalanced blood sugar can lead to insulin resistance, where the cells become desensitised to the effects of insulin and a high blood sugar becomes the norm. This can eventually lead to metabolic syndrome and type 2 diabetes as well as weight gain, high blood pressure and fat accumulation. Type 2 diabetes is different to type 1 diabetes where the blood sugar is high because your body can't make insulin, in which case you need specific medical treatment to manage your condition.

Do you need help balancing your blood sugar?

- Do you carry excess weight?
- Do you suffer from low energy?
- Do you have headaches?
- Do you suffer from mood swings?
- Do you get hungry more than you should?
- Do you crave sugary foods throughout the day?
- Is your sleep disturbed and of poor quality?
- Do you find it hard to concentrate?

If you answer yes to lots of these questions, chances are you need help to balance your blood sugar, which can be achieved through diet and lifestyle interventions. To balance blood sugar you need to slow the speed at which sugar is released into the bloodstream. Using the rollercoaster analogy, what goes up must come down but what you eat depends on how fast the ride is. The obvious solution is to reduce refined sugars and use complex carbohydrates found in starch such as wholegrains, as these foods take longer to break down in the body and do not cause spikes in your blood sugar. Examples are oats, brown rice and wholegrain pasta and noodles. In addition to the above, scientists are beginning to understand the role that your gut bacteria play in helping you manage your blood sugar.[8]

Food labels
'If you don't understand an ingredient on the label then chances are it's not healthy'

Pay attention to labels as they can be deceptive but understanding food labels can make it easy for you to stay on track with your health goals. Labels contain two sets of information: the amount of product per 100g and the serving size in grams. Information you can get from a label includes calories, the amount of protein, carbohydrate, fat, fibre and salt contained in the food. If you don't understand an ingredient on the label then chances are it's not healthy.

Ingredients are listed in the order of most to least and often you will see sugar as the first ingredient – this should be a wake-up call to put the product back on the shelf. In some cases, different types of sugar can be included in a food item and listed under different names. Common names for sugar include: agave, agave nectar, anhydrous dextrose, cane crystals, cane juice, corn sweetener, corn syrup solids, dates, dextrose, dulcin, erythritol, evaporated cane juice, fructose, fruit juice concentrates, glucin, glucose, honey, juice, liquid fructose, lactose, maltose, maple syrup, molasses, sorghum syrup, sucrose, sugar (brown, cane, coconut, date, granulated, invert, powdered, raw, turbinado, white) and syrup (brown rice, cane, corn, high-fructose corn, flavoured and malt). Added sugar can also be found in products you may not expect such as nut butters, low fat yoghurt, breakfast cereals and bars, baked beans and sauces. It's important not to demonise sugar in all forms as there are vitamins and minerals in foods such as honey and maple syrup. However, you still need to limit the amount you have as ultimately it all turns into the same thing after it is consumed.

Manufacturers will also use words like 'natural' and 'wholesome' to draw you when it means nothing. Similarly, sometimes products are advertised as being fortified with vitamins and minerals. Often these are synthetic vitamins and minerals which are nothing like the natural form so are less readily absorbed by the body. By going back to fresh unprocessed food, you don't really need to consider checking labels as the food in its natural state is loaded with vitamins and minerals.

How to balance your blood sugar

We know now that refined sugar causes blood sugar fluctuations, but there are other measures you can take with your diet to ensure your blood sugar is controlled and these are quite easy to implement in your diet.

Add protein to each meal and snack

Protein slows down the digestion of carbohydrates and release of sugar into the blood. Good protein sources are meat, poultry, fish, shellfish, eggs, beans and legumes, dairy products, nuts and seeds and protein powders. Protein should equal a quarter of your plate at meal times or about the size of your phone.

Opt for complex carbohydrates where possible

Wholemeal bread, brown rice, quinoa and oats are all examples of complex carbohydrates. These options are better than refined carbohydrates such as white bread, white rice, breakfast cereal and pastries etc. as they have more fibre and are digested more slowly. These carbohydrates should make up a quarter of your plate at meal times, which is approximately a handful.

Don't skip the good fats

The presence of fat in a meal will lessen the impact of the food on your blood sugar and help keep you full. Consult page 17 for good fats to include, but examples include avocados, nuts, seeds, olive oil and oily fish.

Reduce caffeine consumption

Relying on stimulants to keep you going through the day can cause an imbalanced blood sugar through the release of adrenaline. Adrenaline is a hormone released in times of stress to keep you alert and energised. Additionally, you can become reliant on stimulants and also need more and more to yield the desired effect. This can lead to peaks and troughs of your blood sugar. Caffeine is principally found in coffee, chocolate, green tea, cola and energy drinks. Depending on the person, one to two cups of coffee can in fact be beneficial, but also consider drinking water, herbal teas and coffee alternatives. A simple test to see if you are addicted to caffeine is not to drink it for two or three days. If you get a headache, that's your body withdrawing from caffeine.

Hydrate

Make sure you are drinking enough water throughout the day. This may be supportive in balancing your blood sugar but it's common sense for general health too. As a rule of thumb, drink two to three litres per day. If you struggle to enjoy water then drink sparkling water or flavour water with lemons, limes, oranges or cucumbers. It's a good idea to have a large bottle close by and make sure you get through it during the day.

Limit alcohol

Alcohol is quickly absorbed by the body so can cause fluctuations in blood sugar levels. It's best to limit the frequency and amount you drink but also the type of alcohol you consume. Spirits may be better than beer, cider and sweet wines as the carbohydrate content in their pure form is zero and therefore they have less chance of spiking your blood sugar. You also need to be mindful of the mixer as fruit juice also contains sugar, even if naturally occurring.

Work out when best to eat
Some people need three meals and two snacks at intervals around the clock. Others can thrive on three meals per day or even two meals and a snack. When to eat is a very individualised thing so just listen to your body and work out what system of eating is best for your physiology. If you are going to snack, make sure it's a snack which is rich in protein and not just carbohydrate. Examples of good snacks include two boiled eggs, a handful of nuts or seeds, a couple of slices of meat or fish, three oatcakes with nut butter or a small smoothie with a scoop of protein powder.

Get your vegetables in
Vegetables contain a lot of vitamins, minerals and phytonutrients. You should be aiming for eight portions of fruit and vegetables per day (a portion size being roughly the size of your fist). Ideally, this should be six portions of vegetables and two portions of fruit, and try to get a mix of different vegetables rather than relying on the same ones all the time. I have lost count

of the number of clients I see who batch cook chicken, broccoli and brown rice and eat this through the week, thinking they are being super healthy but their diet lacks variety.

As a general rule (there are exceptions), vegetables grown above the ground such as leafy vegetables can be eaten in abundance as they contain very little sugar. Root vegetables such as carrots, swede, parsnips and sweet potatoes, while being healthy foods, contain more sugar so should be eaten as part of the quarter carbohydrate section of your plate.

Blood sugar responses to food can vary due to many factors including genetics where responses to metabolism, appetite and blood sugar control can be individual. You may consider testing for genetic variations, which personal health company Lifecode Gx offers through a simple saliva swab. You can also use technology to support your blood sugar by wearing a FreeStyle Libre blood sugar monitor continuously for fourteen days. This can give you a picture of your blood sugar through the day and also when you sleep. Wearing this helps you to work out what foods are causing you to have those unwanted blood sugar spikes so you can adjust your diet as necessary. You may even find you are sensitive to grains and therefore better suited to a low carbohydrate diet.

Blood sugar balance is the key to health so should be the first foundational step when addressing your nutrition. Balancing your blood sugar also goes further to keep a healthy weight and provide lasting energy through the day. Once you have taken these foundational steps you can move on to an LGBTQ+ specific intervention as appropriate.

A word on veganism

Veganism has seen a huge rise in popularity in the last few years with many choosing a plant-based diet over an omnivore diet. Seasoned vegans will understand that there are some dietary considerations when adopting the diet. My views on veganism have nothing to do with ethics. I fully appreciate the ethical reasons why people choose to be vegan, but I'm going to discuss the diet strictly from a nutritional standpoint and what you need to do if you are considering becoming vegan.

Protein

Plant proteins do not match up to animal proteins. Most plant proteins are not considered complete proteins, which means they do not have an adequate proportion of each of the nine amino acids essential in the human diet. Animal sources are complete proteins and you may need to combine vegan proteins to match the animal equivalent. Many vegan alternatives do not match up in terms of the amount of protein per serving. For example, a serving of vegan cheese has little or no protein in comparison to dairy cheese and therefore is not conducive to blood sugar management. I notice jackfruit being used a lot and, while not junk food, it is quite high in sugar. If you are on a vegan diet, you may find it beneficial to use a complete vegan protein powder as well as protein-rich vegan food to help hit your protein needs for the day and also support blood sugar balance.

Vitamins
You will most likely need to supplement with vitamins A and B12, iron, calcium and omega-3 as a vegan diet tends to lack these, or the plant sources of these vitamins do not compare.

Many people use processed junk substitutions for meat such as vegan nuggets, vegan cheeses and vegan pies etc. so don't have a healthy diet. Vegan foods may also contain a lot of beans and fibre, which may not work well for those with digestive issues. Plan veganism carefully and adapt it as best you can to make it as healthy as possible.

Many people turn vegan after reading *The China Study* or watching the documentary *The Game Changers*. *The China Study* by T. Colin Campbell and Thomas M. Campbell concluded that all animal protein causes cancer, a conclusion partly drawn from research involving animals being fed a dairy protein, casein. The problem with this research was that it was done on rats and the result may be different in humans, and did not take into account the way the animal protein was prepared, stored or what the animal ate. Similarly, *The Game Changers* showed shocking research on animal-based diets based on flawed research and did not consider variables other than diet. This is not a valid investigation on which to base an argument that veganism is a healthy diet. I'm more than happy advocating a plant-based diet, getting plenty of fresh produce and fruit and vegetables but not based on biased unsound research.

A vegan diet may not suit everyone but eating more plants is beneficial for the majority of people. Many still aren't hitting eight portions of vegetables per day. Cutting down the amount of meat we eat is important, but you could consider more sustainable and better quality animal products, and eating them less frequently, rather than going totally vegan.

Examples of simple blood sugar balancing meals
Breakfast

- Porridge or soaked oats with nut butter and berries
- Scrambled eggs with spinach and avocado on rye bread
- Full fat natural yoghurt with fruit
- Smoothie containing protein powder, nut butter, berries and spinach

Lunch/Dinner

- Meat/fish with salad leaves, beetroot, grated carrot, olives, avocado and sunflower seeds

- Stir fry with tofu/prawns/meat with chopped courgette, onion, mushroom, peppers, with brown rice
- Chicken or chickpea curry with wholegrain noodles and vegetables
- Open sandwich with wholegrain or rye bread and salad
- Omelette with feta cheese and vegetables

Get to grips with your digestion

'Try closing your eyes when you eat and see how much slower you chew. This is the first thing you should do when trying to improve your digestive health.'

If you're lucky enough never to have digestive symptoms then you don't need to read this section in detail. However, most individuals at some point in their life have had some digestive symptoms, whether it's bloating, heartburn, pain, loose stools or even constipation. I always make sure I review someone's digestive health when I see them even if that is not the issue they are seeing me for; you would be surprised how much addressing digestive health helps overall feelings of well-being. Digestive symptoms can also cause anxiety for those who have anal sex, never knowing if they are going to be ready and be accident-free during sex. This anxiety can be so high that it actually ruins intimacy and you can never truly relax or trust your bowel movements.

Digestion is so important in how we use and absorb the nutrients in food, and studies have shown how digestive health is linked to the immune system, mood and mental health, skin health and cancer.[9]

You may have been to the doctor who diagnoses you with irritable bowel syndrome (IBS) and prescribes some laxatives or anti-cramp medication. Neither you nor the doctor know the cause, and in fact the IBS label doesn't mean anything. The government guidelines on IBS don't actually mention what causes IBS, rather it is just a label for a collection of symptoms and the definition can be applied to anyone with some sort of digestive malfunction.[10]

While it is imperative that you should seek medical advice for a digestive concern, the functional holistic approach to digestive disorders seeks to find the cause of the issue and there may be many of these. I summarise them below.

Food sensitivities

Your body can be sensitive to foods you are consuming. This is very different to a food allergy such as nut allergy or coeliac disease, or intolerances such as lactose intolerance – when you lack the enzyme to break down the sugar lactose in milk.

The main culprits for food sensitivities are gluten (the general name for proteins found in the grains wheat, barley, spelt and rye), dairy, eggs and soy. You can consume one food and react to it as much as seven days later, so it's very hard to isolate and know if it is a problem and it doesn't necessarily always correlate with digestive health issues.

Food sensitivity testing is quite complex and expensive, and there are validity concerns, so the gold standard is to consider an elimination diet of foods which you think are causing an issue over a three-week period. It's best to do this with a nutrition practitioner as they can advise you on the reintroduction of the food and challenge testing.

Low stomach acid (hypochlorhydria)

When your stomach acid is low, it can mean key minerals and proteins aren't absorbed properly and leave the body vulnerable to harmful bacteria. Low stomach acid can be caused by ageing, zinc deficiency, stress, a high sugar diet, not chewing properly, chronic illness, infections, allergies and medications. The main symptoms are gas and bloating after meals but can also be heartburn, constipation, acid reflux, weak nails and hair loss.

If you suspect you have low stomach acid then you can consider the following:

- Chew your food thoroughly. Try closing your eyes when you eat and see how much slower you chew. This is the first thing you should do when trying to improve your digestive health.
- Cook your own food. The digestion starts in the kitchen when preparing your meal.

- Try ½tsp of apple cider vinegar in a little water before meals, swish and swallow (be mindful that this may not be suitable for everyone and can interact with some medications so check with a nutrition professional).
- Use a zinc supplement or increase zinc-rich foods.
- Manage stress.
- Increase fermented foods in the diet.

An issue digesting fats or low levels of pancreatic enzymes

Your pancreas may not be working as it should be to produce the enzymes to break down food. In addition, your liver could be under stress because of factors such as environmental toxins (these include alcohol and drugs, both prescription/over the counter and recreational), hormone imbalances or inflammation. Additionally, bile flow can be an issue; bile assists in the breakdown of fats during digestion and carries away waste. Poor bile flow can result in your inability to tolerate fatty food and even to the formation of fatty gallstones.

Constipation

Most of the time this is caused by low levels of fibre in the diet but can also be due to other reasons such as dehydration, an overgrowth of bacteria in the small intestine or underactive thyroid. If you are suffering from constipation, try to increase the amount of fibre in your diet with fruit, vegetables and wholegrains and see if it solves the issue. However, there are some digestive conditions where fibre may be making the problem worse. Usually, this is when the gut is inflamed.

Inflammatory bowel disease (IBD)

If your digestive symptoms are ongoing, there is a history of IBD in the family and blood in your stool then you should make it a priority to visit your doctor to rule out conditions such as ulcerative colitis and Crohn's Disease. If the gut is inflamed, you need to work out why and get the appropriate medical care and testing, while also supporting these with the correct diet and lifestyle interventions.

Bacterial imbalance

The overuse of antibiotics and diets which are high in sugar and low in fibre can lead to dysbiosis or, simply, not enough beneficial bacteria in the gut. It can be a cause of digestive issues but can also lead to bad breath, a coated tongue and even fungal nails.

Small intestine bacterial overgrowth (SIBO)

This is a particular type of dysbiosis in which normal flora found in the colon makes its way into the small bowel, causing symptoms including chronic bloating and gas. You would need to do a breath test to fully understand if this is present and it can be a bit tricky to get rid of. Typical removal regimes include the use of antibiotics and/or herbal antimicrobials and a restrictive diet such as a Specific Carbohydrate Diet or a low FODMAP (Fermentable Oligo-, Di-, Mono-saccharides and Polyols) diet, where certain fermentable carbohydrates are removed.

Infections
Helicobacter pylori, parasites and yeasts can all play a role in digestive problems, even if you don't have any noticeable symptoms. A stool test can help you pick up active infections so you can do something about them.

Stress
This just wreaks havoc on your physiology. The result can lead to any of the above issues. Consider the stress reduction strategies on page 41.

Leaky gut
Otherwise known as intestinal permeability, this occurs when the intestines which normally control what enters the bloodstream become leaky, allowing undigested food, toxins and bacteria to enter the bloodstream. This can be caused by poor diet, high alcohol intake, coeliac disease, poor gut health, inflammation, non-steroidal anti-inflammatory drugs (NSAIDs), nutritional deficiencies and stress. There is debate in the medical community as to whether leaky gut exists but now

there is a fair amount of scientific evidence showing that it does and may be linked to autoimmune disease.[11]

You may be reading this and still not be sure about your digestive concern as your symptoms relate to quite a number of the possible causes above. If this is the case and you have been suffering for a long time, it is worth considering a stool test to understand what exactly is going on in the gut. I recommend Invivo Diagnostics for functional testing as the company offers a stool test which can give you a great foundation to understanding your gut health. A test is not essential but it allows you to be more targeted with nutrition interventions.

Gut health interventions

The 5R gut health protocol is probably the best way to address any gut health issue. It's a system which you work through systematically to help alleviate symptoms and hopefully achieve balance with your digestive health.

Remove

Remove any infection or overgrowth if present and foods that you may be sensitive to. This may mean using an elimination diet or involve medication from the doctor and/or herbs to eradicate a particular infection.

Replace

Replace stomach acid, enzymes and bile if needed.

Reinoculate

Promote the balance of bacteria in the gut by consuming high soluble-fibre foods called prebiotics – these help stimulate the growth of beneficial bacteria in the gut known as probiotics. Prebiotics are available in many foods including artichokes, garlic, leeks, onion, chicory, tofu and other soy products, flax and oats. You can also eat probiotics in the form of foods or supplements. Fermented foods such as yoghurt, miso, kimchi, kombucha, sauerkraut and tempeh are examples of probiotics. If you are going to supplement with a probiotic, try a multi-strain probiotic to encourage diversity of bacteria in the gut.

Repair

Repair the gut lining by supplying key nutrients which support the healing of the gut barrier such as vitamins A, C, E, fish oil and the amino acid glutamine.

Rebalance

Control stress by paying attention to lifestyle choices that can impact digestive health.

Stress

'Chronic stress is a silent killer'

LGBTQ+ individuals have all experienced some stress or trauma in their lives. Whether it is stress from school for not being accepted, understanding one's gender identity or sexual orientation and even coming out of the closet, it can leave a big emotional stress-scar on the body. Add this to the unavoidable life stressors such as work, family, health, finance and other emotional stress such as social interactions, discrimination, microaggressions and homophobia/transphobia, it can end up having detrimental effects on your physiology if the stress is prolonged.

Having been rejected by others throughout my childhood and living in my own head for most of my younger years, afraid to show the real me, I put up a huge defence wall. This stress had a significant impact on my body. I felt nervous all the time, I became a ball of anxiety and ate my feelings, which did nothing but add inches to my waist. I now feel my stress response is substantially altered from past life events and it can take me a long time to unwind from a period of high stress.

Humans deal with stress differently to animals. For example, a cat may be chased by a dog but after the stressful event is over it calms down and goes about its day. A human, on the other hand, can perceive stress in the ways mentioned above. We can have the same stress physiology as animals, we don't calm down quite as quickly and the stressful triggers can come from multiple angles at the same time, meaning a prolonged fight or flight stress response.

The body is great at adapting and tries to keep things working well with three main stress hormones adrenaline, noradrenaline and cortisol, which are released from the adrenal glands. Adrenaline and noradrenaline allow you to deal with the immediate stress by priming the body for an emergency. Your heart beats faster, you become more aroused and focused, blood flow moves to areas like muscles and the brain so the body can get out of the stressful situation and we can think clearer, and the body makes glucose more available to be used as energy. Cortisol is the other stress hormone which is naturally produced in the body throughout the day. It is what helps us get out of bed in the morning as it should be at its highest secretion level, then gradually falling through the day to allow us to sleep easily. Those under prolonged stress may see that their cortisol reading is high in the evening and low in the morning, for example.

Chronic stress is a silent killer. Your body should be capable of handling acute stress by releasing these hormones when needed, but at times of prolonged stress these hormones can be released more frequently than desired and lead to implications for our health. These include compromised digestion and immunity, increased blood pressure and blood sugar, poor sleep, more preference for fattier, more sugary and salty foods, decreased libido and sexual function, obesity, hair loss, diabetes and heart disease.[12]

People deal with stress differently and some are more resilient to its effects than others. You can test your stress hormones to understand how stress may be affecting you by doing a four-point saliva or urine stress hormone test. I prefer this to the blood test as the blood only reveals your stress hormones at one given moment.

Supporting stress through diet and lifestyle

The obvious solution to deal with stress is to stop the stress happening in the first place but I appreciate that this may not be the easiest thing to do. However, there are some diet and lifestyle interventions which help ease the burden of stress on the body.

- You should be aware now how important it is to balance your blood sugar for general health but it's also important for dealing with stress and lessening the burden on the adrenal glands.
- In times of stress, you are also prone to using up nutrients quicker. In particular vitamins B and C and magnesium. Make sure you are including plenty of vitamins B and C and magnesium-rich foods in your diet; it may even be worth considering supplementing these.
- There are also traditional herbs known as adaptogens to help increase resilience to stress, reduce fatigue and improve mental performance. These are rhodiola, Siberian ginseng and ashwagandha. These are usually sold as a complex and taking these as a supplement may support cortisol balance and help you manage stress better.

- Reduce stimulants. Coffee may give short-term energy but it also adds to stress by releasing cortisol and adrenaline. Plus the more coffee you have, the more you need to get the same effect: the brain becomes desensitised to the effects of caffeine yet the cortisol production is still pumping, leaving you tired but wired. Try to limit coffee after 1 p.m. and switch to green tea, which has a relaxing amino acid called L-theanine and contains less caffeine.
- Consider your lifestyle. Sometimes it's important to take yourself out of the stress and do something to reduce stress hormones and nourish the body. If I'm stressed or overwhelmed overwhelmed, especially working from home, I find the best medicine is to take my little dachshund to the local park, making sure I leave my phone at home. You may not have a puppy to do this with but any of the following can help transform stress and lower cortisol in the body:

  - Go for a walk
  - Practise meditation, deep breathing or other relaxation techniques
  - Journal
  - Bring out your creative side and draw, paint, knit
  - Have a massage

- Spend time with friends and laugh
- Do yoga or tai chi
- Take a break from your phone, remove social media apps or use them to do something that is actually relaxing, like listening to a podcast while you're on 'do not disturb'

Hack your sleep

'Sleep allows your body to repair, take the rubbish out and metaphorically clean the house for the next day'

Think of your energy as a bank account. If you have bad sleep then you simply are going into overdraft the next day. This also applies if you miss a night's sleep through partying, working or any other reason.

There are two aspects to getting a good night's sleep. One is falling asleep and the other is staying asleep. Addressing both of these is fundamental in the foundations of health as sleep allows your body to repair, take the rubbish out and metaphorically clean the house for the next day.

Sleep quality is associated with the following:

- Skin health
- Blood sugar and insulin response
- Hunger and satiety
- Obesity
- Energy production
- Stress resilience

Supporting restful sleep

Melatonin

If you are a seasoned traveller, you will have come across melatonin for jet lag. Melatonin is a hormone which influences our body clock known as circadian rhythm. Melatonin is released from the pineal gland in the brain in response to low light levels such as night-time and is what makes you want to go to sleep at night. The problem is we are staring at screens all day and using artificial lights which can suppress the production of melatonin. Additionally, if your job involves a lot of shift work, this will further disrupt your melatonin production as your body clock is always out of balance. It can take several days to adjust to a new rhythm. There is even research to suggest a link between shift work and immune system dysregulation.[13] So if you are a shift worker, you need to pay a lot more attention to supporting your immune system by eating a healthy diet. Increase foods which support melatonin production. Eat foods high in tryptophan, which is then converted to melatonin. Examples include turkey, cottage cheese and eggs. Melatonin is a prescription drug in the UK but available as a supplement in the USA, so speak to your doctor if you feel a prescription would be suitable for you.

Magnesium

This mineral has a role in muscle and nerve relaxation, so it is a good idea to eat magnesium-rich foods before bed. If you are taking a magnesium supplement, the best form for quality sleep is magnesium glycinate as it contains the calming amino acid glycine.

Stress

Cortisol (our stress hormone) should be at its lowest point when we are sleeping, but if we are under a lot of stress the natural rhythm of cortisol production is disturbed, which results in us not being able to fall asleep and waking in the night. That said, it can be a double-edged sword as not sleeping can be stressful in itself. The stress can be psychological but also diet related. If your blood sugar is imbalanced, this can lead to night-waking.

Wearables

Modern technology has allowed us to track our sleep with apps and wearables. Sleep Cycle is an app which can analyse your sleep, your breathing and movements while asleep, and tell you how much deep sleep you are getting; you can ask the app to wake you up when you are in your lightest sleep. The other option is a wearable Oura Ring, which, as well as offering sleep analysis, tracks your body temperature and heart rate variability. Heart rate variability is a good indicator to understand how stressed you are so you can make adjustments to your lifestyle and the effect can be measured.

Reduce blue light sources in the bedroom
This is known as junk light, which you get from your phone, TV or computer. Keep electronics out of the bedroom if possible and get a red lamp rather than bright white light in the bedroom. You can also wear special glasses to protect your eyes from blue light. You may be in the habit of chatting to a potential date/hookup just before you go to bed but try to keep an hour before bed phone-free. Not just for the light that the phone emits but you need to start to wind down your brain before bed. Practise a different night-time habit such as reading or having a bath before bed.

Keep the room dark
If you can, invest in blackout blinds as a dark room (not that kind, an actual dark room) means you're going to get better sleep. This is especially important for shift workers who are sleeping during the day.

Snoring
If your sleep is interrupted by a partner snoring then your first step is to address their underlying reasons for snoring. Snoring can be a sign of a blocked airway which can be linked to inflammation, which may be caused by consuming a food which is mucus-forming like dairy, a food you are sensitive to, excess sugar consumption, smoking, alcohol consumption and obesity.

Overtraining

If you are training hard at the gym and your sleep is suffering as a result so you aren't waking up feeling refreshed on gym days, you need to adjust your gym routine. You are either not eating enough, overtraining or training when you have had poor sleep the night before. Training earlier in the day may be better for your body and sleep than training in the evening. Remember, your recovery will be better if your sleep is better and this also means better gains from your gym sessions as sleep impacts both testosterone and growth hormone.

If after trying all of these, you still can't sleep then just get up and read a bit or listen to music for a while until you feel tired again. However, try to work out the cause for not sleeping well and adjust your routine as you see fit.

Skin health
'Skin can be an indicator of the health of the body'
Browsing the internet one Friday evening while researching this book, I came across a forum started in 2013 where one user asked 'Would you think a male who used skin care products was gay?' Smirking at this, it made me realise how far we have come from having to question a man's sexuality if he uses moisturiser to being a lot more open and free of judgement if someone wants to take care of their skin and even wear makeup if they wish. Empowerment and visibility of the LGBTQ+ community have enabled expression. Historically, makeup was

reserved for women and beauty brands targeted white cisgendered women, but more beauty brands now cater for men, non-binary and transgender people.

Everyone wants to have healthy-looking skin, fewer wrinkles, spots and sun damage, but there is more to skin health than choosing the right serum, cleanser or makeup. Skin can be an indicator of the health of the body. Your skin can largely reflect what you eat, how you absorb food, as well as show the impact of stress and daily pollutants of the modern world. So apart from working out how to use hyaluronic acid or when to use toner, you should look within to achieve glowing skin, hair and nails.

The skin is the largest biological structure of the body and often is a telling sign of someone's health and nutrition status. The healthier you eat, the better your skin will look. Inversely, if you have an unhealthy diet, it may show in your complexion. If you are suffering from any kind of skin disorder, you need to consider your current diet. Is the diet akin to the foundations of this book or can it be improved? If your diet is unhealthy or there is a functional imbalance, no matter what cream you use or supplement you take, you will not get the results you desire on a permanent basis.

Skin disorders can have many possible causes, which can include:

- Nutrient deficiencies
- Food sensitivities

- Digestion and absorption issues
- Hormone imbalances
- Stress
- Toxin overload
- Genetics
- Environmental factors and allergies

It's therefore important to consider each of these factors in cases of long-standing skin issues. There are, nevertheless, some things you can do which can help you achieve healthy, glowing skin. Apart from trying to implement a healthy diet, in line with the foundations of this book, consider the following:

Deficiencies of vitamins, minerals and fatty acids

Deficiencies may be due either to not getting enough nutrients in your diet, absorption issues or extra demand on nutrients from factors like stress and inflammation. Nutrients that can be deficient include protein, vitamins A, B, C and E, zinc and essential fatty acids (omega-3).[14]

Eat rainbow-coloured foods

As mentioned previously, consuming bright-coloured foods rich in antioxidants can help protect our skin from free radicals caused by factors such as smoking and pollution.

Consume fermented foods

The relationship between skin health and the gut is being researched closely and more links are being drawn between poor gut health and skin health. Aside from addressing gut health, fermented foods may support good skin health and improvement of skin disorders.[15]

Consider vitamin C intake as it acts as a cofactor in collagen synthesis

Collagen is the most abundant protein in the body and is found in tendons, fat and ligaments. Having enough collagen helps your skin appear strong and youthful. There are also many collagen supplements available which show promise in improving skin quality.[16]

Drink water

Most people don't drink enough water, but it's important to help hydrate the skin, help the body flush toxins and get rid of waste products. This in turn may contribute to better skin and help prevent breakouts.

Have a green smoothie

Vegetables are packed with fibre and nutrition so having a smoothie can help you reach your vegetable intake for the day, leading to more vitamin, mineral and antioxidant intake. An example is:

250ml water
1 apple or pear

1 kiwi
¼ cucumber
Handful of spinach
1 knob of fresh ginger
Collagen powder supplement (optional)

What to reduce

- Smoking: this ages and depletes nutrients from the skin as well as damaging collagen and elastin (which keep your skin firm and supple), which can result in premature ageing and wrinkles.
- Sun exposure: sunlight in moderation is good for us but excess sun exposure can damage the skin, allowing wrinkles to develop and increasing the risk of skin cancer.
- Stress: raised levels of the stress hormone cortisol can make skin conditions flare.
- Alcohol: this is dehydrating for the skin and acts as an anti-nutrient for the body.
- Sugar: imbalanced blood sugar and excess consumption of sugar can exacerbate skin problems as well as impact general skin health by increasing inflammation and ageing of the skin by loss of collagen and elasticity.
- Foods which you may be sensitive to: skin disorders can be a result of sensitivities to some foods. Common foods include dairy and

gluten. You may benefit from doing a trial of removing gluten or dairy (or both) for a period of three weeks and see how it impacts your skin.

You could write a whole book on skin health and so the above is a short summary of what can be useful if you want to improve your complexion or alleviate a skin disorder. Start with the foundations of a healthy diet then add further considerations when you are ready. Skin improvements can take some time so it can be useful to take skin progress pictures to note any changes.

Supplements

'Supplements have a use but the idea is to supplement *where the diet can't provide. They are not a* replacement *for diet.'*

You may already be taking a number of supplements daily as you feel they benefit your well-being. Inversely, you could be one of those who do not believe in supplements and just think they are expensive urine. Regardless of which camp you are in, let's clear up the confusion around supplements.

Supplements have a use but the idea is to *supplement* where the diet can't provide. They are not a *replacement* for diet. Most people just use a multivitamin but there are many different supplements for different reasons. How do you tell what is good or not? For supplements, you tend to get what you pay for. Chances are if you have bought a supermarket or generic supplement, it will have either very small amounts in terms of dose of the said vitamin, or the vitamin is made from cheap ingredients so may have little effect on the body. An example is folic acid, which is the synthetic inactive form of folate (B9) we get from eating green vegetables. Folic acid from supplements needs to be converted to the active form MTHF (5-methyltetrahydrofolate or L-methylfolate).[17] This involves a number of steps in the body and there may be reasons why the body can't do this well which include a person's genetics so it's always good to get the preferred active forms. While this may sound quite advanced, you can simply look at your multivitamin packet to see whether it lists folate as folic acid or L-methylfolate.

The other factor you need to consider is what 'other' ingredients the manufacturers put in the capsule. Examples can be sucrose (sugar), binders, fillers and preservatives, which are often used to bulk out the capsule or preserve the ingredients. Ideally look for a supplement which has as few additives as possible.

The Natural Dispensary is an online outlet which offers a range of good quality brands. Details are in Appendix 2.

Supplementation should be given under guidance of a knowledgeable health professional, and be mindful of supplementing while you are on medication. Many supplements can interact with medication so ask your doctor or nutrition practitioner who can check the interactions for you. In an ideal world you would test to understand what supplements you actually need rather than taking supplements for the sake of it. I understand testing can be expensive, so if this is not feasible for you then adopt the less is more approach.

3. FAT LOSS AND MUSCLE GAIN

As mentioned in Chapter 1, weight loss, fitness and muscle gain are what most people think about when considering gay health. Pick up any gay-focused magazine and look at the health pages – chances are you will find that it repeats the same cycle of articles on how to get bigger arms, lose weight and get in shape for summer, including a list of foods you should be eating to get those gains. While this type of information can be very valid, there are some problems with it:

- It's unrealistic: the cover model promoting the programme probably had a very restricted diet in order to get those sculpted abs you may or may not be drooling over.
- It offers mixed information: you can read one thing in a magazine one month and the next month it says something completely different, which can be confusing. A lot of the time information may not be science-based and

is only covered because it's a trend at the moment... a typical example is 'the celery juice diet' and its overinflated health claims such as a cure for autoimmune disease, chronic fatigue, skin disorders and shedding weight with ease.

- It does not take into account your health status: it assumes you are a perfectly fit and well-abled adult without any ailments.
- It's limited in focus: often the information is mainly targeted at cisgendered gay men and not the wider LGBTQ+ community.
- It's not functional: it does not consider anything but training and the amounts of food to eat, rather than looking at the body as a whole and taking into account the person as well as lifestyle.
- It's an all or nothing approach: it's usually a programme which requires giving up your lifestyle in order to lose 2kg, which you just end up putting back on after you start eating normally again.
- It's not individual: the programme or advice is usually a one-size-fits-all guide. While it is hard to give personalised advice to a mass audience, it is possible to offer adaptations for certain circumstances and explanations of how you can make a programme work for you.

In this chapter I try to give you the most holistic approach to fat loss, fitness and muscle gain which can be adapted to your individual circumstances. I hope when reading this, you will also evaluate your health and assess any potential imbalances which are important for your health and achieving any goals you may set yourself.

Your health check-up

'The most important thing is to listen to your body and give yourself a bit of self-care when you need it. It will tell you what is wrong.'

Start by doing a scan of your body from top to bottom:

- How do you feel?
- Do you have any ailments, aches or long-standing chronic health issues that you have been ignoring?
- How is your emotional health?
- Have you noticed mood changes? Sadness, anxiety, wanting to isolate more or feeling overwhelmed?
- Are you burnt out from work stress or other external stress?
- Do you feel you have to be on the go the whole time and not allow yourself to relax?

I'm pretty sure most people reading this will be able to identify with some of the above. The reason why I have included this list is not to hinder you in starting a weight loss or muscle-building programme, but to make sure you keep this in mind throughout. The most important thing is to listen to your body and give yourself a bit of self-care when you need it. It will tell you what is wrong. If you are exhausted after working a long shift, just rest – the gym class can wait till another day. The more you practise self-care and let go of the guilt of skipping a gym session, the more at peace you will be in your mind. This will reinforce a positive mindset, which then results in you actually reaching your goals and – more importantly – maintaining them once you're there.

The other aspect of looking after your health is to understand your physical health. A lot of clients I see have never had any testing on their bodies but suffer from chronic health issues. Regardless of whether you have a health issue or not, it's good to get some baseline testing done to see your current health status before embarking on a health programme.

Consider the tests below. Some may be available from your doctor but you may be denied testing if you aren't showing symptoms. There are, however, many reasonably priced private labs which offer testing that you can do in your own home if you have the budget. Markers that are useful to understand are complete blood chemistry, liver health, kidney health, sugar and lipids, sex hormones, thyroid hormones, iron and vitamin D. If you are looking for more functional testing, there are options for vitamins and mineral status, essential fatty acid levels, stool testing for digestive overview, four-point stress hormone testing and even genetics. I recommend you work with a nutrition practitioner to work out what tests are most relevant for you, get help interpreting them and create a personalised health programme for you.

The principles of weight loss

Ultimately, you should be achieving weight loss by following the foundations of this book. Since weight loss is probably one of the most talked-about topics and many offer their own view or method on it, I think it is helpful to talk about some of the theories and methods people use, whether they work and if they are healthy. Weight loss is very individual and I'm not talking just biochemically. You need to find out what works best for you to fit your taste, preference and lifestyle. There is no point jumping on the bandwagon of food prepping and an intensive twenty-eight-day programme if you don't have the time for it, as you will eventually fail. I believe one of the most important things when it comes to weight loss is to have a positive mindset. If that means you only change one or two things until you're used to it then great. This is what forms habits and then you can slowly add more changes when you are ready.

Calories

The 'calories in, calories out' model assumes that if

you eat fewer calories than you burn you will lose weight. While it is correct that weight loss requires a calorie deficit, not all calories are equal. Using a calorie model does not account for your health, so achieving your body goals is more than just calories, it's also about the food you actually eat. Think of foods as having a barcode which your body scans when the food is consumed. That barcode can impact your hormones and your metabolism, which will ultimately influence your calorie intake and how you feel. If you do not eat enough or eat healthily, you will have less energy and your brain will not function as well as it should.

Additionally, focusing on calories alone can mean less satiety, more cravings, less energy, and you can enter a catabolic state whereby you lose both fat and muscle. A good diet limits loss of muscle, maximises energy and gets rid of unwanted cravings.

So while overeating will cause weight gain, your focus should be on improving the nutrient density of your diet by picking foods that contain vitamins, minerals and plant compounds. These are known as unprocessed foods, similar to the basis of the Mediterranean diet. As with the foundations of this book, your diet should be made up of good quality lean meat, fish, poultry, dairy (if you eat these things), vegetables, wholegrains, beans and legumes, nuts and seeds. So it's not surprising that processed foods that are high in sugar, refined flours etc. are regarded as low nutrient density.

Hunger hormones

Weight is largely controlled by hormones which are responsible for your appetite and fat storage in the body. This is most likely the reason why diets are so hard to stick to, particularly low calorie ones which don't look at the quality of food. The main hormones of note are:

Leptin

This helps reduce your appetite and make you feel full. People who are overweight may have problems with leptin signalling so their brain thinks it's starving so they want to eat more. When you lose weight, leptin levels decrease as well and so you feel hungrier, which goes against the wind when you are trying hard to reach a goal.

Insulin

This is released from the pancreas and allows cells to take sugar into the blood for energy or storage as fat. Overeating and eating the wrong type of food can drive up insulin levels and lead to insulin resistance, which then can result in metabolic diseases.

Ghrelin

This hormone is released from your stomach and sends a message to your brain to prompt you to eat. So naturally these levels are high before a meal and low after. Studies show that people who are obese have lower levels of ghrelin and these levels may only decrease slightly after eating, which therefore leads to overconsumption.[1]

Cortisol

This stress hormone is vital for survival and when chronically elevated can lead to overeating and weight gain.

Dopamine

This hormone activates the reward centres in the brain which can impact the amount you eat, your mood and motivation. If you are overeating and particularly eating highly palatable foods, you are more likely to have an impaired dopamine response which leads you to seek more food. This can explain binge eating and lacking enjoyment from food.

Oestrogen

Known as the female sex hormone, high and low levels of oestrogen can cause weight gain. Age and other factors impact whether this causes weight gain.

There are other hunger hormones that are relevant and you could write a whole book explaining their actions, but the above is just a summary of the important hormones to show there is more than calories at play when considering dieting.

Genetics and weight

There are certain genetic variants which can affect your weight. Genetics is a very complex subject, but generally speaking there are genes involved in the regulation of food intake (fat mass and obesity-associated gene), genes which reduce satiety and increase hunger, and genes which impact how dopamine and other neurotransmitters work in the body. Understanding genetics can be helpful when taken in context of other factors such as other biomarkers, diet and lifestyle. There are many genetic testing companies available. The company I use for my clients is Lifecode Gx, which offers various reports to understand your health better.

In summary, you can be genetically wired to crave certain foods, feel hungrier and have reduced satiety, and there are also imbalanced hormones which make you feel demotivated about wanting to eat healthily. Then you finally get the energy to start eating well, but as you start to reduce food intake, your body goes into a crisis and prompts you to feel hungrier and break your diet – this is why weight loss can be so hard!

While you can't change your genetics, you can change your lifestyle and eating habits, which in turn can help stabilise your hunger hormone. The following principles are recommended to support your appetite and cravings when embarking on a weight loss programme:

- Eat protein with every meal and snack
- Avoid sugar as much as possible

- Get plenty of healthy fats including omega-3 fats found in oily fish
- Exercise regularly
- Get enough sleep
- Find ways to relax to lower stress levels

This all sounds straightforward but still many find it hard to lose weight. Or even get started on losing weight. Remember, taking one or two steps at a time can help you get in the right mindset to start taking on more things. Try doing some exercise or movement first thing in the morning and then see how this results in fewer sugar cravings, for example.

What about specialised diets?

Many reading this will have tried various diets in the past, bought diet books and even sought professional help. The easiest explanation of what works is to just say that most diets work if you stick to them. Sticking to a diet is in fact the hard part – I'm sure many of you can relate to going full force into a diet programme on Monday for a week or so and then life gets in the way and you end up breaking it. So you just need to find a programme that works for you, but the best tip I can suggest is to ensure it is healthy and includes fresh produce. This is far better for you and more achievable than embarking on fad diets where you put your body into the hunger crisis described above.

Some people will work well on a food plan which limits carbohydrates, some need carbohydrates, some prefer periods of intermittent fasting. It really is down to the individual, their likes and dislikes, and also what is going on in their life at that time. Make goals easy to accomplish, and then this reinforces a positive mindset to make the changes lasting.

But I want to be a 'bear'

In the gay community, the word 'bear' is often used to describe someone who has a larger frame and is usually hairy. Those who call themselves a bear usually enjoy the fact they have a larger build and some even aim to get bigger in order to appear more attractive. Members of the bear community most likely will have higher percentage levels of fat on their body so it's common sense to know that there are health risks associated with fitting into this community. A 2015 literature review states that the bear population needs to consider the health complications surrounding it such as obesity, hypertension, type 2 diabetes, heart attack and stroke. In addition, it found that bears are more likely to have lower self-esteem which can lead to episodes of compulsive eating.[2] If you are reading this and you feel you identify as a bear, ask yourself: do you actually want to be a bear, or do you feel you have to be because you find it difficult to lose weight? If the former is true then that is one thing, and my advice is just to make sure you are eating healthy food. You still need to support your health in order to lower your risk of metabolic diseases, and I urge you to take advice on this from the foundations of this book. If you are more the person who struggles to lose weight and just feels you will now have to fit into the bear community, perhaps try finding a healthy eating pattern that works for you, address your relationship with food and other trauma that may be affecting you. You will be surprised at how a change in attitude to your body and eating habits impacts your mental well-being and how you identify in the community.

While diet is completely individual and following the foundations in Chapter 2 is supportive of losing weight, there can be factors to consider in order to find out what works well for your body aside from the actual food you eat and how much.

Structure
Find a structure of eating that works well for you. Some find that eating little and often works well for them, others find that it leads to overeating. Experiment with eating patterns such as three meals and one to two snacks per day or three meals without snacking to see what feels right. The key is to feel you are losing weight but also not craving foods too much. The three meals and two snacks option may be good for those who are particularly stressed or those with hormonal support needs. You may start on two snacks per day and then transition into no snacking or mix it up. The

key factor is focusing on the quality of the food to keep your blood sugar stable.

Intermittent fasting

This has become popular in recent years. Intermittent fasting simply means having an extended fasting period compared to when you are eating. There are many ways to practise intermittent fasting but the most common is to have an eating window of eight hours, which means you are fasting for sixteen hours per day. For example, eating hours can be 12 p.m. to 8 p.m., or 8 a.m. to 4 p.m. In the fasting period, you should not have anything to eat but you can drink water, black tea and coffee. By practising intermittent fasting, you may eat less but it can also improve insulin sensitivity and reduce fasting blood sugar, therefore offering a weight loss aid among other benefits such as brain, anti-ageing and heart health benefits. You do not need to practise this every day, but if you like it there is no reason not to. These methods may not be suitable for those who suffer from chronic fatigue, stress burnout or who need to take medication with food in fasting times.

Water

Most of us don't drink enough water. You should be drinking approximately two litres per day to ensure adequate hydration.

Sleep

Are you getting good quality sleep each night? If you are having trouble getting to sleep or staying asleep, this will need to be addressed in order to support your weight loss journey. Consult the information on hacking your sleep on page 46.

Medical conditions

Are you taking any medications that can make it harder to lose weight such as insulin or corticosteroids? You may also have an underactive thyroid which will make it harder for you to lose weight as your metabolism is slowed. This is why getting a health MOT is important to understand your body better.

'Treat' meals

I'm not really a fan of the word 'treat' or 'cheat' as it feels like you are doing something wrong. Realistically, you are not going to eat perfect all the time and that's never my intention when working with my clients. I try not to demonise any food but rather to naturally navigate towards healthier options. Decide how you want to approach eating a 'treat'. Some like to have a day at the weekend where they are relaxed about what they eat and others prefer to do it with a single meal. I suggest you avoid overeating, so don't go to all-you-can-eat buffets, make sure you take time to eat your meal, don't get crazy drunk or binge eat; everything in moderation. The suggestion of a treat meal can make some people nervous so it's up to you if you want to include it but it can bring some positive reinforcement of shelving the craving of sugar until the weekend. You also don't have to have unhealthy food for your treat meal, it could just be some bread with a meal if you are following a low carb programme.

Exercise

Yes, exercise is important for mental and physical health and well-being. Diet and exercise go hand in hand, but if you are new to both and perhaps nervous about taking on too much, bring the exercise in a couple of weeks after beginning to eat healthily. It's also important to find a form of exercise that you enjoy as then you will stick to it.

Your three-day sample meal planner for weight loss

If you feel you need more portion control than suggested in Chapter 2, try the sample meal programme below to see if it suits you. You can adapt the structure to suit your preference as mentioned above.

This table is a guide and meals can be interchanged as needed. For example, you can have eggs for lunch one day or have the fish option on Day 3.

	Day 1	Day 2	Day 3
Meal 1	2–3 poached or boiled eggs	1 scoop of protein powder	220g full fat natural yoghurt
	Vegetables/salad	Handful of leafy greens	1 piece of fruit
		½ banana	
		Flaxseed	
		Frozen blueberries	
		Oat or nut milk (blend together)	
Meal 2	Grilled or stir-fried tofu	100g lentils	Grilled or oven-baked chicken
	Vegetables/salad	Vegetables/salad	Vegetables/salad
Meal 3	Grilled or oven-baked fish	Grilled or oven-baked turkey	Grilled or oven-baked meat
	Vegetables/salad	Vegetables/salad	Vegetables/salad

As a rule of thumb, vegetables grown above the ground can be eaten in abundance: lettuce, celery, runner beans, green beans, onions, cabbage, asparagus, spinach, okra, broccoli, rocket, peppers, courgettes, cauliflower, spring greens etc. Focus should be on roughage (dark leafy greens). Root vegetables count as your starch portion below.

If you want starch, then one small sweet potato or other root vegetable or a slice of rye bread or palm-sized portion of cooked oats, quinoa or brown rice can be added to the meal options above.

You may add one piece of fruit to each meal: one apple, pear etc. or handful of berries (100g) if not already included.

With these rules, your main meals should be protein and veg, an optional starch option and an optional fruit option.

Remember to drink two litres of water daily. Herbal and green teas and green juices count towards that.

You may add sea salt, pepper, herbs and spices to each meal. Good quality oils are to be used moderately.

Snacks are optional and ideas include: vegetable sticks and half a small tub of hummus, a protein shake and apple, two boiled eggs with cherry tomatoes, a handful of nuts or seeds, beef jerky, seaweed thins, two slices of meat with cucumber or salad, a small portion of homemade soup with some lentils, a couple of squares of dark chocolate, or half an avocado with some seeds and seasoning.

Remember self-care

Many weight loss programmes neglect to inform you that self-care is needed to support your weight loss journey. It's that point in the day where you take some guilt-free time for yourself. Try thirty minutes of your chosen activity per day. Examples include meditation, gentle yoga, walking, stretching, tai chi, qigong, taking a bath, doing a beauty regime, practising gratitude, reading, writing, practising a hobby or learning a new skill.

Being accountable

Weight loss can be a lonely journey if you are doing it

alone. There are going to be times when you are finding it hard, times when you don't think you are getting the results you want, and times when you need to try new things. It's also a very vulnerable experience, and for some, it can bring up a lot of trauma as well as the realisation that you comfort eat to mask certain feelings. A suggestion is to find someone you can go through the process with, or someone to be accountable to like a health coach or nutritionist who can help personalise the programme for you. It may also be good to speak to a psychotherapist about your past trauma or stress, which can help you stay on track and also maintain weight loss.

Muscle gain

The thought of a muscle-building programme can conjure up an image of someone who is pumped, with veins popping, the type you see in many locker room selfies. This can make you feel a little intimidated about going to the gym or embarking on such a programme. The truth is building muscle is relevant for everyone and isn't just limited to gay men. Improving lean mass has many other health benefits other than aesthetics, such as posture, balance, bone health and prevention of bone injury.

It's also important that you embark on a muscle-building programme for your own benefit, not because you feel you need to fit in or to be accepted. Ultimately, I find going to the gym and lifting weights is good for my body and mind, but if it's not for you don't force it; find something else to help condition your body.

You may also be familiar with the frustration of lifting weights but finding that your physique is not improving. This is usually down to not training hard enough and not having adequate nutrition in place, but can also be linked to stress, sleep and other lifestyle factors. Now is the time to look at your lifestyle and training and see if they suit your goals. However, no matter how advanced you are in your training, you still need to stick to any changes you make, so be mindful of not taking on more than you can handle at once.

Can you burn fat and gain muscle at the same time?

You may also be thinking about gaining muscle and losing weight at the same time. While this is achievable, if you have fat to lose then focus on this first before embarking on a muscle-building programme. For muscle gain, you need to eat more calories than you burn to build muscle. So if your primary goal is losing fat, you don't want to be overeating, but you can find a balance to help build some muscles while you are losing weight. I recommend you mainly pursue the fat-loss programme above while ensuring the following:

- Include both strength and cardio exercises in your workout programme.

- Make sure you are eating adequate amounts of protein to help keep you full and support muscle growth.
- Eat or drink protein within thirty minutes of a workout.

How do you build muscle?
'Put simply, you have to challenge the body'

There is a misconception that you need to be in the gym every hour of the day to build muscle. This couldn't be further from the truth, especially if you are trying to build muscle more for health than aesthetics. With a focus on aesthetics, you can easily slip into thinking this as you don't see results straight away. In reality, working out about three times per week is enough if you cover the major muscle groups. You shouldn't jump to lifting heavy weights immediately as this can result in bad form leading to injury. Focus on form and the rest will come. We have learned from COVID-19 lockdown measures across the world that you can still develop a nice physique by doing bodyweight movements, dumbbell exercises and using resistance bands, so you don't need to wait till you have joined a gym to start on your body goals.

For the more experienced gym-goer who is struggling to see results, I would question if you are training hard enough. You will no doubt agree that, looking round any gym, you can see a lot of people hogging benches while on their phone. You should also question if you are doing the wrong type of training. If you are someone who does the same routine each week and is not really pushing yourself then you need to freshen things up. Put simply, you have to challenge the body as doing the same workout can cause adaptation, meaning your progress can plateau. So consider changing things up if you are stuck in a routine like this:

Monday: Chest
Tuesday: Arms
Wednesday: Back
Thursday: Legs
Friday: Abs and shoulders

Similarly, if you just do three sets of twelve of the same weight for each exercise then your body will get used to it and this may hinder results. And don't be shy of training legs, as this can support muscle growth for the whole body. I want you to switch things up a bit with your routine and the number of reps you do. The weight should be tough enough to make the last rep the hardest such that you can hardly do it. Familiarise yourself with supersets, rest pauses, drop sets and muscle rounds as all this keeps surprising your body and shocks it into growth. If you are looking for muscle bulking, don't do too much high intensity exercise.

Muscle rounds: six sets of 6–8 reps with 10 seconds rest between each set

Drop set: one normal set, wait 10 seconds then do another set with a slightly lighter weight

Superset: two different exercises back to back with no rest

Rest pause: a rest of 10–15 seconds between sets with the same weight

Hiring a personal trainer can also be good to help vary the exercises and create an individual training programme for you.

Sample gym routine

The following is a sample routine which you can adapt how you wish. The idea is to complete all the workouts in a week. If you go to the gym fewer than four times a week, continue sequentially through the workouts you have not completed before starting with Workout 1 again. It's a good idea to change your routine every four to six weeks. If you're unsure of any exercise, watch YouTube for a demonstration.

Rest

You need to give your body rest from training to help growth and prevent injury. As a rule of thumb, take two rest days per week and don't train the same muscle group two days in a row. For example, the routine below could be implemented as follows:

Monday: Workout 1 – Upper
Tuesday: Workout 2 – Legs
Wednesday: Workout 3 – Upper
Thursday: Rest day
Friday: Rest day
Saturday: Workout 4 – Upper
Sunday: Rest day

After each workout, do ten minutes of abs and stretching.

Workout 1: Upper	
Incline chest press (dumbbell or barbell)	4 sets 12–15 reps
Cable fly	2 sets 15 reps
	1 set 15 reps then drop set
Wide-grip lat pulldown	3 sets 12–15 reps
Rope triceps extension	Muscle rounds 6 sets 8 reps
Weighted dips	3 sets 15 reps

Workout 2: Legs	
Leg extension	Warm-up: 2 sets 15 reps light weight
	2 work sets 15 reps
	1 work set 15 reps with 25 partial reps and holding for 10 seconds

Leg curl	Warm-up: 2 sets 15 reps light weight
	2 work sets 15 reps
	1 work set 15 reps with 25 partial reps and holding for 10 seconds
Squat	4 sets 8–10 reps
Leg press	30 reps rest pause then 20 reps
Body weight single lunges	2 sets 20 reps

Workout 3: Upper	
Dumbbell rows	4 sets 12–15 reps
Dumbbell biceps curl	Superset after rows (until failure)
Smith machine shoulder press	Warm-up: 15 reps Muscle round 6 sets 6 reps
Barbell/t-bar row	1 set 12–15 reps 1 set rest pause 15 reps then failure 1 drop set
EZ bar curls	4 sets 12 reps

Workout 4: Upper	
Smith machine chest press	4 sets 12–15 reps with pause at bottom of rep
Skull crushers	3 sets 12–15 reps
Underhand pulldown	1 warm-up set 15 reps 2 work sets 10–12 reps 1 drop set
Dumbbell side lat raise	3 sets 20 reps (medium weight)
Dumbbells triceps kickbacks	3 sets 20 reps
Weighted back extensions	1 set 25 reps

Body weight push-ups	1 set until failure
	Rest pause
	1 more set until failure

Bodybuilding nutrition principles

You may have heard of the saying that you can't out-train a bad diet – it's completely true. Many don't see results because they aren't training well but are either eating unhealthily or not eating enough to fuel their desired growth. You need to make sure you are eating a surplus to gain muscle. This is roughly about 20% of your daily calorie needs for maintaining weight.[3] I provide some examples below, but this is quite an individual thing so it is best to look at a calculator online that can factor in age, height and lifestyle.

Bodybuilders often use terminology such as bulking and cutting, which represents a period where they focus on eating more for a number of weeks (usually in winter) and then spend time cutting fat (usually in summer).

Protein

Protein is probably the most important nutrient for muscle growth. There are different opinions on how much protein you need for muscle growth and this depends on factors such as age, health, physique, goals and activity. Research shows that it is around 1.5–2.2g per kg of body weight per day.[4]

It's not just about the amount of protein you eat but also about the quality of that protein. Protein is made from amino acids, which are like Lego blocks linked together. Some of these amino acids are made in the body but some need to be obtained from food. Animal protein provides all amino acids in good enough amounts but vegetable sources of protein are inferior. So if you do not eat meat, you need to be mindful of how to food-combine to hit your protein targets for muscle growth. For example, someone weighing 80kg would need to hit between 128g and 176g of protein per day, which can be quite a lot when you think of food intake; a chicken breast, say, is around 30–40g of protein. This is why a lot of bodybuilders eat many meals per day and often use protein powders.

Carbohydrates
Carbohydrates are not the enemy you may think they are. Again, it's about the quality of the carbohydrates as discussed in Chapter 2. In terms of bodybuilding and gaining mass, you need around 4–7g of carbohydrates per kg of body weight per day. As carbohydrates are the main source of fuel for the body, you can tell if you aren't eating enough as you will have less energy throughout the day and during workouts. While carbohydrates are important for bulk, they can also mean more fat storage and the goal is to have a lean bulk. If you have a higher percentage body fat, you

may want to opt for the lower end of the carbohydrate range or reduce even further, whatever works for you.

Fats

As discussed in Chapter 2, fats have been demonised but they are essential. They also help you feel full and the bonus is that they are higher in calories than protein and carbohydrates so are a way to help hit your calorie allowance per day. This is particularly useful if you are a hardgainer (see page 96) or if increasing carbohydrates causes bloating. Additionally, fat can influence testosterone, which is important in building muscle. Fats should make up about 20–30% of your calories when bulking and focus should be on the beneficial fats such as oily fish, nuts, seeds and olive oil.[5]

In summary, in order to fuel muscle growth, you need to:

- Make sure you are eating enough calories
- Eat enough protein and carbohydrates to fuel muscle growth and recover
- Train hard but make sure you have adequate recovery time

Functional considerations

Sleep
It's important to get adequate sleep to fuel muscle growth and recovery. Consider the sleep strategies in Chapter 2 to address this.

Stress hormones
Elevations of the stress hormone cortisol can make it harder for you to gain muscle. As well as lifestyle stress, training hard in the gym can impact your stress hormones too. It's important to address the cause of your lifestyle stress and focus on stress reduction techniques.

Overtraining
The more you train doesn't necessarily mean the more you will grow. You need to plan adequate rest days to support your growth. If you want to go to the gym more, do something light like stretching, yoga or gentle swimming.

Gut health
You aren't just what you eat but what you absorb also. If you're having digestive difficulties, you may not be absorbing your meals. Consider the digestive advice given on page 34 and focus on this first. Increasing food intake may exacerbate your digestive symptoms so it is important to work out what exactly is going

on in the gut first. If you're constantly bloated, have 'temperamental' toilet habits – like stools that are always loose, too hard to pass, or a combination of both – you may benefit from taking a stool test to identify any potential issues with your gut bacteria, such as too little, too much (known as overgrowth) or simply dysfunctional, which I referred to previously as dysbiosis.

Supporting healthy testosterone levels

Testosterone is often looked at as the male hormone but it's produced by everyone. It plays a role in sex drive, mood, cognition, bone density, sperm production, libido, blood sugar management, heart health, energy and also improves strength and increases muscle mass. As there are so many benefits of healthy testosterone levels, it's not surprising that some cisgendered men seek to maximise their testosterone production. Testosterone also naturally declines as we age, which could be a reason why you feel keeping in shape is harder than in your youth.

When embarking on a muscle-building programme, it is always good to understand your levels of testosterone. This can be done with your doctor or many online labs offer inexpensive at-home testing for male hormones. It's important to check both testosterone and free testosterone, as well as levels of sex hormone binding globulin (SHBG), which can impact how testosterone is used in the body. If your testosterone is low, you can speak to your doctor about hormone replacement therapy and/or address the factors which may be causing it to be low. Symptoms of low testosterone in cisgendered men include low energy, weight gain, lack of motivation and low libido. Diet and lifestyle factors could be the cause of low testosterone and so addressing these may improve your symptoms but also help to improve performance in the gym and increased strength and muscle size.

Check your vitamin D as deficiency can be linked to low testosterone.[6] While there are food sources of vitamin D, it's best to spend some time in the sun as one of the best sources of this vitamin. If you are low in vitamin D then consider supplementing; make sure the form is vitamin D3 (it will say this on the label). Similarly, research has found links between zinc deficiency and low testosterone levels, so if your zinc levels are low zinc-rich foods may help boost testosterone levels.[7]

As for lifestyle, there are general well-being factors which can impact testosterone as well as performance and appetite. These include:

Stress

Chronic stress is associated with a reduction in testosterone production.[8] When you are stressed, you are in survival mode so your body doesn't need to prioritise making a reproductive hormone. Stress can promote comfort eating, overeating and fat accumulation, especially around the middle which can impact testosterone levels. Look at the stress management section on page 44 for support on managing stress.

Exercise

Increasing exercise can help increase your testosterone if you are a cisgendered male, but this is not the case with cisgendered females where it has little or no effect in increasing testosterone.[9] So for cisgendered males, the advice would be to add in some daily exercise. Be mindful, not all exercises are created equal; the ones to focus on should be resistance exercises such as weight training or high intensity workouts.

Sleep

Get plenty of good quality sleep. Poor sleep patterns can negatively affect testosterone levels.[10] The effects can be seen after just a week of disrupted short sleep. If sleep is an issue for you then take note of the sleep tips on page 46.

The muscle-building programme

There are two versions of this programme. One version is for people who are fairly new to sports nutrition and don't have much time to prepare food or don't want to fuss over counting protein, carbohydrate and fat amounts. The other is a programme designed for more advanced users wanting to bring their nutrition to the next level. If you're not sure which programme to follow, ask yourself the following questions:

1. Have you implemented any nutrition programme before?
2. Do you have time to prepare meals?
3. Are you a seasoned gym-goer?
4. Do you train hard?

If you answered no to any of these questions, I would suggest you begin with the foundation programme, which is easy to fit into your life, and then step it up when you are ready to do so.

Foundation

Start here if you are just starting out with nutrition or haven't had any structure before with what you are eating. It should be easy to follow, but the important thing is to remember to have protein with every meal and avoid junk food where possible.

As I have already explained, you need to eat enough to achieve desired growth. This translates into eating more, therefore opting for an extra meal (or meals) during the day is helpful to achieve a surplus in calories. The sample structure below means eating at least four times a day, and making sure you pay attention to the programme notes in the advanced programme. You don't need to count macronutrients but each meal should be roughly balanced according to the advice on how to balance your plate on page 22.

The example below is for three possible days. You can adjust them as you see fit and mix the meals around a bit. As long as you follow the structure you will be fine.

	Example Day 1	Example Day 2	Example Day 3
Meal 1	3 eggs Vegetables/salad 1–2 slices of rye bread	1 scoop of protein powder Handful of leafy greens 50g oats 1 piece of fruit Oat or nut milk Ice (blend together)	220g full fat natural yoghurt 50g oats 1 piece of fruit
Meal 2	1 chicken breast Brown rice Vegetables/salad	100g lentils & 2 eggs Vegetables/salad	1 chicken breast Quinoa Vegetables/salad
Meal 3	1 scoop of protein powder Banana Oat or nut milk 1tbsp of nut butter (blend together)	Protein bar Apple	1 scoop of protein powder 50g oats Oat or nut milk Nuts/seeds (blend together)
Meal 4	1 large steak Vegetables/salad Brown rice	2 salmon fillets Vegetables/salad Wholegrain pasta	2 medium pork chops Vegetables/salad Brown rice

Advanced

The following programme is designed for the more advanced gym-goer who is able to train hard and eat according to set amounts of protein, carbohydrates and fat. Collectively, these are your macronutrients and are referred to as macros in the programme. Please read the information carefully and apply it how best you can.

This is probably the only time I recommend counting macronutrients because you need to make sure you are eating enough food. You don't need to be religious at weighing everything all the time but this is at least recommended in the beginning to understand the amounts.

Macros

The following is calculated based on your weight range in kg. If you weigh yourself in lb then divide your weight by 2.2 to get the kg.

You will need to work out your calorie need, which is best done with a calculator online. You work out your Total Daily Energy Expenditure and increase it by 20%. So if your Total Daily Energy Expenditure came to 2,000 calories, you would increase it to 2,400 calories. (An example is here: www.mytecbits.com/tools/medical/tdeecalculator.) Alternatively, if you don't want to be too specific, I recommend you work out your protein and carbohydrate needs and then assume a moderate fat allowance which can occur naturally. The calculations are based on:

- Protein: 1.5–2.2g per kg of body weight per day (middle value 1.9g rounded up)
- Carbohydrate: 4–7g per kg of body weight per day (middle of range 5.5g)
- Fat: to make up rest of calories (approximately 20%)

Use your own judgement when deciding quantities of food to eat. At the end of the day, nutrition is very individual and you need to find out what works for you when considering your goals.

Weight	70kg	80kg	90kg	100kg
Protein intake per day 1.9g per kg body weight	133g	152g	171g	190g
Carbohydrate intake per day 5.5g per kg body weight	385g	440g	495g	550g

You will break the macros down into five or six meals per day to comfortably fit your food amounts into your day, ideally having an equal gap between meals. You can opt for a different meal frequency structure as long as the overall intake is the same.

You should also have protein and carbohydrates within thirty minutes of your workout. You may feel this is easiest to do with a shake so make sure it has around 30g protein and 60g carbohydrate. You can use carbohydrate powder or fruit such as bananas.

This will mean your calories are slightly less on non-workout days when you don't have a shake.

Example day

Meal 1	Eggs
	Porridge
	Apple
Meal 2	Turkey
	Brown rice
	Vegetables
Meal 3	Chicken
	Brown rice
	Vegetables
Meal 4	Salmon
	Sweet potato
	Vegetables
Meal 5 (post-workout)	Steak
	Quinoa
	Vegetables
Additional post-workout shake	1 scoop of protein powder
	1 scoop of carbohydrate powder (60g carbs)
	Mix with water and shake

The food programme is designed for people who train four to six times per week. This is the optimal amount of time needed in the gym to make the best gains possible while following this food plan. You may wish to begin by taking measurements of your chest, waist, biceps, top of leg and calf, and your weight so you can monitor progress.

I understand that you may find it hard to fit in all the meals or training sessions. You need to be as prepared as you can but also don't beat yourself up if you don't fit in all your macros for the day. In time you will get there so just adjust the programme to what way works best for you. It's a good idea to make a shopping list, do a big shop and schedule two prep days per week.

You will benefit from a kitchen scale to work out weights of food. The protein, carbohydrate and fat amounts suggested above are the actual grams of protein, carbohydrate and fat, not the weight of the food. For example, 100g of chicken breast is approximately 30g of protein. Be mindful of amounts changing when they are cooked, so 100g of raw chicken will weigh less than 100g when it's cooked due to moisture loss. For consistency and accuracy, measure foods in their raw state.

Tips

- Your carbohydrate options should ideally be from slow-releasing complex sources such as oats, brown rice, quinoa and sweet potato.
- You will be using good fat sources such as olive oil, coconut oil, oily fish, eggs, avocado, nuts and seeds.
- It's important to get at least six portions of vegetables per day. There is no need to count these in your calculations.

- You can have a variety of drinks. Stay clear of diet sodas and artificial sweeteners. Try to get three litres of water per day, slightly more liquid to compensate for exercise and recovery. You can use herbal teas to help get you to this amount. Ideally you will limit coffee after 1 p.m.
- Relaxed meals can be included but ideally after training legs and back as these are big muscle groups. Stick to two relaxed meals per week maximum, and have a sensible meal of your choice plus a small dessert if you like.

Hardgainers

There are those people who, however much they try, can't seem to hold onto weight. If you are one of these people, you need first to consider if you have good nutrition as outlined above and if you are training hard and frequently in the gym. If you are doing this then consider the following:

- Add 3tbsp of olive oil to your meal plan per day. This is a source of good calories without having to resort to dirty bulking (eating junk food). You can add this to meals as a dressing.
- Pick the upper protein and carbohydrate grams per kg of bodyweight.
- Check your stress hormones and testosterone markers. I recommend doing the DUTCH Test (Dried Urine Test for Comprehensive Hormones)

which looks at all of these markers and metabolites (see the resources section on page 264 for more information). Low testosterone and high cortisol may be a reason why you aren't gaining muscle in the gym.

- Limit the amount of cardiovascular exercise you do.

After bulking

Once you have finished the bulk, you may consider what is known as a cut. This is where you reduce your food intake and create a calorie deficit to improve your definition. Ideally you would do this gradually to preserve muscle. My advice is to keep the protein at the same amount per day and reduce the carbohydrates by 10% per week until you see the results happen. Some people use a low carbohydrate approach when cutting but this is very much down to the individual response to carbohydrates.

Supplements

Whey protein
This is to support daily protein needs and also to use post-workout. Ideally use a good quality grass-fed whey protein that is free from sweeteners. If you need flavouring, try to get one sweetened with stevia rather than sucralose.

Non-dairy protein
If you can't tolerate whey protein, consider switching

to a plant-based source. Usually these are made from combining protein sources so you get the full complement of amino acids. You can also consider using collagen as a protein source although it's not vegetarian.

Carbohydrate powder

Use this in your post-workout shake to maximise protein and glycogen synthesis. You can also use fruit or eat another carbohydrate source such as rice cakes instead.

Creatine

This is probably one of the best bodybuilding supplements you can take to improve muscle growth and performance.[11]

Depending on individual need, you may also want to consider:

- A good quality multivitamin to cover essential nutrients
- Probiotics to support gut health
- A digestive enzyme to support digestion of food considering the large number of meals
- Adaptogenic herbs which can support stress and the impact of weight training
- Magnesium to support muscle recovery and nervous system

Body Dysmorphic Disorder

Body image issues are widespread in the LGBTQ+ community. With scene pressures, social media and other social pressures to look good, LGBTQ+ individuals can be plagued by Body Dysmorphic Disorder (BDD), a condition where someone is overly critical of their physical appearance and persistently focuses on what they perceive as flaws which are often unnoticeable to others. Someone with BDD may feel the need to constantly groom themselves, do excessive exercise, or check themselves out in the mirror, and are programmed to seek validation. People with BDD don't see what others see. They look in the mirror and feel they are small or fat or constantly examine the need for improvement. Usually they find it hard to take compliments even though being physically attractive has become their number one goal.

Most have some sort of rejection trauma, and possibly as a result of that they build a strong 'perfect' body to act as a defence wall that yearns to be wanted and accepted. You can control what your body looks like, get temporarily validated by posting selfies on apps and having countless one-night stands. But if you don't address your past trauma, you will never deal with BDD. Learn to work with, not against, that inner child and then you will begin to feel you are enough and have fewer cravings for inauthentic validation. Working on this is a hard process and you may always have to work with BDD in mind. Learning to accept yourself for who you truly are and, more importantly, loving yourself and being kind to yourself are skills that take time to learn. Don't be afraid to talk to a therapist if this is something that resonates with you.

Performance enhancing drugs

Anabolic steroid use is common in some sections of the gay community. People opt to use steroids to increase muscle, decrease body fat and improve performance in the gym. This is often fuelled by BDD, low self-esteem, wanting to appear more attractive or fit into a group.

One day when I was working as a drug addiction counsellor a young gay man came into the service asking for a needle exchange. I took him into the room and asked him the usual questions. He said that he'd never been to the gym but felt he needed to start using steroids to be more attractive to other guys on the gay scene. He was adamant that using steroids would be the answer and, sad to say, as much as I tried to counsel him otherwise, he had his heart set on doing his first cycle of anabolic steroids. All I could do was give him harm reduction advice and provide the service he was looking for. If I had refused, chances are he would have injected wrongly and shared equipment. This wasn't the only time I experienced an exchange like this. Many gay men who came to the service spoke about using steroids for aesthetic reasons, to be more attractive, get ready for circuit parties and boost their confidence and self-esteem. There was often very little regard for the side-effects and, unsurprisingly, many did not even know what steroids really were or what they did in their body. If this sounds familiar, don't be embarrassed – now is your chance to read how anabolic steroids work, the potential side-effects and tips on safer using.

I am not condoning the use of anabolic steroids. Regardless of how I frame that using anabolic steroids is unhealthy and damaging to the body, it will not deter someone from wanting to use them. My hope is that if you are using or contemplating using them, you will make better choices as you will now have the knowledge about how they work and the side-effects, which include physical and psychological changes as well as potentially dangerous medical conditions.

Anabolic steroids are synthetic versions of the hormone testosterone. They work to increase muscle mass and strength while reducing body fat. Anabolic steroids are not to be confused with corticosteroids, which are medications prescribed to treat conditions like asthma and skin problems. For ease, I will use the word 'steroids', which refers to anabolic steroids.

The goal when taking steroids is to speed up the natural muscle-building process. Steroids add to the natural testosterone in the body which attaches to muscle cells, boosting growth as well as having other effects around the body. Some steroids are testosterone itself, some are testosterone precursors, and some are related compounds that act similar to testosterone. Steroids are mostly in the form of liquid injection or a tablet. They are normally used on a 'cycle' for durations of six to twelve weeks and you will often find that they are used as a 'stack', where more than one steroid is used. You may also come across terms such as 'blasting' and 'cruising', which describe a period of high doses followed by a maintenance dose.

Steroids are bought on the black market so you have no idea of the quality or amount of drug you are actually taking. There are many brands that you may come across but there is no guarantee of the ingredients actually being what the bottle says, whether they are fake or produced in a sterile environment. Additionally, the oils used can irritate the skin, cause swelling, thicken and scar the skin tissue and lead to cysts.

Steroids are not often used as a single agent and often there are other drugs that are used in conjunction to limit side-effects or accentuate the effect of the steroids. These include but are not limited to:

- Insulin to promote muscle growth
- Human growth hormone to promote muscle growth, body composition, strength and sleep
- Anastrozole and tamoxifen to mitigate the effects of oestrogen
- Antibiotics to reduce acne
- Diuretics to limit water retention
- Fat burners such as clenbuterol and ephedrine
- Sleeping aids to counteract insomnia

It's very rare for someone to have no side-effects when taking steroids. The side-effects include:

- Acne
- Depression
- Baldness
- Gynaecomastia (man boobs)
- Aggression
- Joint pain
- Changes in sex drive
- Erectile dysfunction
- Fluid retention
- Low sperm count
- Changes to blood chemistry
- Reduction of HDL cholesterol (known as the good cholesterol)
- Enlargement of clitoris
- Reduction in testicle size
- Increased facial and body hair

Knowing the side-effects, you should try to refrain from using recreational drugs while on steroids as it may increase risk of cardiovascular events and liver damage.

Steroid use may also lead to long-term side-effects such as blood pressure, heart disease, liver damage and mood disorders. Steroids are also very addictive as the user sees the results but, once they finish using steroids, they tend to lose weight and find it hard to keep up with the effort needed to maintain the results. Some steroids also make the body hold water which your body loses within a few weeks when you stop using, which shows on the scales too. For this reason, many do not 'come off' completely or give enough time between cycles for their body to rest, which can be extremely dangerous.

Steroids are not a magic bullet. You still have to put in the work at the gym by training hard. You also need to eat sufficient amounts, ensuring adequate intake of protein and carbohydrates to fuel muscle growth. If you are thinking of using steroids but are new to training or do not eat right to match your training, I urge you to begin by addressing that rather than jump to using steroids. You will see benefits of increased muscle mass just by applying the diet and training principles outlined above.

There is very little scientific evidence around anabolic steroids in terms of how to use, how much to use, how long to use and how to come off steroids. It's all a bit of a guessing game. So it's important you start by taking small doses and monitor your progress and side-effects. Taking more and more won't necessarily give you the results you want as there is a limit to how much of a steroid your body can handle and will use; more will not give you more results, just more side-effects. In addition, the diversity of your gut bacteria – known as microbial diversity – also plays a role in your ability to clear these drugs out of your system. The only way to find out whether your gut bugs are diverse enough to help you optimise this process is to do a stool test.[12]

If you are looking to begin using steroids or are currently using them, I recommend you try to get a complete blood test which assesses your blood chemistry, lipids, liver and kidney health and inflammation markers. If you have any health issues then I suggest addressing these before beginning the use of steroids. And if you use steroids on a regular basis, I would advise including a stool test to fully understand your digestive health.

Safer using

It's vital that you understand how to inject steroids safely. If you are in doubt, ask for advice from your local substance use charity or needle exchange. They will advise you on how to inject, what paraphernalia to use and also supply you with sterile equipment if needed.

How nutrition can support steroid use

Nutrition can go some way in helping to limit some of the possible side-effects of being on a cycle. The key take-away is to eat to support muscle growth – this means following the nutrition and supplement guidelines in the muscle-building section on page 76. It also means eating healthily and not 'dirty bulking' which may lead to fat gain and increased associated health risks.

Support your liver

As discussed above, steroids have side-effects and they also put the body under a considerable amount of strain. They can cause harm to your liver. It's important to monitor this with regular liver function testing but it is also important to support your liver the best way you can when on a steroid cycle. The following should be included where possible to support your cycle.

Consume liver-supporting foods such as:

- Watercress
- Turmeric
- Ginger
- Cruciferous vegetables such as Brussels sprouts, broccoli, cabbage, cauliflower, collard greens, kale and turnips
- Sulphur-rich foods
- Vitamin C-rich foods
- Whey protein, which can encourage glutathione (a master antioxidant) production
- Coffee
- Green tea

Cruciferous vegetables are important as they contain a compound called indole-3-carbinol, which our bodies convert upon digestion into diindolylmethane (DIM). This can help balance oestrogen, which is important as many steroids convert to oestrogen in the body, resulting in side-effects such as gynaecomastia (man boobs), fluid retention, prostate issues, libido loss and acne.[13] Bodybuilders are conscious of this, which is why they opt to take aromatase-inhibitor drugs such as tamoxifen and anastrozole, but adding more unprescribed drugs to the pile can also add more side-effects. The compound DIM works by blocking the enzyme that converts testosterone to oestrogen but also helps in the metabolism of oestrogen, so it's helpful to increase the intake of cruciferous vegetables when on a steroid cycle.

The role of oestrogen in cisgendered women bodybuilders is very different as you wouldn't want to block the effects of oestrogen. However, it is still of benefit to eat cruciferous vegetables to help balance and metabolise oestrogen in the body.

N-acetylcysteine (NAC)

This can be useful in supporting liver function and helping prevent liver injury from the use of steroids.[14] I prefer to recommend this over the liver-supporting herb milk thistle, as milk thistle can have interactions with medications including PrEP (pre-exposure prophylaxis) and other HIV drugs.

B vitamins

In particular, B6, B12 and folate (B9) are supportive of prevention of heart disease. Using anabolic steroids can raise your levels of homocysteine in the blood.[15] Homocysteine is an amino acid that your body uses to make proteins. B6, B12 and folate (in L-methylfolate form) can be supportive of lowering homocysteine.[16]

Curcumin

Using steroids can put a stress burden on the body and so curcumin may be useful. Curcumin is the active compound in turmeric and is shown to have anti-inflammatory properties; it acts as an antioxidant in the body as well as supporting joint health.[17] Make sure you find a supplement that contains piperine (black pepper extract) to increase absorption.

Omega-3 fish oil

Fish oil has many benefits including supporting heart health, lower blood pressure and healthy cholesterol levels.[18] Consuming fish oils may help with the cardiovascular side-effects associated with taking steroids.

Chances are that you have read this chapter thinking about doing your first cycle of steroids or are experienced with using them. Highlighting the risks may not change your mind but do take into account how to use them safely and follow my advice on protecting yourself the best way you can. Think hard about the true reason why you are taking steroids and begin to work on that one step at a time.

4. LET'S TALK ABOUT SEX

When you think about sex and LGBTQ+, there are a lot of things you can talk about. For some, their mind may go straight to thoughts about anal sex and not being clean for their partner when bottoming; some may consider vaginal health concerns and the impact on their sex life; some may think about penis-related issues; while others may be more concerned about pain which may prevent them from enjoying sex or recovering from sex. Nutrition can have an impact on these topics which are not always discussed in detail both within and outside the community. The purpose of this chapter is to unpick these intimate subjects and give easy-to-implement advice so sex is more enjoyable and less stressful.

Sex positivity

'One of the biggest issues in the community is that we are all walking around with our walls up ready to defend ourselves; this creates judgement and so we disengage with our authentic and vulnerable self.'
I'm lucky to have grown up in a household which was

pretty liberal and we were encouraged to talk about sex (even if my parents were talking to me about the birds and the bees when they should have educated me on the birds and the birds or the bees and the bees). However, I did grow up in a wider society that gave labels to men who have sex with men which came from both outside and within the gay community. You may be familiar with the phrase 'bottom shaming' where someone ridicules another for being a bottom. This can be done in jest or intended with malice to imply that someone who is bottom is more feminine or 'the girl in the relationship'. The person who makes these judgements from within the community may themselves be dealing with insecurities about being gay and is probably the type to put 'masc 4 masc' as the title of their profile on hookup apps. Shaming, whether in jest or maliciously, is bullying and can have an impact on the target, making them feel inadequate, which ultimately leads to less enjoyment of sex. The same can go for those who prefer to be top. Thanks to porn, there is a view that in order to be top, you need to have big muscles and be well endowed; this can lead to self-esteem issues if you don't quite fit that build but prefer to be top during sex. Likewise, people can shame someone who may describe themselves as versatile or versatile-bottom. They can be ridiculed for not admitting what they really like – insinuating they are bottom only. While this may be light banter, it again promotes the view that someone is ashamed of their position in bed, or that they can't be a top if they enjoy bottoming.

Shaming also happens when it comes to fetishes or promiscuity. What someone enjoys is none of your business if it's consensual, safe, legal and causing no harm to society. Again, judgement of what other people get turned on by can impact self-esteem and ultimately lead to someone not enjoying sex or feeling they may need to take substances to have sex. What you enjoy sexually has nothing to do with the person you are outside of the bedroom. You can and should embrace femininity if that is you, be a bottom if that is what you enjoy, be a top even if you are slim-build and even be versatile if you like both ways. Just do what feels right for you, that person behind the wall of defence – a wall that has been built to protect yourself from being bullied growing up and beyond. One of the biggest issues in the community is that we are all walking around with our walls up ready to defend ourselves; this creates judgement and we disengage with our authentic and vulnerable self.

Bottoming 101

Most people who bottom think about their hygiene when it comes to sex. Accidents or the fear of accidents can really get in the way of enjoying sex and relaxing completely. No matter how much you have prepared, you unconsciously say or think 'Is it clean?' at the end. You may be completely ready to be penetrated but have such a fear of a mess, which is probably fuelled by a time when you had an accident, that it ruins your enjoyment.

People want to know how they can be a cleaner bottom but it's not something that is really talked about other than making sure you clean yourself properly by douching. We all know douching is a way to help prevent this from happening but this does not always work. In fact it can cause damage to the lining of the anus if you are consistently doing this for about thirty minutes. Douching can impact the levels of friendly gut bacteria and naturally occurring mucus in the colon which is protective and part of the immune system. These probiotic strains have been revealed to support gut health but also to help with diabetes, food allergies, immunity, skin health, oral health, mood disorders and hypertension. There is also preliminary research showing the possible benefits of helping prevent sexually transmitted diseases.[1] So you really need to be supporting your gut health as a preventative measure to stay healthy.

What if I were to say that there are some things you can do to get ready so you only need to think about douching once or twice or not need to douche at all?

Follow these simple steps and you'll feel more ready than ever
Drink water
Aim for two to three litres per day. It's an obvious

one but many people do not drink enough water. Constipation is related to dehydration in the colon so the more hydrated you are the softer and easier to pass your stools will be. You can use herbal teas, sparkling water or you can flavour water with cucumbers, limes or other fruit to help increase your water intake.

Fibre

As a general rule you need your fibre, but when it comes to anal sex it's a little more complex than just having more fibre in the diet. Generally speaking, it is healthy to eat vegetables and wholegrains. Besides the pack of nutrition they give you, you're also getting a hit of dietary fibre which can help push things along nicely. Fibre, while not providing energy, helps the intestines function properly. Government guidelines suggest we consume 30g of fibre a day but most adults only eat around 18g a day so this is something to keep in mind. Fibre foods include wholegrains, beans, pulses, fruits and vegetables, so eating a mix will help you get the benefits of each fibre variety. If you are not used to eating a lot of fibre, you may want to increase slowly as this can lead to excess wind, which can defeat the point of increasing fibre to improve your sex life!

Now with regard to sex, it's important to understand the different types of fibre, which are determined by how they dissolve in water. Soluble fibre has metabolic health benefits as well as helping avoid constipation and prevent haemorrhoids. Insoluble fibre works mainly as a bulking agent and helps the motility of the colon. Most plant foods have a combination of both soluble and insoluble fibres; an example is an apple where the flesh is soluble fibre and the skin is insoluble fibre.

Examples of foods containing fibre are:

Insoluble: wholegrains such as brown rice, wheat bran, nuts, beans, and some vegetables (like cauliflower, potatoes and green beans).

Soluble: oat bran, barley, nuts, seeds, beans, lentils, peas, and most fruits and vegetables. It is also found in psyllium husk, a common fibre supplement and often the main ingredient in many supplements on the market for gay men.

When it comes to bottoming, as a rule of thumb, you may want to avoid some of the insoluble fibre twenty-four hours before you have sex. So in those periods, you would want to switch to white rice instead of brown rice, going easy on wholegrains. Similarly, you may want to peel your vegetables, such as potatoes, tomatoes and peppers (you can do this easily by roasting them). If you aren't sure about when you are going to have sex then try to work out which of the fibrous vegetables are going to be your trigger foods. If you know that at the weekend you are going to be enjoying yourself, go easy on the insoluble fibre about twenty-four hours before (depending on your digestive cycle). Remember also to make sure you're getting a mix of both fibres in your diet in general for overall health.

Chew your food

As well as increasing fibre in your diet, you need to break your food down by chewing. Most people don't chew their food properly and this can lead to it coming out the other end in large bits. If you chew, you break the food particles down and digest them better.

Dairy

Sometimes dairy can be the cause of things getting all gooey down there. Have a think about what you eat and if it's going to have an effect. Big culprits are milk, cream, yoghurt, cheese and whey protein shakes. By simply removing dairy for a couple of days, you can see if it helps improve your stool consistency. If you are worried about losing your gains in the gym from stopping whey protein then switch to a vegan brand or collagen protein.

Red meat

I often see people listing red meat as a big no for bottoming as it can lead to greasier stools. I am not entirely convinced by this, and if it is the case for you then perhaps it's down to your ability to digest protein or fat sufficiently. Consider trialling a digestive enzyme with meals if this is the case or chewing as described above.

Understand your digestion

Adding to the point above, if you're suffering with a

digestive disorder or other digestive discomfort, you need to understand what is going on at a deeper level. Sufferers will know that it's hard to identify when you are ready for sex. Digestive issues can be caused by many things including food sensitivities, not being able to digest food properly, infections, bacteria imbalance, inflammation and a compromised gut lining. Stress is also a big factor in digestive disorders as well as impacting the regularity of producing stools. There is more information about digestive health concerns in the foundations of this book on page 34.

Reduce fat intake

Loading up the fries, meats and oils? Perhaps take a look at the amount of fat you are consuming. Maybe you aren't digesting it well, which can cause issues with your stool, making it greasier. As a general rule, if your stool floats then perhaps you're having an issue with fat digestion and need some support with that.

Add good bacteria

I'm not talking about those probiotic drinks full of sugar you see in the supermarket, but getting good bacteria into your gut either as a supplement or via fermented foods such as miso, kimchi, kombucha, sauerkraut and tempeh. This can help improve levels of beneficial bacteria which can play a role in gut and stool health. If you're not keen on these foods then a multi-strain probiotic may be helpful in supplying live bacteria to the gut.

Know your food triggers
If there are still things that are not quite right, you may need to consider if some foods in your diet aren't working well for you. Common triggers are spicy foods, eggs, red meat, caffeine, alcohol and junk food. Perhaps try limiting one or two of these a few days before you have sex again.

You may not need to do all of these steps but try working your way through them to see what is the best thing for you. You can only be healthier by following them anyway!

Anal douching

Even if you've been following the steps above, you may still feel like you need to douche. Advice on douching is simple:

- In an ideal world you should douche as little as possible, because it can strip the mucosal layer of your gut, which may impact your health in the long term.
- Purchase a douche shower attachment and use a thick emollient cream such as Epaderm on both you and the attachment. Make sure you clean the attachment after use with disinfectant.

- Run water at a low temperature and low pressure as the inside of your anus is a lot more sensitive than the outside. Be as gentle as possible and try not to do this in a rush.
- Choose between a complete clean or a quick clean. A complete clean may take an hour but a quick clean can be completed in a few minutes. A complete clean is more suitable for longer sex sessions or sexual practices such as fisting.
- For a quick clean, don't hold the hose for longer than three seconds at a time as this may travel further than the sigmoid colon and dislodge faeces further up, which can make you need to go again after having been clean.
- Some pharmacies sell disposable douches or you can buy home douche kits. These may be slightly more of a chore to use but they often contain just the right amount of water so you don't over-douche. The only disadvantage is you may not feel completely clean compared to using a shower attachment.

Anti-diarrhoea medication

I think it's important to mention that many people use these medications before they go out or plan on having a long sex session. The problem with these over-the-counter medications is that they interrupt your internal 'gut clock' which is set to know when you are eating and sleeping. While they work to serve a purpose, it's not going to be beneficial to use them on a regular basis. You may also be using such medications alongside other recreational drugs on a party weekend, which clear from the body through the gut. Stopping the motility of your gut can create a more toxic environment in the body. But if you are going to do this, make sure you are super caring to your gut and body the week after and keep use for this reason to a bare minimum.

Antibiotics prophylaxis

Many people may use antibiotics a few days before, during and after a planned event where there will be a lot of sexual activity to help prevent sexually transmitted infections (STIs). In a small clinical trial, the antibiotic Doxycycline helped reduce the occurrence of STIs in men who have sex with men.[2] This sounds all well and good but there is a problem. The success of treatment was only 47% and drug-related gastrointestinal events were reported more commonly in those who took the antibiotic. So it's still a bit of a Russian roulette situation. You may still get STIs even though you are taking Doxycycline, plus taking it can lead to gut problems. Further, if you then test positive for gonorrhoea, syphilis or chlamydia, you will need more antibiotics, which causes more impact on your gut. Think of this as, every time you take antibiotics you are pouring bleach into the gut and it takes the good bacteria away as well as the bad. While antibiotics are lifesavers, they should only be used when they are needed and prescribed by a doctor for their intended purpose. Another reason to take them only for their intended purpose is that the more frequently and the longer antibiotics are used, the less effective they become.

Pain

You may have completed all of these steps but are still finding it painful when passing a stool or having sex. You may also want to know how to recover from a big weekend of having a lot of sex or certain sex practices which stretch, challenge or overuse the anus.

The first and most important step is to make sure you have checked any health issue with a doctor, particularly if there is bleeding involved and it's dark blood. If you wipe with toilet paper and it's bright red, it is most probably coming from the entrance to the anus, which is inflamed, but do speak to your doctor. There could be many reasons for this, including:

- Not having enough water or fibre in the diet in general
- Straining to go to the bathroom or constipation
- Irritation from wiping, douching or sex
- Using wet wipes (DO NOT USE WET WIPES TO CLEAN – they can dry the area too much)
- STIs, bacterial or yeast infection
- Irritable bowel syndrome

- A skin condition such as psoriasis
- A fissure or tear around the anus caused from the above or other reasons

If your doctor has examined you and said everything is fine, and working on the above steps does not help, then consider any dietary triggers such as food sensitivities. There are prescription creams which can help address the symptoms you are experiencing, but the problem will keep coming back if you do not address the cause of the issue. To see if you have a food sensitivity try an elimination diet for two to three weeks to see if it gets any better. Common food sensitivities include gluten, dairy, soy and egg. Be mindful that if you take more than one food out at a time, you will need to reintroduce them one by one (seven days apart) to identify the offending food.

My final comment is about products for the anal area which are meant to make sex more enjoyable. You may have sensitivity to some of the chemicals in lube. The skin around the anus is a very sensitive area and some brands of lubricant may not suit you. You'd need to do research to find out what brands of lubricant suit you. As a general rule, try to get the most natural (and effective) lubricant possible; you should be able to eat what goes on your skin, especially in intimate areas. This advice also applies to how you clean your anus. Highly perfumed shower gels or lotions may be irritating and so you should use products that are as natural as possible.

Supplements

Fibre supplements

I have seen many supplements online which are designed to be taken regularly to support digestive function in order to be 'ready'. However, the truth is these can be very expensive for the ingredients they offer. Likewise, you need to make sure you are not taking these at the same time as PrEP or other medications as the supplements may interfere with medication and the way it is absorbed. This important information is often omitted from these brands' labels, which is a bugbear of mine.

There are some reputable brands on the market which do have some wholesome ingredients, but don't just buy randomly without checking out the company or the ingredients. If the capsule just contains psyllium husk, it's very expensive for what it is and you can simply order some psyllium husk powder online and drink it in water or add it to your protein shake. You should do this according to your body but I suggest starting with 1tsp and then building up to 1tbsp if needed per day. It's pure fibre and acts as a mild laxative, soaking up water as it makes its way through your colon. Some find taking this before bed most beneficial as it will encourage a complete movement the next morning. You should make sure you leave a gap of two to four hours between taking a fibre supplement and any medication you are taking. Speak to your doctor or health professional if you are not sure about taking this.

Probiotics

Taking a probiotic may also be useful if you don't like fermented foods or are travelling. Try to find one that you don't need to put in the fridge. I prefer multi-strain probiotics as it's like a multivitamin and covers most bases. You may find you have to go slow when taking a probiotic as it may lead to gas, bloating or changes in stool consistency. This can be normal – in essence you've sent the good guys in to do battle with the bad guys, so the gut can be a little upset as it gets used to it.

Coconut oil

If your anus is irritated and sore, I recommend making sure the area is moistened by a hypoallergenic and non-perfumed cream or oil. My preference is to use coconut oil as it has antimicrobial properties due to its lauric acid content and may be of additional help if there is a bacterial or fungal skin issue.[3]

Aloe vera

Aloe vera gel is the clear, jelly-like substance found in the inner part of the aloe plant leaf. It may support wound healing so using topically may help if your anus is inflamed.

Magnesium

Taking a magnesium supplement may help with regular bowel movements. It works by drawing water into the intestines which stimulates bowel motility. It's best to use magnesium citrate for this purpose as it acts as a gentler laxative than the other forms. Typical doses are around 500mg per tablet but consult the label for the suggested dose as well as checking for any potential interactions with medication.

When it comes to the vagina

Vulvo-vaginal health is important for overall well-being but also pertinent to sexual health, including the enjoyment of sex, the desire to have sex, as well as impacting confidence or causing anxiety.

A healthy vagina can:

- Lower your risk of STIs, human papillomavirus (HPV) infection, pelvic inflammatory disease, cervical cancer and genital warts
- Lower your risk of urinary tract infections (UTIs) and yeast/fungal infections
- Positively impact fertility, including increasing chances of successful fertility treatment, reduction of pregnancy complications and even confer benefits to the baby during vaginal delivery

The vagina microbiome

The human body contains bacteria, viruses and fungi which are known as the microbiome. Some bacteria can cause problems and be associated with disease risk but others are beneficial and essential for many aspects of our health. You may have heard the term 'microbiome' before in relation to gut health but there are also other areas where these microorganisms live such as the skin, mouth, nose and vagina. Further, the vaginal environment prefers to be acidic with a pH of around 3.8–4.5, which is protective. If the pH level rises, it can put you at risk of infections.

The vaginal microbiome is very sensitive so even small changes can impact vaginal health and therefore increase risk of infection, disease or negatively impact fertility. Nutrition can have a positive impact on the vaginal microbiome, so the following advice can be your journey to a healthier vagina.

- Balance your blood sugar – yeast and pathogenic bacteria thrive on sugar. So ditch the refined sugar in your diet and follow the advice in Chapter 2.
- Do not use fragrances, scented creams and products with chemicals in the vaginal area as these may cause irritation and even infection. This is even the case with hygiene products as conventional products such as tampons and sanitary towels can be bleached, contain chemicals and scent. There are some natural hygiene alternatives or even washable reusable products made out of organic materials if budget is a concern.
- Support your gut. Digestive health bacteria

imbalances can also mean vaginal health bacteria imbalances. Assess and address your gut health with the advice in Chapter 2. You may find a probiotic supplement supportive of vaginal health that is also available as a suppository, which can be more targeted at supporting the vaginal microbiome.

- Consider your partner and their health. They have their own microbiome and anything from semen, saliva, sex toys and penetrative sex can influence your vaginal microbiome.

Transgender neovaginal microbiome
The research on the vaginal microbiomes of transgender women who have undergone gender-reassignment surgery is fairly limited. It is debatable whether trans women have a neovaginal microbiome akin to a cisgendered woman's vagina, as well as the neovagina environment being less acidic.[4] Nevertheless, trans women are still susceptible to STIs, UTIs and yeast infections and the environment can still be supported by the strategies above, especially with the use of a probiotic supplement containing lactobacilli strains.[5] Trans women may also not produce natural lubricant, which may increase the risk of tears during intercourse or other mechanical stress; a good vagina-friendly natural lubricant is therefore advised.

Vaginal health is important for transgender men who have frontal genital openings. There is still risk of infections, but testosterone therapy can also cause dryness or pain. As well as the advice above, see page 149 for more detail on pelvic pain for transgender men.

If following the advice above does not have any success, you may want to investigate further with a health professional. There is a test you can do with Invivo Diagnostics to analyse vaginal health including bacteria makeup, vaginal pH, pathogens and yeast infection markers.

When it comes to the penis

Erectile dysfunction

The inability to attain or maintain an erection for sex may be something you give yourself a bit of a hard time over. If you can't achieve or maintain an erection then you may feel ashamed and emasculated. The truth is that it is perfectly normal to experience this occasionally and most partners will understand if it happens.

Erectile dysfunction often develops gradually. You may feel softer, take longer to achieve an erection or have difficulty keeping an erection. This then sends your mind into overdrive, which in turn makes the situation worse.

There are many root causes of erectile dysfunction. It's important to speak to your doctor if you are experiencing this and request that the root cause is looked into. While treatments like Viagra, Cialis, Trimix and Caverject may help temporarily, they do not tackle the root cause so it's important to address this if possible. While there is a psychological element, there can also be physical conditions which impact blood flow or nerve functioning.

Typical causes of erectile dysfunction include:

- Side-effects of medications
- Hair loss medication such as finasteride
- Alcoholism
- Diabetes
- Kidney disease
- Multiple sclerosis
- Cardiovascular disease
- Hypertension
- Prostate disease and prostate cancer
- Prostatitis (inflammation of the prostate)
- Hormonal imbalance
- Hormone therapy
- Depression
- Stress, anxiety and psychological trauma
- Substance use
- Sleep disorder
- Smoking
- Age

Go to your doctor and request the following tests to be conducted:

- Prostate Specific Antigen (PSA) to understand prostate health
- Hormone profile to assess hormone levels including testosterone, Free Androgen Index, prolactin, sex hormone binding globulin (SHBG) and thyroid markers
- Vitamin D levels
- Metabolic and cardiovascular testing to include cholesterol, triglycerides, homocysteine, glucose, HbA1c (a marker that represents blood sugar over time) and c-reactive protein (a marker of inflammation). Also ask for your blood pressure to be taken
- Ask for a referral for a sleep clinic to assess sleep apnoea (where your breathing stops and starts during sleep) if you think there is a possibility your sleep is an issue and you are snoring a lot
- Check if there are any side-effects to medications you are taking which may explain the issue

If you believe there may be a psychological factor, you may benefit from a talking therapy to address the root cause. This can include addressing stress, anxiety, sexual feelings and confidence and relationship issues.

The next step is to understand your health. Assess whether your diet is healthy and take steps to improve it based on the foundations of this book. Focus should be on including fresh fruit and vegetables, quitting smoking and only drinking alcohol in moderation. Exercise within your limits but also try calming exercises like breath work, meditation, yoga and acupuncture therapy.

There are some supplements which may help but these will do little if you aren't addressing the root cause of the problem. So the information above should be your first port of call rather than relying on a supplement to mask the issue. Such supplements include:

- Herbs such as Panax ginseng[6]
- Rhodiola, which may improve energy and fatigue and support stress adaptation therefore impacting libido[7]
- L-arginine, an amino acid naturally present in the body that helps make nitric oxide, which helps relax the blood vessels and improve erections[8]

What about premature ejaculation?
Slightly different to erectile dysfunction, premature ejaculation is when you climax a lot sooner than you would like. This can also happen alongside erectile dysfunction and there could be similar reasons why you may be experiencing this. This can also include performance anxiety, stress, depression, self-esteem as well as a hormonal link. I encourage you to work through the steps above with emphasis on addressing the psychological root cause of the issue.

Maintaining healthy testosterone levels

When you think of male hormones, your mind may immediately go to testosterone. Testosterone functions to control sex drive, promote muscle mass, increase energy and regulate sperm production. Levels of testosterone naturally are highest in adolescence and fall as we age, which can result in decreased sex drive.

Symptoms of low testosterone include:

- Reduced sexual desire
- Fewer erections
- Erectile dysfunction
- Infertility
- Depression
- Low energy and motivation
- Reduced muscle
- Gynaecomastia (man boobs)

As before, you should speak to your doctor about your concerns and request a male hormone test profile which include the markers listed on page 129. There may be reasons other than medical why you have low testosterone. These may be diet and lifestyle mediated, including:

- High alcohol consumption
- Obesity
- Lack of exercise
- Depression

- Stress
- Poor sleep
- Finishing a course of anabolic steroids

Try the following steps to help raise your testosterone naturally:

- Weight loss.
- Exercise: according to research, the best exercise you can do for your testosterone levels is resistance training.[9]
- Eat enough: dieting all the time can impact testosterone. You need to make sure you are eating enough protein and carbohydrates as well as healthy fats which support testosterone production.
- Reduce stress: can you remember a time when you were overwhelmed with stress? Were you horny then? Stress can lead to consistently high levels of cortisol, which can reduce testosterone levels.[10]
- Vitamin D: this can raise testosterone.[11] Testing for vitamin D status is inexpensive and you should supplement if low (choose vitamin D3). You are particularly at risk if you have dark skin or do not go out in sunlight or if you live in a cold climate.
- Zinc: this can help boost low testosterone levels. Try to consume zinc-rich foods

regularly, but note that most zinc food sources are non-vegan so you should think about supplementation if you are a vegan or do not eat much shellfish or other zinc-rich foods.

- Get good quality sleep: poor sleep is linked with lower testosterone levels.[12] Try limiting your use of technology before bedtime, spending an hour or more winding down and making the bedroom a cool and dark environment to sleep in.

What else to consider

Research into 'natural testosterone boosters' is still in its infancy. You may, however, benefit from taking some herbs to support the adrenal gland such as ashwagandha. This may support stress adaptation and lower cortisol levels and therefore aid testosterone production.

Minimise exposure to plastics as these may impact testosterone levels due to the oestrogen-like chemicals found in bisphenol A (BPA).[13]

Your testosterone levels are impacted by what is happening in your body such as the levels of a marker called sex hormone binding globulin (SHBG), and how it is converted. SHBG is a protein that binds to hormones like testosterone and helps transport them into tissues to do their job. You can have a normal testosterone level but high SHBG level; high SHBG can cause symptoms associated with testosterone deficiency and cause erectile dysfunction and decreased sex drive.[14] SHBG can be raised in those with high oestrogen levels, low testosterone, anorexia, hyperthyroidism, liver disease, pituitary or calorie restriction, or who are ageing. It's important these factors are ruled out if your SHBG is elevated. A healthy balanced diet rich in protein helps to normalise SHBG levels.

This list of actions may be tough to work through by yourself so you may find it beneficial to work with a functional medicine practitioner or nutritionist who can individualise a programme for you. The first port of call is to understand your body so work through these sections one by one and see what applies to you. Testing privately or with a doctor is recommended to rule out any medical reasons for low testosterone.

There also is the option of testosterone replacement therapy. Your doctor can offer guidance on this and discuss the pros and cons of treatment with you. Testosterone is a controlled substance by UK law so do not try to buy this online as it is illegal. You also do not know if what you are buying is real or dosed correctly.

Finally, it is vital to promote positive psychology, both by yourself and within a relationship. This can have an impact on physical issues such as sex, erectile dysfunction, premature ejaculation, stress and more. Be patient with this as it's not an overnight change; just start by being curious about your own feelings, thoughts and emotions. Most of all, be compassionate to yourself around this vulnerable subject.

5. TRANSGENDER NUTRITION

'Transgender individuals have unique nutrition needs, which may vary according to the stage of social and medical transition'
Hormone Therapy, Health Outcomes and the Role of Nutrition in Transgender Individuals[1]

I wanted to start this chapter by first acknowledging that I am writing as a cisgendered gay male. My experience of transgender nutrition is mostly from a professional standpoint. My understanding of transitioning, hormone treatment, side-effects of medications, surgery and the emotional journey has come mainly from interaction with clients, research and speaking with charities, doctors and transgendered individuals. While my knowledge is detailed enough to provide nutritional considerations to support transgender health, I will never be able to put myself in the place of someone who identifies as transgender. I thought it was hard enough to come out as a gay man so I can only imagine the extra mile that transgender individuals have to go to be their true self. While we live in a more tolerant world than we did twenty years ago, transgender rights are being taken away in some places. Just as I am writing this, Hungary has voted to end legal recognition of transgendered people, and in other parts of the world, transgender rights are constantly threatened and under political debate. So while the rest of the community are honoured to stand alongside transgender individuals in the fight for equality, there is a long way to go to reach the point where your gender identity isn't the factor that decides whether you deserve equal rights.

Transitioning is a long process which not only includes medical appointments, medication, surgery, adapting to a new life, but is also about accepting yourself for who you really are. As with other members of the community, transgendered individuals grow up with shame, rejection, guilt and anxiety around acceptance. Every day there are micro-stressors which are unique to being transgender such as using public bathrooms and changing rooms. Not only does this impact your personal psychology but it can also impact your physical health due to the elevations in the stress hormone cortisol. In the short term, stress is meant to help you deal with a situation by either fighting it or fleeing from it. However, as we discussed in Chapter 2, long-term elevations of stress hormones can compromise your health and lead to issues such as high blood pressure, heart attack, stroke, type 2 diabetes, reduced immune function and cognitive issues.[2] It takes a very strong person to learn to be resilient, and transgender individuals are just that. Yet even the most resilient person can still be impacted by the stress, trauma and anxiety. The good news is there are things you can do to support your health to become more resilient to stress. This encompasses making changes to your nutrition and lifestyle which not only create a healthier you, but also help create a positive mindset. This may be one of the last things you are thinking about as you already have a lot going on, but even one or two changes can alter your outlook on life and help you feel that you have achieved something, which in turn creates positive messaging internally and promotes better health.

What exactly is transgender health?

Aside from the impact of stress on daily life, there are other individual health aspects experienced by the transgender community. This chapter focuses on transgender health from two perspectives: female–male (FTM) and male–female (MTF). FTM and MTF have different medications, and with medications come side-effects and health challenges. Nutrition can play a part in minimising the side-effects and risks of taking such medications and help create hormone balance in the body, helping you lead a healthier, more relaxed life.

In order to benefit from this chapter, you will need to start with the foundations of this book. There is no magic pill to take, and adding one special ingredient into your diet won't do much if the rest of your diet and lifestyle is unhealthy. First, identify where your diet is most unhealthy and work on that. It could be reducing sugary drinks or eating more vegetables, for example. Even if you haven't started hormone therapy yet, this chapter can still apply to you, and it is even more important to get the foundations right to fully prepare you for hormone therapy.

For Parents

If you are a parent, carer or supportive person reading this and want to know how best to help someone who has told you they are transgender, I hope this chapter allows you to understand the physical and emotional changes so you can truly be there for someone undergoing treatment. It's a huge journey for someone to embark on and can take many years to feel the person who they are. Transitioning is a very intimate and vulnerable process which may feel lonely at times. It's important to show empathy, love and support to someone beginning this journey. This can be done without much effort: helping someone to eat healthier, educating them, encouraging self-care practice or just being there to listen when needed.

What hormones do

Hormones are powerful messengers which control the whole of your physiology, far beyond the reproductive system. They drive how a person thinks, feels and acts in certain situations. They are involved in many areas of the body including reproduction, growth, immunity and balancing blood sugar. Hormones have to be released from an endocrine gland in the body such as the thyroid, adrenal gland, testes or ovaries. Once released, they travel through the body to reach their destination where they relay a message. They naturally fluctuate through your lifetime, such as during puberty, pregnancy, breastfeeding, menopause and as you get older, or when under hormone therapy.

Everyone has what are considered 'male' and 'female' sex hormones. The main hormones when thinking about transgender nutrition are oestrogen and testosterone. When someone is transitioning from male to female, hormone replacement therapy helps increase levels of oestrogen and reduce testosterone to induce feminine secondary sex characteristics. Oestrogen is commonly known as the major female hormone and is naturally produced in the ovaries, the adrenal glands and fat. It plays a role in female sexual development as well as impacting the brain, cardiovascular and skeletal systems, hair, skin and urinary tract. Someone transitioning from female to male can be prescribed hormone replacement therapy to help increase levels of testosterone and reduce oestrogen to induce masculine secondary sex characteristics. Testosterone is typically known as the male hormone and plays a role in sexual desire, bone density, muscle, insulin sensitivity, energy, cognitive function as well as regulation of the menstrual cycle in females.

What influences your hormones?
By understanding what influences hormones, you can understand how to adjust diet and lifestyle to support hormonal balance. This is particularly important when using hormone therapy as is the case with transgender individuals. Taking hormones to assist with transitioning can lead to some side-effects. To fully support your body in balancing your hormones healthily, you need to look after the systems which process and remove hormones from the body. It's therefore particularly important to look after your liver health and digestion health to understand your transition from a functional viewpoint. This can mean fewer unwanted side-effects, making your transition more comfortable as well as helping prevent known risks associated with transitioning.

The liver

The liver is a powerful machine. It acts like a filter gathering toxins and biological substances like hormones from the bloodstream; it processes them, then either stores them or returns them to circulation for removal in the urine, or deposits them in bile for excretion by the digestive system. The liver works hard and is very effective but it can be overworked, leading to imbalanced liver function. This can impact the body's ability to handle toxins, as well as creating a hormone imbalance.

Extra hormones taken during transition can make a lot of extra work for the liver so supporting liver function is very important when transitioning, as, just like drugs and toxins, sex hormones are metabolised in the liver. The good news is that diet and lifestyle can support your liver health. It's important not to jump into detox diets or a juice cleanse, as not eating may do more harm than good and can lead to a lack of protein, which is very important for your liver to function well. During hormone therapy, I suggest the following to support liver health.

Things to consider avoiding or limiting

- Exposure to pollution
- Pesticides and herbicides
- Heavy metals such as mercury (mainly found in contaminated water, some fish and dental amalgam fillings) and lead (mainly found in lead paints and some cosmetics)
- Bisphenol A (BPA), a chemical used to manufacture some plastics (some water bottles and food storage containers)
- Parabens in toiletries
- Stress
- Fried foods
- Sugar
- Alcohol
- Smoking
- Recreational drugs

Things to consider increasing

- Water: to help prevent constipation and help your kidneys filter the waste your liver has broken down.
- Coffee: a superfood for your liver yielding many benefits. Research suggests drinking three cups a day but base this on your tolerance. See earlier advice on caffeine on page 28.[3]
- Green tea: can help improve markers of liver health which are usually one of the concerns of those undergoing hormone therapy.[4]
- Berries: such as blueberries, raspberries and cranberries. These contain antioxidants (nutrients that destroy free radicals in the body), helping to keep the liver healthy.
- Cruciferous vegetables: such as Brussels sprouts, broccoli, cauliflower, cabbage, kale, bok choy, rocket, collards, watercress and radishes. These are the best foods for your liver as they can increase the natural detoxification enzymes.
- Oily fish: contains healthy omega-3 fats which help keep liver enzymes in normal range and lower inflammation.[5]
- Olive oil: not only does extra virgin olive oil have positive effects on heart health and metabolism, it can also decrease levels of fat and improve liver enzyme markers.[6]
- B-complex vitamin foods: the liver

detoxification pathways rely on B vitamins to work effectively, in particular B3, B6, folate (B9) and B12.[7]

It can also be of benefit to switch to natural detergents and natural toiletries without parabens, buy organic food as far as possible, and use glass or ceramic food storage containers to help reduce the burden of chemicals on the body.

Digestion

Digestion also plays a role in hormone metabolism. Once the liver has done its job, some of the waste products are taken from the liver to the gallbladder and then out to the digestive system to be removed in faeces. Your gut health is important in this process; if it is in a poor state it can lead to hormones being reabsorbed which can then cause symptoms of hormonal imbalance. This can occur mostly when you are constipated or lack fibre in the diet, have poor levels of beneficial gut bacteria, are on a high protein and saturated fat diet, or experiencing stress which may slow digestion.

The key take-away in supporting your digestion is to address the foundation advice in Chapters 2 and 4 but also ensure you are getting adequate amounts of fibre in the form of wholegrains, fruit and vegetables. Eating a diet rich in fermented foods also supports gut health and some may benefit from taking a probiotic to support digestive health.

Blood sugar

Imbalanced blood sugar can also impact hormone balance. Eating a large amount of sugar or refined carbohydrates in one go can cause a large amount of the hormone insulin to be released in the body to bring the sugar level down. This hormone is usually associated with diabetes but it can also be linked to hormone balance.

Hormones work together so there is a connection between blood sugar regulation, insulin and our other hormones. A bit of sugar here and there isn't going to do much to upset your hormones, but constantly eating a diet high in sugar can lead to an imbalance of the body's hormones which in turn can cause health issues and risk of heart disease, diabetes and cancer. A high sugar diet can also cause symptoms such as anxiety, dizziness, sweating, brain fog, fatigue, food cravings and mood changes. Interestingly, these are similar to symptoms of hormone imbalance. If you are taking hormone replacement therapy, these symptoms can be exacerbated so it's vital to support your blood sugar to be a healthy transgender individual. Consult the advice on page 23 for tips on blood sugar management.

Stress

Stress can play havoc with anyone's health including hormone health. One of the functions of the stress hormone cortisol is to increase blood sugar to enable the body in the fight or flight response. This can impact overall blood sugar balance and contribute to the symptoms described above. The stress response becomes the priority for the body over other metabolic functions such as growth, digestion and reproduction. With regard to hormone metabolism, stress causes its processes not to function as well as they should, which can cause the symptoms of hormone imbalance. The body's stress response is designed to get us out of immediate danger occasionally, but the problem with human beings is that we have many psychological stressors, so in reality we are being exposed to stressors multiple times a day. Add to that the extra stressors of being transgender, and it can mean stress hormones are elevated even more. The important thing is to work out how to address the stressors which you can control and seek professional help if you feel there are some stressors which are out of your control. By following the stress reduction tips in previous chapters, you can support your body to deal with stress and therefore avoid almost full line above centred heading if possible.

Buying medication online

There are several online pharmacies and forums which offer hormone treatment without prescription. It's important to take advice about hormone therapy medications from a doctor and not someone who has merely been using it or read about it. Buying online has risks which include unregulated or fake medications.

Additionally, varying levels of hormone in the medication may mean more side-effects, resulting in changes you don't necessarily want to see. Please try to be patient and seek the help of a doctor or transgender service; go through the necessary steps so you can be monitored by a professional carefully during your transition.

Female to male – testosterone hormone therapy

The primary objective in undergoing hormone therapy is to develop male secondary sex characteristics and to minimise female secondary sex characteristics.

Physical and emotional changes include:

- Skin becomes thicker and more oily
- Pores become larger
- Acne may develop
- Sweat and urine odour changes
- Perception of touch and pain differs
- Fat will diminish around hips and thighs
- More muscle definition around arms and legs
- Fat accumulation around abdomen
- Eyes and face develop a more male appearance
- Vocal cord thickens to develop a deeper voice
- Body hair thickens, darkens and grows faster
- Facial hair grows
- Male-pattern baldness may develop
- Changes in feelings, emotional state and behaviour

- Libido changes
- Clitoris changes
- Orgasms may feel different
- Periods may change in appearance, duration and regularity

Medications used in FTM hormone therapy
Testosterone
The primary medication used in FTM transgender hormone treatment is testosterone. It comes in many types and forms such as gels, patches, creams and injections. You should be patient when first starting testosterone therapy and do so within treatment guidelines with your doctor. Taking more or higher doses of testosterone will not make changes happen more quickly and could risk converting to oestrogen in the body and unwanted side-effects such as uterine imbalance, increased cancer risk and increased cholesterol.

Anti-oestrogens
Medications such as anastrozole or tamoxifen can be used to reduce the effect of high levels of oestrogen in transgender men.

5-alpha reductase inhibitors
Medications such as finasteride can be used to help prevent the unwanted side-effects of testosterone replacement therapy such as hair loss.

Progestogens
Medication such as medroxyprogesterone may be used to control menstruation in transgender men. This is often used prior to starting testosterone therapy.

Considerations
Polycystic ovary syndrome (PCOS)
After long-term testosterone therapy, there is a risk of PCOS.[8] This is a hormone condition characterised by symptoms of or measured high levels of androgen hormones (known as the male hormones), cysts developing on your ovaries and irregular menstrual cycles. This can lead to symptoms such as excessive hair growth, acne, infertility, weight gain, high levels of insulin, risk of insulin resistance and type 2 diabetes. FTM transgender persons on hormone therapy are likely to have elevated androgens and therefore risk of PCOS. A lower carbohydrate diet may be supportive for PCOS by lowering insulin levels in the body and supporting a healthy body weight. I don't mean adopting a diet like the Atkins Diet but rather following the foundations laid out in Chapter 2. Your diet will be balanced with protein, fruits, nuts and seeds, while limiting refined sugars. Additionally, take regular exercise to support overall health but it also may be supportive of PCOS and insulin resistance.

Hair loss and acne
These symptoms may happen after commencing hormone therapy. Medication may be offered to

support these conditions, such as finasteride, which is a 5-alpha reductase inhibitor, but this can also lead to reduced libido or sexual dysfunction. However, this may not occur at the dose used to prevent hair loss.

Cardiovascular risk

There is not enough evidence to suggest that transgender men have an increased risk of cardiovascular disease, although associations have been found between hormone therapy and an increase in fats that circulate in the blood such as LDL ('bad') cholesterol and triglycerides, which are risk factors for cardiovascular disease.[9] There is, though, no harm in supporting a reduction in risk of cardiovascular disease by following a healthy diet akin to the Mediterranean diet. As I have already advocated, a healthy diet consists of unprocessed foods, nuts, seeds, fruit and vegetables and wholegrains. If high cholesterol or triglycerides is an issue then supplementing a fish oil may support good cholesterol and triglyceride levels. Additionally, managing your weight and quitting smoking will also reduce your risk, as with cisgender males.

Pelvic pain

Pain may result from different issues so it's important to seek testing to understand the root cause with your doctor. Testosterone therapy can lead to vagina tissue changes and thinning of the lining, which increases the pH of the vagina and the bacterial environment, leading in turn to an increased risk of bacterial vaginosis, cystitis or cervicitis.[10] It is therefore good to support your levels of beneficial bacteria through the use of fermented foods or a probiotic supplement. As a preventative, you may want to use a natural lubricant but also consuming sea buckthorn oil as a supplement has been shown to improve vaginal health.[11]

Persistent menses

Testosterone therapy should be enough to stop your period. This can depend on the type and dose of the testosterone. In some, this can take longer than normal, especially in those who have a history of irregular cycles before transition. There can be many root causes of this so it's important to speak to your doctor about reasons why this is occurring. Your doctor may prescribe higher doses of testosterone, and while this may work, it can lead to more side-effects. The hormone-balancing tips on page 141 can help to support this.

Migraines

These may be caused by the fluctuation of oestrogen levels in the body or as a side-effect of testosterone therapy itself. Magnesium may help in addressing the symptom of headaches. Additionally, a magnesium supplement or using a magnesium oil spray topically on the neck to relieve tension may provide symptomatic relief.

Muscle support

Transitioning can mean there is an increase in muscle mass from testosterone, which can mean you have a greater need for protein. Aim to have a source of protein at each main meal and snack to support this. As a rule of thumb, you should be trying to get 1g of protein per kg of body weight. So for someone who is 70kg, this is 70g of protein, which looks like: two to three eggs, one medium chicken breast and one fillet of salmon per day.

Testing

Your doctor will most likely be running testing before and during hormone therapy. This is usually to see how the hormones are working to bring you into the desired range but also to monitor your overall health such as blood chemistry, blood sugar and HbA1c (a marker of blood sugar over time), cholesterol, liver and kidney health. Testosterone therapy may also result in an increase in haemoglobin and haematocrit, which can increase your red blood cell count.[12] This can lead to circulation problems, heart attack, stroke and blood clots so it is important this is monitored for you. It may not be necessary to check testosterone levels regularly, but your doctor will usually check these if you are having unpleasant symptoms. An overall picture of testosterone includes total testosterone (amount attached to proteins), free testosterone (amount in unbound state – free), SHBG and albumin.

Be mindful also to screen for breast cancer as there still may be some tissue present after surgery. While the risk lowers, it does not lower to the level of a cisgender male. Likewise, it is also important to have routine screening for cervical, endometrial and ovarian cancer if you have not yet had a hysterectomy (womb removed) or oophorectomy (ovaries removed).

Overall, testing should be taken in context as there are different result ranges in different labs conducting the test. Note, too, that ranges may be set for what sex the lab has on your medical records and therefore result ranges may be set to female. This can mean you appear over the range for female results but under the range for male results. This can therefore lead to some interpretation problems. If the clinic does not have an understanding of how to interpret a transgender person's blood test, ask for both male and female report ranges.

Male to female – oestrogen hormone therapy

The primary objective in undergoing hormone therapy is to develop female secondary sex characteristics and to minimise male secondary sex characteristics.

Physical and emotional changes include:

- Skin becomes drier and thinner
- Pores will become smaller and less oily
- Odour of sweat and urine changes and most likely you will sweat less

- Perception of pain and temperature can change
- Breast development which can be slightly painful initially
- Body fat will change and is more likely to accumulate on hips and thighs
- Muscle mass can decrease and appear less defined
- Facial features change to a more female appearance
- Face and body hair will decrease, grow slower and less thick
- Balding can slow or stop
- Emotions may change
- Libido may change and the number of erections decreases
- Testicles shrink
- Arousal and pleasure can feel different and orgasms last longer
- Reproductive changes occur which can make you infertile

Medications used in FTM hormone therapy
Hormone therapy for transgender women can include three different medications: oestrogen, testosterone blockers, and some people may be prescribed progesterone.

Oestrogen
This is known as the female hormone. It is the hormone

that drives the development of female secondary sex characteristics when transitioning. Oestrogen is available as injection, pills, patches, creams, gels and spray.

Testosterone blockers

These medications can block the production of testosterone and also block the action of it. The most common testosterone blocker is spironolactone, which can cause potassium levels in the body to rise. For this reason, I would suggest avoiding potassium supplements and get your potassium checked regularly. Other medications may be offered as an alternative such as finasteride if spironolactone is not suitable.

Progesterone

Some have progesterone (another female sex hormone) as part of their hormone replacement therapy. Reported benefits are improvement of breast development but there is little evidence to support this. Progesterone is usually not recommended as it can cause mood changes and weight gain as well as increase the risks associated with hormone replacement therapy.

Considerations
Cardiovascular health

There may be a slightly higher risk of cardiovascular events when on an oestrogen hormone replacement therapy.[13] This can be linked to the method of administration of oestrogen. The research is mixed on the risk elements but it's better to support your heart health as a preventative. Additionally, the use of oestrogen can mean increased body fat and higher levels of insulin in your body and increased risk of insulin resistance. This can also alter your blood lipid balance and therefore increase your risk of cardiovascular health events. As with FTM, adopting a Mediterranean diet is the foundation for good heart health.

Bone health

Research on bone health for the transgender population has yielded mixed results. Bone health and risk of osteoporosis (a condition which weakens your bones and increases risks of fractures) is gauged on many factors which aren't completely related to hormone therapy. Risk factors include how much weight-bearing exercise you do, your muscle mass and vitamin D and calcium levels. For transgender men, there is no change in risk of decreased bone mineral density, whereas there are some studies showing slightly increased risk of osteoporosis for transgender women.[14] Regardless of risk, it's important to make sure you are optimising your levels of calcium and vitamin D and fitting some daily exercise into your life. Vitamin D levels can be tested cheaply online or by your GP. The natural source is sunlight so try to get some exposure daily, which can be hard if you live in a cold climate. If you are going to supplement then make sure the form is vitamin D3.

Smoking

If you smoke and are on oestrogen therapy, it is important that you quit. There is an increased risk of venous thromboembolism, which is where a blood clot forms in the vein. Ask your doctor for advice on smoking cessation.

Headaches

Headaches are common for transgender women so eating magnesium-rich foods and possibly taking a magnesium supplement may give some relief.

Eating disorders

Transgender women are more at risk of developing an eating disorder because they may feel they need to weigh less to have a slighter build. This can lead to inadequate nutrition and not fuelling the body with what it needs to support your health and your transition. You simply do not need to count or restrict calories if you eat healthy, unprocessed food, particularly if you are in a normal weight range. Follow the advice in Chapter 2 on balancing your blood sugar and chewing your food, and take some daily exercise.

Testing

As with FTM transgender people, there are issues with how testing is conducted, and at the time of writing there are no set reference ranges for those who have transitioned. This can make it difficult for your doctor to monitor your hormone levels. For a comprehensive health picture, it is useful to test kidney health, cardiovascular health, potassium levels (if using spironolactone), thyroid markers, diabetes markers, oestrogen, luteinising hormone, follicle stimulating hormone and a full testosterone panel which shows free testosterone and SHBG.

Hormones in the blood don't show the full picture of how the hormones are working inside your body, and with hormone therapy there are potential side-effects which can occur. This can be explained by how the hormones are broken down through the body. A personal favourite of mine when it comes to hormone testing is to use the DUTCH Test (see the resources section on page 264). You can personalise the results to make nutrition recommendations. While this test is easy to collect in your home (it tests your urine), the report can be complicated so it would be good to work with a functional medicine practitioner to fully understand the report. The testing company will also provide the report as two documents, one as male and one as female, so the reference ranges can be examined carefully.

Even if you have undergone surgery, you will still have a prostate gland and should be conscious of your prostate health, particularly for those aged over fifty or with a history of prostate cancer.

Surgery

Those having surgery will need support in their recovery.

This can mean increased nutritional needs so it is important to eat more for recovery, starting a few days before surgery and continuing throughout the recovery period. You will also need more protein so ensure you eat protein with every meal; i.e. don't just have a piece of toast for breakfast. A protein supplement may be useful (see page 160). Post-surgery, you will want to promote wound healing by consuming a high protein diet and vitamin C- and zinc-rich foods. Additionally, antibiotics may be prescribed for your surgery and if any infections occur after, which may impact your gut health. As a precautionary measure, it's good to take a probiotic suitable for antibiotic therapy, best taken a few hours after your antibiotic, or eat fermented foods while you are on antibiotics to assist with minimising digestive unrest.

Transgender children and adolescents

Transgender children are treated with puberty/hormone blockers known as gonadotropin-releasing hormone (GnRH) analogues. These prevent someone from experiencing unwanted hormone changes until they can be prescribed gender-affirming hormones. The advice is to support a young transgender person in the best way possible using a food programme which supports their blood sugar, liver health and mental health, so, when the time is right, they will be in the best positon to deal with the effects of hormone therapy on the body.

Supplements

Supplements may be useful according to the medication you may be taking, but there can be interactions. You should therefore speak to your doctor before embarking on any supplement regime.

Multivitamin

Taking a multivitamin can help ensure you get adequate levels of nutrients which can support your body through transition. If you are a transgender woman, you do not need to take a multivitamin designed for women. This is because of the iron content, and as you don't menstruate your iron need is less. The same argument could be given for transgender men. Look for a good multivitamin which covers most of the bases and in good doses and active forms. Refer to my section on supplements on page 55.

Fish oil

Hormone therapy may increase risk of cardiovascular events, particularly in transgender women. Taking fish oil may help reduce that risk as it can lower the risk of blood clots and lower triglyceride levels, but it may also help with some of the mood changes associated with hormone therapy, particularly if your diet lacks oily fish. Choose a supplement with both the omega-3 fatty acids – eicosapentaenoic acid (EPA) and docosahexaenoic acid (DHA) – and made from good quality fish. If you are vegan, you can use algae-sourced omega-3 instead.

Vitamin D3

Vitamin D is needed for calcium absorption in the body so can be protective of bone health. It also can help mood, immune function and lower cardiovascular risk. Supplements range in dose and too much vitamin D can be toxic for you so it is important to get your levels tested. Choose vitamin D3 as this is better absorbed than D2. Dosages vary but a typical maintenance dose is about 600–1,000iu, although if you are deficient, you may require a higher dose.

Vitamin C and zinc

These may support wound healing after surgery. A typical dose of vitamin C is 500–1,000mg per day and a typical dose of zinc is 15–30mg per day.

Protein powders

These may be useful to support muscle mass and also support you through surgery and recovery. There are many different protein powders on the market, including whey which is dairy sourced and may not be suitable for everyone. Others include collagen and vegan protein powders. Try to find one that is organic and/or free from artificial sweeteners. This can be used in smoothies, yoghurts or just put into a shaker with water, making a good snack to have on the go.

Magnesium

Taking magnesium may help with stress and migraines.

The best form to take is magnesium glycinate or magnesium citrate, so look for a supplement that contains this form as there are many other forms available.

Sea buckthorn oil

This may be a promising supplement for transgender men who want to prevent dryness in intimate areas. Research shows that it supports vaginal health at the daily dose of 3,000mg. Most supplements come in a dose of 1,000mg but you may not need to take the full recommended dose of 3,000mg to get the effect.

Probiotic

Taking a multi-strain probiotic can be supportive of gut health and therefore support hormone balance, but it can also help while you are taking antibiotics to prevent side-effects and for a few weeks after. Look for a reputable brand which has different strains as some products only have one. If you are using probiotics to support antibiotic side-effects, there are also brands which offer probiotics designed for those on antibiotics.

Hormone-balancing meal suggestions

The following are some hormone-balancing meal suggestions aligned with the foundation principles in Chapter 2 and suitable for all transgender persons at any stage during the transition process. They are particularly supportive of hormone balance as they promote blood sugar balance and contain liver-supporting foods.

Breakfast

- Poached eggs with sautéed spinach and mushroom on rye toast
- Porridge with pumpkin seeds, nuts and berries
- Green smoothie
- Natural yoghurt with berries and a sprinkle of low sugar granola

Lunch

- Grilled chicken salad with red peppers, avocado and olives
- Lentil soup
- Greek salad with tuna on a bed of watercress
- Sweet potato with curried chickpeas and a dollop of yoghurt

Dinner

- Salmon fillet, broccoli and brown rice
- Chilli with lean mince with cauliflower rice
- Tofu curry with vegetables and brown rice
- Chicken with roasted vegetables

Snacks

- Broccoli, radish and cauliflower crudités with hummus
- Protein shake or smoothie
- Handful of nuts and seeds
- Yoghurt and apple
- Boiled egg

Smoothie suggestions to help increase vegetables in your diet to support hormone balance

Love is Green

- 4 broccoli florets
- Handful of kale
- 2 kiwi fruits
- Handful of flat-leaf parsley
- ¼ cucumber
- Juice of ½ lemon
- 300ml coconut water, apple juice, nut or oat milk or water

Pride

- 1 apple
- ½ banana
- ½ avocado
- Handful of watercress

- 300ml coconut water, apple juice, nut or oat milk or water

Proud Green

- Handful of spinach
- 1tbsp of pumpkin seeds
- 1 pear
- Handful of frozen mango chunks
- 300ml coconut water, apple juice, nut or oat milk or water

Rainbow Red

- 2 small beetroots cooked and chilled
- 1 celery stick
- ½ apple
- 2 radishes
- Handful of sliced red cabbage
- 1 cup of frozen berries
- 300ml coconut water, apple juice, nut or oat milk or water

Self-care – thirty minutes a day

Self-care is a very important practice as part of your transition and is often overlooked. It is an important step in learning to make time for yourself, love yourself and accept yourself. It should be something you want to do and something that you make a priority.

Below are some examples of some self-care exercises which you should try to do for at least thirty minutes every day.

- Taking a bath
- Beauty regime
- Practising gratitude
- Reading
- Writing
- Practising a hobby
- Learning
- Meditation
- Hatha yoga
- Tai chi
- Qigong
- Walking
- Running
- Cycling
- Boxing
- Rowing
- Weight training
- Resistance band workout
- Stretching
- Pilates
- HIIT class
- Zumba

6. HIV AND NUTRITION

One of my first memories of HIV was as a child, watching Princess Diana on the news shaking hands with a patient with Acquired Immunodeficiency Syndrome (AIDS) in Middlesex Hospital. Even as a young child I was mildly aware of HIV and the AIDS epidemic. While I didn't live through the 1980s as a gay man witnessing the many deaths in the community, I was brought up passively viewing the destruction AIDS caused in a very homophobic society, where it was wrongly seen at first as solely a gay disease. Therefore I am fuelled by respect for my elders who experienced it first-hand.

Eventually I became a young (and ignorant) gay man on the scene with an incredible fear that I would get diagnosed with HIV and my life would be over. I would go for an HIV test and almost faint with fear in the waiting room; friends would ensure I carried a condom with me at all times; I would receive constant lectures on safe sex and panic unnecessarily any time I had sex, even if protected. Fast forward twenty years and thankfully there is more education and less stigma surrounding HIV. We know that an undetectable person cannot pass on HIV to someone else; we have instant testing and amazing medications that help someone living with HIV have a healthy and long life; and we also have PrEP treatment, a daily medicine to prevent HIV. We must never forget, though, that the fight against HIV isn't over until there is a cure, and HIV-positive people can be some of the most vulnerable in the community.

The good news is that nutrition and lifestyle measures can help those living with HIV improve their overall health, fight HIV, minimise symptoms and side-effects from medications and maintain a healthy weight. The focus of this chapter is how best to support your body if you are living with HIV but it is also intended to educate those in the wider community and beyond to reduce the stigma of HIV even further.

What are HIV and AIDS?

HIV is a virus which attacks and weakens your immune system making you vulnerable to infections and diseases. Without drug treatment, HIV can lead to AIDS whereby your immune system becomes extremely weak and you may become ill from certain opportunistic infections and cancers. HIV specifically attacks and destroys the various immune cells called CD4 cells, which reduces someone's response to the virus. CD4 count is measured to check the health of someone who is living with HIV. If their CD4 count falls below 200 cells/mm or if they have certain opportunistic infections, it's a sign that their immunity is severely compromised and a person has progressed to AIDS.

HIV is passed on through blood, semen, vaginal fluid, anal mucus and breast milk. People can get HIV through having unprotected sex, sharing needles, sharing sex toys, coming in contact with contaminated blood, and from mother to baby during pregnancy, childbirth and breastfeeding.

No cure for HIV exists but an HIV drug treatment regime known as antiretroviral therapy reduces the viral load in the body to an undetectable level and prevents HIV from advancing to AIDS, helping people live long, healthy lives.

Someone who is HIV-positive and on antiretroviral therapy with an undetectable viral load cannot pass on the virus.

Terrence Higgins Trust recommends testing at least once a year for HIV and other sexually transmitted infections if you are sexually active, and every three months if you are having sex without a condom with new or casual partners. Testing regularly is crucial to prevent passing HIV to anyone else and to starting treatment early. A drug called PrEP is also available which is taken by HIV-negative people to reduce the risk of getting HIV.

A combination of antiretroviral therapy with good nutrition is fundamental in people who are living with HIV. Nutrition can support your body to fight HIV and support the immune response, and help manage symptoms that may occur as a result of HIV or side-effects from treatment.

Where to begin

The first step is to address your overall health. This is where you should go back to the advice in Chapter 2 and look at the foundations of a healthy diet and lifestyle. Once you feel you have a semi-healthy diet and have addressed lifestyle factors, come back to this chapter for tailored support for living with HIV. A healthy diet can:

- Support weight and muscle goals
- Support energy levels
- Support your immune system
- Minimise side-effects from medication

It's important not to put more stress on yourself to have the perfect diet and lifestyle as this may lead to breaking what you have achieved so far – in fact the perfect diet does not exist. Even by focusing on just two changes at once, you can create a positive mindset and you are likely to stick to what you have changed. Examples could be reducing added sugar or taking thirty minutes of physical activity three times per week.

During the AIDS epidemic, many people were dealing with symptoms as a result of HIV. This ranged from opportunistic infections to muscle wasting. Now, HIV can be asymptomatic and drug advancements mean that there are far fewer side-effects than there used to be from taking medications, or they are only mild. That said, we are all individual and some may experience symptoms and side-effects from medications. Weight loss, appetite loss, fatigue, digestive health issues such as diarrhoea, body fat changes (although this is more associated with older HIV medication), rashes, nausea, headaches, liver and kidney implications and changes to blood lipids are just some side-effects associated with antiretroviral therapy.

While there are some HIV-specific nutrition considerations such as supporting the immune system, it's hard to give generic advice when it comes to HIV as nutrition should really be tailored to the individual, and the recommendations do not apply to everyone due to variations of symptoms and nutritional need. The important thing is to read these recommendations and then apply what is relevant to you. In any case, opting for a healthy lifestyle is key, regardless of whether someone is HIV-positive or not.

If you are living with HIV, you most likely have regular blood testing at your health visit. This will include your viral count, blood chemistry, iron, cholesterol and triglycerides, sugars, proteins, liver and kidney function and electrolytes. You can then use this information to tailor nutrition intervention to you. I also recommend getting your vitamin D and vitamin B12 tested regularly.

The food we eat turns to energy which supports growth and repair and provides us with energy to function day to day. People living with HIV may have an increased need for energy and nutritional requirements. This is important to support the immune system to fight HIV and other infections, but HIV itself may lessen the absorption of food and nutrients. The World Health Organization recommends that HIV-positive individuals who are not experiencing symptoms should increase their calorie intake by 10% per day to maintain body weight.[1] This is roughly 250 calories for the average person, which translates to an extra snack per day. While I don't encourage calorie counting for general health, if you are losing weight then I would suggest adding an extra protein-rich snack which can also support energy levels and your immune system. Ideas for appropriate snacks are an apple with 1tbsp of nut butter, a protein shake, one pita bread and hummus or a handful of almonds.

Supporting your immunity

Supporting your immunity is probably at the forefront of your mind when you think about nutrition. Put simply, a regular healthy diet rich in fruit and vegetables is supportive of immune health. As a general rule, aim for six portions of vegetables and two pieces of fruit every day and try to pick a variety of colours of vegetables, keeping in mind the 'eat a rainbow' principle in the foundations chapter to support your immune system and encourage gut bacteria diversity. The additional fruit and vegetables in your diet will mean you are getting more fibre, which will also support your gut health and absorption of nutrients.

With HIV (even if you are on medication and have an undetectable viral load), your immune system is always activated. This can cause chronic inflammation in the body, which can lead to increased risk of age-related diseases such as cardiovascular disease, osteoporosis, liver disease, kidney disease, cancer and cognitive decline. Further, if you have other viruses such as hepatitis B or C, this can also contribute to a heightened inflammatory state. While the health consequences may not come to the surface at all or only much later in life, you can do your best to minimise inflammation in the body with diet and lifestyle modifications such as eating healthily, not smoking or using recreational drugs, exercising regularly and doing your best to limit stress. There are also some functional foods which can fight inflammation in the body so it is wise to consume the following regularly:

- Berries such as blueberries, raspberries, blackberries and strawberries
- Fatty fish such as salmon, sardines, mackerel and anchovies
- Broccoli
- Avocados
- Green tea

- Red, green and yellow peppers
- Asian mushrooms such as shiitake, reishi and oyster
- Grapes
- Turmeric
- Extra virgin olive oil
- Dark chocolate
- Tomatoes

It then makes sense that you should do your best to avoid the foods that can increase inflammation, namely sugar, refined carbohydrates, junk food, fried foods, trans fats and processed meats.

Deficiencies

Increased activation of the immune system and increased energy expenditure can mean nutrients are being used up quicker and you may be at risk of developing deficiencies. The immune system relies on vitamins A, C, D, E, B6, B9 (folate) and B12, zinc, iron, copper and selenium to support function and the daily need may be higher in those with HIV.[2]

Now, don't run off to your nearest supplement store so quick, as research into nutritional deficiencies in people living with HIV has not been able to conclude whether taking immune supportive supplements is worthwhile and safe. Some studies note benefits from supplementation, while others find no effect or question the safety in an HIV-positive population. Until there is more evidence and clinical trials to determine safety and effectiveness, I recommend you use either a food-first approach to support your immune system, supplement in cases of deficiency or a multivitamin without iron (iron is another mineral which causes controversy in HIV research).

The following are foods you can include to support your immune system:

- Vitamin A-rich foods
- B-complex vitamin-rich foods
- Vitamin C-rich foods
- Vitamin E-rich foods
- Selenium-rich foods
- Zinc-rich foods

Never overlook food in place of supplements. It's hard to overdose and cause medication interactions using food. It's also the way nature intended, so absorption can be better. Furthermore, a study found that using a selenium supplement at 200mcg per day was supportive to those living with HIV.[3] The food equivalent is only consuming approximately four Brazil nuts. This is not to discount the use of supplements as they have a place but always think about food first. If you do decide to use supplements, remember to shop for a multivitamin the way you should shop for food. The cheaper multivitamins will tend to be lower quality and either have low levels of nutrients or are not in active forms.

Check the supplement section on page 55 for how to pick good quality supplements.

A lot of the clinical studies that show benefit from using supplements involve people who are not on antiretroviral treatment. Now, as this book is intended for the LGBTQ+ population, I assume that some readers will be on medication. The problem here is that medication can interact with supplements you may be taking so you need to consider the possible interactions that they may cause, even if minor. Whatever supplement you consider taking either from recommendations in this book or elsewhere, you should check with your HIV doctor. Ultimately you should begin a food-first approach by ensuring a balanced diet.

Supplements that show interactions with common HIV drugs include St John's Wort, garlic, Sutherlandia, African Potato and high doses of vitamins A, C, E and B6, zinc and selenium. Be mindful to check ingredients to make sure these are not listed.

Oxidative stress
As a by-product of your body dealing with HIV, it leaves behind a trail of destruction in the form of molecules called free radicals. Free radicals need to be calmed down by the body's antioxidant reserves to stop damage to the cells and tissues. This is a relatively automatic process if there are adequate antioxidant reserves in the body and a person has adequate antioxidant intake from their diet; bright-coloured

fruit and vegetables are the main source. However, there is research to show that HIV-positive individuals may have lower levels of glutathione, the body's most important antioxidant, which can lead to increased oxidative stress and increased risk of liver function problems and immune dysfunction.[4] It's therefore vital that people living with HIV consider boosting their levels of glutathione. There are some foods which are naturally high in glutathione such as avocado, spinach and okra, but there are also foods which can help your body manufacture the antioxidant:

- Sulphur-rich foods
- Vitamin C-rich foods
- Selenium-rich foods
- Cysteine-rich foods

What about absorption?

HIV-positive individuals may have difficulty absorbing nutrients from their diet. This can be linked to difficulty absorbing fat (which is a symptom of HIV), damage to the gut lining, diarrhoea (which some HIV-positive people can experience), or as a possible side-effect to medication.[5] This can further impact nutritional deficiencies such as the fat-soluble vitamins A, D, E and K.

If you are reading this and think that you have digestive issues then I urge you to address these. Your digestive issues may not be related to fat absorption issues or side-effects to medication, so look back at the digestion section in Chapter 2. If you are suffering with diarrhoea, you may benefit from taking a beneficial yeast strain called Saccharomyces boulardii which is useful at supporting episodes of diarrhoea.[6] Additionally, taking a probiotic or consuming fermented foods such as yoghurt, sauerkraut, kimchi or kombucha may further support your digestive health.[7]

Someone with fat malabsorption may have symptoms such as foul-smelling or greasy stools. You can be assessed for this by having a stool test to understand if there is excess faecal fat in your stool (steatorrhea). If this is the case, you can benefit from taking a digestive enzyme which can help support fat digestion. Additionally, fat malabsorption can be improved by following a lower fat diet.

Some of the above supplements are not vegetarian so be mindful when choosing. As with all supplements, check to make sure there are no possible interactions with your medications before taking them.

Side-effects of medication

Even though antiretroviral drugs have improved since they were first available, they can still cause side-effects. Below are some tips on helping to manage some of the possible side-effects from medication.

Appetite loss

- Spread out your food intake into smaller meals throughout the day. You don't

necessarily need to stick to the three meals per day structure.
- Drink your food in the form of soups or smoothies.
- Have more calorie-dense meals containing good quality fats as they have higher calories per gram.

Nausea

- Fresh ginger juice or ginger tea may help.
- Limit caffeine.
- Eat smaller meals throughout the day.
- Eat bland foods such as rice cakes or crackers.

Fatigue

- Support your blood sugar using the foundations of this book, ensuring meals and snacks are high in protein and low in sugar.
- Limit caffeine as it can cause energy imbalances and interfere with sleep.
- Consider slower-paced exercise such as yoga, tai chi or breathing exercises.
- Consider sleep hygiene advice in Chapter 2.

Elevated cholesterol and triglycerides

- Eat foods rich in omega-3 fatty acids.

- Aim to be physically active every day within your limits.
- Limit refined and processed sugar.
- Avoid smoking and limit alcohol.

Diarrhoea

- Eat fermented foods and follow the digestion advice in Chapter 2.
- Limit high fat, dairy and spicy foods.
- Consider Saccharomyces boulardii supplement as discussed above.

Insomnia

- Consider sleep hygiene advice in Chapter 2.
- Limit screen use an hour before bedtime.
- Limit caffeine after 1 p.m.
- Make sure your bedroom is well ventilated.
- Practise meditation before bed.

Rash

- Try using natural laundry and soap products.
- Shower with cooler water on the affected area.

If any of these symptoms are new or prolonged then you must speak to your doctor. They will be able to offer advice on symptom management and review your medication.

What about PrEP?

As discussed above, PrEP is used by HIV-negative people to reduce the risk of getting HIV. Some people use this medication daily and may be part of a trial. Others take what is known as event-based dosing (two tablets two to twenty-four hours before sex, one tablet twenty-four hours after sex and a further tablet forty-eight hours after sex). Although there are very few side-effects with PrEP, they can include nausea, headaches, digestive unrest and fatigue, but they mostly subside very quickly. In rare cases, PrEP may impact kidney function and also cause slight decline in bone mineral density which can weaken bones and increase risk of osteoporosis.[8]

You can eat to support bone and kidney health by:

- Drinking enough water through the day to support kidney health
- Increasing weight-bearing and resistance exercises such as weight-lifting to help strengthen your bones
- Increasing calcium-rich foods to support bone health
- Getting adequate sun exposure to support healthy vitamin D levels and increasing intake of vitamin D-rich foods

It's important to speak to a sexual health clinic if you are concerned about the risks with PrEP. If you are not monitored by a clinic then make sure you are having regular testing for other STIs as well as liver and kidney function.

Functional foods

The term 'functional food' describes food or ingredients which yield particular benefits to health. The following foods have benefits beyond supporting general health so are naturally classed as a superfood in my eyes.

- Whey protein: not only a rich protein source which can help build and preserve lean muscle, it is also rich in immunoglobulins which support immunity, and also helps increase the potent antioxidant glutathione.[9]
- Mushrooms: rich in beta-glucans, a natural polysaccharide which supports the immune system directly.[10] Choose Asian mushrooms for more potency such as shiitake, reishi and oyster.
- Broccoli: this member of the cruciferous vegetable family is rich in vitamin C and sulforaphane which has anti-viral activity.[11]
- Turmeric: the yellow spice which goes into many curry dishes. The active ingredient, curcumin, supports the liver and is also shown to reduce inflammation and act as an important antioxidant.[12] Black pepper can support absorption of turmeric when used.

- Fermented foods: may support digestive health and help ease side-effects of medications. Early research is showing they are also supportive of the immune system, CD4 count and gut health.

Lifestyle

Many of you will have your health in the forefront of your mind since being diagnosed with HIV. Addressing the diet is only about 60% of the journey; you need to consider your lifestyle too.

Exercise

Physical activity can support weight management, build muscle and strong bones, which is important for those living with HIV. You may struggle to get motivated to exercise at first but it gets easier to do each time, particularly if you actually do something you enjoy.

Stress

Where people fall down is on combating stress and learning to have some down time, relax and unwind. It's something you need to practise daily as self-care is something that goes out of the window when you don't have enough time in the day. Put simply, stress interferes directly with immune function and increases inflammation in the body.[13] Everyone can do more for themselves; take a day off, don't check emails, or cancel plans. It's OK to do what you need to do for yourself and not others. While there are some active relaxation exercises which are good for supporting your immunity and stress levels such as yoga, tai chi, qigong and meditation, you may be one of the many who find the difficulty lies with saying no. Being able to say no sometimes is more immune supportive than anything. You will never go through life without stress but you can have more boundaries. For more stress reduction advice, see page 44.

Psychological support

I recommend to all of my LGBTQ+ clients, not just those living with HIV, to find someone to talk to; whether it's psychotherapy, counselling or another form of talking therapy. Having some sort of therapy can help you deal with stress, manage daily life, address past trauma and also come to terms with your diagnosis. Therapy can help you connect your mind and body, create new positive thought patterns and learn to live your true authentic self. If you are looking for a therapist, look for one you can relate to and who also understands LGBTQ+ well-being. There are specific LGTBQ+ directories available which list therapists and specialisms, some of which are listed here in Appendix 2. It may take a lot of courage to reach out to speak to someone so do this in your own time and when you are ready.

7. BLACK TUESDAY

'"Black Tuesday" is when the comedown hits and the energy and brain chemicals that were borrowed from the overdraft at the weekend need to be paid back'

I want to state clearly my intentions in writing this chapter. Substance use happens, period. I want to present the idea of recovering from a weekend of partying in the best way possible. I'm not here to endorse drug use or anything remotely related to it, but I feel it is important to provide tips and strategies to minimise the harm from drug use. I think this well-rounded approach is realistic and genuine. Good nutrition can have a significant impact on brain chemistry, and minimising the effects of the comedown ultimately means you are less likely to call in sick the next week, eat junk food or skip working out for two weeks after a party.

It's important to acknowledge that substance use happens regardless of sexual orientation or gender identity. However, there is evidence to suggest that the LGBTQ+ groups have higher rates of substance use than heterosexual groups.[1] There are also certain substances which are more highly concentrated in the

LGBTQ+ community, such as gamma-hydroxybutyrate (known as G, GHB or GBL) and methamphetamine (crystal meth, Tina).[2]

This chapter will mainly focus on substances which tend to be used in a club setting and known as 'club drugs'. These include G/GHB/GBL, methamphetamine, MDMA (often referred to as ecstasy), ketamine, mephedrone and cocaine. While I acknowledge that the LGBTQ+ community may use other drugs, club drugs are the focus here, looking at how these work on the body when taken, how to support the body after using, and advice for limiting the comedown impact as much as possible.

During my career as a drug and alcohol recovery therapist, I saw the damaging effects of drugs and alcohol on both the individual and community. This included mainstream addiction drugs, but also club drugs, which the individual may have started off by using recreationally but then ended up addicted. Many people understand that drugs like cocaine and crystal meth can be highly addictive, but they don't think that taking G can be physically addictive so their body becomes dependent on it and they have to dose it hourly to avoid dangerous withdrawal symptoms. I saw many people who attended my drug recovery service not understanding that they were withdrawing from G even though they had to dose every hour in order to function normally and eventually required in-patient medical detox.

Substance use and even poly drug use is dangerous and I acknowledge it happens; you just have to look around at a dance party to know that most revellers are on some sort of drug to get their thrill. The people at circuit parties or in LGBTQ+ venues also tend to be well educated and financially secure. It seems the reward of substance use outweighs the risks at these events and often the use does not end when the club closes; people using club drugs can carry on for days at afterparties and chillouts with little or no sleep or food, which is a huge tax on the body itself, in addition to the effects of drugs. People who use club drugs often use more than one substance at a time and this can lead to engaging in 'chemsex' – sex under the influence of drugs. Substances may allow the user to experience disinhibition, but also heighten sexual arousal so can be attractive to the user; this often means they prefer using chems for sex over sex without drugs, or sober sex.

If you are concerned about substance use either for yourself or a loved one, please reach out to the experts who can provide the support you need. I have listed a number of relevant services in Appendix 2. They can help provide advice for those who do not acknowledge they have a problem with substance use. In the therapy world, we call this precontemplation in the cycle of change. It's when the user is beyond a recreational user, but in denial about possible addiction. Someone in the precontemplation stage is challenging, as the initial drive to get better needs to start with the individual, but the right services can work to help move someone into a contemplation stage, where they are thinking about the impact of their substance use and considering options. If you are reading this and you suddenly feel that this may be you, please reach out to a local treatment service. When individuals presented themselves for assessment at the drug and alcohol service where I worked, they were mostly shy and shameful and expecting judgement about their drug use. Drug and alcohol recovery workers are not there to judge and to insist you cease using substances but to do their best to give you confidential advice and the best support options available. So make that call and enquire about an assessment of your needs!

My training in nutrition coupled with my background in substance use recovery allows me to understand what drug use does to the body and brain chemistry and to support it with nutrition. This is probably one of the questions I get asked most when I tell someone at a party what I do for a job – 'What can I do not to feel awful next week?' If you read the title of this chapter and got the context then you've been there and understand the pain of 'black Tuesday'. It's called this because this is usually when the comedown hits from partying the previous weekend. You're sitting in the office wishing you hadn't gone out at the weekend, you're feeling a bit emotional, on your third iced coffee before 11 a.m. because you can't keep your eyes open, you only want to eat sugar and junk food to give some pleasure to your senses, and you probably have 'chemmy sweats' so your shirt has sweat patches like dinner plates. How did we get here, and why, if there is a comedown, do we take these substances? Well, what goes up must come down so 'black Tuesday' is essentially when the comedown hits and the energy and brain chemicals that were borrowed from the overdraft at the weekend need to be paid back. While I do not claim to be able to cure your comedown, my education and experience allow me to understand the body and what substances do to it, and therefore I am able to offer advice which may support the body pre-, during and post-party.

What happens when we party?

In order to understand how to support party weekends and mitigate the dreaded comedown, it's important to look at what happens in the body when we party and take substances. Having some knowledge of what happens when we party can help you make conscious decisions about safer partying. The body is a wonderful adaptive machine but some of the life choices we make, and indeed when we party, make our body work overtime to mop up the damage we have done to it.

Whether you are in a club or at a circuit party, it usually means many hours on the dance floor. Whether a seasoned partier or the new kid on the block, you will know that spending a whole weekend raving away can be quite taxing on the body. Not only is your brain fired up and alert for extended periods, your muscles get tired from dancing, you're probably not eating for a long time, and you're more likely to be dehydrated. In fact, the whole process doesn't just begin when you walk into the party, it starts with the ritual of getting ready, choosing an outfit, getting a pump at the gym earlier that day and limiting your diet in case you have sex later on. It's similar to the ritual of making coffee in the morning: the chemical messages in the brain start to release even before you have dropped an ecstasy pill. For if they didn't, you wouldn't have any desire to go to a circuit party or get the summer body primed for Mykonos. Remember the first time you went to a circuit party or got into Berghain? You senses were overloaded from doing things you perhaps don't normally do, hot people around you, sex happening, music that creates euphoria and of course the use of drugs which lighten the mood, lower inhibitions and relax you. Your brain remembers this cocktail of events, and while you may experience a comedown from using drugs, the reward of attending parties is far greater than the lows you experience the week after. This is why you forget the comedown the next time your friends plan a party weekend.

Club drugs are similar to chemicals that are already in our body. They work by changing the way nerves in the brain send and receive information. These messengers in the brain are called neurotransmitters; they are chemicals in your body which relay messages while controlling reflexes, emotion and memory. Normally this process is tightly controlled by the body which produces and breaks down neurotransmitters at a steady rate. Drugs can interfere with this process; they either imitate the natural chemical messengers the brain releases, release large amounts of natural neurotransmitters or prevent the reabsorption of these brain chemicals. This means you feel high when taking drugs.[3] There are many neurotransmitters in the brain but we will focus on those involved in the reward pathway such as dopamine, serotonin, noradrenaline, glutamate and gamma-aminobutyric acid (GABA). These are the main neurotransmitters affected by drug use in the short and long term.

Dopamine
Dopamine is our reward neurotransmitter. It's responsible for our pleasure-seeking behaviour and is involved in any pleasurable activity such as shopping, gambling, food, sex and drugs. It helps you focus to complete a task to receive the reward at the end of the process. Without dopamine, you would be lazy and unmotivated to do anything in life, but too much can lead to irritability.

Dopamine production can be increased by improving the diet as it is synthesised from the amino acid tyrosine. Other nutrients involved in the production and metabolism of dopamine are vitamins B6, B9 (folate), B12 and C, copper, iron, magnesium and zinc.

When drugs like cocaine and methamphetamine are taken, they interfere with the natural production and metabolism of dopamine, causing excessive dopamine stimulation which results in the user feeling high.

Serotonin

Serotonin controls appetite, sleep, learning and mood. When something great happens in your life, serotonin is produced, making you feel happy. This is released in everyday life but even more so when partying with your friends when you feel the euphoria of your favourite song being played; your body gets a hit of serotonin alongside other chemicals such as dopamine and noradrenaline to intensify the happiness and feeling of contentment. Serotonin is primarily associated with the use of MDMA (ecstasy) and LSD.

Serotonin is synthesised from the amino acid tryptophan, which is obtained from eating meat, fish and eggs. Vitamins B6, B9 (folate), B12 and C and magnesium are needed to support the production and metabolism of serotonin.

Noradrenaline

Noradrenaline is one of our stress hormones and is

responsible for alertness and arousal. It is produced from dopamine so the same dietary factors that support the production and metabolism of dopamine also support noradrenaline production. Cocaine, methamphetamine and speed interfere with normal functioning of noradrenaline and lead to anxiety, among other effects.

Glutamate

Glutamate is one of the most abundant neurotransmitters in the brain and central nervous system. It's an excitatory neurotransmitter, which means its job is to fire up nervous activity. In short, drugs force a release of a massive amount of glutamate when using and, once over, lead to a deficiency in glutamate. This change can mean someone is primed for addiction and crave further drug use.

Gamma-aminobutyric acid (GABA)

GABA is the exact opposite of glutamate and known as the calming neurotransmitter. It serves to calm things down in the body and the ratio of glutamate to GABA in normal circumstances is regulated to feel balance. Drugs such as benzodiazepines (benzos) like Valium, Xanax, G and alcohol make you feel calmer and sleepy due to activation of the GABA receptor system.

The comedown

The cocktail of these chemicals may mean you're feeling

in the mood to party at the time of use, but when you get home it's hard to sleep until your brain breaks down the neurotransmitters and you are back to a natural state. You can feel quite tired, suffer from low mood and be unmotivated the following week as it takes a time to build the serotonin back up to normal levels.[4]

Aside from impacting brain chemistry, substance use and partying for extended hours also have other physical effects which need to be considered and understood.

Your liver gets overloaded
Your body has a sophisticated way of eliminating toxins that involves the liver, kidneys, digestive system, skin and lungs. The liver in particular does the dirty work of filtering and disposing of all the unhealthy things we consume. While your liver is great at doing its job and managing all the stress from daily life, you can overwhelm it by partying, which can mean the poor thing is overworked with many jobs piling up. Activities such as drinking too much and substance abuse can mean your body has a reduced ability to carry out its normal functions such as detoxifying.[5]

You have more chance of being dehydrated
Hours in the sun dancing or even in a sweaty club can mean you're at higher risk from suffering from dehydration. Your body regularly loses water through sweating and urination. Additionally, important

electrolytes are lost in sweat, including sodium and potassium. If the water and electrolytes aren't replaced, you become dehydrated. Symptoms can be mild to severe and include fatigue, dry mouth, dizziness and headaches.

You lose sleep

Chances are if you are going to a party then your regular sleep routine is going to get out of kilter. You may even find when you get to bed that you can't sleep, feeling wired from the night. Sleep allows your brain to recharge itself and remove toxic by-products accumulated throughout the day.[6] Not sleeping well or missing a night's sleep can impact your quality of life and lead to health consequences including emotional stress and mood disorders.[7]

Your muscles get tired

Dancing for hours on end can be considered a good workout but can lead to exhaustion and muscle fatigue. This usually isn't a long-term issue with one or two nights out but can lead to some muscle cramps and soreness the next day. Logically, you could also say that the jaw clench, otherwise known as gurning, which is caused by the use of certain drugs could be related to stiffness in the jaw muscles.

You're more likely to suffer from stress

Taking drugs and not sleeping can be a massive tax

on your adrenal stress hormones. Imbalances in cortisol, your stress hormone, can lead to a decreased ability to deal with normal daily stress, as well as further health issues such as compromised immunity, digestion, poor sleep, obesity, blood pressure and blood sugar issues.

Summary

Regularly taking substances can yield long-term health consequences. Partying and bombarding your brain with substances to alter its chemistry can mean you don't just need more to get a hit from the drug but you may never feel life's pleasures in the way you used to. This is called neuron death and the source of the phrase 'chasing the dragon' – you are constantly trying to chase that first high. Increased oxidative stress is another consequence of drug use. It is the imbalance between free radicals and antioxidants; higher free radicals mean the body ages both inside and out.

Aside from psychological and genetic factors, altered brain chemistry from substance use can mean you are more prone to addiction as the brain is now wired to seek the drug of choice and therefore you are at higher risk.

Let's focus on what you can now do pre-, during and post-party to support your body to keep healthy, limit the comedown and stabilise brain chemistry, which in turn can lower the risk of addiction.

Safer using

Apart from familiarising yourself with the various support groups that are available, there are some general guidelines when using substances that should be adhered to. You may be tempted to skim over this, thinking that you know this already, but this information could save your life – or someone else's – so I urge you to read this carefully. There is also a resource section in Appendix 2 if you feel you could benefit from speaking to someone for advice about drugs or confidential treatment options.

Substance use is not a safe practice. Drugs not only impact brain circuitry and behaviour leading to addiction, but can also lead to medical complications and death in the event of an overdose. By following this harm reduction advice, you can help to minimise the damage caused by taking substances.

Alcohol

Work out how much you usually drink. In the UK there is a unit system which lets you compare different drinks and how much you drink. A pint of regular lager is 2 units, strong lager is 3 units, 25ml of spirits is 1 unit and a 250ml glass of wine is 3 units. Aim to keep your units below 14 per week as a rule of thumb and spread your drinking out. It's also a good idea to have some days where you don't drink alcohol and not binge drink on the days that you do.

G/GHB/GBL

G should not be mixed with alcohol or ketamine as it increases your chance of 'going under', having fits or a coma. Make sure you measure your dose correctly, ideally with a syringe barrel. Do not use other people's G as it may be stronger than yours to which you know your tolerance. Set a timer when taking a dose and do not redose for three hours. G is very abrasive so make sure you are drinking it with a mixer or it will burn your throat and can damage teeth and gut lining. G can also cause nausea and sickness so a good way to avoid this is not to consume it on an empty stomach. Make sure you eat a meal before partying and have a quick-releasing energy snack in your bag such as a chocolate bar or banana which can help minimise nausea.

Use G in a safe environment and make sure people are aware of the risks. Agree collectively to call an ambulance if someone shows signs of overdose.

As mentioned previously, regular G use can lead to dependency. This can mean you are anxious, shaky and suffer from insomnia. This can happen quite easily after a long party weekend, so do not use more than 15ml in a twenty-four-hour period and not for two days in a row. If you are feeling withdrawal symptoms, it's best to go to A&E or call your local drug service for advice on what to do.

Methamphetamine/crystal meth (Tina)

Crystal meth is not physically addictive, but it is very

psychologically addictive as it produces effects the user wants to repeat. Crystal meth is usually smoked in a pipe or injected into a vein. It leaves the user with a high but there are some dangers associated with using. It can lead to high-risk sexual practices as inhibitions are lowered and perspectives can be distorted. Do not use crystal meth every weekend as your brain chemistry needs time to settle; so do not buy large quantities to keep in the house, as you are likely to use more in one session because it is there.

Do not mix crystal meth with other drugs (especially stimulants) as you run the risk of stroke and heart attacks. Do not share equipment such as needles or pipes. Avoid injecting crystal meth as the high may not be controlled and you're probably not going to be injecting safely. Unsafe injection practices can lead to hepatitis C.

Crystal meth use can result in horrendous comedowns and there may be little nutrition can do to limit these. If you plan to use then make sure you take time away from your work and social life to fully recover from it.

Other stimulants
Other stimulants like mephedrone and cocaine can lead to anxiety, palpitations, hallucinations and paranoia. Use can also lead to a comedown the week after. Snorting can be an irritant to the nose and lead to bleeding. You should not share notes, straws or other paraphernalia because of the risk of exposure to hepatitis B and C.

Do not use cocaine and alcohol together as this combination produces cocaethylene in the liver, which increases toxicity.[8]

Ketamine
Using a large amount of ketamine can cause the user to hallucinate or be in a 'K hole' where there is limited perception of reality. So if you are planning to use ketamine, only use very small amounts. Ketamine can also lead to bladder damage which can result in incontinence or pain. If you experience this, you should speak to your doctor immediately.

MDMA (ecstasy)
Keep to a safe dose of MDMA. If using ecstasy pills, do not do a whole pill at once as they vary in strength. Start small and work up to a dose that is effective but within safer guidelines.

Make sure you are drinking enough water when taking MDMA. It's a good idea to take an electrolyte drink when partying such as coconut water or even an isotonic sports drink. If you can't get this at the party then consume when you arrive home.

Once again, I would like to point you to the resource section at the end of this book if you want to speak to someone for advice about using drugs or confidential treatment options.

Supporting comedowns

The experience of a comedown is individual. We all have that one friend who does not get any comedown at all yet they can be the biggest partier. However, for most people there is a period after drug use where you feel a comedown. The extent to which you have a comedown depends on the substances you have taken, how much sleep you missed while using substances, the impurities in the substances, your state of health, and your diet and lifestyle pre- and post-partying.

Nevertheless, there are steps you can take which can help to minimise the after-effects of partying so you can function better the week after, putting an end to or reducing the 'black Tuesday' feeling.

In general, having a healthy diet will help to mitigate some of the comedown. If your blood sugar is imbalanced, you may experience more intense comedowns. Good nutrition is not only healthy for your body but can also be conducive to recovery the week after. It's a good idea to revisit the foundations in Chapter 2 to support your diet and lifestyle choices.

Before the party, it is essential to eat. I know you may not wish to eat as you may not want to feel bloated, or you think the drug will have less effect or you may not be able to have sex if you eat too much. However, you should have a healthy meal around four hours before you party, especially if you are going to be dancing all night. If you are worried about feeling bloated or not being able to have sex, eat something which is protein and vegetable only such as chicken or eggs with vegetables.

When you are partying you probably won't have much of an appetite and this can mean you can go for a long time without food, particularly if the party has extended hours or you end up at an afterparty. The best solution here is to drink your food in the form of a smoothie when you get home before sleeping. This can support your blood sugar when you crash which may mean fewer ill-effects post-partying. If you don't have a blender, put protein powder in a shaker with milk or water. Be mindful to drink this slowly, as some people may find it hard to digest food straight after partying. You may find it helpful to prepare the smoothie or ingredients to blend and keep it in the fridge before going out as you may not feel like doing it when you get home.

An example post-party smoothie

Serves 2:
1 scoop of vegan protein powder
1 banana
¼ cucumber
½ apple
Knob of ginger
Handful of spinach
200ml coconut water
Ice

How to eat the week after the party
People automatically think about supplements when considering party recovery but there is quite a lot you can do with food to support your body and normalise brain circuitry. Supporting diet may also help in addiction by helping to prevent unwanted cravings.

What to avoid

- Excess refined sugars and carbohydrates which result in unstable blood sugar levels
- Unhealthy vegetable oils and trans fats which are pro-inflammatory for the body
- Processed foods, which often have additives to increase shelf-life, provide colour or enhance flavour

What to include

- High protein foods such as lean meat, fish, eggs, nuts, seeds and dairy
- Healthy fats such as olive oil, oily fish, nuts and seeds
- Eight portions of vegetables per day (six vegetables and two fruit)

Functional foods
Vitamins B6, B9 (folate) and B12 are cofactors involved in the production and metabolism of neurotransmitters

(chemical messengers). Neurotransmitter production is altered when taking drugs and so will most likely need support post-party so aim to include food sources of these vitamins the week after.

Essential fatty acids also play a role in normal brain functioning and development so aim to consume at least two portions of foods rich in omega-3 the week after taking drugs.

Gut health

It's up to your brain to make serotonin from what you eat. You can't directly get serotonin from food, but you can get tryptophan, an amino acid that's converted to serotonin in your brain. Food sources of tryptophan are eggs, fish, poultry, nuts, seeds, spinach and soy, but due to the way it is metabolised in the body, tryptophan-containing foods may not be fully used by the brain in the days recovering from substance use.

Most serotonin receptors are located in the gut and so gut health can positively or negatively affect your mood. There is a two-way communication between the gut and the brain, so you could argue that supporting gut health is also conducive to supporting comedowns.

- Eat enough fibre and include wholegrains and legumes in your diet.
- Include fermented foods in your diet.
- Add a range of colourful fresh fruits and vegetables as these are high in polyphenols,

the special plant chemicals contained in the pigments of many foods. These colours generously feed good bacteria in your gut and help them to thrive and help make you healthy. Examples are berries, plums, pomegranates, red chicory, black grapes, red onions, thyme, olive oil and sage.

G can also be very abrasive to the gut so it's a good idea to support this by making a bone broth. Simply boil chicken bones with some vegetables for a few hours and then drink the broth. This is rich in vitamins, minerals, amino acids and collagen which can help support and heal the mucosal lining of the digestive tract. Aim to have one cup of this per day the week after partying.

Support your liver
Drugs are metabolised in the liver and not eating may also slow your detoxification pathways. Consume liver-supporting foods such as:

- Watercress
- Turmeric
- Ginger
- Cruciferous vegetables such as Brussels sprouts, broccoli, cabbage, cauliflower, collard greens, kale and turnips
- Sulphur-rich foods

- Vitamin C-rich foods
- Whey protein, which can encourage glutathione (a master antioxidant) production
- Coffee
- Green tea

You also want to ensure you are not constipated to enable healthy removal of toxins. Reasons for constipation can include a low fibre diet, magnesium need or food sensitivities. Take note of the digestive advice in Chapter 2 on page 34.

Sleeping

By partying at night, you are missing out on normal sleep so your sleep pattern will be unbalanced. To help minimise this, I would advise you to get adequate sleep on the nights leading up to the party and even try to have a 'disco nap' in the afternoon before the party. For circuit festivals and cruises with continuous parties, the rule of thumb is to get sleep each day and not go a day where you have been up for more than twenty-four hours. Try at least to get four hours each night and ideally more when on these trips. You may find it hard to sleep when taking substances so take time to relax before sleeping, by having a bath or watching TV, for example.

Exercise

Exercise may seem like the last thing you want to do

after partying but it's fundamental to the recovery following a heavy weekend. Exercise can be supportive of neurotransmitter production such as dopamine and serotonin, can improve brain functioning and also reduce stress levels. If you have to, pack your gym bag before you go to the party – just getting to the gym is often part of the struggle. I advise a less strenuous workout for a couple of days following a party before resuming your normal intensity.

Meditation and mindfulness
Both meditation and mindfulness can be supportive of brain chemistry, help normalise neurotransmitters, lower stress and support changes to the brain known as neuroplasticity, which can help with addiction and dependency. Find what suits you as you may experience what is known as a grasshopper mind if you try to meditate for the first time. There are many apps to help you, or simply time breathing in for five seconds and out for five seconds. If you are addicted to your phone, perhaps start with having a mini digital detox at night one to two hours before bed.

Supplements

The following supplements may be supportive in normalising brain chemistry following drug use. As always, seek expert advice if you are planning on taking any of the following and enquire about possible interactions if you are taking any medication.

Vitamins B6, B9 (folate) and B12

As mentioned above, these B-complex vitamins help produce and break down the neurotransmitters serotonin, dopamine, noradrenaline, glutamate and GABA. It's probably best to take these in a good quality B-complex formula.

Stress adaptogens

Herbal adaptogens such as ginseng, rhodiola and ashwagandha can be supportive of the stress response as taking drugs is a stress on the body. These can be sold in a complex or on their own.

L-Tyrosine

L-Tyrosine is an amino acid and precursor to dopamine which can be supportive of neurotransmitters. You would take this on an empty stomach first thing in the morning and usual doses are 500–1,000mg in the days after partying.

5-hydroxytryptophan (5-HTP)

You are probably familiar with 5-HTP as it seems to be the most common afterparty supplement. It comes from the seeds of Griffonia simplicifolia and is the immediate precursor to serotonin. Usual doses are 50–100mg per day in the days after partying.

For optimum neurotransmitter balance, it is recommended to supplement L-Tyrosine AND 5-HTP together, the reason being a potential competition for absorption between these two molecules.[9] For example, taking 5-HTP alone may affect the synthesis and metabolism of dopamine, and supplementing L-Tyrosine may impact serotonin levels.[10] Additionally, if you are on medication which impacts serotonin, dopamine and noradrenaline levels, it's not advised to supplement with these precursors as you increase risk of toxicity.

Magnesium

Magnesium is a key nutrient in supporting the health of the nervous system. It may also help the muscles to relax after extended periods on the dance floor, which is something to consider when you get home from partying. You should consider an absorbable form such as magnesium glycinate or magnesium citrate and a standard daily dose is around 300–500mg.

Antioxidants

When our body breaks down a drug, it creates oxidative stress. Think of oxidative stress like a bad drunk at a party causing damage to the house. The good thing is that there is a defence mechanism in the body which is like a buddy who takes the bad drunk with them and calms them down. These are known as antioxidants; they're chemicals which help stop the body rusting and prevent damage to its cells. In this process, antioxidants get used up so you need to make sure they are essentially refuelled in the diet. Antioxidants in food tend to come from anything with bright colours but also in supplements such as vitamin C, vitamin E, alpha-lipoic acid (ALA) and glutathione. Speaking logically, you would take these pre- and post-party to help give your body the army it needs to break down the oxidative stress from substance use. One study showed that mice fed MDMA on a low vitamin E diet suffered more neurotoxicity compared to the mice with sufficient vitamin E in their diet.[11] If you decide to supplement with antioxidants, you can either use antioxidant complexes or single nutrients like vitamin C (choose one with bioflavonoids for better absorption). A typical dose of vitamin C is 500–1,000mg daily which can be taken pre- and post-party, but also ensure your diet is far from beige in colour the week after.

Fish oil
If you do not eat fish in your diet then it would be wise to consider a fish oil for omega-3 content. Fish oil contains two types of omega-3 fatty acids, eicosapentaenoic acid (EPA) and docosahexaenoic acid (DHA), which play a role in normal brain functioning, synthesis and breakdown of neurotransmitters, helping increase antioxidant reserves and supporting the stress response. A dose of 1,000–2,000mg of omega-3 fatty acids from fish oil is a standard dose and well within the upper safe limit.

Activated charcoal
Traditionally used in cases of poisoning and treatment

for overdoses, activated charcoal works by trapping toxins in the gut, preventing their absorption.[12] It's the by-product of burning wood or coconut shells which are heated to high temperatures to change the structure and increase surface area making them more absorbent. Activated charcoal may be useful when you get home from partying, and there is even research on its use for G intoxication.[13] Be mindful not to take this with other medications as it may reduce their effectiveness; nor should this be used in the event of G overdose, in which case you should call an ambulance.

There are many more supplements that I could include here but sometimes less is more in terms of supplements. Vitamin D, zinc, copper, iron and selenium all may play a role in brain health and functioning so, generally speaking, a good quality daily multivitamin will cover the bases and then use the supplements above as and when necessary.

Bottom line

If you are going to be a party regular, you need to understand what it is doing to your body in order to help mitigate some of the potential physical effects. As well as supporting recovery from occasional partying, nutrition can go a long way in the management of addictions and preventing relapse in the recovering user. As much as you may want junk food the week after partying, try to avoid it, get some exercise straight away and keep sugar low and protein high so your body will recover quicker. There are some supplements which may help your body to repair the damage from using but they are designed to supplement a healthy diet and you should consider these based on your individual health, lifestyle and medical needs.

8. LGBTQ+ MENTAL HEALTH

If you do an online book search for 'LGBTQ+ health' or 'gay health', most of the results show titles related to mental health. While as a population we are so much more than mental health issues, people who identify as LGBTQ+ are at high risk of developing poor mental health. This can be down to a number of factors, such as having to hide your true self, suffering rejection, not accepting yourself or not being accepted by others, dealing with inequalities, trauma from your past, anger, violence, loneliness, low self-worth, anxiety, depression, addiction, homophobia, transphobia and more. Although in today's society LGBTQ+ people are accepted more than ever, every day freedoms and rights are being threatened around the world, and at ground level there are daily microaggressions that LGBTQ+ people face.

Within the community there are also mental health triggers such as comparability, shame, vulnerability issues, internal discrimination, fat shaming, slut shaming, racism, body dysmorphia and perfectionism. The list could go on and on but internal and external triggers can leave someone feeling quite overwhelmed, suffering low self-esteem, experiencing loneliness, struggling to find authentic relationships, misusing drugs and suffering low mood which can ultimately lead to suicidal ideations. All of this can be a lot for someone to deal with and process, so it can be quite daunting being someone who is LGBTQ+ in a heteronormative world. People learn to build a big wall of defence to protect themselves but behind it is a scared inner child wanting to be loved and accepted like anyone else. This wall can stop feelings and emotions on the outside, but if broken down, it reveals anger, fear, rejection, trauma, depression, anxiety and more. It can also prevent you connecting with your body and listening to it when you are tired, stressed, worn out or anxious. All of this can contribute to the development of mental health issues which can have a profound effect on daily life, impact sleep, make you more tired or lose interest in daily life and limit your ability to function at your best. It can also lead to controlling parts of your life because you feel you can't control some other parts, which can draw you into behaviours such as eating disorders, obsessive working out or unhealthy perfectionism.

While I'm not a mental health expert in terms of psychology, I have had my fair share of rejection issues growing up and within the gay community. I have suffered from extreme anxiety and burnt myself out trying to deal with imposter syndrome as I never felt I was quite good enough. In fact, I've had four years of therapy and I can honestly say it has saved my life. I am a different person now and, most importantly, I am learning to love and accept myself and feel less need to care what others think or to seek validation. This is an ongoing process and you have to practise daily at being perfectly imperfect. My advice to you is to start somewhere, even if it is just making that step to begin talking to someone about what is going on in your head.

Mental health difficulties affect each and every one of us at some point in our life. Mental health is a broad subject and can include anxiety, depression, obsessive-compulsive disorder, post-traumatic stress disorder, schizophrenia, bi-polar disorder and eating disorders. Mental health issues may cause you to withdraw from family and friends, lack motivation and feel like there is a cloud above you which follows you everywhere you go; it may feel like nobody understands you or you may not be taken seriously. You may be unable to explain why you are suffering with mental health issues and it can be down to your brain chemistry. Mental health issues can also run in the family as there is a strong genetic link with mood disorders. There are no direct blood tests for mental health disorders, so the first port of call is to see your doctor who can advise the best referral route. A doctor or psychiatrist can diagnose you and organise a treatment plan with you. This can include medication and there are times when this is absolutely essential. If the mental health problem is due to a psychological trauma, you may benefit from a talking therapy such as cognitive behavioural therapy (CBT), psychotherapy or counselling.

Looking after your mental health can help you live a more fulfilled life and you should not be afraid to ask for help if you need it. Don't suffer in silence – maybe just tell one person you are not OK if that is how you really feel. Unveil the vulnerable you and it can be life-changing. The good news is nutrition and lifestyle measures can help you develop a healthy mind. You probably are fully aware by now of the benefits of good nutrition on physical health, but nutrition can also support mental wellness, as well as mood disorders such as depression and anxiety. The purpose of this chapter is to explain what nutritional factors can be linked to mental health issues and how to support them.

The food we eat impacts how we feel in different ways. For example, you can go on a diet and lose some weight, which then makes you feel happier and more content in your body so contributes to better mental health. You can also eat healthily to prevent chronic debilitating health which triggers poor mental health as you have to live with health conditions. Nutrition can act as a therapy for mental health conditions as well as contributing to overall mood and well-being. Examples include the impact of sugar and mental health, deficiencies in nutrients such as certain fats, vitamins and minerals, the quality of food in the food chain, and overconsumption of processed foods, all of which can influence mood and behaviour. A diet that is rich in lean protein, complex carbohydrates, fruit and vegetables can help protect your mental health. So this is where you need to begin, starting with the foundations in Chapter 2.

One of the keys to a healthy mind is to make the right food choices. Eating healthily can help you feel more mentally balanced, enabling you to take further steps at supporting your mental health. I can appreciate, however, that when you are feeling low or anxious, changing your diet and lifestyle can be difficult and you can lack motivation. You don't need to change everything at once, but even taking just one or two actions means that the rest of the journey can be easier.

How neurotransmitter imbalances can contribute to mental health problems

Neurotransmitters are chemical messengers which impact how the brain and body function by sending messages throughout the body. Neurotransmitters are covered in the previous chapter on page 189 but here's a recap with regard to mental health. The most important neurotransmitters in relation to mental health disorders are serotonin, dopamine, noradrenaline and GABA.

Serotonin
This impacts how you feel, your mood, appetite and sleep. Those with anxiety and depression may have low

levels of serotonin.[1] Antidepressant medication works by blocking the reuptake of serotonin leaving more in the system to help elevate mood.

Dopamine
This helps you seek reward and keeps you motivated to complete a task. Low levels of dopamine may impact low mood due to low motivation but it has also been linked to attention deficit hyperactivity disorder (ADHD) and schizophrenia.[2] Imbalanced levels may cause anxiety and increased risk of addictive behaviours.[3]

Noradrenaline
This neurotransmitter is involved in our flight or fight response in terms of stress so is related to feelings of anxiety.

Gamma-amino butyric acid (GABA)
This is an amino acid that acts as a neurotransmitter. GABA limits nervous activity in the body; if your body doesn't have enough, this may lead to anxiety disorders.[4]

Supporting neurotransmitters with nutrition

Food precursors
It may be of benefit to eat certain foods known as neurotransmitter precursors. These are the raw materials from which your brain makes neurotransmitters.

- Tryptophan foods which are the precursor to serotonin: meat, eggs, bananas, yoghurt, milk and cheese
- Tyrosine foods which are the precursor to dopamine and noradrenaline: milk, meat, fish and legumes

Blood sugar
Too much sugar and refined carbohydrates in your diet, smoking, alcohol and insufficient protein and fibre can cause blood sugar fluctuations which can lead to mood changes including feelings of anxiety and inability to handle stress. Further, there are studies which link the consumption of ultra-processed foods to depression.[5]

Importance of protein
If you don't eat enough protein, you may be deficient in amino acids which are needed to make neurotransmitters that impact mood and motivation. Ensure you are getting protein with each meal and snack to support your body in the best way possible.

Low vitamin D
Vitamin D is known as the sunshine vitamin so if you live in a colder climate or spend most of your time indoors you may be at risk of vitamin D deficiency. For some, low levels of vitamin D can contribute to low mood.[6] A simple test by your doctor can assess vitamin D levels and I suggest that you supplement if deficient.

Importance of fats

The balance of essential fats is important in your diet. Eating too many fried foods, hydrogenated fats and vegetable-based damaged oils and not enough omega-3 fatty acids can impact mood, as this sort of diet affects how neurotransmitters such as dopamine and serotonin work in the brain. There are two types of omega-3 fatty acids – eicosapentaenoic acid (EPA) and docosahexaenoic acid (DHA). They are important for maintenance of normal brain function and there is strong evidence that omega-3 fatty acids can improve depressive symptoms.[7] If you do not consume oily fish regularly, you may want to consider starting to eat oily fish two days a week, taking a fish oil supplement or a plant-based algae supplement.

Vitamins and minerals

When we don't get enough of certain vitamins and minerals, not just physical health but mental health can suffer. In particular, the B-complex vitamins such as B9 (folate), B6 and B12 are essential to produce neurotransmitters, so a deficiency in these can lead to mood disorders. These nutrients are also needed for the metabolism of homocysteine, an amino acid which plays a role in maintaining balance in the nervous system. High levels of homocysteine are linked to depression and anxiety.[8] You are able to measure homocysteine through a blood test, and if your levels are high, you may want to consider increasing foods rich in folate, B6 and B12 as well as taking a B-complex supplement.

Magnesium

Magnesium is an essential mineral for brain function and there is emerging evidence that deficiency is associated with an increased risk of depression and anxiety.[9] Ensuring adequate food sources but also taking a magnesium supplement may be helpful. It is usually bound to other substances to help the absorption. Best forms include magnesium glycinate or magnesium citrate as these can be easily absorbed by the body and may also give benefits to sleep, constipation, muscle aches and headaches. A typical dose is around 350mg per day, and be mindful that higher doses can lead to loose stools, nausea and low blood pressure.

Gut and mood

Research shows that our gut bacteria play a role in how we feel. The gut produces 90% of the serotonin your body makes and there is growing interest in the gut–brain axis, a two-way communication pathway between the gut and the nervous system.[10] This means how you feel is linked to your gut health. So if you have feelings of anxiety or low mood, it could be something to do with your gut health that is impacting your mental health. Everything you eat and drink interacts with your gut processes and your bacteria. Certain strains of gut bacteria can impact your mood by helping mental health conditions such as anxiety and depression.[11]

If you are suffering with digestive issues, you need to support your gut by following the advice in the digestive health section in Chapter 2 (see page 34). There is even a relationship with gluten sensitivity and mood disorders, so it is worth considering either a trial of removing gluten from your diet, or getting tested for coeliac disease or gluten sensitivity.[12] A nutrition practitioner can help organise this for you.

Ultimately, you should ensure your diet has a variety of different fibres as these contain prebiotics which are good for your gut bacteria. Examples of such foods include wholegrains, nuts, seeds, fruit and vegetables. You can also include polyphenol-rich foods such as green tea, cocoa, olive oil and coffee. As discussed on page 41, fermented foods can be a useful addition to help boost gut bacteria numbers. By adding these foods, you can alter the types of bacteria in your gut and therefore possibly improve your mental well-being.

Stress
People with depression tend to have elevated levels of the stress hormone cortisol.[13] As discussed on page 42, elevated cortisol can be a problem when you face ongoing stress, which can exhaust the body and impact levels of serotonin in the brain. Introducing stress management techniques and adjusting your diet to

support stress can help reduce levels of cortisol in the body. Examples of lifestyle changes include:

- Relaxing: take your mind off work, turn your phone off and spend some time outside. It's OK to take a day off from the gym too. Although relaxing is something that can be very difficult for people to do as they feel they need to be working and ticking off that to-do list, you should charge yourself as much as you charge your phone.
- Do something you enjoy every day: playing music, baking and drawing are just some examples. Too often, we push ourselves and prioritise work, which leaves little 'me' time.
- Meditation: a proven technique to reduce stress and anxiety.[14] There are many apps which can help you with guided meditation and breathing exercises. People get frustrated with meditation but it works the same way as going to the gym: you don't get fit overnight, nor can you train your brain to meditate in one session.
- Exercise: it is well documented that exercise can increase levels of serotonin in the brain.[15] Exercise also increases levels of brain-derived neurotrophic factor (BDNF), which is important for brain health and plasticity.[16] It's important to do exercise that you enjoy or you will not stick to it. Don't feel pressured to

go to the gym if you hate it. Perhaps taking part in a team sport can also help elevate your mood if you feel loneliness is contributing to your mental health state.

Genetics

You may have a family member with mental health issues or feel you can't explain your mental health. While genetics are just one piece of the puzzle, there are some variants which are linked to mental health issues. Examples include the methylenetetrahydrofolate reductase (MTHFR) gene and the catechol-O-methyltransferase (COMT) gene, which can impact neurotransmitter production and metabolism therefore resulting in anxiety and depression.[17]

Sleep

Living with stress or worries can impact your ability to sleep but poor sleep can also have an impact on your mental health. Our circadian rhythm or internal body clock tells the body naturally to go to sleep at night. Factors such as lack of sunlight, shift work and jet lag can impact sleep patterns. If sleep quality suffers, it can impact alertness and cause anxiety and depression symptoms.[18]

Modern day lifestyles can also mean you do not get sun exposure and spend too much time exposed to artificial light. The biggest example of this is your phone which emits blue light; this can suppress the sleep hormone melatonin so can impact sleep quality.[19] To combat this, you may want to invest in blue-light blocking glasses to wear in the evening and try not to use your phone two hours before bedtime. Adjusting your bedroom with blackout blinds, making it a cool temperature and also using red lights may help improve your sleep, as well as eating well and trying to limit caffeine.

What testing can I do to understand my mental health better?

As there is no direct blood test to diagnose a mental health condition, it is usually done by talking to the patient and a series of questionnaires and assessment by the doctor.

There are, however, some functional medicine tests which may be of use if you can't explain your symptoms and you want to try to find the root cause of a mental health issue. The results can be used to create nutrition and lifestyle changes which can support your mental health.

- Genetics: consider a nervous system test to understand dopamine metabolism and serotonin metabolism pathways. I recommend Lifecode Gx as its reports are the most thorough, but you will need to work with a functional medicine practitioner to understand yours fully and how to apply it.

- Stress hormone: four-point cortisol testing can help you identify if stress is an issue in mood disorders.
- Blood testing: to check levels of vitamins B9 (folate), B12 and D and homocysteine.
- Organic acid testing: to understand neurotransmitter health and nutrient need.
- Essential fatty acids: to identify levels and balance of omega-3 and omega-6 fatty acids.

What about being vegetarian or vegan?

If you are vegetarian or vegan, you should be mindful of the quality of your diet. As already mentioned, protein and omega-3 fatty acids are specifically important for mental well-being. You need to ensure you are getting food which is classed as a complete protein source. As vegan sources of protein tend to be inferior to animal protein, they may not contain all the amino acids (building blocks) which help make neurotransmitters. As I discussed in the foundations chapter, some people consider food combining if they are vegan, or they could include vegan protein shakes made from different sources of protein. If you don't eat fish, you rely on nuts and seeds for your omega-3 fatty acids. The problem here is with the conversion of these fatty acids that work to support brain function. Your body has to work harder to convert them, but in any case, you should make sure you are eating flaxseed, chia seeds and walnuts daily and perhaps consider an algae supplement which is rich in omega-3 fatty acids. For more discussion on plant-based diets, see page 31.

Eating disorders

Studies show that LGBTQ+ individuals are at a higher risk of developing an eating disorder compared to heterosexual populations.[20] For example, transgender or non-binary persons may feel they need to conform to gender constructs so they may restrict the amount of food they eat. Or gay men with body dissatisfaction might try to conform to a specific societal physical ideal. This could take the form of pressure to keep a low body fat percentage so they restrict eating, or they want to be heavier to be more accepted into groups of men who like bigger men, and so have episodes of binge eating. Additionally, trauma, shame, low self-esteem and feelings of rejection can all play a role in making an individual more vulnerable to an eating disorder.

These factors can cause unhealthy eating patterns to develop and obsession with food or a particular body shape. The most common eating disorders include anorexia, bulimia, binge eating and orthorexia nervosa, which is an unhealthy obsession with eating healthily.

You may feel it's an impossible cycle to break out of but it's vital that you get help if you feel you are suffering with unhealthy eating habits. There is support available so it is important to make contact either with your doctor who can refer you for assessment, or with some of the listed services on page 267.

Working with eating disorders can feel like an uphill struggle but there are some things you can do to help improve your quality of life. The most crucial tip is to let go of feeling you need to diet, which can be a journey you have to take step by step. A sensible intuitive eating approach without dietary rules is what you want to aim for. It may sound daunting but letting go of calorie counting, macro counting, elimination of food groups, allowing yourself to enjoy a bit of sugar with reassurance that it won't harm you etc. can be so stress relieving and ultimately lead you to start loving the body you are in, which creates positive psychology. I recommend working with an eating disorder nutrition specialist alongside psychological support while you are in the recovery process.

Anabolic steroids and recreational drugs

A side-effect of using anabolic steroids can be feelings of anxiety and depression. You can also feel low when you stop using steroids as hormone levels change and you may struggle to keep the body you have while on steroids. So if you have a sudden change in mood from either using steroids or stopping them, it is probably associated with this.

The same goes for recreational drugs. We discussed

in Chapter 7 what goes up must come down, so if you are using recreational drugs feelings of low mood and anxiety the week after may be attributed to this. When you use stimulants, they cause a surge in neurotransmitters in the brain, and once the effects have worn off, you can be left with low levels or imbalanced neurotransmitters.

Supplements

5-Hydroxytryptophan (5-HTP)
This is a serotonin precursor. Some small studies show that it may help increase levels of serotonin in the body which can improve mood and help sleep.[21] Be mindful not to use 5-HTP when using antidepressant medication.

B complex
B-complex vitamins are what the body needs to make neurotransmitters such as dopamine and serotonin. A B-complex supplement can also support maintenance of normal homocysteine levels as discussed above.

Zinc
Supplementing with zinc can support the nervous system to function well and has been shown to be a useful therapy when used in conjunction with antidepressant medication.[22]

Psychology

Nutrition will only get you so far in helping your mental health. A functional medicine approach looks deeper at the source of what could be impacting your mental health. This includes lifestyle factors and psychological factors that could either be the reason for mental health conditions, or keep you from recovering from them.

I want you to take a moment from reading this and just be curious about your emotions, your feelings. What do your mind and body want to feel? Sometimes we are too cerebral and so focused on the anxieties, pressures and conflicts that we don't give our bodies the chance to feel and be heard. I have been guilty of this myself. A prime example was when I was in an unhealthy relationship but the anxiety was drawing me in. I was far from myself, and my friends described me as a constant ball of anxiety. But I did not understand why I was feeling anxious, nor did I notice when I was breathless on the way to my boyfriend's house. It took my first session of psychotherapy to make me stop and really listen to my body; then it clicked that my body was actually aware of times that it felt 'danger' even if I was not conscious of this. The first step in working on yourself is listening to your body and helping connect it to your mind. Actioning and learning to act differently can take years of work, and like a muscle, the brain needs constant training or it can quite easily slip back into old ways.

'What does it feel like when someone asks you if you love yourself?' This question can make you stop in your tracks, or at least make you think about the answer for a while afterwards. Being LGBTQ+ is not the easiest way to be. Many of us grew up with a lot of rejection and shame in a heteronormative society. We were told to toughen up and not cry as kids so we managed to build this great wall of defence which is often so thick that nobody can penetrate it. This can sometimes mean that we feel alone in relationships as our past trauma haunts us. We may also be attracted to rejection, perhaps because of daddy issues or other trauma from the past. We may not realise what true love is and be drawn to anxious or jealous love and pick a partner who may represent a figure from our past.

We all have a scared child inside us. If you look back to your childhood, there was most likely trauma of some sort. As a result, there may be a scared child within you that is quite vulnerable. Perhaps they are under thick layers you have built up to protect yourself and survive as a minority in this world. This can result in your emotions and feelings being blocked, which ultimately makes your mental health worse. Fundamentally the inner child wants to be loved and respected, both by you and by others – sometimes being loved by you can be the hardest part. This is about accepting yourself for who you are without shame and giving less thought to what others think of you. As long as what you do is safe, legal and consensual, it should be free from judgement and opinion. Once you allow yourself to be who you are without worrying about what you think you should be, you will be a happier person. This will also allow you to accept love from yourself and authentic love from others.

Loving yourself will help you establish boundaries, which can be an issue across the board from friendships, relationships, work and beyond. Can you say no? Do you know when to let go of unhealthy relationships? Being assertive, setting boundaries and saying no may sound daunting and also make you feel anxious but it's your fundamental right. For every time you do something you don't want to, it feels like you are chipping away at your core bit by bit. The 'people pleaser' springs to mind as I write this, and examples can include helping a friend move house when you don't feel able to, lending someone money when you know you won't get it back, taking drugs when you don't want to or thinking you have to go to party when you are tired. It may be tempting to be a 'yes' person for the sake of ease, but the result can be very draining for your psychology and well-being.

There are ways to begin unlearning the defence-first approach and probably the best way is to begin a talking therapy. It may be a bit of a step to begin this process, but trust me, you can change your whole outlook on life.

It took a while in therapy for me to learn what vulnerability meant and how it applied to being gay. It has also helped me question relationships, rejection, communication, jealousy, shame and, most important, knowing when it's time to leave and stop flogging a dead horse. You should be able to feel accepted by your partner and not have to make excuses if you like something or want to do something. Sometimes people project their shame and insecurities on you, and if you are an empath, you take and absorb that energy. People can't be rescued from their shame but you must do what you can to rescue yourself from your own feelings. We are all imperfect to some degree and we can't help it. Learning to be vulnerable is probably one of the hardest things you have to do. It goes against the grain to come out from behind the wall of defence as there is a possibility of rejection when you express vulnerability. This is essentially what we fear the most, yet we have, as a community, been constantly rejected, so hiding behind a defence wall is what we do best.

Social media and apps can trigger a rollercoaster of emotions. You can easily forget that in their posts people put their best filtered foot forward and it can play with your brain circuitry. A gym locker room progress pic, a beach selfie or 'luxe life' shopping trip can all make you feel you aren't enough compared to others, and arouse jealousy. This will happen whether you like it or not: social media is designed for the user to seek validation from others, get more likes and comments. Can you imagine taking a picture and uploading the first shot without a filter? No, you wouldn't, but this is not an authentic presence. In fact, some of the most stressed individuals out there can be influencers because they have to look perfect in every single picture.

The same can be said, or even worse, for dating apps. These dig deep into your core feelings of rejection and not being good enough. These apps have a lot to answer for in their ability to impact LGBTQ+ individuals' lives. In addition to the social media trauma, people experience rejection, racism, discrimination and sex shaming to the point they don't feel good enough. This can happen both directly and indirectly and sometimes you may not notice the effect these apps are having on your well-being. The pressure of society can make you feel burnt out and fatigued by life, and the knock-on effect is that your mental health suffers. If you feel social media or dating apps are impacting your mental health, one of the most empowering things you can do is take a break. You don't need to post if you don't want to and you don't need to be on dating apps if they aren't working for you. The peer pressure you give yourself can easily be relieved by stopping and evaluating your use of them. Perhaps you're not into casual sex but you feel you should be engaging in it because everyone else is and if you're not using the apps then you will never find love. Yes, this is the dialogue you tell yourself and it actually just masks what you truly want in life. Sometimes unfollowing those who don't make you feel great or giving yourself a break from social media or dating apps can be so refreshing and you may find other ways to date or seek company.

One other pressure we have taken from heterosexual norms is the need to find 'the one'. I remember speaking to my therapist, concerned about who would be 'the one' in my life. He simply replied that the unlikely combination of Disney and porn have made us feel we need to find that perfect person to fall in love with, that they need to tick every single box and be faultless. In reality, this person doesn't exist but we naturally seek them out. Often, we can be so quick to pass on someone because they made a mistake or they don't fit a certain profile. This can lead to endless searching because nobody will be good enough. It goes without saying that you need to find someone who respects you, but, like you, they will not be perfect. They will have faults, wind you up sometimes and just be themselves. Relationships are about establishing boundaries, having mutual respect but also not pressuring someone to be something that they are not.

As you get older, you realise that a partnership is more than looks and sex. It's about how someone treats you and if they can be vulnerable with you. However, like you, a relationship needs work and won't always be perfect so it's important you have open communication, and where one falls down, the other picks up.

You can also learn to communicate effectively and approach arguments with an open mind, listening with intent rather than listening with intent to reply. It's amazing the power of vulnerability in arguments. If you go into battle with your wall up, you will be met with another wall. Try a different approach next time you have an argument with your partner or loved one; it may be the very thing that opens up communication to your partner and you both feeling valued and respected in the relationship. Two people do have to come to the party, though, so it can't just be one person expressing vulnerability.

There is a difference between expressing vulnerability and fixing someone. That you can't do. You can be there for someone but they must address their own scared inner child the same way you have been working on yours. You also need to find a way to hold onto your own identity and boundaries when you find love as this helps your overall well-being and helps contribute to a successful relationship. Finally, you do need to know when a relationship is over and it's time to walk away – when it's affecting your mental health and limiting your ability to live your true authentic self.

Writing this chapter has come from deep within my heart. I have been through everything I have described above and I'm still learning every single day. While nutrition is my profession, it would be wrong to write this book without discussing the psychosocial factors that contribute to mental well-being. I want to reiterate my words in the beginning that if you feel your mental health is suffering for any reason, please don't suffer in silence. There is so much support out there, you just have to be vulnerable enough to take it.

9. LGBTQ+ FERTILITY NUTRITION

Traditionally, having a baby required a man's sperm and a woman's egg and therefore having biological children was restricted to heterosexual relationships. For LGBTQ+ individuals, there were limited options so many chose the adoption route to create a family. Now, with advances in technology and equality legislation, LGBTQ+ individuals can have a biological child using fertility treatment with a third party donor, providing eggs, sperm or acting as a surrogate to carry the pregnancy.

Cisgendered males and men in same-sex relationships need to find a surrogate, and either the surrogate supplies their own eggs or a donor egg is used.

Cisgendered females and women in lesbian relationships need a donor sperm and have the option of intrauterine insemination (IUI) or in vitro fertilisation (IVF).

Transgender people have options depending on the partner they have. Transgender males have the option to become pregnant if they have a functioning vagina, ovaries and uterus and stop hormone treatment. Those with a cisgender female partner may also elect for her to be inseminated with donor sperm. Transgender females, before hormone replacement therapy, can act as a sperm donor or, if they have a cisgendered male partner, have the option of surrogacy and egg donation. It is also possible for transgender people to freeze eggs or ovarian tissue and sperm to consider fertility options at a later date. This would be conducted before gender-affirming hormone and surgical treatments as these may affect fertility.

Non-binary people with functional reproductive systems may be able to give birth and access fertility treatments as appropriate.

Treatment options

Intrauterine insemination (IUI)
IUI is also known as artificial insemination. The higher quality sperm are separated and injected directly into the uterus where they are left to fertilise eggs naturally. IUI is a more natural process than IVF so can mean fewer drugs. It is less expensive than IVF but also less successful.

In vitro fertilisation (IVF)
IVF is different from IUI, as eggs are removed from the body and fertilised in the lab then the best embryos

are put back into the womb. A person undergoing IVF will have various medical appointments and it can take some time for the appointments and tests to be completed. A cycle of IVF treatment can be three to six weeks and involves a number of stages:

- Medication to stimulate the ovaries to produce eggs
- Egg collection
- Sperm sample generated or donor sperm taken from the freezer
- Medication to prepare the womb lining
- Eggs mixed with sperm in the laboratory
- Two to five days after, embryo(s) are transferred to the womb
- Date given to take a pregnancy test

IVF is a better treatment in older people or if you have fertility or gynaecological issues. Couples where both partners have a uterus have the option of reciprocal IVF, where one partner provides eggs and one partner carries the pregnancy.

Surrogacy

This is the main treatment for gay men or male couples who want to have a biological child. It means finding someone who will carry a child and give birth to it for you. The process involves using sperm with the surrogate's eggs or donor eggs.

Nutrition and fertility

Addressing your nutrition and lifestyle prior to fertility can help promote hormone balance as well as the quality of eggs and therefore improve chances of successful treatment and a healthy, successful pregnancy. It can also help improve sperm health including helping with reduced sperm count, quality and motility, as well as erectile dysfunction.

Below are recommendations to give your body the best support and chance of successful fertility.

The first step is to begin to work on your current diet and lifestyle. You should start to prepare your body for a successful pregnancy three months prior to your fertility treatment. There is even research backing up the use of a Mediterranean diet in improving the chances of successful IVF treatment.[1] If you are unsure of what exactly the Mediterranean diet is, it's similar to the foundations set out in Chapter 2. Focus should be on lean meats, fish, eggs, wholegrains, healthy fats, legumes, fruit and vegetables, while minimising processed foods and refined sugars. Not only can this help with the success of treatment, it can also help you keep a healthy weight, which can support hormonal health, regulate the menstrual cycle and support energy production while you are going through the treatment process.

Diet can also support sperm health so don't forget the male role in fertility.

Fertility treatment as well as changing your diet can be stressful. You may feel the burden of wanting to give it your best chance so you try to be 'perfect'. It's important you are kind to yourself, and even if you make just a few changes a week that is great. Start by reducing sugar and increasing the proportion of vegetables in your diet and go from there. If you start gradually as you lead up to your treatment, by the time you have got to it, you should be feeling the benefits of good health.

How to support your fertility and pregnancy

Eat your greens!
Green vegetables such as asparagus, broccoli, cabbage, kale and spinach are rich in folate. Folate is a B vitamin which is important for pregnancy as it can help prevent neural tube defects (incomplete development of the brain or spinal cord) and promote healthy growth and development. Your doctor will recommend you take folic acid, the synthetic version of folate, when trying to get pregnant and during the first few months of pregnancy. It's recommended to take 400mcg of folic acid per day both prior to conception and in the early stages of pregnancy.

Fibre
Fibre is essential for keeping your digestion moving and can help promote hormone balance by helping to reduce excess levels of hormones by removing them through your colon.

Constipation can cause hormones to be reabsorbed by the body leading to hormone balance symptoms such as painful or heavy periods, bloating and other symptoms involving excess oestrogens. If you are prone to constipation, try to include wholegrains such as oats, brown rice, quinoa, rye, spelt, millet and buckwheat with each main meal, as well as making sure you have adequate amounts of fruit and vegetables in your diet.

Water
You need more water when you are pregnant. Water is needed to pass nutrients to your baby and also helps increase amniotic fluid levels, the fluid that surrounds your baby and an important part in fetal development. It's therefore important to make sure you are making a special effort to maintain healthy fluid levels.

Calcium
Calcium is a key mineral during pregnancy to aid the development of the baby. It helps form bones as well as support heart, muscles, hormones and nerves.

Iron
Blood volume increases in the body when you are pregnant so your body needs to produce more haemoglobin. Iron is an essential mineral in this process. While pregnant, you should ensure you get adequate levels of lean meat as well as green leafy vegetables.

If you do not have enough iron, you can be at risk of iron-deficiency anaemia, which is quite common in pregnant individuals.

Vitamin A

It's recommended to avoid high doses of vitamin A as this can build up in the liver and cause harm to the baby. This means you should avoid eating high amounts of foods rich in vitamin A. Vitamin A in the harmless carotenoid form is found in vegetables, and it is hard to eat too much of this form. Your baby still needs some amounts of vitamin A to support immunity and aid embryonic development of the heart, lungs and central nervous system. So it is safe to eat plenty of vegetables.

Vitamin D

Adequate levels of vitamin D can help your baby develop strong and healthy bones. As mentioned in previous chapters, vitamin D comes mainly from sunlight so if you don't get outside much or if you live in a cold climate, you may not be getting enough. Try to go outside each day, allowing your skin to be exposed to sunlight. But if you are deficient, you may benefit from supplementing to correct this.

Oily fish

Oily fish are a source of omega-3 fatty acids needed to make hormones, so if you don't eat fish it can impact fertility. There are, however, some fish to avoid due to their high mercury content which may affect the baby's nervous system. This amount would normally need to be high to have an effect, but to err on the safe side avoid excess tuna, marlin, swordfish and shark.

Iodine
Iodine helps develop the baby's brain and it is important to get 200mcg a day when pregnant or breastfeeding. Seaweed is a very concentrated source so don't eat excess amounts as there is risk of toxicity. If in doubt, ask your doctor or nutrition practitioner.

Selenium
Selenium is an antioxidant which helps protect DNA and minimise birth defects. It is useful for both sperm and egg health and can support sperm motility, so it is important for those donating sperm to consume selenium.

Zinc
Zinc is important for sperm health. It can help improve sperm motility, even in those with poor sperm motility.

Avoid certain cheeses and undercooked foods
While pregnant, you should avoid certain cheeses such as blue cheese, brie and camembert. These contain a bacteria called listeria which can be harmful to your baby. Additionally, eggs should be cooked fully as well as meat, fish and shellfish. The current NHS advice

on egg consumption states you can eat raw, partially cooked and fully cooked eggs as long as they have the British Lion stamp on them.

What can impact fertility?

Your weight
Having a healthy body fat percentage can help maintain healthy hormone levels and aid getting pregnant. Those who are underweight may find their periods become irregular or stop altogether. The process of trying to gain weight can be just as stressful as losing weight so again take your time with it. Gaining weight doesn't mean gorging on unhealthy food but nor does it mean denying yourself food if you are craving it. The middle line is having a healthy relationship with food and using food as a tool, such as increasing the amount of healthy fats in your diet as these are calorie dense so can help you reach a surplus in the day. Evaluating your output is also a good idea; by this I mean the amount of exercise you are doing as this can interfere with weight gain and hormone health.

Stress
Fertility treatments can be a source of stress. There is always the fear that the treatment may not work or that you may suffer a miscarriage. You can find yourself in quite a vulnerable and defeated state if you are not getting the results you want. While nutrition is

a big consideration when you want to optimise your fertility, emotional well-being is equally important. It's hard to say definitively if stress impacts fertility directly but stress reduction techniques may support you while you are going through assisted fertility treatment.[2] They can help your relationship, help you persevere and deal with other aspects of your lifestyle not related to fertility. We all cope with stress differently. Some may find an evening laughing with their friends can be therapeutic but there are more focused ways such as yoga, mindfulness, tai chi or meditation, or you may benefit from speaking with a professional. Take time to review the stress reduction tips on page 44.

Smoking

Smoking impacts fertility and chances of a successful fertility treatment. It can impact sperm quality, hormone health, egg and ovary health, the success rate of IVF, increase risk of pregnancy and birth complications, and affect the physical and mental health of offspring.[3] To get help with giving up smoking, you may want to explore treatment options with a smoking cessation clinic. The primary factor in regard to diet is ensuring your blood sugar is balanced, which can lessen cravings.

Alcohol

The safest advice is not to drink alcohol during pregnancy but it may also impact your chances of successful fertility treatment and live birth rates.[4]

Caffeine

Too much caffeine increases the risk of miscarriage and of babies being born with low birthweight. The NHS suggests that a person should limit caffeine to 200mg per day, which is equivalent to about two daily espressos. Be mindful that caffeine is found in tea, coffee, energy drinks, sodas and chocolate, and amounts of caffeine can differ in different shops or brands.

Plastics

Evidence shows that exposure to plastics, particularly the chemical bisphenol A (BPA), may impact fertility and chances of successful IVF treatment as well as male fertility.[5] BPA acts as an endocrine disruptor that mimics the hormone oestrogen. BPA is commonly found in plastic containers, canned foods, toiletries, intimate hygiene products, till receipts, electronics, CDs and DVDs and even dental filling sealants. It's best to switch to glass and stainless steel for storage as replacements for BPA and phthalates (found in other plastics) may also negatively impact fertility.

Anabolic steroids and testosterone

A side-effect of using anabolic steroids or testosterone is that it can lower fertility. Using testosterone can mean natural production of testosterone is switched off, which can lead to reduced sperm counts and reduction in the size of the testes. It's recommended to stop using testosterone six months prior to donating sperm, by which time quality and count should have returned to normal levels.

If you are a transgender male on hormone therapy wishing to get pregnant, you will need to stop taking testosterone as this can impact ovulation and hormone levels, and can cause birth defects.[6]

Recreational drugs

This area isn't studied as much as alcohol and smoking but what we do know is that using drugs such as cannabis can reduce fertility in terms of sperm quality, ovulation and egg development. Other drugs may also contribute to fertility problems and so it is advisable to stop taking drugs before treatment, donation and during pregnancy.

Health conditions

Polycystic ovary syndrome (PCOS), ovarian cysts, endometriosis, fibroids, damage to fallopian tubes, uterine or cervical disorders and other hormone imbalances can impact fertility. If you feel you are suffering with any of these and are not getting any relief by following the foundations of this book, do reach out to someone who is a fertility nutrition specialist trained in functional medicine. They can help you find the root cause of the problem and coach you through fertility treatment. There are directories listed in the resource section on page 263.

Dealing with morning sickness

Some of you may experience morning sickness when pregnant. It usually lasts for the first three months of pregnancy but sometimes longer. Below are some ideas you can try to help limit the intensity of morning sickness:

- Eat smaller meals and snacks to support your blood sugar.
- Limit sugar as much as possible.
- Cold foods may be more tolerable than warm foods, as warm foods smell stronger.
- Stay clear of tea and coffee.
- Drink ginger tea: just steep slices of fresh ginger root in hot water for a few minutes.
- Sip on a homemade smoothie or soup.
- A B6 supplement may help with nausea and is regarded as safe during pregnancy, although check with your doctor who understands your medical history.

Testing

As part of your fertility treatment, you will most likely undergo a range of testing to understand your hormones, as well as a sexual health screen and semen analysis for the donor. Screening can assess if you are ovulating, why not if you aren't ovulating, reveal any sexually transmitted infections as well as assess sperm quality.

If you are having issues with fertility and are at risk of miscarriage, I recommend having genetic testing for the gene methylenetetrahydrofolate reductase (MTHFR). This gene breaks down folic acid into the active form for the body to use and there are some associations between MTHFR and fertility.[7] Those with a variant in the gene may have difficulty metabolising folic acid and it is therefore recommended that they supplement with L-methylfolate, which is the active form and ready for the body to use. Genetic testing can be completed with many companies but I recommend Lifecode Gx as it offers full testing of the folate pathway. I suggest you speak to a trained nutrition practitioner who can help you interpret the results.

Additionally, the DUTCH Test is helpful to fully evaluate stress hormones and reproductive hormones, and how they are metabolising in the body (see the resources section on page 264. A comprehensive fertility evaluation can improve your health and the chances of successful fertility treatment and pregnancy. Sperm DNA Fragmentation Testing may also be something to consider. It is a more advanced sperm analysis which can assess sperm DNA quality, which if badly damaged, can impact fertility success. Markers assess the ability of the sperm to reach the egg, likelihood of fertilisation and whether fertilisation is likely to achieve a full-term pregnancy. You can use the results of this test to make lifestyle changes to improve sperm DNA health. Sperm DNA Fragmentation Testing is available through Examen Labs (https://examenlab.com/).

Supplements

Supplements are quite tricky to navigate with fertility treatment and through pregnancy so you should always check anything you are taking with your doctor.

Generally speaking, a good prenatal multivitamin should cover everything you need to support fertility and pregnancy. Your doctor may recommend extra supplementing if you are vegan, have vitamin D deficiency or if extra folate is warranted.

Bottom line

I can understand that this is a lot of information to consider if you are about to embark on fertility treatment, so to reiterate, you should try to limit the stress of having to improve your diet as much as possible. You may be eager and impatient to conceive and have a healthy pregnancy but nutrition is not a quick fix and nor do you get results overnight, which is why many individuals get frustrated when they don't see change straight away. Fertility can be a long and sometimes lonely journey, so don't be hesitant to speak to a professional, either for nutrition advice or psychological support to help you along the way. But, in summary:

- Apply the foundations in Chapter 2 to diet

- Achieve a healthy weight
- Have a healthy exercise routine
- Add functional fertility foods
- Limit and support factors which can impact fertility and pregnancy

10. FINAL THOUGHTS

This book has given you many things to think about. I have tried to cover most of the subjects that are relevant to LGBTQ+ health and some of you can benefit from the information in every single chapter. This may make you feel a little overwhelmed, not knowing where to start and what to prioritise. The golden rule is not to feel burdened by anything you can do to improve your health. This is why I emphasise in each chapter to start with just one or two changes and build from there. This is less effort than a whole programme and you are more likely to stick to it as you're creating a positive mindset.

Adhering to the nutrition advice gets easier over time. As you begin to see improvements in your energy, skin, weight, digestion etc., you will be more motivated to continue to do things to support your health. I don't ever expect anyone to be perfect and nor should you feel any shame about eating sugar occasionally, having fast food now and then or even going to a party. What you will feel, though, is that when you have moments like this, they may not be as enjoyable if you're in a run of healthy eating, as you will feel nourished and not so keen to do things that take you out of that bubble. If you do have a late night party, for example, do it without guilt but know what you need to do to get back on track.

Remember it's not just about healthy eating – lifestyle plays a huge role in feeling well. It's important to take regular exercise within your means but most important to support your lifestyle and help reduce stress. Everyone has their own stressors and yet self-care seems to be the one thing we lack. As LGBTQ+ individuals, we have been brought up feeling less in society, fighting for equality and always feeling the need to outshine to impress others. Dealing with these daily microaggressions and imposter syndrome adds to your stress levels. Be curious about this stress and your reluctance to relax and have some self-care. Just as with diet, you need to take some steps to heal your lifestyle; and for it to be long-lasting, follow the bit-by-bit approach.

The world has changed due to the Covid-19 pandemic. For LGBTQ+ individuals, this can mean several things. They may be at home with their family and aren't able to be their true self, come out or they feel they have to live a secret life. They don't have the usual satisfaction of meeting others or travelling; they may be experiencing loneliness, feelings of impending doom, unemployment, financial difficulties, sickness and other lifestyle changes. The world is now a very different place and social tensions are running high; unfortunately we just need to adapt to living in this new state, while we try to get fulfilment in our daily lives.

There is no place for in-fighting within the LGBTQ+ community. It's time we let go of stereotypes, stop shaming, end discrimination and racism, and come together as a unit to help others who need our support. Yes, this is like moving a mountain but even small things can make a change. Try saying hi to someone you've seen in the coffee shop or gym time and time again, smile at someone at a dance party, be kinder to yourself and others and educate yourself about the community and its history.

You now have the knowledge to support your health in the best way. LGBTQ+ health needs are very valid and no longer ignored. This book has a very special place in my heart and I'm honoured to have the platform but also to be able to use my skill to help those who need it. I invite you to share what you have learned from this book with others. Many people could benefit from the knowledge you have gained from this book. You could be in a bar, gym, café, at work or even at a dance party and strike up a conversation about health. You most likely will know when someone can benefit from some of the support in this book. They may not listen straight away or have other ideas about what is healthy but you have planted the seed. Helping others helps to counter the way the world is going and makes you feel more connected.

I invite you to stay in touch with me, let me know how you are getting on and follow the conversation on social media, my podcast or through my website thenakednutritionist.co.uk. I am indebted to those who believed in me, supported this book project and stuck by me throughout the crowdfunding campaign and the writing process. Thank you from the bottom of my heart.

Daniel

APPENDIX I: FOOD SOURCES OF VITAMINS AND MINERALS

Vitamin A
Bok choy, cantaloupe, carrots, dark leafy greens (beet greens, mustard greens, spinach, Swiss chard, turnip greens, etc.), fish, milk, liver, sweet potato, red, green and yellow peppers, tropical fruits

Vitamin D
Egg yolks, fortified foods (milk, oat and nut milk, etc.), liver (beef), mackerel, salmon, sardines, tuna. Sunlight is the best source of vitamin D.

Vitamin E
Almonds, asparagus, avocado, dark leafy greens, sunflower seeds

Vitamin K
Asparagus, bok choy, broccoli, Brussels sprouts, cabbage, cauliflower, dark leafy greens, parsley

Vitamin B1 (thiamin)
Barley, beans (black, lima, navy, pinto, etc.), lentils, oats, peas, sunflower seeds

Vitamin B2 (riboflavin)
Almonds, asparagus, beef, broccoli, cheese, dark leafy greens, eggs, halibut, milk, mushrooms, poultry, salmon, soybeans, spinach, yoghurt

Vitamin B3 (niacin)
Beef, lamb, rice (brown), poultry, salmon, sardines, shrimp, tuna

Vitamin B6 (pyridoxine)
Bananas, beef, potato, poultry, salmon, spinach, sunflower seeds, sweet potato, tuna

Vitamin B9 (folate)
Asparagus, beans (black, garbanzo, kidney, navy, pinto, etc.), broccoli, dark leafy greens, lentils

Vitamin B12 (cobalamin)
Beef, cheese, clams, cod, crab, eggs, lamb, mackerel, milk (cow), mussels, poultry, salmon, sardines, scallops, shrimp, tuna, yoghurt

Vitamin C
Broccoli, Brussels sprouts, cabbage, cantaloupe, cauliflower, dark leafy greens, grapefruit, kiwi, lemons,

limes, oranges, papaya, pineapple, potato, red, green and yellow peppers, spinach, strawberries, tomatoes

Calcium
Cheese, dark leafy greens, sardines, sesame seeds, tofu, yoghurt

Chloride
Soy sauce, table salt

Copper
Apricots (dried), asparagus, dark chocolate, dark leafy greens, lentils, liver (beef), mushrooms, nuts, seeds

Cysteine
Beef, cheese, eggs, poultry, sunflower seeds, whey protein, yoghurt

Fluoride
Drinking water, fish, tea

Iodine
Cod, eggs, milk (cow), salmon, sardines, scallops, sea vegetables (seaweeds and algae), shrimp, strawberries, tuna

Iron
Asparagus, beans, bok choy, cumin, dark leafy greens,

eggs, leeks, lentils, offal, parsley, poultry, red meat, shellfish, turmeric

Magnesium
Beans (black, navy, soy), cashews, dark leafy greens, quinoa, seeds (pumpkin, sesame, sunflower)

Manganese
Beans (lima, chickpea, white, navy), cinnamon, cloves, dark leafy greens, oats, pineapple, rice (brown), seeds, turmeric

Molybdenum
Barley, beans (lima, kidney, black, soy, pinto, and chickpea), lentils, oats, peas

Selenium
Asparagus, beef, Brazil nuts, clams, cod, mushrooms, offal (liver, kidney), oysters, poultry, salmon, sardines, shrimp, tofu, tuna

Sodium
Almost all foods contain sodium

Sulphur
Beans (soybeans, black beans, kidney beans, split peas, and white beans), eggs, fish, meat, milk, nuts, poultry

Phosphorus
Fish, eggs, meat, milk, poultry

Potassium
Avocado, banana, beans (lima, soy), beets, dark leafy greens, lentils, potato, sweet potato, yoghurt

Zinc
Asparagus, all beans, beef, lamb, mushrooms, oysters, poultry, scallops, seeds (pumpkin, sesame), shrimp, spinach

APPENDIX 2: RESOURCES

Nutrition practitioner directories

The British Association for Nutrition and Lifestyle Medicine (BANT) is a professional body for Registered Nutrition Practitioners. https://bant.org.uk

Institute for Functional Medicine (IFM) Certified Practitioners are recognised as the most thoroughly trained and tested functional medicine clinicians in their fields. https://www.ifm.org

Testing companies

Invivo Healthcare provides diagnostic functional testing services for many areas of your health including stool, hormones, cardiovascular health and nutritional needs. https://invivohealthcare.com

Genetic testing
Lifecode Gx is a personal health company applying

the latest genomics science to enable a preventative, proactive and personalised approach to health. https://www.lifecodegx.com

Precision Analytical offers the DUTCH Test (Dried Urine Test for Comprehensive Hormones), which is a comprehensive assessment of sex and adrenal hormones and their metabolites. This urine test shows the levels of your hormones as well as how they are breaking down in the body. It also shows your stress hormones throughout the day, which can be useful to understand if high stress is impacting your health and energy. https://dutchtest.com

Supplements

The Natural Dispensary is an independent nutritional supplement company that sells good quality supplement brands, health foods and natural toiletries. https://naturaldispensary.co.uk

Support

Switchboard is a confidential listening service for the LGBTQ+ communities. https://switchboard.lgbt

Stonewall campaigns for the equality of lesbian, gay, bi and trans people across Britain. https://www.stonewall.org.uk 0800 0502020, 9.30 a.m.–4.30 p.m. Monday to Friday (answerphone available outside these hours)

LGBT Foundation is a national charity delivering advice, support and information services to LGBTQ+ communities. https://lgbt.foundation

LGBT Health and Wellbeing works to improve the health, well-being and equality of LGBTQ+ people in Scotland. https://www.lgbthealth.org.uk

LGBT Cymru Helpline offers support and information to the LGBTQ+ community in Wales. https://www.lgbtcymru.org.uk

Imaan is the UK's leading LGBTQ+ Muslim charity. https://imaanlondon.wordpress.com

Drugs and alcohol

Antidote at London Friend is one of the UK's only LGBTQ+ run and targeted drug and alcohol support services. https://londonfriend.org.uk/antidote-drugs-alcohol 020 7833 1674, 10 a.m.–6 p.m., Monday to Friday

Nationwide Twelve-Step groups
A twelve-step programme is a set of guiding principles outlining a course of action for recovery from addiction, compulsion or other behavioural problems. Some have specific LGBTQ+ meetings so look at what your local meeting provides.

- Alcoholics Anonymous UK: 0800 9177 650, https://www.alcoholics-anonymous.org.uk
- Anorexics and Bulimics Anonymous: https://aba12steps.org
- Codependents Anonymous: https://codauk.org
- Cocaine Anonymous: https://cocaineanonymous.org.uk
- Crystal Meth Anonymous UK: https://www.crystalmeth.org.uk
- Narcotics Anonymous UK: https://www.ukna.org
- Overeaters Anonymous: https://www.oagb.org.uk
- Sex Addicts Anonymous: http://saauk.info/en

Sexual health and HIV

56 Dean Street is a friendly, convenient and free NHS sexual health clinic in the heart of London. The Soho-based service also offers full outpatient HIV clinic services. https://dean.st/56deanstreet

GMFA is a gay men's health and sexual health project. https://www.gmfa.org.uk

Terrence Higgins Trust is a national HIV and sexual health charity with information on HIV, sexually transmitted infections and where to get tested. https://www.tht.org.uk

Positively UK can support any aspect of your diagnosis, care and living with HIV. https://positivelyuk.org

Therapy

The following are databases to seek help from a qualified therapist. Ensure that the therapist you choose understands LGBTQ+ issues.

- British Association for Counselling and Psychotherapy: https://www.bacp.co.uk
- UK Council for Psychotherapy: https://www.psychotherapy.org.uk
- Pink Therapy: directory of LGBTQ+ therapists: http://www.pinktherapy.com

Mental health

Beat is a directory of support services and information targeted at those with eating disorders. https://www.beateatingdisorders.org.uk

Mind gives information about mental health support. https://www.mind.org.uk

Mind Out is a mental health service run by and for LGBTQ+ people with experience of mental health issues. https://www.mindout.org.uk

Samaritans offers a safe place for you to talk about whatever's on your mind, at any time. Call free on 116 123 any time. https://www.samaritans.org

Transgender

Mermaids support gender-diverse children and young people until their twentieth birthday, as well as their families and professionals involved in their care. https://mermaidsuk.org.uk

GIRES is a charity that hears and gives a voice to trans and gender non-conforming individuals, including those who are non-binary and non-gender, as well as their families. https://www.gires.org.uk

Fertility

New Family Social is a charity for LGBTQ+ adoptive and foster parents. https://www.newfamilysocial.org.uk

Proud 2B Parents is an inclusive organisation for all routes to parenthood. http://www.proud2bparents.co.uk

First 4 Adoption can help you find an adoption agency. https://www.first4adoption.org.uk

Surrogacy UK is a one stop shop for all information about surrogacy in the UK. https://surrogacyuk.org

LGBTQ+ Financial Family Building Support has compiled a list of charities to help you through the process of fertility treatment or adoption. https://www. gayparentstobe.com/financial/grants-charities

Family Equality lists opportunities for LGBTQ+ family building grants. https://www.familyequality.org/ resources/lgbtq-family-building-grants

Human Fertilisation & Embryology Authority provides information for trans and non-binary people seeking fertility treatment. https://www.hfea.gov.uk

The Fertility Nutrition Centre has a directory of qualified fertility specialist nutrition practitioners. https://fertilitynutritioncentre.org

Housing

Albert Kennedy Trust helps young LGBTQ+ people who are made homeless or living in a hostile environment by providing housing and services to help them live independently. https://www.akt.org.uk

APPENDIX 3: REFERENCES

1. Introduction

1   Blashill, A. J., & Safren, S. A. (2014). 'Sexual orientation and anabolic-androgenic steroids in U.S. adolescent boys'. *Pediatrics*, 133(3), 469–75. https://doi.org/10.1542/peds.2013-2768

2. The Foundations

1   Monteiro, C. A., et al. (2017). 'Commentary: The UN Decade of Nutrition, the NOVA food classification and the trouble with ultra-processing'. *Public Health Nutrition* 21(1), 5–17. https://doi.org/10.1017/S1368980017000234

2   Louzada, M. L., et al. (2015). 'Consumption of ultra-processed foods and obesity in Brazilian adolescents and adults'. *Preventive Medicine*, 81, 9–15. https://doi.org/10.1016/j.ypmed.2015.07.018

    Rico-Campà, A., et al. (2019). 'Association between consumption of ultra-processed foods and all cause mortality: SUN prospective cohort study', *British Medical Journal*, 365, 1949. https://doi.org/10.1136/bmj.l1949

    Schnabel, L., et al. (2018). 'Association Between Ultra-Processed Food Consumption and Functional Gastrointestinal Disorders: Results from the French NutriNet-Santé Cohort'. *American Journal of Gastroenterology*, 113, 8, 1217–8. https://doi.org/10.1038/s41395-018-0137-1

3   Nicolopoulou-Stamati, P., Maipas, S., Kotampasi, C., Stamatis, P., & Hens, L. (2016). 'Chemical Pesticides and Human Health: The Urgent Need for a New Concept in Agriculture'. *Frontiers in Public Health*, 4, 148. https://doi.org/10.3389/fpubh.2016.00148

4   Pesticide Action Network UK. (2020). 'Pesticides in Our Food'. Available at: https://www.pan-uk.org/dirty-dozen-and-clean-fifteen/. [Accessed 9 August 2020]

5   Daley, C. A., Abbott, A., Doyle, P. S., Nader, G. A., & Larson, S. (2010). 'A review of fatty acid profiles and antioxidant content in grass-fed and grain-fed beef'. *Nutrition Journal*, 9, 10. https://doi.org/10.1186/1475-2891-9-10

6   Della Corte, K. W., Perrar, I., Penczynski, K. J., Schwingshackl, L., Herder, C., & Buyken, A. E. (2018). 'Effect of Dietary Sugar Intake on Biomarkers of Subclinical Inflammation: A Systematic Review and Meta-Analysis of Intervention Studies'. *Nutrients*, 10(5), 606. https://doi.org/10.3390/nu10050606

7   Hunter, D., Foster, M., McArthur, J. O., Ojha, R., Petocz, P., & Samman, S. (2011). 'Evaluation of the micronutrient composition of plant foods produced by organic and conventional agricultural methods'. *Critical Reviews in Food Science and Nutrition*, 51(6), 571–82. https://doi.org/10.1080/10408391003721701

8   Berry, S. E., Valdes, A. M., Drew, D. A., et al. (2020). 'Human postprandial responses to food and potential for precision nutrition'. *Nature Medicine*, 6(6), 964–73. https://doi.org/10.1038/s41591-020-0934-0

9   Carabotti, M., Scirocco, A., Maselli, M. A., & Severi, C. (2015). 'The gut-brain axis: interactions between enteric microbiota, central and enteric nervous systems'. *Annals of Gastroenterology*, 28(2), 203–9. https://www.ncbi.nlm.nih.gov/pmc/articles/PMC4367209
    Salem, I., Ramser, A., Isham, N., & Ghannoum, M. A. (2018). 'The Gut Microbiome as a Major Regulator of the Gut-Skin Axis'. *Frontiers in Microbiology*, 9, 1459. https://doi.org/10.3389/fmicb.2018.01459
    Hullar, M. A., Burnett-Hartman, A. N., & Lampe, J. W. (2014). 'Gut Microbes, Diet, and Cancer'. *Cancer Treatment and Research*, 159, 377–99. https://doi.org/10.1007/978-3-642-38007-5_22

10 National Institute for Health and Care Excellence (2008). 'Irritable Bowel Syndrome in Adults: Diagnosis and Management (Clinical guideline [CG61])'. Available at: https://www.nice.org.uk/guidance/cg61/chapter/1-Recommendations. [Accessed 9 August 2020]

Talley, N. J., Zinsmeister, A. R., Dyke, C. V., & Melton, L. (1991). 'Epidemiology of Colonic Symptoms and the Irritable Bowel Syndrome'. *Gastroenterology*, 101(4), 927–34. https://doi.org/10.1016/0016-5085(91)90717-y

11 Arrieta, M. C., Bistritz, L., & Meddings, J. B. (2006). 'Alterations in intestinal permeability'. *Gut*, 55(10), 1512–20. https://doi.org/10.1136/gut.2005.085373

12 Yaribeygi, H., Panahi, Y., Sahraei, H., Johnston, T. P., & Sahebkar, A. (2017). 'The impact of stress on body function: A review'. *EXCLI Journal*, 16, 1057–72. https://doi.org/10.17179/excli2017-480
Yau, Y. H., & Potenza, M. N. (2013). 'Stress and eating behaviors'. *Minerva endocrinologica*, 38(3), 255–67. PMID: 24126546; PMCID: PMC4214609. https://www.ncbi.nlm.nih.gov/pmc/articles/PMC4214609

13 Almeida, C. M., & Malheiro, A. (2016). 'Sleep, immunity and shift workers: A review'. *Sleep Science* (São Paulo, Brazil), 9(3), 164–8. https://doi.org/10.1016/j.slsci.2016.10.007

14 Basavaraj, K. H., Seemanthini, C., & Rashmi, R. (2010). 'Diet in dermatology: present perspectives'. *Indian Journal of Dermatology*, 55(3), 205–10. https://doi.org/10.4103/0019-5154.70662

15 Kober, M. M., & Bowe, W. P. (2015). 'The effect of probiotics on immune regulation, acne, and photoaging'. *International Journal of Women's Dermatology*, 1(2), 85–9. https://doi.org/10.1016/j.ijwd.2015.02.001

16 Proksch, E., Segger, D., Degwert, J., Schunck, M., Zague, V., & Oesser, S. (2014). 'Oral supplementation of specific collagen peptides has beneficial effects on human skin physiology: a double-blind, placebo-controlled study'. *Skin Pharmacology and Physiology*, 27(1), 47–55. https://doi.org/10.1159/000351376

17 Smith, A. D. (2007). 'Folic acid fortification: the good, the bad, and the puzzle of vitamin B-12'. *The American Journal of Clinical Nutrition*, 85(1), 3–5. https://doi.org/10.1093/ajcn/85.1.3

3. Fat Loss and Muscle Gain

1 Daghestani, M. H. (2009). 'A preprandial and postprandial plasma levels of ghrelin hormone in lean, overweight and obese

Saudi females'. *Journal of King Saud University – Science*, 21(2), 119–24. https://doi.org/10.1016/j.jksus.2009.05.001

2   Quidley-Rodriguez, N., & De Santis, J. P. (2017). 'A Literature Review of Health Risks in the Bear Community, a Gay Subculture'. *American Journal of Men's Health*, 11(6), 1673–9. https://doi.org/10.1177/1557988315624507

3   Iraki, J., Fitschen, P., Espinar, S., & Helms, E. (2019). 'Nutrition Recommendations for Bodybuilders in the Off-Season: A Narrative Review'. *Sports* (Basel, Switzerland), 7(7), 154. https://doi.org/10.3390/sports7070154

4   Schoenfeld, B. J., & Aragon, A. A. (2018). 'How much protein can the body use in a single meal for muscle-building? Implications for daily protein distribution'. *Journal of the International Society of Sports Nutrition*, 15, 10. https://doi.org/10.1186/s12970-018-0215-1
Mettler, S., Mitchell, N., & Tipton, K. D. (2010). 'Increased Protein Intake Reduces Lean Body Mass Loss During Weight Loss in Athletes'. *Medicine and Science in Sports and Exercise*, 42(2), 326–37. https://doi.org/10.1249/MSS.0b013e3181b2ef8e

5   Helms, E. R., Aragon, A. A., & Fitschen, P. J. (2014). 'Evidence-based recommendations for natural bodybuilding contest preparation: nutrition and supplementation'. *Journal of the International Society of Sports Nutrition*, 11, 20. https://doi.org/10.1186/1550-2783-11-20

6   Pilz, S., Frisch, S., Koertke, H., Kuhn, J., Dreier, J., Obermayer-Pietsch, B., Wehr, E., & Zittermann, A. (2011). 'Effect of Vitamin D Supplementation on Testosterone Levels in Men'. *Hormone and Metabolic Research*, 43(3), 223–5. https://doi.org/10.1055/s-0030-1269854

7   Prasad, A. S., Mantzoros, C. S., Beck, F. W., Hess, J. W., & Brewer, G. J. (1996). 'Zinc status and serum testosterone levels of healthy adults'. *Nutrition* (Burbank, Calif.), 12(5), 344–8. https://doi.org/10.1016/s0899-9007(96)80058-x

8   Brownlee, K. K., Moore, A. W., & Hackney, A. C. (2005). 'Relationship Between Circulating Cortisol and Testosterone: Influence of Physical Exercise'. *Journal of Sports Science & Medicine*, 4(1), 76–83. https://pubmed.ncbi.nlm.nih.gov/24431964

9   Kumagai, H., Zempo-Miyaki, A., Yoshikawa, T., Tsujimoto, T., Tanaka, K., & Maeda, S. (2016). 'Increased physical activity

has a greater effect than reduced energy intake on lifestyle modification-induced increases in testosterone'. *Journal of Clinical Biochemistry and Nutrition*, 58(1), 84–9. https://doi.org/10.3164/jcbn.15-48

10 Leproult, R., & Van Cauter, E. (2011). 'Effect of 1 Week of Sleep Restriction on Testosterone Levels in Young Healthy Men'. *JAMA*, 305(21), 2173–4. https://doi.org/10.1001/jama.2011.710

11 Nissen, S. L., & Sharp, R. L. (2003). 'Effect of dietary supplements on lean mass and strength gains with resistance exercise: a meta-analysis'. *Journal of Applied Physiology* (Bethesda, Md.: 1985), 94(2), 651–9. https://doi.org/10.1152/japplphysiol.00755.2002

12 Shin, J. H., Park, Y. H., Sim, M., Kim, S. A., Joung, H., & Shin, D. M. (2019). 'Serum level of sex steroid hormone is associated with diversity and profiles of human gut microbiome'. *Research in Microbiology*, 170(4–5), 192–201. https://doi.org/10.1016/j.resmic.2019.03.003

13 Ishikawa, T., Glidewell-Kenney, C., & Jameson, J. L. (2006). 'Aromatase-independent testosterone conversion into estrogenic steroids is inhibited by a 5 alpha-reductase inhibitor'. *Journal of Steroid Biochemistry and Molecular Biology*, 98(2–3), 133–8. https://doi.org/10.1016/j.jsbmb.2005.09.004

14 Khoshbaten, M., Aliasgarzadeh, A., Masnadi, K., Tarzamani, M. K., Farhang, S., Babaei, H., Kiani, J., Zaare, M., & Najafipoor, F. (2010). 'N-acetylcysteine improves liver function in patients with non-alcoholic Fatty liver disease'. *Hepatitis Monthly*, 10(1), 12–16. https://pubmed.ncbi.nlm.nih.gov/22308119

15 Graham, M. R., Grace, F. M., Boobier, W., Hullin, D., Kicman, A., Cowan, D., Davies, B., & Baker, J. S. (2006). 'Homocysteine induced cardiovascular events: a consequence of long term anabolic-androgenic steroid (AAS) abuse'. *British Journal of Sports Medicine*, 40(7), 644–8. https://doi.org/10.1136/bjsm.2005.025668

16 Schnyder, G., Roffi, M., Flammer, Y., Pin, R., & Hess, O. M. (2002). 'Effect of Homocysteine-Lowering Therapy With Folic Acid, Vitamin B12, and Vitamin B6 on Clinical Outcome After Percutaneous Coronary Intervention: The Swiss Heart Study: A Randomized Controlled Trial'. *JAMA*, 288(8), 973–9. https://doi.org/10.1001/jama.288.8.973

17 Zhao, F., Gong, Y., Hu, Y., Lu, M., Wang, J., Dong, J., Chen, D., Chen, L., Fu, F., & Qiu, F. (2015). 'Curcumin and its major metabolites inhibit the inflammatory response induced by lipopolysaccharide: Translocation of nuclear factor-κB as potential target'. *Molecular Medicine Reports*, 11(4), 3087–93. https://doi.org/10.3892/mmr.2014.3079

Hewlings, S. J., & Kalman, D. S. (2017). Curcumin: A Review of Its Effects on Human Health. *Foods* (Basel, Switzerland), 6(10), 92. https://doi.org/10.3390/foods6100092

18 Wang, Q., Liang, X., Wang, L., Lu, X., Huang, J., Cao, J., Li, H., & Gu, D. (2012). 'Effect of omega-3 fatty acids supplementation on endothelial function: a meta-analysis of randomized controlled trials'. *Atherosclerosis*, 221(2), 536–43. https://doi.org/10.1016/j.atherosclerosis.2012.01.006

Minihane, A. M., Armah, C. K., Miles, E. A., Madden, J. M., Clark, A. B., Caslake, M. J., Packard, C. J., Kofler, B. M., Lietz, G., Curtis, P. J., Mathers, J. C., Williams, C. M., & Calder, P. C. (2016). 'Consumption of Fish Oil Providing Amounts of Eicosapentaenoic Acid and Docosahexaenoic Acid That Can Be Obtained from the Diet Reduces Blood Pressure in Adults with Systolic Hypertension: A Retrospective Analysis'. *Journal of Nutrition*, 146(3), 516–23. https://doi.org/10.3945/jn.115.220475

Petersen, M., Pedersen, H., Major-Pedersen, A., Jensen, T., & Marckmann, P. (2002). 'Effect of Fish Oil Versus Corn Oil Supplementation on LDL and HDL Subclasses in Type 2 Diabetic Patients'. *Diabetes Care*, 25(10), 1704–8. https://doi.org/10.2337/diacare.25.10.1704

4. Let's Talk about Sex

1 Parolin, C., Frisco, G., Foschi, C., Giordani, B., Salvo, M., Vitali, B., Marangoni, A., & Calonghi, N. (2018). '*Lactobacillus crispatus* BC5 Interferes With *Chlamydia trachomatis* Infectivity Through Integrin Modulation in Cervical Cells'. *Frontiers in Microbiology*, 9, 2630. https://doi.org/10.3389/fmicb.2018.02630

2 Molina, J. M., Charreau, I., Chidiac, C., Pialoux, G., Cua, E., Delaugerre, et al. for the ANRS IPERGAY Study Group (2018). 'Post-exposure prophylaxis with doxycycline to prevent

sexually transmitted infections in men who have sex with men: an open-label randomised substudy of the ANRS IPERGAY trial'. *Lancet. Infectious Diseases*, 18(3), 308–17. https://doi.org/10.1016/S1473-3099(17)30725-9

3   Kabara, J. J., Swieczkowski, D. M., Conley, A. J., & Truant, J. P. (1972). 'Fatty acids and derivatives as antimicrobial agents'. *Antimicrobial Agents and Chemotherapy*, 2(1), 23–8. https://doi.org/10.1128/aac.2.1.23

4   Petricevic, L., Kaufmann, U., Domig, K. J., Kraler, M., Marschalek, J., Kneifel, W., & Kiss, H. (2014). 'Molecular detection of *Lactobacillus* species in the neovagina of male-to-female transsexual women'. *Scientific Reports*, 4, 3746. https://doi.org/10.1038/srep03746

5   Kaufmann, U., Domig, K. J., Lippitsch, C. I., Kraler, M., Marschalek, J., Kneifel, W., Kiss, H., & Petricevic, L. (2014). 'Ability of an orally administered lactobacilli preparation to improve the quality of the neovaginal microflora in male to female transsexual women'. *European Journal of Obstetrics, Gynecology, and Reproductive Biology*, 172, 102–5. https://doi.org/10.1016/j.ejogrb.2013.10.019

6   Jang, D. J., Lee, M. S., Shin, B. C., Lee, Y. C., & Ernst, E. (2008). 'Red ginseng for treating erectile dysfunction: a systematic review'. *British Journal of Clinical Pharmacology*, 66(4), 444–50. https://doi.org/10.1111/j.1365-2125.2008.03236.x

7   Chan S. W. (2012). '*Panax ginseng, Rhodiola rosea* and *Schisandra chinensis*'. *International Journal of Food Sciences and Nutrition*, 63 Supplement 1, 75–81. https://doi.org/10.3109/09637486.2011.627840

8   Chen, J., Wollman, Y., Chernichovsky, T., Iaina, A., Sofer, M., & Matzkin, H. (1999). 'Effect of oral administration of high-dose nitric oxide donor L-arginine in men with organic erectile dysfunction: results of a double-blind, randomized, placebo-controlled study'. *BJU International*, 83(3), 269–73. https://doi.org/10.1046/j.1464-410x.1999.00906.x

9   Timón Andrada, R., Maynar Mariño, M., Muñoz Marín, D., Olcina Camacho, G. J., Caballero, M. J., & Maynar Mariño, J. I. (2007). 'Variations in urine excretion of steroid hormones after an acute session and after a 4-week programme of strength training'. *European Journal of Applied Physiology*, 99(1), 65–71. https://doi.org/10.1007/s00421-006-0319-1

10 Cumming, D. C., Quigley, M. E., & Yen, S. S. (1983). 'Acute Suppression of Circulating Testosterone Levels by Cortisol in Men'. *Journal of Clinical Endocrinology and Metabolism*, 57(3), 671–3. https://doi.org/10.1210/jcem-57-3-671

11 Pilz, S., Frisch, S., Koertke, H., Kuhn, J., Dreier, J., Obermayer-Pietsch, B., Wehr, E., & Zittermann, A. (2011). 'Effect of Vitamin D Supplementation on Testosterone Levels in Men'. *Hormone and Metabolic Research*, 43(3), 223–5. https://doi.org/10.1055/s-0030-1269854

12 Leproult, R., & Van Cauter, E. (2011). 'Effect of 1 Week of Sleep Restriction on Testosterone Levels in Young Healthy Men'. *JAMA*, 305(21), 2173–4. https://doi.org/10.1001/jama.2011.710

13 Li, D., Zhou, Z., Qing, D., He, Y., Wu, T., Miao, M., Wang, J., Weng, X., Ferber, J. R., Herrinton, L. J., Zhu, Q., Gao, E., Checkoway, H., & Yuan, W. (2010). 'Occupational exposure to bisphenol-A (BPA) and the risk of Self-Reported Male Sexual Dysfunction'. *Human Reproduction*, 25(2), 519–27. https://doi.org/10.1093/humrep/dep381

14 Ahn, H. S., C. M. Park, and S. W. Lee. (2002). 'The clinical relevance of sex hormone levels and sexual activity in the ageing male.' *BJU International* 89.6, 526–30. https://doi.org/10.1046/j.1464-410X.2002.02650.x

5. Transgender Nutrition

1 Rozga, M., Gradwell, E., Wood, J. C., Darst, V., & Linsenmeyer, W. (2020). 'Hormone Therapy, Health Outcomes and the Role of Nutrition in Transgender Individuals: A Scoping Review'. *Current Developments in Nutrition*, 4(Suppl 2), 1481. https://doi.org/10.1093/cdn/nzaa061_109)

2 Lundberg U. (2005). 'Stress hormones in health and illness: The roles of work and gender'. *Psychoneuroendocrinology*, 30(10), 1017–21. https://doi.org/10.1016/j.psyneuen. 2005.03.014
White Hughto, J. M., Reisner, S. L., & Pachankis, J. E. (2015). 'Transgender stigma and health: A critical review of stigma determinants, mechanisms, and interventions'. *Social Science & Medicine* (1982), 147, 222–31. https://doi.org/10.1016/j.socscimed.2015.11.010

3 Wadhawan, M., & Anand, A. C. (2016). 'Coffee and Liver Disease'. *Journal of Clinical and Experimental Hepatology*, 6(1), 40–46. https://doi.org/10.1016/j.jceh.2016.02.003

4   Imai, K., & Nakachi, K. (1995). 'Cross sectional study of effects of drinking green tea on cardiovascular and liver diseases'. *British Medical Journal* (Clinical Research ed.), 310(6981), 693–6. https://doi.org/10.1136/bmj.310.6981.693

5   Gupta, V., Mah, X. J., Garcia, M. C., Antonypillai, C., & van der Poorten, D. (2015). 'Oily fish, coffee and walnuts: Dietary treatment for nonalcoholic fatty liver disease'. *World Journal of Gastroenterology*, 21(37), 10621–35. https://doi.org/10.3748/wjg.v21.i37.10621

6   Nigam, P., Bhatt, S., Misra, A., Chadha, D. S., Vaidya, M., Dasgupta, J., & Pasha, Q. M. (2014). 'Effect of a 6-Month Intervention with Cooking Oils Containing a High Concentration of Monounsaturated Fatty Acids (Olive and Canola Oils) Compared with Control Oil in Male Asian Indians with Nonalcoholic Fatty Liver Disease'. *Diabetes Technology & Therapeutics*, 16(4), 255–61. https://doi.org/10.1089/dia.2013.0178

7   Hodges, R. E., & Minich, D. M. (2015). 'Modulation of Metabolic Detoxification Pathways Using Foods and Food-Derived Components: A Scientific Review with Clinical Application'. *Journal of Nutrition and Metabolism*, 2015, 760689. https://doi.org/10.1155/2015/760689

8   Baba, T., Endo, T., Honnma, H., Kitajima, Y., Hayashi, T., Ikeda, H., Masumori, N., Kamiya, H., Moriwaka, O., & Saito, T. (2007). 'Association between polycystic ovary syndrome and female-to-male transsexuality'. *Human Reproduction*, 22(4), 1011–16. https://doi.org/10.1093/humrep/del474

9   Maraka, S., Singh Ospina, N., Rodriguez-Gutierrez, R., Davidge-Pitts, C. J., Nippoldt, T. B., Prokop, L. J., & Murad, M. H. (2017). 'Sex Steroids and Cardiovascular Outcomes in Transgender Individuals: A Systematic Review and Meta-Analysis'. *Journal of Clinical Endocrinology and Metabolism*, 102(11), 3914–23. https://doi.org/10.1210/jc.2017-01643

10 Perrone, A. M., Cerpolini, S., Maria Salfi, N. C., Ceccarelli, C., De Giorgi, L. B., Formelli, G., Casadio, P., Ghi, T., Pelusi, G., Pelusi, C., & Meriggiola, M. C. (2009). 'Effect of Long-Term Testosterone Administration on the Endometrium of Female-to-Male (FtM) Transsexuals'. *Journal of Sexual Medicine*, 6(11), 3193–200. https://doi.org/10.1111/j.1743-6109.2009.01380.x

11 Larmo, P. S., Yang, B., Hyssälä, J., Kallio, H. P., & Erkkola, R. (2014). 'Effects of sea buckthorn oil intake on vaginal atrophy in postmenopausal women: A randomized, double-blind, placebo-controlled study'. *Maturitas*, 79(3), 316–21. https://doi.org/10.1016/j.maturitas.2014.07.010

12 Ederveen, E., van Hunsel, F., Wondergem, M. J., & van Puijenbroek, E. P. (2018). 'Severe Secondary Polycythemia in a Female-to-Male Transgender Patient While Using Lifelong Hormonal Therapy: A Patient's Perspective'. *Drug Safety – Case Reports*, 5(1), 6. https://doi.org/10.1007/s40800-018-0075-2

13 Irwig M. S. (2018). 'Cardiovascular health in transgender people'. *Reviews in Endocrine & Metabolic Disorders*, 19(3), 243–51. https://doi.org/10.1007/s11154-018-9454-3

14 Rothman, M. S., & Iwamoto, S. J. (2019). 'Bone Health in the Transgender Population'. *Clinical Reviews in Bone and Mineral Metabolism*, 17(2), 77–85. https://doi.org/10.1007/s12018-019-09261-3

6. HIV and Nutrition

1 World Health Organization. (2004). 'Nutrient requirements for people living with HIV/AIDS: report of a technical consultation', 13–15 May 2003, Geneva. https://apps.who.int/iris/handle/10665/42853

2 Gombart, A. F., Pierre, A., & Maggini, S. (2020). 'A Review of Micronutrients and the Immune System – Working in Harmony to Reduce the Risk of Infection'. *Nutrients*, 12(1), 236. https://doi.org/10.3390/nu12010236

3 Kamwesiga, J., Mutabazi, V., Kayumba, J., Tayari, J. C., Uwimbabazi, J. C., Batanage, G., Uwera, G., Baziruwiha, M., Ntizimira, C., Murebwayire, A., Haguma, J. P., Nyiransabimana, J., Nzabandora, J. B., Nzamwita, P., Mukazayire, E., & Rwanda Selenium Authorship Group (2015). 'Effect of selenium supplementation on CD4+ T-cell recovery, viral suppression and morbidity of HIV-infected patients in Rwanda: A randomized controlled trial'. *AIDS*, 29(9), 1045–52. https://doi.org/10.1097/QAD.0000000000000673

4 Borges-Santos, M. D., Moreto, F., Pereira, P. C., Ming-Yu, Y., & Burini, R. C. (2012). 'Plasma glutathione of HIV+ patients responded positively and differently to dietary supplementation

with cysteine or glutamine'. *Nutrition* (Burbank, Calif.), 28(7–8), 753–6. https://doi.org/10.1016/j.nut.2011.10.014

5 Poles, M. A., Fuerst, M., McGowan, I., Elliott, J., Rezaei, A., Mark, D., Taing, P., & Anton, P. A. (2001). 'HIV-related diarrhea is multifactorial and fat malabsorption is commonly present, independent of HAART'. *American Journal of Gastroenterology*, 96(6), 1831–7. https://doi.org/10.1111/j.1572-0241.2001.03879.x

6 Billoo, A. G., Memon, M. A., Khaskheli, S. A., Murtaza, G., Iqbal, K., Saeed Shekhani, M., & Siddiqi, A. Q. (2006). 'Role of a probiotic (*Saccharomyces boulardii*) in management and prevention of diarrhoea'. *World Journal of Gastroenterology*, 12(28), 4557–60. https://doi.org/10.3748/wjg.v12.i28.4557

7 Heiser, C. R., Ernst, J. A., Barrett, J. T., French, N., Schutz, M., & Dube, M. P. (2004). 'Probiotics, Soluble Fiber, and L-Glutamine (GLN) Reduce Nelfinavir (NFV)- or Lopinavir/Ritonavir (LPV/r)-related Diarrhea'. *Journal of the International Association of Physicians in AIDS Care (2002)*, 3(4), 121–9. https://doi.org/10.1177/154510970400300403

8 Grant, P. M., & Cotter, A. G. (2016). Tenofovir and bone health. *Current Opinion in HIV and AIDS*, 11(3), 326–332. https://doi.org/10.1097/COH.0000000000000248.

9 Kent, K. D., Harper, W. J., & Bomser, J. A. (2003). 'Effect of whey protein isolate on intracellular glutathione and oxidant-induced cell death in human prostate epithelial cells'. *Toxicology In Vitro: An International Journal Published in Association with BIBRA*, 17(1), 27–33. https://doi.org10.1016s0887-2333(02)00119-4

10 Akramiene, D., Kondrotas, A., Didziapetriene, J., & Kevelaitis, E. (2007). 'Effects of beta-glucans on the immune system'. *Medicina* (Kaunas, Lithuania), 43(8), 597–606. https://pubmed.ncbi.nlm.nih.gov/17895634

11 Furuya, A. K., Sharifi, H. J., Jellinger, R. M., Cristofano, P., Shi, B., & de Noronha, C. M. (2016). 'Sulforaphane Inhibits HIV Infection of Macrophages through Nrf2'. *PLoS Pathogens*, 12(4), e1005581. https://doi.org/10.1371/journal.ppat.1005581

12 Praditya, D., Kirchhoff, L., Brüning, J., Rachmawati, H., Steinmann, J., & Steinmann, E. (2019). 'Anti-infective Properties of the Golden Spice Curcumin'. *Frontiers in Microbiology*, 10, 912. https://doi.org/10.3389/fmicb.2019.00912

13   Morey, J. N., Boggero, I. A., Scott, A. B., & Segerstrom, S. C. (2015). 'Current directions in stress and human immune function'. *Current Opinion in Psychology*, 5, 13–17. https://doi.org/10.1016/j.copsyc.2015.03.007

7. Black Tuesday

1   Home Office. 'Drug Misuse: Findings from the 2013/14 Crime Survey for England and Wales. July 2014'. Available at: https://www.gov.uk/government/statistics/drug-misuse-findings-from-the-2013-to-2014-csew/drug-misuse-findings-from-the-201314-crime-survey-for-england-and-wales

2   Halkitis, P. N., & Palamar, J. J. (2006). 'GHB use among gay and bisexual men'. *Addictive Behaviors*, 31(11), 2135–9. https://doi.org/10.1016/j.addbeh.2006.01.009
     Wood, D. M., Hunter, L., Measham, F., & Dargan, P. I. (2012). 'Limited use of novel psychoactive substances in South London nightclubs'. *QJM: Monthly Journal of the Association of Physicians*, 105(10), 959–64. https://doi.org/10.1093/qjmed/hcs107

3   NIDA. 2020, July 10. 'Drugs and the Brain'. Retrieved from https://www.drugabuse.gov/publications/drugs-brains-behavior-science-addiction/drugs-brain on 8 August 2020.

4   Albert, P. R., Vahid-Ansari, F., & Luckhart, C. (2014). 'Serotonin-prefrontal cortical circuitry in anxiety and depression phenotypes: pivotal role of pre- and post-synaptic 5-HT1A receptor expression'. *Frontiers in Behavioral Neuroscience*, 8, 199. https://doi.org/10.3389/fnbeh.2014.00199

5   Suk, K. T., & Kim, D. J. (2015). 'Staging of liver fibrosis or cirrhosis: The role of hepatic venous pressure gradient measurement'. *World Journal of Hepatology*, 7(3), 607–15. https://doi.org/10.4254/wjh.v7.i3.607

6   Eugene, A. R., & Masiak, J. (2015). 'The Neuroprotective Aspects of Sleep'. *MEDtube science*, 3(1), 35–40. https://www.ncbi.nlm.nih.gov/pmc/articles/PMC4651462

7   Medic, G., Wille, M., & Hemels, M. E. (2017). 'Short- and long-term health consequences of sleep disruption'. *Nature and Science of Sleep*, 9, 151–61. https://doi.org/10.2147/NSS.S134864

8   Jones, A. W. (2019). 'Forensic Drug Profile: Cocaethylene'. *Journal of Analytical Toxicology*, 43(3), 155–60. https://doi.org/10.1093/jat/bkz007

9   Parker, G., and Brotchie, H. (2011). 'Mood effects of the amino acids tryptophan and tyrosine'. *Acta Psychiatrica Scandinavica*, 124: 417–26. https://doi.org/10.1111/j.1600-0447.2011.01706.x

10 Aquili, L. (2020). 'The Role of Tryptophan and Tyrosine in Executive Function and Reward Processing'. *International Journal of Tryptophan Research*: IJTR, 13, 1178646920964825. https://doi.org/10.1177/1178646920964825

    Meyers, S. (2000). 'Use of neurotransmitter precursors for treatment of depression'. *Alternative Medicine Review: a Journal of Clinical Therapeutic*, 5(1), 64–71. https://pubmed.ncbi.nlm.nih.gov/10696120

11 Johnson, E. A., Shvedova, A. A., Kisin, E., O'Callaghan, J. P., Kommineni, C., & Miller, D. B. (2002). '*d*-MDMA during vitamin E deficiency: effects on dopaminergic neurotoxicity and hepatotoxicity'. *Brain Research*, 933(2), 150–63. https://doi.org/10.1016/s0006-8993(02)02313-2

12 Villarreal, J., Kahn, C. A., Dunford, J. V., Patel, E., & Clark, R. F. (2015). 'A retrospective review of the prehospital use of activated charcoal'. *American Journal of Emergency Medicine*, 33(1), 56–9. https://doi.org/10.1016/j.ajem.2014.10.019

13 Neijzen, R., van Ardenne, P., Sikma, M., Egas, A., Ververs, T., & van Maarseveen, E. (2012). 'Activated charcoal for GHB intoxication: An in vitro study'. *European Journal of Pharmaceutical Sciences: Official Journal of the European Federation for Pharmaceutical Sciences*, 47(5), 801–3. https://doi.org/10.1016/j.ejps.2012.09.004

8. LGBTQ+ Mental Health

1   Dayan, P., & Huys, Q. J. (2008). 'Serotonin, Inhibition, and Negative Mood'. *PLoS Computational Viology*, 4(2), e4. https://doi.org/10.1371/journal.pcbi.0040004

2   Volkow, N. D., Wang, G. J., Kollins, S. H., Wigal, T. L., Newcorn, J. H., Telang, F., Fowler, J. S., Zhu, W., Logan, J., Ma, Y., Pradhan, K., Wong, C., & Swanson, J. M. (2009). 'Evaluating Dopamine Reward Pathway in ADHD: Clinical Implications'. *JAMA*, 302(10), 1084–91. https://doi.org/10.1001/jama.2009.1308

    Brisch, R., Saniotis, A., Wolf, R., Bielau, H., Bernstein, H. G., Steiner, J., Bogerts, B., Braun, K., Jankowski, Z.,

Kumaratilake, J., Henneberg, M., & Gos, T. (2014). 'The role of dopamine in schizophrenia from a neurobiological and evolutionary perspective: old fashioned, but still in vogue'. *Frontiers in Psychiatry*, 5, 47. https://doi.org/10.3389/fpsyt.2014.00047

3 Klein, M., Battagello, D., Cardoso, A., et al. (2019). 'Dopamine: Functions, Signaling, and Association with Neurological Diseases. Cellular and Molecular Neurobiology', 39(1), 31–59. https://doi.org/10.1007/s10571-018-0632-3

Solinas, M., Belujon, P., & Fernagut, P., Jaber, M., & Thiriet, N. (2018). 'Dopamine and addiction: what have we learned from 40 years of research'. *Journal of Neural Transmission*, 126. https://doi.org/10.1007/s00702-018-1957-2

4 Nuss, P. (2015). 'Anxiety disorders and GABA neurotransmission: a disturbance of modulation'. *Neuropsychiatric Disease and Treatment*, 11, 165–75. https://doi.org/10.2147/NDT.S58841

5 Adjibade, M., Julia, C., Allès, B., Touvier, M., Lemogne, C., Srour, B., Kesse-Guyot, E. (2019). 'Prospective association between ultra-processed food consumption and incident depressive symptoms in the French NutriNet-Santé cohort'. *BMC Medicine*, 17(1). https://doi.org/10.1186/s12916-019-1312-y

6 Spedding, S. (2014). 'Vitamin D and Depression: A Systematic Review and Meta-Analysis Comparing Studies with and without Biological Flaws'. *Nutrients*, 6(4), 1501–18. https://doi.org/10.3390/nu6041501

7 Mocking, R. J., Harmsen, I., Assies, J., Koeter, M. W., Ruhé, H. G., & Schene, A. H. (2016). 'Meta-analysis and meta-regression of omega-3 polyunsaturated fatty acid supplementation for major depressive disorder'. *Translational Psychiatry*, 6(3), e756. https://doi.org/10.1038/tp.2016.29

8 Chung, K. H., Chiou, H. Y., & Chen, Y. H. (2017). 'Associations between serum homocysteine levels and anxiety and depression among children and adolescents in Taiwan'. *Scientific Reports*, 7(1), 8330. https://doi.org/10.1038/s41598-017-08568-9

9 Tarleton, E. K., & Littenberg, B. (2015). 'Magnesium intake and depression in adults'. *Journal of the American Board of Family Medicine*, 28(2), 249–56. https://doi.org/10.3122/jabfm.2015.02.140176

Boyle, N. B., Lawton, C., & Dye, L. (2017). 'The Effects of Magnesium Supplementation on Subjective Anxiety and Stress – A Systematic Review'. *Nutrients*, 9(5), 429. https://doi.org/10.3390/nu9050429

10 Clapp, M., Aurora, N., Herrera, L., Bhatia, M., Wilen, E., & Wakefield, S. (2017). 'Gut Microbiota's Effect on Mental Health: The Gut-Brain Axis'. *Clinics and Practice*, 7(4), 987. https://doi.org/10.4081/cp.2017.987

11 Messaoudi, M., Violle, N., Bisson, J. F., Desor, D., Javelot, H., & Rougeot, C. (2011). 'Beneficial psychological effects of a probiotic formulation (*Lactobacillus helveticus* R0052 and *Bifidobacterium longum* R0175) in healthy human volunteers'. *Gut Microbes*, 2(4), 256–61. https://doi.org/10.4161/gmic.2.4.16108

Akkasheh, G., Kashani-Poor, Z., Tajabadi-Ebrahimi, M., Jafari, P., Akbari, H., Taghizadeh, M., Memarzadeh, M. R., Asemi, Z., & Esmaillzadeh, A. (2016). 'Clinical and metabolic response to probiotic administration in patients with major depressive disorder: A randomized, double-blind, placebo-controlled trial'. *Nutrition* (Burbank, Calif.), 32(3), 315–20. https://doi.org/10.1016/j.nut.2015.09.003

12 Busby, E., Bold, J., Fellows, L., & Rostami, K. (2018). 'Mood Disorders and Gluten: It's Not All in Your Mind! A Systematic Review with Meta-Analysis'. *Nutrients*, 10(11), 1708. https://doi.org/10.3390/nu10111708

13 Dienes, K. A., Hazel, N. A., & Hammen, C. L. (2013). 'Cortisol secretion in depressed, and at-risk adults'. *Psychoneuroendocrinology*, 38(6), 927–40. https://doi.org/10.1016/j.psyneuen.2012.09.019

14 Marchand, W. R. (2012). 'Mindfulness-Based Stress Reduction, Mindfulness-Based Cognitive Therapy, and Zen Meditation for Depression, Anxiety, Pain, and Psychological Distress'. *Journal of Psychiatric Practice*, 18(4), 233–52. https://doi.org/10.1097/01.pra.0000416014.53215.86

15 Young, S. N. (2007). 'How to increase serotonin in the human brain without drugs'. *Journal of Psychiatry & Neuroscience*, 32(6), 394–99. https://www.ncbi.nlm.nih.gov/pmc/articles/PMC2077351

16 Sleiman, S. F., Henry, J., Al-Haddad, R., El Hayek, L., Abou Haidar, E., Stringer, T., Ulja, D., Karuppagounder, S. S.,

Holson, E. B., Ratan, R. R., Ninan, I., & Chao, M. V. (2016). 'Exercise promotes the expression of brain derived neurotrophic factor (BDNF) through the action of the ketone body β-hydroxybutyrate'. *eLife*, 5, e15092. https://doi.org/10.7554/eLife.15092

17 Wan, L., Li, Y., Zhang, Z., Sun, Z., He, Y., & Li, R. (2018). 'Methylenetetrahydrofolate reductase and psychiatric diseases'. *Translational Psychiatry*, 8(1), 242. https://doi.org/10.1038/s41398-018-0276-6

Montag, C., Jurkiewicz, M., & Reuter, M. (2012). 'The Role of the Catechol-O-Methyltransferase (COMT) Gene in Personality and Related Psychopathological Disorders'. *CNS & Neurological Disorders Drug Targets*, 11(3), 236–50. https://doi.org/10.2174/187152712800672382

18 Alvaro, P. K., Roberts, R. M., & Harris, J. K. (2013). 'A Systematic Review Assessing Bidirectionality between Sleep Disturbances, Anxiety, and Depression'. *Sleep*, 36(7), 1059–68. https://doi.org/10.5665/sleep.2810

19 Gooley, J. J., Chamberlain, K., Smith, K. A., Khalsa, S. B., Rajaratnam, S. M., Van Reen, E., Zeitzer, J. M., Czeisler, C. A., & Lockley, S. W. (2011). 'Exposure to Room Light Before Bedtime Suppresses Melatonin Onset and Shortens Melatonin Duration in Humans'. *Journal of Clinical Endocrinology and Metabolism*, 96(3), E463–E472. https://doi.org/10.1210/jc.2010-2098

20 Feldman, M. B., & Meyer, I. H. (2007). 'Eating disorders in diverse lesbian, gay, and bisexual populations'. *International Journal of Eating Disorders*, 40(3), 218–26. https://doi.org/10.1002/eat.20360

21 Shaw, K., Turner, J., & Del Mar, C. (2002). 'Tryptophan and 5-Hydroxytryptophan for depression'. *The Cochrane Database of Systematic Reviews*, (1), CD003198. https://pubmed.ncbi.nlm.nih.gov/11869656

22 Ranjbar, E., Kasaei, M. S., Mohammad-Shirazi, M., Nasrollahzadeh, J., Rashidkhani, B., Shams, J., Mostafavi, S. A., & Mohammadi, M. R. (2013). 'Effects of zinc supplementation in patients with major depression: a randomized clinical trial'. *Iranian Journal of Psychiatry*, 8(2), 73–9. https://pubmed.ncbi.nlm.nih.gov/24130605

9. LGBTQ+ Fertility Nutrition

1 Karayiannis, D., Kontogianni, M. D., Mendorou, C., Mastrominas, M., & Yiannakouris, N. (2018). 'Adherence to the Mediterranean diet and IVF success rate among non-obese women attempting fertility'. *Human Reproduction*, 33(3), 494–502. https://doi.org/10.1093/humrep/dey003

2 Rooney, K. L., & Domar, A. D. (2018). 'The relationship between stress and infertility'. *Dialogues in Clinical Neuroscience*, 20(1), 41–7. https://doi.org/10.31887/DCNS.2018.20.1/klrooney

3 Waylen, A. L., Metwally, M., Jones, G. L., Wilkinson, A. J., & Ledger, W. L. (2009). 'Effects of cigarette smoking upon clinical outcomes of assisted reproduction: a meta-analysis'. *Human Reproduction Update*, 15(1), 31–44. https://doi.org/10.1093/humupd/dmn046
Pineles, B. L., Park, E., & Samet, J. M. (2014). 'Systematic Review and Meta-Analysis of Miscarriage and Maternal Exposure to Tobacco Smoke During Pregnancy'. *American Journal of Epidemiology*, 179(7), 807–23. https://doi.org/10.1093/aje/kwt334

4 Rossi, B. V., Berry, K. F., Hornstein, M. D., Cramer, D. W., Ehrlich, S., & Missmer, S. A. (2011). 'Effect of Alcohol Consumption on In Vitro Fertilization'. *Obstetrics and Gynecology*, 117(1), 136–42. https://doi.org/10.1097/AOG.0b013e31820090e1

5 Ziv-Gal, A., & Flaws, J. A. (2016). 'Evidence for bisphenol A-induced female infertility: a review (2007–2016)'. *Fertility and Sterility*, 106(4), 827–56. https://doi.org/10.1016/j.fertnstert.2016.06.027
Li, D. K., Zhou, Z., Miao, M., He, Y., Wang, J., Ferber, J., Herrinton, L. J., Gao, E., & Yuan, W. (2011). 'Urine bisphenol-A (BPA) level in relation to semen quality'. *Fertility and Sterility*, 95(2), 625–30.e304. https://doi.org/10.1016/j.fertnstert.2010.09.026

6 T'Sjoen, G., Arcelus, J., Gooren, L., Klink, D. T., & Tangpricha, V. (2019). 'Endocrinology of Transgender Medicine'. *Endocrine Reviews*, 40(1), 97–117. https://doi.org/10.1210/er.2018-00011

7 Merviel, P., Cabry, R., Lourdel, E., Lanta, S., Amant, C., Copin, H., & Benkhalifa, M. (2017). 'Comparison of two preventive

treatments for patients with recurrent miscarriages carrying a C677T methylenetetrahydrofolate reductase mutation: 5-year experience'. *Journal of International Medical Research*, 45(6), 1720–30. https://doi.org/10.1177/0300060516675111

ACKNOWLEDGEMENTS

Those who know me understand it has been a dream of mine to have a book published, particularly on a subject close to my heart that can help my community. Some individuals have helped me along the road to achieving this dream, so I would like to take this opportunity to express my gratitude.

I have to start by thanking my number one supporter in life. She is a very strong woman who has taught me resilience and has always stood by me in my struggles and successes. Thank you, Mum.

To my closest friends in the LGBTQ+ community: Michael Gilchrist, Terry Markle, Ross Henderson, Al Martin, Chris Davis and Cassio Magalhaes. You have all taught me what an authentic friendship is and also put up with my writing frustrations and perhaps being a little extra at times while crowdfunding for this book.

One of my longest friends, Yvonne Aldsworth, who has remained constant throughout my life, that person who always wants the best for you and always offered to help by reading through drafts of chapters.

To Ammar Husseini, you are not only an amazing personal trainer and a close friend, but you are a strong ally of the LGBTQ+ community. You have listened to my life and work stressors, helped to clear my head every training session and given me inspiration for the muscle gain chapter of this book.

I'd also like to express thanks to Sandra Greenbank, a fellow nutritionist and fertility expert for reviewing and providing feedback on the fertility chapter of this book.

Once my tutor, now a good friend, Miguel Toribio-Mateas, you were my first supporter and kept the nutrition field interesting by showing me it didn't need to be so serious. Thank you for your endless support, particularly for the times when I asked you to review drafts and help me sift through evidence.

Special thanks to Tiago Brandao, my psychotherapist, who turned my life around. Tiago taught me that vulnerability is a positive attribute, helped me let go of past trauma, set me on the road to loving myself and gave me the confidence to write this book.

To Janice Gittens, my first manager who took a chance on the twenty-two-year-old man who asked her for a job as a drug addiction therapist. Thank you for your leadership, guidance and diversity teachings. You were the catalyst through which I found my passion for helping people.

Thank you to the team at Unbound who believed in this project and helped bring it to life. In particular,

Fiona Lensvelt, Georgia Odd, Martha Sprackland and Imogen Denny; whose expertise in crowdfunding and publishing is unparalleled.

I'm forever indebted to my wonderful clients and the people who have followed my journey over the last ten years, who trusted me with their health and gave me the experience to be able to write *Naked Nutrition*.

Lastly, thank you to the parents of LGBTQ+ children and allies who have picked up this book to understand the community better. You all play a vital role in the continued fight for equality.

INDEX

Unbound is the world's first crowdfunding publisher, established in 2011.

We believe that wonderful things can happen when you clear a path for people who share a passion. That's why we've built a platform that brings together readers and authors to crowdfund books they believe in – and give fresh ideas that don't fit the traditional mould the chance they deserve.

This book is in your hands because readers made it possible. Everyone who pledged their support is listed below. Join them by visiting unbound.com and supporting a book today.

Lindsay Abbott
Rebecca Acceber
Olivia Addison
Rebecca Adlington
Chris Agostini
Hannah Alderson
Yvonne Aldsworth
Oday Alhamzah
Hamad Almarzouqi
Sarah Anderson
David Andrew
Irene Arango
Cristian Aristi

Paul Armstrong
Klemens Arro
Sabrina Artus
Ben Atkinson
Ant Babajee
Zachari Bach
Mark Balzli
Pedro Bandeira
Philip Beaver
Eric Bergeron
Guy Bernard
Daniel Bernardo
Emma Beswick

Maria Bez
Renaud Billard
Harriet Bindloss
Wojciech Bojko
Lukas Bozik
Tiago Breda
Annie Breen
Lulu Brekalo
Chris Brogan
Christopher Bryan
Beverley Buckner
Yvonne Budden
Paula Burgess
Tommy Burgess
David Butler
Regina Caldart
Colin S Campbell
Robert Carlin
Gabriel Carlos
Ralph Chalfoun
Joao Charruadas
Ben Clark
Scott Clark
Anna Cleary Ikin
Javier Cobo
Kristy Coleman
Therese Conlon-Barratt
Ben Coomes
Graciela Corrales Arias
Jose Cruz
Jonathan Dabush
Justin Daly
Chris Davies
Melanie De Grooth
Dre & Syl
Demi Eleftheriou

Sandra Evans
Sarah Evans
Delfino Falante
Ryan Ferguson
Juan F Fernandez
Pedro Ferreira
Nina Fischer-Yargici
Franziska Florina
David Fossey
Andrew Fox
Marcus Gallimore
Biagio Galotti
Pietro Emanuele Garbelli
Nader Gebran
John Gemayel
Andreas Georgalla
Sasha Georgievski
Alex Georgiou
David Germain
Habib Ghosn
Michael Gilchrist
Nickos Gogolos
Jayme Goldstein
Dr. Yoni Goldwasser
Becky Graham
Sarah Green
Sandra Greenbank
T. Griffiths
Andres Gutierrez
Leonardo Guzman
Nicola Hamilton
James Harrison
Philippe Harvey
Dan Harwood
Ross Henderson
Justin Herne

Ross Higgins
Dalton Holdge
Craig Houston
Charlene Howells
Chris Hulbert
Kamal Hussain
Ammar Husseini
Georgina Hyman
Maurizio Ijzerman
Michael Imber
Invivo Healthcare
Johari Ismail
Martyn Jackson
Danny Jaghab
Sue Jameson
Soraya Janmohamed
Tim Owen Jones
Hani Kalouti
Dan Kieran
Elizabeth King
William Kokay
Christian Kramer
Robert Larsen
Paul Law
Raheem Lee
Andreas Lege
Clarissa Lenherr
Fiona Lensvelt
Rodrigo Lopes
Samuel Ludford
Cassio Magalhaes
Marjan Mahoutchian
Jordan Mair
Ian Marber
Terry Markle
Al Martin

Björn Martin
Jared Martin
Mel Martin
James Masson-Wood
Matt and Dan
Aric McDaniel
Werner Menzinger
John Mitchinson
Karim Mkld
Sean Montoya
Christopher Morgan
Lee Moss
Pierre-Antoine Mudry
Carlo Navato
Stephen Neill
Stefanos Neofytou
Jackson Netto
Ady Norman
Bernadette O'Shaughnessy
Daniel O'Shaughnessy
Tomy Ortiz
Natalia Otero Sancho
Michael Page
Samantha Paget
Jaime Palmera
Monique Parker
Thinus Parreira
Miguel Perez
Alberto Pérez Davila
Luci Perry
Jamie Pizzorno
Justin Pollard
Steve Pont
Iain Potter
Richard Potts
Cliff Price

Jose A Prieto
Ali R
Siobhan Ramjhan
Deborah RaRa
Fiona Renshaw
Mike Reynolds
Ebi Rezaei
Candice Ringsell
Nuno Rodrigues
Alex Rogers
Benoit Rosar
Chris Rose
Helen Ross
Jon Ruano
Ahmad Saleh
Tony Samways
Manolo Sanchez
Michael Sanderson
Margaret Scott
Joanna Scott-Lutyens
Niall Sheehy
David Sheppard
Alex Shillito
Andrew Simmons
Caroline Smales
Eamon Somers
José Sousa
Daniel Spring
Beverley Starkie
Leigh Stewart
Roger Stockwell
Michael Stokes
Tess Strom
Lucy Sugars
Thomas Swallow
Deirdre Swede

Finnegan Szabo
Nandor Szabo
Roland Tan
Janine Tandy
Amy Tavner
Zoë Taylor
Annika Thomas
Rob Thompson
Pepa Toribio
Miguel Toribio-Mateas
Theo Tsipiras
Victor Vasquez Zorrilla
Nichola Vassallo
Ismael Vela
Corinna Venturi
Tiago Vieira
Trung Vu
Waseem NYC
David Webb
Janis Wharton
Paul Whitaker
John Williams
Steven Yeung
Abe Zakhem
Camilla Zeitlin